The
Archives
Fixing Time

Book Two

Christopher E. Cancilla

A brief (yeah right) word from the author

Seriously, have you ever known an author to be brief? I wrote this series for one reason, I wanted to; I hoped people would read and enjoy it, but if not that would not be my loss, that would be the people who made the decision to NOT read the stories. The characters are familiar, we all know people like them. That is the sign of a good and interesting story.

Nevertheless, more to the point, it is fun. I mean it, it really is and if you can believe this next statement, it is an unbiased opinion. Really.....

The story takes place throughout time and space; all of history is at Ben's fingertips. However, the story is more human and at the same time quite alien in nature. This is by design; after all, you need to keep a certain level of not only interest, but also intrigue.

I hope you enjoyed book one, and will read book three, four, and five, because they are all tied together. The inside jokes, the shared history; you will see.

As for me, well, if you read this and wish to send me an email, you can direct it to me (put The Archives in the subject line) and send the email to SnipDawg.Publishing@gmail.com and rest assured that I will not only receive this email, but I will also reply to it.

Have fun in all you read and do!

Chris

ISBN 978-1-304-54378-3

9 781304 543783

Copyright ©2014 by SnipDawg Publishing, First Printing

The copyrighted Leave No Trace Seven Principles have been reprinted with the permission of the

Leave No Trace Center for Outdoor Ethics

The Seven Principles, and their descriptions, are available on the Leave No Trace website at: http://lnt.org/learn/7-principles

ACKNOWLEDGEMENTS

Who to say thank you to….

WOW! I can think of several people off hand, but I suppose I should thank the people who read and edited my story first.

Big thanks go to Bob Clade, Jeff Barstow and Rick Isbell for reading and offering ideas about the story and the writing.

I need to thank my kids, Allison and Gregory; because if it were not for them, I would be boring.

Finally, my wonderful wife (of more than 25 years) Tammy. She does not read Science Fiction, but I get to bounce the story off her verbally. Which helps me out tremendously…

Lastly, my miniature ball of fur and energy, Snip. He has the uncanny ability to magically appear at my laptop the instant I get up from my chair to get a drink or dinner. Then, because he is part cat and part cyborg, he lies on my keyboard and can jiggle just right to delete the last entries I typed in. Thanks to him, I learned to **SAVE**….and save often!

Prologue

Information and Rumor

Brad Jorgen walked down the hall, the same hall he has not seen in a decade as far as he is concerned. At the other end of the hall is a room; he vaguely remembers where his desk is located. He looks a lot older, and has a smell no one can quite identify. Long term assignments can be difficult and take their toll on a person physically and mentally; emotionally draining a person to the point of breaking them. But the smile on his face is telling a different story.

He finds his desk and sits down, still in the clothing of the 'Wild West', and wearing matching silver six-shooters. Touching his terminal, he remembers, slowly, how to activate and send a message. He has no idea where his friend's office is located, so the fastest way is to use the computer. He could simply contact Security Control and request a temporary frequency change, but it has been so long it slipped his memory.

"Computer, open new message to Benjamin Jensen. Subject, URGENT. Ben, I am at my desk. I need to see you NOW. END MESSAGE." Thinking… "Computer, send message to all communications forms you have availability to send to, so recipient will receive the message as fast as possible." Brad sat back in the chair, realizing how comfortable it was and started dozing off to sleep.

Security, which had been following him like puppies since his return a few moments ago, saw him falling asleep and quietly walked over towards him. Brad woke up with a start and looked at him. "Sir, we need your weapons." They told him.

"Oh Man! I forgot I had these. Sorry, they have become a part of me and I don't give them a second thought." He grabbed the pistols and laid them on the desk with the butt's toward the security team. They picked them up and placed them in a bag and they both noticeably relaxed. He had been in the past for more than a decade, closer to two actually, and security policy was such that when a person returned from an extremely long jump they need to be observed and analyzed before clearances can be reissued.

'BEEP!' A few moments later a tone was heard from his desk. Brad looked at it and scrunched his face trying to remember what that noise meant. After a moment he let out a loud chuckle and touched a lighted panel and a terminal appeared in front of him floating above the desktop.

"When did you get back?" The face on the screen asked.

"Benjamin, nice to see you too!" Brad smiled. "About ten minutes ago. Benjamin, four-four-two."

"Understood!" The connection ended and Brad lay back in the chair and dozed off.

The security team accompanying him looked baffled, and amused. They found a couple chairs and sat – facing Brad – and waited. What they were waiting for, they had no idea but when they found out it would be monumental. They understood the reference to a four-four-two, but found it hard to understand how this guy sleeping in the chair could have discovered it, when no one of importance has a clue.

* * * * * * * * * * * * * * * * * * * *

"BRAD! Welcome back to the now…..as it were. You called a four-four-two. Explain."

"I need your boss, and my boss, and security in the security briefing room in five minutes, and then I will explain."

Benjamin keyed his portacom to Matthew Sharp's receptionist and pressed the call button.

"Mr. Sharp's office, this is…."

"This is Benjamin Jensen. Please gather Mr. Sharp, Miss Kimber from LT, and Miss Martinez from Security into the Security Conference Room in twenty minutes. This is a code four-four-two." Benjamin did not say another word he simply turned off his comm and put it away. Leading Brad to his office he closed the entrance and made it soundproof so no one walking near could over hear them. Several months ago he was made supervisor over the new people in the department, he was to train them and make them all valuable researchers. When he was promoted to supervisor he received the walls around his cube, and it was noticeably larger than a standard cube. He ushered Brad to his big, comfy chair, since he had not been in a real chair for a while.

He sat next to Brad but on the desk and, "OK, shoot. Give me the short version. Why did I just call a four-four-two?"

"Benjamin, I watched two travelers appear and rob a bank, then disappear."

Benjamin looked like the rest of the sentence was coming, "…and…"

"You don't understand. I watched researchers, like us, appear in the desert so I followed them in an attempt to say HI, and I'm like you. Then I realized they were not like me. I was able to hear their thoughts but they could not hear mine. Which means they are running on a different set of protocols. A different set of rules. I followed them into town and they walked into a bank and stunned everyone in the room with a small device," Brad touched his left wrist, "…fortunately they missed me by a few centimeters but the effect gave me a reason to stop. I mean I felt tingly and played unconscious while they were there. They grabbed all the money in the bank, robbed all of the patrons of their possessions, and left."

"Did you follow them?"

Brad was noticeably getting a bit frustrated, "Let me put this in plain terms that even you can understand. They jumped into my temporal reference, robbed a bank and its patrons, activated the recall signal and jumped home …taking their loot with them!"

Benjamin finally got it. He also had that feeling again. That feeling like he was about to be given a very large assignment that meant he needed to repair history.

Brad managed to change while he was telling his story to Benjamin and Benjamin sat on the desk with his mouth open, thinking. Fortunately, Brad was about the same size as Benjamin and he always kept an extra set of cloths in his office in case he needed to work long hours, or there was an impromptu game of racquetball during the day to clear the mind.

Activating his implant, *"Security, this is Benjamin Jensen. Please sync my frequency with that of Brad Jorgen for a two-hour time period."*

"Sir, we will need to get approval for the freq...."

"Authorization code four-four-two."

"Code Four-two. Affirmative. Frequencies in sync for two hours. Has Security Control being notified?" The operator asked.

"Yes. Mr. Matthew Sharps secretary is coordinating a meeting in the security conference room in the next ten minutes. Miss Kimber, Mr. Sharp, and Ms. Martinez have been invited and will attend."

"Thank you." And they dropped the connection.

Brad realized Benjamin was in his head and dumped his entire memory core to him all at once. They had gotten used to this transfer since Brad was on the long-term mission; he had been there for more than two years present to Benjamin which equates to about a decade or so to Brad. Benjamin pops back to visit him for a few days every couple of months' present time.

Brad's supervisor, Arianna Kimber, asked that he jump in to visit Brad, get the data, and jump home to upload Brad's current data to her system. She could not spare anyone from the Long Term section for such a short mission; and Benjamin needed the vacation every few months anyway. Arianna and Matthew had planned this for Benjamin while he was on a mission, and let him hear about it after his first trip back to see Brad, when he was supposed to arrest him for temporal infractions. Brad was cleared of all charges, thanks to Benjamin, and time was returned to the way it was supposed to be, but Benjamin became a data courier and his reward was to spend a couple quality weeks with Brad every few months. A chore Benjamin was happy to do. Occasionally he brought one of the newbie's who deserved a reward.

"We need to leave."

They walked into the elevator, and pressed the floor they needed. A subterranean level where the security moles lived in harmony. The security puppies were still sitting in the same seats when they left the room.

Benjamin looked at Brad and thought, *"Heel Security puppies....Good boys...."*

Brad started laughing out loud and the security operatives had no idea they were the object of the humor. They simply stood and began following the two laughing targets. Security was so boring.

The two of them walked to the Security area and on the way stopped for a fast bite to eat from the cart in the lobby.

Chapter 1

The Future is Now

Brad and Benjamin exited the elevator on the lowest level with their security escort in tow and walked down the hall and into the room. As they entered, the room went into secure mode. Lights dimmed, screens activated, doors closed and locked, and a slight hum started and blended into the background indicating that not even sound or electrical impulses can leave the room at this point. Looking around he saw everyone and someone he wished he had not….Will Carter was there. Why him of all people?

Will was in the same class at the academy as Brad and Benjamin, but Will truly hated Benjamin and Benjamin had no real idea why. True, he made fun of Bill and Betty for having a belief in a God of some kind but other people on the planet believed in a deity. However, Benjamin did not let up on them, he needled and poked and prodded until Bill and Betty left the program.

Standing in front of the table, Brad and Benjamin looked at each other. Benjamin turned to everyone at the table and began speaking.

"Thank you all for coming. I am Benjamin Jensen and this is Brad Jorgen. To bring us all up to the same page, Brad is a member of Miss Kimber's LT Department, and as a Long Term researcher he spends a great deal of time back in history. This gives him a distinct advantage in the sense he can see things and people that are out of place. He has had approximately present time two years in temporal reference and has become comfortable in the late 1800's. He has avoided becoming a part of any history or historical event for more than a decade transit time, but has reported on several very minor incidents that have happened during his two years in that specific temporal reference which were corrected."

Pausing to see if it is all sinking in, he wanted to be certain to paint a picture of Brad that was positive, dedicated, and trustworthy.

Benjamin continued, "Mr. Jorgen has recorded some truly frightening images we would like to share with you now." Benjamin silently told Brad to load the images, the video, and the reports onto the local server through the implant.

When Brad was finished uploading the data he looked toward the end of the table where the control panel was located. Will was sitting there, Brad spoke for the first time in this meeting, "Will, please call up video file 1800-96 and display it on the main viewer."

Will looked around and then to his boss, she nodded and he punched a few buttons and the images appeared on the monitor wall. It was an image of the inside of a bank in the late 1800's, and it was paused.

"Before we run the video, let me set the stage." Brad said with a deep thought on his face. "I had my implant deactivated so I was not aware there were other travelers in my timeframe. I had just left a small town where I had spent a couple of days on vacation doing nothing really, and I was on my way to Russellville, Kentucky to witness the James Younger Gang robbing the

Nimrod Long Bank and to document the cities first waterworks system. I was on a ridge just outside the small town of Bowling Green when I looked in a valley and saw a temporal team literally appear. I activated my implant and attempted to see if they were looking for me but all I was able to do was hear what they were discussing."

Brad paused for a moment, excited. "It was obvious they were not able to hear me attempting to communicate with them but I was able to hear their thoughts clearly. I stayed out of their view and followed them until I heard them talking about the bank. They planned to rob the bank of all cash and return home to sell the money as historical items, making a small fortune in the process. I hurried my horse and arrived at the bank nearly 2 hours ahead of them, they were on foot. I waited and entered the bank 7 minutes before they did and spoke to a bank manager about a loan for a home, my way of looking like a patron and not someone waiting for bank robbers to show up."

Brad stopped for a moment and took a deep breath to help slow himself down. Sipped a glass of water he had in front of him and looked at each face around the table. Everyone was looking at him with an intensity he had never before experienced. Brad continued, "I was still able to hear them all this time and knew when they entered the town, and when they were entering the bank. As the three of them entered the bank they had pistols drawn and cocked. When they fired at the bank manager I was speaking to, the weapon did not fire a ball of lead. Instead, it expelled a small red ball of energy I recognized as a stunner blast. This was evidently a well-planned and thought out operation. But to use the jump system for profit…that baffled me. The second shot, fired in my direction, hit the desk near where my hand was resting and the energy discharge threw me to the floor; I remained conscience but dazed. I intentionally fell to the floor as if I was hit and continued to video the entire event from my vantage point. After it was over, all patrons were disabled; the team placed all currency, cash and coins, into large sacks that were not from the current timeframe. They had the appearance of canvas bags but when they poured the coins into the bags the sound was similar to metal mesh."

OK, just about done…Brad was feeling like an encyclopedia with a few pages missing.

"Once they left the timeframe the other patrons began to come to and I gave the appearance I too was under the same influence as they, regaining consciousness slowly and after several of the others to avoid any impropriety. I departed the bank after the Sherriff spoke to me and since I did not see anything useful he let me leave quickly."

Benjamin jumped in, "Let's watch the 3 minutes of video from the exchange." Looking at Will he nodded and Will activated the recording.

Everyone stared at the screen as the video played. It opened with Brad seeing himself in a mirror behind the desk of the bank manager. There was absolute silence in the room as the trio of bandits entered and Brad zoomed in the visual of his implant to click off a crystal clear image of the faces of all three of the thieves. The stunner bolts flew all over the room with one landing on the bank manager. Brad happened to be looking in his direction at the time and the aura of the bolt striking him appeared odd to all in the conference room. During this incident the voices of the three from the future time could be heard on the recording, but they were not speaking verbally.

"Pause." The Security Director ordered. "Rewind back 15 seconds and advance very slowly." As the image advanced she stared at the screen intently, at the moment of impact she had Will pause again. "This item is not from this century. This stun weapon is from our future."

Matthew spoke first, "How can you tell?"

"The impact aura from current stunners creates a localized energy pattern that is absorbed by the skin and causes the stun effect, and also a pain – not serious though – where the blast impacts. This unit is of a stunner that is currently under development, in the planning stages. When the bolt of energy impacts the body it is dissipated over the entire surface of the targets skin causing complete and total nervous system overload and unconsciousness. The effects of this device are theorized to be faster at incapacitation, longer in duration with steps from 5 minutes to 4 hours, less physical side effects, and the power consumption of the device is less than one-quarter of current stunners. Advance again at one quarter normal."

As the video advanced Brad was seen to turn around and face his attacker. As the beam was released it was evident it was installed in what appeared to be a traditional 45 caliber pistol. Brad ducked to the left and his hand instinctively rose to cover his face. As he did the beam missed him and only his pinky finger was grazed by the outer edge of the bolt of energy. Brad dropped like a sack of sand to the ground.

Brad commented, "I don't remember falling like that?"

"Evidently you were affected more than you realized." Brad's boss entered into the conversation. She was smiling as she said it.

Brad smiled back at her and nodded.

A few minutes passed since the altercation began and Brad was still motionless on the floor. When he was stunned his eyes remained opened and recording continued without his assistance.

The three bad guys stood in the center of the room and all of them closed their eyes at the same time and were encased in a soft white glow, then vanished.

"Looking back at this," Matthew Sharp added, "…it appears the three robbers were in telepathic communications. The odd part was they were not aware you were in their timeframe, let alone the same room as they were. It appears they are not fully trained or perhaps using the jump system in such a way, rather….such a time, as there is more than one in the world."

"Wait a moment," Brad looked at Maria. "You said our current stunners are not on par with the stunner you are seeing in this video. Can you call up the specs and image of a current stunner?"

She looked at Will and the image appeared on the screen. In the lower right corner, a video of the unit's operation was running and this was definitely not the same unit that Brad was wearing on his left wrist. This device was several decades junior and did not have the capability to camouflage itself after the wearer puts it on.

Brad looked ill. "Brad? Are you OK?" Will said loudly so everyone could hear.

"No, no I'm not. This ripple goes deeper than a single incursion with this incident. Several months, or actually almost a year your time, Benjamin came back to see me to correct a temporal incursion in which I was suspected of temporal manipulation. I was cleared and the real culprits were apprehended and sentenced to prison. In the process Benjamin was sent to me with a current stunner of the day and before he returned home he left it with me in the event I ever needed it. And boy has it come in handy in one or two events during this research. But it is the exact make and model energy weapon as those pistol weapons we saw in the video. Therefore, time has been affected further than just a simple bank robbery. The technology in which I departed has not yet been created after my return!"

Maria opened her comm unit and began issuing orders to recall all temporal agents with a designation of Alpha through Gamma. These are the agents on assignment in the distant past and completely isolated from all humans. They are the CONTROLS of history. As she spoke agents from the now were jumping back to retrieve the agents, or more to the point to simply download their data modules and return to the present. This way they could pinpoint the exact timeframe where the incursion occurred.

"Mr. Jorgen, can you please show us this stunner?" The leader of the security detachment asked nicely, but it was in no way a request.

Brad pulled up his left sleeve and removed the stunner. After a moment it materialized and it looked like a rather oversize 20th century wrist watch. He placed it in front of him on the conference table. He glanced at Benjamin who looked as amazed as the others at the operation of the device.

"Mr. Jorgen, what can you tell us about the operation of this device?" Arianna asked.

"Everything, actually. When Benjamin came back and gave it to me he uploaded the manual to my implant and over the last eight or so years I have read and reread that manual so I believe you can say I have it memorized."

Matthew stepped in, "Mr. Jorgen did Benjamin frequently upload information to your implant when he visited you for data retrieval?"

"Yes. Sometimes a lot, sometimes a little. Depending on what was happening in the present."

"Give us an example of the types of information he brought to you." Will asked that question.

"Normally entire sporting events, novels, movies, old television shows from the 20th and 21st centuries. My favorite is the recordings of the news broadcasts for the months since his last trip. I was able to experience the news in somewhat real-time. I picked a date, then watched the hour of news and knew what happened on that date back home."

Pausing briefly, he began again, "The best items were the complete historical encyclopedia from 1800 through 2200. I sometimes randomly pick a page and start reading or watching the data. Gives me something to do on those long nights between towns."

Both security people, Maria Martinez and Will Carter, stood at the exact same moment. That made it obvious to all in the room that their implants were on the same frequency.

Ms. Martinez spoke with authority, "This meeting is adjourned. The device in question will be retained and studied by my department. In the event travel is warranted the device will be returned to you since it came from your timeline, for your use on this mission. You will submit to a complete download where we will acquire the data needed to verify the information we heard, and to get the documents such as the encyclopedia, and the stunner's manual, into our possession."

Brad broke in, "Be certain to get the technical manual also. I had needed it to perform periodic maintenance on the device and Benjamin brought it to me on his next trip."

Matthew started to speak. "Brad, if you had to put your finger on a timeframe and using Benjamin as a timeline, which visit do you think would have been the biggest change?"

Brad sat back in his chair and thought for a minute, it felt like a very long minute to everyone else in the room. "If I had to put a question mark on a visit, the strangest one was about two hundred days ago. The news stories were all there but if I remember correctly some of the news towards the end of the reporting period was out of whack. For example, for years they were referring to the Space Station as the Orbital Facility in Earth orbit, or the Orbital Facility in Lunar orbit. From one news day to the next the reference was changed to Ryerson Station for Earth orbit, and Ryerson Two for Lunar orbit. Who is this Ryerson?"

"Ryerson, Mr. Jorgen, is the developer of the temporal jump system. His contributions to humanity were instrumental in colonization of the planets and space flight in general." Ms. Martinez said. She was not only standing with her hands in fists, resting her knuckles on the table; but her attitude became very condescending while she was speaking.

"Never heard of him before. From what I can remember from the academy, the jump system was developed by a team of scientists about a century and a half ago. No one man ever took credit for the creation of the system. That may be a good place for you to start investigating." Brad looked directly at Ms. Martinez, eye to eye, and continued with, "…but that is only my impression."

Benjamin wanted to laugh. The look on Brad's face and the anger in Maria Martinez's face were hysterical.

Ms. Martinez and Will left the room and Arianna and Matthew walked up to Benjamin and Brad.

"Gentlemen, I have a question," Ms. Kimber started, "Ben, do you remember giving Brad that device?"

"Yes"

Matthew added, "…and it was this exact device?"

"Yes"

"Then the temporal error occurred while you were on mission, therefore your memory and my memory of an event will differ. But it appears that your memory and Brad's memory are similar. Not really sure where that gets us, but it is something."

"The worst thing is I never heard of Ryerson either and do not remember ever hearing the name. As for the news vids, I recorded them but never watched them so I had no clue about the temporal modification." Benjamin said flatly.

＊ ＊ ＊ ＊ ＊ ＊ ＊ ＊ ＊ ＊ ＊ ＊ ＊ ＊ ＊ ＊ ＊ ＊ ＊

Several days have passed since the briefing in the conference room, and since Brad had no place to stay Benjamin offered his couch. Brad took him up on the offer and they had been catching up on things and trying new ventures and adventures, for dinner.

Brad had no apartment in this timeframe at the moment, only storage. Since Brad had accepted a very long-term assignment after graduation, he opted to not lease a place and lived in a nearby hotel for the couple of months until the assignment started. He did take Tom up on the offer of the apartment in Benjamin's building if he graduated, but never acted on it. He needs to call Tom to see if he could reinstate the contract so, as Brad put it, he had an address – a place to hang his hat.

Brad spent a lot of time in Benjamin's apartment, with and without Benjamin. His possessions were in storage – mostly – but he had stopped by the facility and picked up a few essentials for use in Benjamin's apartment to tide him over. He also brought back with him his prized possessions before he returned. Most of what he owned was still back in the dessert, buried in the sand in a place only he knew about. If he ever returned at least he had stuff to go find.

As soon as he could find a place of his own he would. After all he had quite a bit of pay all stored up in the bank so poor he was not. And if need be, he could always fall back on his trust fund. Daddy is quite well-off, after all. Being the owner of the largest mining company in the known universe and all.

Benjamin carried communiqués from everyone to Brad during his missions to download data and take time off to relax. Brad responded as if he could only communicate through messaging, as though he was off-planet and out of visual or voice comm range for extended periods of time. Once in a while Benjamin would record a video letter to his parents or someone else and personally deliver it to them in a data module. He liked visiting Brad's parents, since Benjamin's father was killed on a mission, and his mother was injured and not really all there any longer, he felt like they were a great substitute.

This was the only way Brad could communicate in reality. So he spoke to his parents electronically and was able to keep up with his family just fine. He told them he was going on a long-term journey to the outer edge of the mapped universe, and he could only download and reply to communications when he was near a station, planet, or facility that was connected to the matrix.

They said they understood. He gave them Benjamin's contact information in the event of an emergency and Benjamin could get in touch with Brad in a moment, literally.

"BRAD! This place looks like a pawn shop I visited in the 1980's!! Can you at least organize it into chaos? That would be an improvement." Benjamin jibed.

Brad had arrived to the now on a Tuesday afternoon and started all the excitement; he and Benjamin stayed late into the evening working. They went in early and stayed late on Wednesday and Thursday and plan to take a few hours off on Friday. Benjamin was planning to hold his weekly party, but due to workload, he couldn't. He needed to put time in this weekend, as did Brad. Most of his regulars are upset and trying to find a new party and letting him know just how **inconvenient** it is for them since he cancelled the party. It should have been at this precise moment when Benjamin realized his friends were not friends at all, but merely using him…a means to an end. But, since he completely understood and falls into that mentality as well, the thought eluded him and he felt sorry for his friends having to find a new activity where they could drink, eat, and drink some more for free.

"Where do you want to eat this evening?" Brad asked Benjamin.

"I was thinking about the new place I told you about in the Lunar Dome. We can get there and back, and have a great meal and some fun, before 9am tomorrow." Benjamin smiled one of those smiles.

"Sounds good!" Brad laughed.

"Computer, contact Maria Williamette." The wall vid opened with her face.

"Benjamin....Brad!! Great to see you. Last I heard, Brad, you were on a long term....trip." Maria Williamette said with real excitement in her voice to hear from two of her former classmates.

"Well, I'm back now. But Benjamin and I need a travel agent. Know a good one?"

"As a matter of fact, I do" When she left the class she opted to become a travel agent and has become one of the best in the Solar System. She still had a position at the Archives and her implant but she was not a Temporal Researcher.

"OK, Let's see.....can you please reserve two seats to the Lunar Dome, a reservation in the primary suite at the Lunar Hilton – a room with two bedrooms, and a dinner table for four at Le Chandra for this evening at say 9pm lunar time."

"Hmmmm....no. But I can reserve two seats on the Lunar shuttle to the Lunar dome, two suites at the Tranquility Hilton, and a table at Le Chandra with complimentary hors d'ovres. Now, when do you want to leave for the Moon?"

"Impressive. What are my choices?"

"Arrival times vary depending on your departure time. There are three choices. You can leave at 1pm from the port from pad 16 and arrive 9 hours later at Luna Port; you can leave at 2:15pm and arrive at Luna Port at 4:15pm; or you can leave at 6pm and arrive at 8:30pm. The variance is the difference in a layover at the Earth orbital facility for the 6pm flight, and a layover at both the Earth and the Lunar facilities for the 1pm flight. The 2:15pm flight is direct; the cost is slightly higher."

Brad looked at Benjamin, "Allow me....book passage for two, first class, for the 2:15pm flight and the return trip will be through the drop ship to arrive as close as possible to 10am tomorrow."

"Nice..." Benjamin said to Brad.

Maria continued, "To arrive at 10am you will need to be on the shuttle from Luna Port at 6am where you will change vessels at the Earth Orbital facility to the drop ship. Surface arrival is scheduled at 10:03am."

"Perfect. Book the entire plan." Turning to Brad, "That will get us to the Island just before 10:30am. Let's schedule an 11am meeting, and we can call it a weekend."

"Acknowledged. Plan booked. You may pick up your itinerary at the Spaceport Complex. Check in no later than 1:45pm." Maria said, someone was talking to her off screen. "I need to run, gotta book a vacation to a colony. Now THAT is where the income is generated. Save me a dance!" She was gone in a flash.

"Save her a dance?" Brad looks at Benjamin.

"Her way of saying ..talk to you later...remember"

"It has been ten years you know; I am getting old!!" They both smiled. "OK, why reservations for four?" Brad asked.

"I'm sure we are going to meet a couple companions on the flight. I've been on the 2:15 before, mostly women looking for a weekend romance. Any luck and we will have companionship all weekend. When we leave, the romance never existed."

"Sounds strange. Remember me, the guy who spent the last decade or so living in a place where moral fortitude was important."

"Let's play it by ear."

"And I thought we were working this weekend?"

"As I said, let's play it by ear...."

"So, for dinner this evening," Brad continued, "How about Pluto's?"

"Sure thing. Give me a few minutes to finish up the documents. Hey, tell you what. Computer, organize all images from Project B into a slide show and add appropriate music. Delay each image for 8 seconds. Play on the main wall."

Brad looked at Benjamin and cocked his head like a curious puppy. "Huh..."

"You'll see."

A few moments later the images began. It was a collection of still images Benjamin collected whenever he went back to visit with Brad. Brad sat on the sofa and watched intently, and laughed at the memories that surfaced when he saw the images.

* *

"Hi Ya Bennie!" Were the first words out of Barbara's mouth as she sat a beer in front of Benjamin and Brad...and then a revelation as she remembered "BRAD!! You're back. Welcome back to Earth. A two-year trip has to be hard to do. Where did you go, what did you see?"

"I have plenty of time to tell you but essentially let's just say that for the few stops I made I find this establishment SO much better than floating through space between points A...B...C...and so on. I already know what I want to order. I have been dreaming about it for months, once I knew I was on my way home. I want a Pluto Burger, all the way."

"You want fries with that order?" Barbara asked.

"Fries?" Brad had no idea what she was talking about.

"After the place was destroyed and Benny helped us rebuild he gave us a new recipe for fries. Essentially, they are crispy potato sticks?

"Definitely." Benjamin replied for him and Brad.

"Benny?" Barbara asked.

"Same thing. Oh, and ask Mike if he remembers how to make a Temporal Rift. We'll take two if he does."

She smiled and walked away. Brad looked at him in amazement. "Destroyed?"

"I'll tell you all about the meteor that tried to kill me and destroyed Pluto's Bar, and how my grandson popped in and saved my butt." Brad's mouth started to open and Benjamin continued. "But not now, not here. Tomorrow on the flight we can link and get some preliminary work done and I will tell you about it then. Silently..."

"OK....uh...your grandson?" Brad asked slowly.

"Tomorrow....on the flight.....through the Sub-Q, not before."

"OK" Brad shook his head.

"HEY BEN!! Do I remember how to make a Temporal Rift? I should come over there and give you a piece of my mind." Mike yelled from the bar.

Benjamin yelled back, "Mike, not a good idea. You need all the little pieces of your mind that you have. But you are welcomed to stop over and say hi to Brad. Back from the nether regions of the universe."

"Who's back Benjamin?" Tom Wolski walked it at that moment and chimed in.

"Tom, join us. Barbara, repeat it all for Tom." Benjamin motioned to Barbara. If she heard him or not, she understood.

"Tom, you remember Brad. Brad Jorgen, this is Tom Wolski. He is the current owner and landlord of the planet Earth." Benjamin laughed.

Tom chuckled uncontrollably and "Brad. I do remember you. You were one of the few I made the contract with in Benjamin's class and who never took me up on the offer. I have two openings in Benjamin's building if you are interested. Since you are back from somewhere I am guessing you will need a place to live."

"What floors?"

"One is on Benjamin's floor, right next door actually…"

"Are you kidding. He is a noisy neighbor…" Brad smiled at Benjamin and Tom.

"The other is one floor up, DIRECTLY one floor up."

"I want that one. How soon can I move in?"

"Well, sign the lease in the morning. Move in tomorrow afternoon. The place is already clean and ready to go."

"Consider it a done deal." Brad and Tom shook hands.

"Hey, do I get a commission?" Benjamin laughed.

"You sure do!! BARBARA, this round is on me." Tom smiled at them both.

"Not exactly what I had in mind, but dinner and drinks works for me." Benjamin added.

"Dinner....and drinks." It was at that moment Barbara arrived with three burgers, all the way, and three Temporal Rifts; and of course three more beers. Barbara looked at Tom who keyed in his code and paid for the meals and drinks. Tom looked at his dinner companions and smiled. "The building will never be the same again."

Chapter 2

A Working Vacation

Walking into the terminal to get the shuttle was always a long and drawn out affair, especially trying to go through security. But, since Brad and Benjamin worked at Archive Island, and were Temporal Researcher, the government considered them to be trusted members of society. As they entered the terminal they simply walked in the out door. Security began to run toward them but they both showed their ID and they were left alone.

However, all of the people standing in line saw the incident and were not happy with the fact they walked through so quickly.

They made it to their gate and sat down, waiting to be called to enter the shuttle. A short time later, it was time to board.

As Brad and Benjamin entered the shuttle to take them to the Lunar Colony, they were escorted to the first class compartment, which was actually nothing more than free drinks and a larger seat just inside the airlock to the ship. The greatest advantage was the fact that you were able to board and leave the craft first and rapid progression through customs since you paid the extra for the seat. Customs feels that if you show that much attention to yourself you are more than likely not trying to hide anything.

Also, since they were both trusted members of the Archive Island Research Team, there was an unwritten level of trust that made the process even smoother. So, for Benjamin and Brad, this was a simple 'look what I can do' exercise and not a flamboyant display of wealth.

Brad looked at Benjamin, "That was the absolute best meal I have had in dec…uh…a long time. I may not eat again till dinner on the Moon."

They just arrived at the SpacePort after a lunch at a retro early 21st century restaurant. Although it was all vegetarian cuisine, the creative use of spices, ingredients, and textures made the meal exquisite and wonderful.

"Me too. I am still full." Benjamin replied. "Don't worry, although the food is excellent, it does not last all that long and you will be hungry again about the time we are getting ready to sit down for dinner. I am, however, very glad that you have a place to live though. I get my living room back! When we get back I will help you get your things moved and get you set up with Auto-Maids. They are wonderful."

"Sure…that sounds good. What is Auto-Mai…." Brad was cut off in mid-sentence by the flight attendant.

"Mr. Jorgen…Mr. Jensen. Your seats are ready." The attendant escorted them through the wall of people to the ramp that took them to the elevator which let them off at the airlock of the ship. A few steps and they were in their seats sipping on champagne and watching the other passengers walk past them a few minutes later. Several of the other passengers looked at them with distaste, but most could care less.

The flight attendant arrived seat side to remove their empty cups, "Is there anything else I can do for you?"

Benjamin simply looked at her and smiled until she caught what he was trying not to say. As soon as he could see they were on the same wavelength, "Actually, there is. We were just notified that our associates will not be able to join us for our meeting so this weekend has gone from a boring meeting session to that of a mini-vacation. We have reservation for four at Le Chandra at 9pm. How would you and your friend like to join us?"

"Ah…Mr. Jensen."

"Before you say anything else, ask your friend. After all, it is dinner on us at the BEST restaurant on Earth's only natural satellite…" Brad started to chuckle at the obvious line he was tossing at the flight attendant.

"Well…." She started.

"We also have the dome for our private use from 11pm till 2am. What time is your next flight?"

"1pm tomorrow. OK, I'll ask Gloria." She walked away.

"Brad, I am so glad our bosses agreed to this mini-vacation for a couple days. I used words like Brad needs to relax and he has been on assignment for two years… OH, and my favorite, if he relaxes this mission will be easier to accomplish." Benjamin whispered to Brad.

"I am happy they agreed, but I was not stressed out. I was rather content and relaxed to start with, but I have to say that being pampered is a big change from what I put up with while on assignment." Brad took a deep breath and exhaled a nice relaxing exhale, nuzzled himself into his seat and gave the general impression he was all comfy and cozy. "Flight dome for our private use?"

"Yep" Benjamin smiled. "I am friends with the owners."

A few moments later Gloria and her friend returned.

Benjamin and Brad were in the center seats, in the front row of the craft. Between them was the center aisle. On either side of them was an empty seat. Gloria sat next to Brad who had a smile on his face from ear to ear.

The woman they asked sat next to Benjamin, "Well, I'm Tiffany and this is Gloria and it would be our pleasure to dine with you this evening. It may be fun too."

As if on cue, Brad and Benjamin grabbed, ever so gently, the right hand of the woman closest to them and gently kissed it, "My name is Benjamin Jensen and this is Brad Jorgen. Tonight will be a memorable evening for sure."

"Jorgen…I know that name. Are you related to the mining people?"

"Well, yes. I am. My father is the owner and the rest of my family does various things at the company."

"What do you do at the company?" Gloria asked.

"Nothing, just have fun and spend money." He smiled…. again.

Benjamin thought to himself…. that just sealed the deal. Brad must have heard his thoughts and smiled to himself. Naturally, both women knew they worked for the Archives.

* * * * * * * * * * * * * * * * * * * *

The foursome would meet later that night at the restaurant; the girls had post-flight duties but said they would be there on time. Brad and Benjamin left their rooms at the same time and turned to each other, as if on cue, and winked at each other. They started walking toward the elevator, Brad in the lead since the elevator was a bit closer to his room. Benjamin, not too concerned, met up a moment later as Brad pressed the call button. They looked at each other and smiled, they were having fun. A weekend of hooky then off to save humanity. Entering the car, the doors closed and Brad was hit with a revelation. He knew exactly how he needed to move forward to resolve the temporal situation.

"Security, please match frequencies with myself and Benjamin Jensen. Authorization code 442." Brad thought silently into his implant.

"Approved. Duration?" Came back from Security.

"Indefinite." Brad thought back.

"Connection complete." And Security severed the link.

"Benjamin...." Brad thought to him and Benjamin stopped dead in his tracks.

"...and I assume there is a reason we are sharing a brain..." Benjamin thought back.

"Not really. Just wanted to let them think...uh...know we are working; and also to have some fun with our dates."

"OK.....and...." Benjamin said out loud.

"And I have a few thoughts I wanted to relay to you regarding how to move forward with the corporate issues we are attempting to resolve."

"Work stuff. Works for me. Could be fun too."

The doors opened and they exited without really seeing where they were. They stopped a few steps into what sounded like pure chaos and anarchy. This had to be the casino level. Wrong floor… as if using a single mind, they both did an about face and re-entered the lift before the door closed. Benjamin pressed the correct button and they stood there in silence for a moment.

"I hate noise." Brad said quietly, slowly, and with an intensity that made you believe him.

"I know." Is all Benjamin could reply.

The doors reopened and soft dinner music could be heard, hushed voices whispering about any number of unintelligible conversations could almost be heard. They exited and at the same time said, "BETTER…."

"Ben, Brad!" They turned and saw their dates. Gloria was waving slightly. They both wore something a little formal, but not evening attire. Since they were all going to the dome later for a flight, a dress would not be the best idea. Benjamin and Brad wore a light shirt and dress slacks, and a dinner jacket.

"So, how was the debriefing?" Benjamin asked.

"Standard. It is not so much the debriefing part that takes the most time, but the fact we are being required to perform more and more maintenance on the ship." Gloria was talking. "Since Tiffany is the senior member, she is required to complete all of the paperwork. Whoever finishes first helps the other."

"You do maintenance on the ship?" Brad asked.

"Yes, big advantage in that. In the event of an in-flight emergency we can fix it!" Tiffany smiled as she said it.

During this short conversation they were walking toward the entrance to the restaurant. As they arrived, the hostess said, "All reservations are full, we have no available seats."

Benjamin looked her in the eye and said, "I have a reservation, Jensen."

The hostess scanned her display for a moment, "Yes you do. Table for four next to the fireplace, with an external view. Give me a few minutes to make certain all is ready. You may go into the bar for a complimentary glass of champagne."

"Thanks…..uh…is the owner here today?"

"Yes, she is. May I ask why?"

"Can you please give Miss Sharp the following message, exactly?"

"Sure, what is it?" She said tentatively.

"8-6-7-5-3-OH-9" he paused a moment and repeated it, "8-6-7-5-3-OH-9, just like that. Nothing else needs to be said. Don't modify a thing, and you need to say it exactly as I did. Now let's hear it."

"8-6-7-5-3-OH-9" She recited.

"Perfect!" Benjamin nodded and turned to go to the bar.

She nodded back to him and headed to the kitchen, where Benjamin's former neighbor and friend liked to be more than anywhere else. Good thing too since she was also an expert chef and owner of several restaurants. Benjamin knew she would understand the reference to the 20th Century music lyric; she was well versed in what he and Brad did for a living since she was his bosses – Matthew Sharps – Niece. Hiding what they did from her did not make any sense since she had trained to be a temporal researcher but opted out of the program in lieu of becoming the solar systems best and most sought after chef and restaurateur.

She had considered reapplying to the school and joining the class after Benjamin at one point in her life, but cooking got into her blood. She and Benjamin were inseparable for a time, but they grew apart and she moved on, as did he. Their friendship lasted through it all and they enjoy seeing each other every once in a while. The message he sent her was the access code to his apartment. Only she would know exactly what it was and who sent it.

As they entered the bar they were handed a glass of champagne. Benjamin tasted it, it was alright. Brad tasted it and realized it had been a LONG time since he had anything like champagne.

They made small talk and waited for their table, learning a little more about each other. They were, at this time, a group; not two couples.

"So Gloria, where are you from?" Brad asked.

"My family is from the west coast of the North American continent. I was born in San Francisco and grew up in Napa Valley. My favorite uncle owns and runs the best vineyard in the area." She said with pride.

Everyone looked at Tiffany and she started, "I am from the exact opposite location from her. Sometimes we even refer to each other as the evil twin."

Brad broke in, "Are you from the Eastern Coast?"

She continued, "Not exactly....I am from Perth, Australia. I grew up on the Swan River near Bristle Park. From my bedroom I could see the river. I kinda miss it. But as far as the planet Earth is concerned, if you ran a stick from her house to mine, it would pass extremely close to the center of the planet. So, Evil Twins!"

"What did your parents do?" Brad asked, addressing the question to both women.

"My Mum designed clothing and my father owned several fast food dining establishments in Western Australia. Both parents knew that the sciences and mechanics were important, so I had to take all of the mechanics and shop classes in school. When I went to University, I majored in engineering and restaurant management. I never could make up my mind. So I spent an extra year and got both degrees before I graduated." Tiffany realized her accent was coming back a little as she reminisced about home and looked embarrassed.

Gloria took over, "I really like when she is flustered, or tired. That is when the REAL accent gets thick."

"BENJAMIN JENSEN!" The female voice came from behind him somewhere. He recognized the voice and got a grin like he was the cat that ate the canary. "Do you know how long it has been since you have visited my little eatery? I should tossed out and shoot you back home on the next mag-lev."

"Yes ma'am. Been at least a year and I really miss your food. No one cooks like Ramona Sharp."

Brad perked up when he heard her name, "As in Matthew Sharp....your boss?"

"Yes" She said back to him, "My uncle!" She grinned.

Benjamin stood and they grabbed each other in a big hug. Not a hug of passion but the hug of two very good friends who have not seen each other in a long while. Well, hug is not exactly what it was, she jumped up into his arms and wrapped her legs around him and gave him the biggest hug anyone in the bar had ever seen. Including the hostess with the attitude.

"Are you four at your favorite table, Ben?"

"Yes we are. Why?"

"Does anyone have any food allergies" everyone shook their head. "Does everyone like seafood?" Everyone nodded. "GOOD! I will give you a preview of a menu item I found a few months ago on New Sydney. It's a seafood delicacy that will have you wanting more. Do you trust me?"

Everyone nodded and was smiling from ear to ear. The rumors of the amazing seafood from New Sydney were all over the media, and she had some….this is going to be great.

"Mr. Jensen, your table is ready." The hostess said in a peaceful calm voice. "Please follow me." Ramona nodded to the hostess and waved to Benjamin and his party as she disappeared into the kitchen.

Thinking to Brad, *"Let the drooling begin!"*

Brad chuckled and shook his head, *"Yep, that's Benjamin."* He replied through the link.

As the hostess led them through the restaurant Brad noticed that each and every table was in use. He would have wondered how they were able to get a table if he had not seen the reception by the executive chef.

"She is not only the executive chef, Brad; she is also the owner of this and five other four star restaurants in the solar system. She

even owns the Burger Deli on the station, my idea. She named it Jump Burgers at my suggestion. As in jumping to and from Earth. We can stop there tomorrow on the way to the drop-ship. It's right next door." Benjamin passed on the information through the link. Brad had forgotten it was active. It has been a long time since he had a direct link with anyone in this way so he was a bit rusty.

The table they were led to was a meter square, and next to the exterior view of the lunar surface. There were two views that could be chosen; a view of the Earth or a view of the dark side of the Moon, and the vastness of deep space. Benjamin's standing table reservation was for the latter. Although a view of the Earth, and full Earth it is at the moment, these women travel back and forth constantly, and see the Earth in all its glory and majesty. So, it is logical that the view of space 'could' be more appealing; and at the very least, it is beautiful.

"So ladies, what do you think of the view?" Brad motioned to the vastness of the view to his right.

The table was positioned so everyone at the table had a spectacular view. The window was actually a point jutting out over the lunar landscape as if pointing to some landmark or curiosity in the distance, with one corner of the table pointing toward this same destination. Brad and Gloria were sitting nuzzled, somewhat, in this corner with Brad's right side facing the great unknown. Benjamin sat across from Brad which placed Tiffany across from Gloria. It also made for a boy-girl-boy-girl setting, which is more intimate and prompts conversation at the table.

As they were staring into the darkness of space trying to remember the names of all those points of light, Benjamin reached under the table and touched a panel. He knew it was there because when the restaurant was built he suggested it be installed on all the tables near windows. As he touched the toggle the window became ever so slightly opaque and the star names, planets, constellations, and other points of light became alive. The names appeared as if hovering next to each and the others at the table all participated in a collective gasp, then an ahhhhh.

"Benjamin, what did you do?" Gloria asked.

"Why do you think I did something?" Benjamin replied innocently.

"Multiple reasons, but mainly this seems like you're doing." Tiffany added.

"Uh, Benjamin. Is this the chef you talked about last year?" Brad asked.

"Yep! She is." Benjamin nodded.

Tiffany looked rather upset and asked, "So, were you two an item?"

Benjamin smiled and shook his head, "No, not at all. She lived next door to me for a while and I assisted her in refining her menu and her recipes."

They all just looked at him waiting for him to continue.

"OK, her uncle is my boss. We are good friends and like some of the same things. We tried dating for a while but decided we were better as friends, so, that's where we are; and have been that way for more than a year and happy with it."

"How long did you date?" Tiffany asked.

"Less than a month. When she was opening her first restaurant. I had a weekend party at my apartment whenever I was in town and she catered the event. Her catering menu was unique every week because she was testing and experimenting with new recipes trying to perfect them or give them a 'Ramona' flair and feel. As a researcher for the archives I come across a lot of things and some of them are really old recipes. I print them and pass them to her and she plays with them till she is happy, and then finds guinea pigs, oh…I mean taste testers to try and critique the results."

They all stared and were shaking their heads. Not disbelief, but amazement.

Gloria asked slowly, "You do work for the Archives?"

"Uh, yes we do." Brad answered.

Gloria snuggled closer to Brad, and Tiffany placed her hand on Benjamin's. The women looked at the guys differently. If they had looked at their identification, it would have been obvious, but there was no reason to look at their ID.

"Brad, what just happened?" Benjamin asked through the Sub-Q link.

"Not sure. They seem to think that since we are employees of the archive we are celebrities or something." Brad thought back to him.

"I'm not sure if this is a good or a bad thing. But I will have fun trying to figure it out!" Benjamin smiled when he sent that to Brad, both inside, and on his face.

"Mr. Jensen." The maitre d' arrived at the table with a bottle of champagne. "This is compliments of the Executive Chef and

Owner." He said with a matter of fact tone, but gracefully and a hint of arrogance tossed in for effect.

"Thank you. You may open and pour the table. I trust the judgment of Chef Sharp so I am certain, without smelling the cork or tasting the wine, that it will be excellent."

Taken somewhat by surprise the gentleman in his mid 30's began opening the cage. Interesting, after all these centuries of wine making technology, that wine is always best when made in the traditional method, and bottled and capped as it has been for centuries.

POP! A small pop could be heard under the towel and after a moment he poured a half glass for each of the four. Together they all toasted silently, ringing their goblets together in the center of the table. As they all drank they realized this was the best wine they had ever had...

Setting their glasses on the table the maitre d' refilled them this time to the top in the anticipation their meals were about to arrive.

He placed the remainder of the bottle in the ice bucket and left. There was enough in the bottle for one more refill for each person, as this bottle was nearly two liters' in volume.

Benjamin picked up the bottle to look at the label. He had the shock of his life. His eyes were open all the way and his mouth hung open slightly.

"What is it?" Gloria asked.

The other two stared at him for a moment then he was able to speak.

"Uh…" Benjamin started to talk then closed his mouth. The others could see Ramona Sharp, the executive chef and owner, walking up from behind him.

"So, do you like the wine?" Yes's and nods all around.

Ramona took the bottle from Benjamin and explained. "I decided a long time ago, with the assistance of a very close and dear friend, that if you do ANYTHING you should do it to the best of your ability. Wine is no different. I stock a variety of vintages but this label, my house wine, is the best tasting and least expensive on the menu…at least in my restaurants. This friend suggested I create my wines and bottle them and sell them at select locations for a very impressive amount, a lot more than it is worth, in a sense, but a lot more than it needs to be. It would increase the profit margin drastically and give me a niche market to the wealthy."

She read the label silently to herself, then out loud. "A robust wine with a slightly cherry and smoky aftertaste that pairs well with life, and dinner. Suggested accompaniments are good food and good friends." She paused.

"He then suggested that each bottle cost so little when consumed in the restaurant with dinner, that people would eat here just to get the wine. I thought that was a strange and unique idea, and since we had a strange and unique relationship…I did it. You don't get rich on wine, but you do get rich on food and ambiance. Been my motto ever since. Give it away hear for 7 credits a bottle, and on Earth in a wine store it goes for sixty-three credits a bottle. The alcohol content is lower than most wines and it is just a joy to sit and sip with friends."

Benjamin was shaking his head ever so slightly and Ramona gave him a hug and left. As she was walking away she stopped a few paces from their table, looked at the maitre d' and said flatly, but with emotion, "Bring my friends another bottle of Ben's Friendship, on me."

They were all speechless. Gloria had something in her eye and Brad started clearing his throat.

"You had no idea she did that?" Tiffany asked.

"No" He replied. Still staring at the bottle.

"She must be one special friend. You owe her big time." Gloria added.

"No, actually, we owe each other. We owe each other a lot."

*   *   *   *   *   *   *   *   *   *   *   *

The appetizers were definitely different. The dinner however was a different story. All in all it was going well. At first they were afraid to touch, let alone eat, the ugly little sea creature in front of them. They were all given a different meal and were told to share. There was enough seafood on these four plates for eight to ten people so that seemed logical. Brad was the most daring and tasted his meal with the chef standing next to him. Slowly, cautiously, he carved off a slice. It was very tender. He placed it in his mouth expecting to taste something alien.

"OH MY GOODNESS!!" Brad exclaimed. "That is the best fish I have ever tasted."

The rest of them were so impressed that they dug in and really enjoyed their meal. After a few minutes they started sharing and found they all liked all five meals. That's when they realized Ramona pulled up a chair between Benjamin and Gloria and had something really different on her plate.

Benjamin turned and asked her, "When did you get here?"

"Several years ago, while you were eating." She answered. That was it. When they all had enough she, Ramona, handed them each a sheet of interactive myoply.

It was a questionnaire on the meals. That's when they realized there were five different color plates rather than numbers or names. They all liked that. Order the RED meal and you knew exactly what you were getting. Ramona's idea to take the alien seafood worldwide with a method of identification that was so simple anyone could remember which they liked the best.

Each finished tapping their sheet of questions and handed them to Ramona who also filled one out. They sat at the table and the cocktail waiter brought them each a drink of their choice and discussed the results until just after 11pm Lunar Time.

"WOW! We have the dome from NOW till 2am." Brad exclaimed. "Ramona, wanna join us? Not too often you can fly for free and with only a few others. Bring a date."

"I will. Give me thirty minutes and we will be there." She got up and left. The restaurant closed more than 45 minutes ago, 10:30pm to be exact. Clean up and then some low-grav flight. Nice night.

The foursome left the restaurant and strolled – but quickly – towards the dome. Brad suddenly started humming in his head a tune he heard during a mission.

"Let's all fly like the birdies fly" Brad started.

Benjamin continued, *"Cheap....Cheap Cheap....Cheap Cheap!"*

They both started laughing and the girls just stared at them.

* * * * * * * * * * * *

As they entered the dome Benjamin remembered his favorite moments flying through the one hundred and fifty-meter-high dome. It was quite a bit larger across than high, but that left for some interesting maneuvers when learning to use the wings.

A few moments later the video of Benjamin crashing into a wall during their school break was piped from Brad's Sub-Q to his. He smiled and sent him back the image of a very sun burnt Brad, wincing slightly, remembering the pain and the embarrassment at falling asleep in the island Sun during break, and the special mission he and Benjamin had to make to correct history when Benjamin tried to change time just to see if it would work. Man, did he get in trouble with the school; he was nearly expelled from the Academy.

Looking at each other they nodded and smiled. That was all that needed to be said. There was a bond between them, a very strong bond that could not be loosened or broken. They were closer than brothers.

Walking into the dome the man standing near the door asked, "Mr. Jensen?....BENJAMIN! `Bout time you got here, I need someone to crash into that wall over there to make the room more balanced." The man was pointing to the opposite wall Benjamin crashed into all that time ago.

"...And I supposed you're going to give me those substandard wings, and that nasty drink, and those awful ... what did you call them again?" Benjamin said, but sounding like he was having fun.

"..NACHO'S, what is it with you. With that memory of yours I am surprised you remember how to get TO the dome."

"OK, now what…." Benjamin said as if trying to not look like he was having fun.

From the back corner of the reception area, about 2 meters away or so, a female voice could be heard. "Would you to just FINALLY say hello already!"

They did, they ran the two steps and grabbed each other. It was definitely an embrace of old friends. Since he was here in school he and this man had become friends.

The woman came up and pulled him away from the man, he grabbed her and gave her the biggest hug, and a really nice kiss.

"HEY! That's my wife!" The man said.

"I'll give her back." Benjamin replied.

"Later…" The woman added.

"OK!" The man added.

They all separated and Benjamin stood between them with his arm around this married couple. As they all turned to the other three who were all left out of this welcoming, they looked at their faces and nearly fell on the floor laughing. "If you three could see your faces right now." Benjamin finally was able to say.

"Uh….I am assuming that you know these people Benjamin." Brad said, still a little in shock.

"I guess he knows us a little. Spends more money here than the shuttle has rivets." The man said.

Tiffany was about to say that the shuttle contains no rivets, it is completely assembled with molecular bonding. No weak points at all in the skin or anywhere else. Gloria stopped her.

"My name is Tim and this is Jan, we own this place and "Crash" Jensen here is our interior decorator."

Benjamin started laughing, "You honestly remember that crash all those years ago?"

"My boy, I remember each and every crash. It is simply rare, however, for the crashee to want to take up residence until he, now how did he put it dear...."

"...got it right!" She added and squeezed Benjamin a little around the waist.

Benjamin nodded and replied, "Yes, and in the process I made some really good friends, oh, and you two also.... ANYWAY!. This is Brad, Gloria, and Tiffany."

Tim nodded and asked, "So, who wants their wings first?" Benjamin looked at Tim and Jan. They all raised their hands at the same time. "Like a bunch of kids in a candy store." Jan replied. "Strap on a pair of oversized wings and give the tourists a chance to fly like little birds and they regress to teenagers." Tim smiled. So did they.

Since Benjamin had frequented the dome whenever he had the chance he knew the set he wanted. "I would like wing-set Alpha seven please."

"Sir," The woman paused formally. "Are you certain?"

"Yes. I have used them several times in the past. They are very comfortable and after hitting the walls a few times to break them in I got quite used to them. Besides, with that set I will not need an assisted take-off."

"True. Wait, I remember you now. Didn't you slam into a wall a few years ago? If I remember correctly we refer to that hole up there…" She pointed about seventy five meters up and to her right. "…as the Jensen porthole. It went straight through to the swimming pool. The debris landed in a sand dune, but no one was injured; the hole is still there however. We never fixed it by design. We did cover the hole with a transparent sheet to make it air-tight and put a little plaque on it with the name of the person who made it and the date. Don't worry; you are not the only one to cause damage to this facility. We believe this place is the personality of the patrons so therefore we 'NAME' every incident and commemorate it with a plaque."

Benjamin blushed. The girls laughed. Brad snickered and chuckled, and shook his head.

Once they all had their wings Benjamin took off. Flapped his arms and flew. The others were a bit less graceful and needed a running start off a small platform, but they all did quite well. Benjamin flew up to the hole – a hole he had no idea he created by the way – and hovered to read the plaque. Name…date…and the statement you need to not lose focus when operating a set of wings. A little humor but highly accurate. In all the times he had been here afterwards, he never noticed the hole or the plaque.

The incident occurred during his training at the archives. They, his class top six, had just received their Sub-Q devices. Since the device allows them to communicate and transmit video to anyone on the same frequency, they tested it out. Benjamin was flying in the dome, another classmate was taking a stroll on the dark-side on the Moon; a couple others were playing around in the asteroid belt; one went home to Siberia; and the last stayed right at the school. Brad was not one of the six elected class leaders but later when the remainder of the class received their implants the video was shared, at the expense of Benjamin. But he did not mind. Brad has always saved that vid in protected memory. He watches it from time to time just to get a chuckle.

They all looked at the entrance far below them and saw Ramona enter the facility. She had someone with them, it was the maître d'.

Benjamin and Brad landed a few meters away from them. "Hi there, glad you made it." Brad said, slightly out of breath.

"You know Henry, right." She looked at Benjamin and smiled.

"Of course we do. Nice to meet you Henry. Now grab some wings and we can all compete. You have thirty minutes till the games begin."

"Games." Henry said. "What games?"

*   *   *   *   *   *   *   *   *   *   *   *   *   *   *

"OK, time for the games to begin. Will everyone please join me at the flashing blue light." The voice echoed through the facility and everyone heard and began to fly towards the blue pulsating strobe.

"Games." Henry said. "What games?"

"Why the games of skill and daring we set up for private parties. We put them on once a quarter here for all to compete. The winner of the public games gets a year of free flight. The winner of today's games a small trophy." Jan, who was also an owner of the facility, looked like it was going to be fun. She looked genuinely excited about the games.

Tim continued. "There will be three competitions, all accomplished alone and your timed scores will be tallied to determine a winner. Number one, take-off race; you will each take-off and fly to the apex of the dome where you will invert and press the panel with your feet. That will illuminate a light and ring a bell. You will then land in the red circle. Timer starts when you leave the ground and ends when you are landed in the circle."

Jan took over, "Number two, my favorite, you will take-off and fly around the dome counter clockwise twice, then land as close as possible to the yellow star on the floor. Not a timed event but accuracy." She pointed to the spot and they all saw it. Not the biggest landing area.

"And the last round," he continued, "was to take-off, hover for fifteen seconds while the ring moves into place, then fly through the four holo-rings that will be in front of you. When you take-off, you will see a yellow holographic box in mid-air. Hover in the box facing the back wall, the big blue wall. The rest will unfold in front of you. Timer starts when the box disappears, which is fifteen seconds after you are hovering in the box. Any questions?"

No questions.

"I have one." Gloria voiced up. "What are the stakes?"

Benjamin spoke up quickly. "If either of you beautiful ladies win, dinner for the four of us at the restaurant of your choosing anywhere in the Solar system. Transportation and lodging included if there is travel involved." They both agreed. "…and if either of us wins?"

Tiffany spoke up quickly. "We can discuss that in private."

Benjamin and Brad both agreed to a very vague prize, but they got the idea. Ramona and Henry laughed. "What if one of us win? Ramona asked.

Henry chimed in, "Guys against girls?"

A resounding YES and the games began.

"The computer will choose the competitor's order randomly for each test, Benjamin…you are first." The man who owns the facility spoke. "We have been here as the proprietors of the dome flight experience since its inception ten years ago. I expect to see you out-do everyone before. OK, Benjamin, ready?" Jan added in a quiet voice, "NO PRESSURE THERE!" Tim continued, "When you hear the horn you take off and fly to the light at the apex of the dome. As you approach the panel you will need to stall and kick your feet up above you. Press the panel with your feet then land in the red circle…there." He traced the route with his hand and a green laser so each item was identified.

"Ready." Benjamin whispered. He was standing poised to spring into the air.

"OK, try not to crash again…." Tim verbally poked him. They all chuckled.

When he heard the sound he leapt into the air and flapped as hard as he could. So hard in fact that he reached the ceiling a lot faster than he anticipated, spreading his arms he caught a large amount of air and nearly came to a stop, with his speed his feet kicked up without even trying and stepped on the panel. He bent his knees so the momentum he built up would compress him to the ceiling and he could get a spring board effect and flapped a couple times to balance, then coasted to the ground. He was coming in hot; a lot faster than anyone watching thought would be safe. Just before the last moment he flared his arms and caught big time air and it instantly slowed him to a landing velocity in the dead center of the circle.

"Time was 11.4 seconds." Jan yelled out. "You tied the record."

"Who's record?" Benjamin asked.

Jan replied, "Mine!"

"Excellent!" Benjamin added. "I need something to drink."

Tim chimed in, "Got the perfect concoction for you. It's called the Misty Jacks. Do you trust me?" Benjamin nodded.

Jan took over while Tim made a few drinks and passed them around to the six competitors. "This is good" Ramona exclaimed. "What's in it?"

"Thanks, my creation. Ancient Chinese secret!" Tim answered with a smile and half.

"Why is it called a Misty Jacks?" Henry asked.

Well, in a large pitcher you put in ENOUGH Jack Daniels, and ENOUGH Canadian Mist, fill it with a light citrus soda and ice and pour into glasses. Add a splash of apricot brandy to the glass and drink.

"Please sir, may I have another." Brad said making those puppy dog eyes.

"Benjamin, these people are as nuts as you, no ALMOST as nuts as you." Jan added to the humor.

"OK, now, how did it get its name, well, let's see. Before Jan and I left Earth to live here we had a couple pets, a cat named Misty and a dog named Jack, Jackson actually, but we called him Jacks. They live with our son in Texas now. We get to visit them every once in a while."

Jan took over, "A half year after we started this business our son brought Jack up here to visit. He was so excited he ran and jumped at us. He did not understand the concept of gravity, but if you look over there…" She pointed to a hole in the wall outlined with small lights, "That's where he landed. Hard!"

Tim continued, "He never ran again up here, but it only took one time to understand gravity in his little doggie mind."

As the competition continued the six people became friends. They even allowed Tim and Jan to join their little band of friendship.

Benjamin bonded with Tim and Jan, and by the end of the evening Jan was like his little sister. Tim was like another brother. Not nearly as close as Brad, but yes, a brother none the less.

Chapter 3

A Vacation from Reality

As Brad and Benjamin entered the shuttle to take them to the home from the Lunar Colony, they were escorted to the first class compartment by Tiffany and Gloria. Benjamin was smiling from ear to ear and Brad had the look on his face of peace and calm.

"Tiff, ok, where would you like to have dinner? You beat me by .01 seconds. If I did not have the best wings out there I would have beat you easily. But getting those giant wings through the rings without touching the borders was not easy. How was I to know that touching adds a whole second for each touch? I could have won by almost 14 seconds."

"But you didn't. I did. And I will tell you where and when as soon as you return from your trip. Where are you two going anyway?"

Brad started, "We need to do some research on a few of the databases at the colonies. Unfortunately, these databases are not on the central net so we need to be there in person. We should be back in a few weeks, private charter for this mission. Thankfully direct flights and Brad and I are the only passengers."

They were seated and the girls needed to attend to their duties aboard ship. Brad tapped his head and Benjamin knew that was the sign to reactivate his implant so they could communicate with no one listening on their conversation.

"You there?" They both asked at the same time. They started laughing out loud and then looked around in case anyone was watching them.

"Good. Here is what I see, and what we need to do and in what order. Number one, we need to jump back to when you saw them and get their finger prints or if at all possible their DNA. Then we could determine their lineage or their person and trace it to a generation or so. We know we can go less than one hundred years in the future with no ill effects, more and we will suffer. Once we can ..."

"Gentlemen...." A voice boomed through their heads like an amplified sound system. *"Upon arrival at the orbital facility please redirect your path to visit me. We will discuss your next step."*

They both were sitting back in their seats with their eyes closed, it was the easiest way to appear to be resting and give full focus on the conversation. But when Mr. Winchester's voice punched through, they both jumped as though they were hit by lightning.

Their eyes opened together and they looked at each other in shock, but the shock wore off quickly. *"Sir,"* Benjamin thought. *"We will be arriving in several hours but we will need to book transport on the shuttle to your orbital facility."*

"The booking is complete. Your new itinerary can be viewed on your comm unit. Check your messages, the update should have reached you already." Mr. Winchester stated.

Checking their messages, they see the update with an arrival about nine hours later than originally planned. One-hour flight to see Mr. Winchester and a one-hour flight for the return trip from the station to the drop ship; forty-five-minute layover then a thirty-minute ride on the drop ship. "That leaves about six hours with Mr. Winchester." Benjamin said out loud, but not loud enough to be overheard

"Very good gentlemen, I see you can still add." They forgot he could hear their thoughts. *"I will see you in a few hours, oh…and dinner is on me. I hope you like meat loaf? Something Mr. Jensen found in the past that I have taken a liking too. That, and in zero gravity it is the easiest item to consume without making too much of a mess."*

"Uh, Mr. Winchester, I have a suggestion on that." Benjamin added. *"If you make the meatloaf into a sandwich, the mess factor lowers considerably."*

"Nice idea. We will try it when you arrive." Slight pause. *"I will leave you to your thoughts."* They heard the telltale sound of a high pitched hiss that was barely noticeable unless you were looking for it, which signified the connection was broken. They were alone again.

"Brad, while connected he sent me a file. Hang on…" Benjamin opened and reviewed the file. It contained the bulk of the research data for the last few centuries compared to the last few centuries of the controls located in the past. The differences were amazing. Benjamin sent a copy to Brad who was looking at it also.

"DAMN!" Brad said out loud.

"Is there something wrong? Can I get you something?" Gloria was standing between them looking curious at the outburst.

"No, thanks. I simply remember I had a meeting after we land and it is not a meeting I am looking forward to, thanks for asking though." Brad created the excuse like a pro. Benjamin must be rubbing off on him more than he thought.

"Uh..Gloria. Can you please let Tiffany know that Brad and I were just informed our assignment starts when we dock? We will be transferring to another shuttle to go to a different station where we will begin our next assignment. We have your contact info and believe me, we will make good on the bet. It just may be a few weeks before we get back in the system." Benjamin tried to sound sincere, and did a fair job of it. He was an accomplished liar to one extent, and he did teach the course at the academy which taught thinking on your feet. Still taught but by someone he recommended. So, it was no surprise.

"We know. We received the updated travel plan for the two of you and were instructed to ensure you are the first off the ship and safe in your transfer shuttle. This must be one heck of an assignment. Research, and a higher priority than any VIP. Can you tell me anything?"

"No, we have no idea what we will be doing, simply to report to the station for a briefing. I am getting a feeling about this, and I hope I am wrong."

Gloria and Tiffany resumed their duties on the shuttle and Brad and Benjamin sat in their seats looking as though they were either asleep, resting, or jotting notes on a pad. In reality, Mr. Winchester was beginning the briefing through the Sub-Q and there were a great many people on the link at the same time.

The remainder of the flight went as planned, and the girls escorted them to the next set of hands to escort them to the shuttle that would take them to visit Mr. Winchester were a burly, over muscled pair of security types. They kissed the girls and walked down the corridor and into the shuttle, which undocked and left within minutes for Station Sigma Five.

* * * * * * * * * * * * * * *

"Mr. Jensen, Mr. Jorgen. How nice of you to visit?" Mr. Winchester said sarcastically.

"Brad and Benjamin spoke at the same time, Benjamin said, "We were in the neighborhood" and Brad said, "Well, did we have a choice?" almost under his breath. Benjamin heard him but chose to ignore it.

"No Mr. Jorgen, you did not. Now, let's get down to business. Are you two ok with no gravity?"

Brad spoke up, "I'm fine"

"As am I" Benjamin added.

"Good. Now here is what we have discovered."

For the next few hours they all interfaced with the main security conference room on the island and chipped away at the plan to correct the historical errors. The first thing they discovered was there was an anomaly in early seventeen ninety-one. It seems the Bill of Rights for the Constitution of the United States of America was never ratified due to what we would refer to today as an act of terrorism. Alexander Hamilton was taken hostage and released only if the Bill of Rights was voted on and denied. That is exactly what happened and within a few months, all of the representatives who supported the Bill were dead of what appeared to be natural causes.

Mr. Carter from Security continued, "It seems to be natural causes but knowing what we know now it is a safe bet they were poisoned with something from the future and is invisible to the law enforcement agencies of the time."

"So, first order of business is to visit several of the persons and keep an eye on them. We have developed, using the technology given to us by Mr. Jorgen, a device which emits a signal that will disrupt the return signal. If you activate it, the person you are interested in talking to cannot depart until you let them. Additionally, it limits the range of the Sub-Q to one meter."

"Which means they can't call for help, pop out, or hide anything from you thanks to that one little device." Mr. Sharp added loudly and with pride.

"That is part one. Part two is to find out where this person comes from, when actually, and who they are and who they work for. Once you activate the device and hijack their Sub-Q, it will be tuned to your secondary frequency, which fixes it so they can't contact their friends. You are to incapacitate this person after you get the information and then inject him with a wide-band transponder. This specific frequency will be coded to this event for all of history so we will know when and why this person is of interest. The transponder, when interrogated by the main computer at the archives, will transmit all relative data. Which mean they will not get away with it?"

Will continued, "Second, you must stop the bank robbery; but Brad, your other self cannot be a part of this action. This is where improvisation and stealth come into play. When it comes to covert, Benjamin is the best." Was that a barb on the end of the hook?

For the next few hours they learned how they were to correct history and they set up the jump plan. They would need three sets of clothing; rustic west, business attire from the 20th century, and security force attire from the 23rd century.

The meeting ended a bit early and Mr. Winchester made them stay for dinner. Very nice dinner and a fine wine, even though it was served in zero gravity in a bag with a straw.

Having the debilitating illness, and living on the station, gave him freedom and mobility in the microgravity. But now it is time to leave.

"Gentleman, the shuttle will return you to the drop ship. You leave in the morning for your mission. Good luck."

"We have nearly an hour layover on the station before the drop ship departs. I want to stop by Jump Burgers."

Sounds good is all Brad could think of saying.

The restaurant is nothing more than a hole in the wall, literally. You walk up to a hole that is in the wall and place your order. The guy makes your food and hands it to you through the hole. You pay, leave, eat, and enjoy.

Since Benjamin and Ramona were still an item when this place opened, Benjamin and the on-site manager became friends, since he was here so much. The guy was busy and Benjamin stuck his head in the hole and yelled, "Got any fresh rat?"

"BENJAMIN!" The guy yelled back.

He made them a meal and took his break so he could sit and talk to them while they ate. Then, on to the drop ship.

*   *   *   *   *   *   *   *   *   *   *   *   *   *   *

"Brad, let's stop by the quartermaster's office and pick up a few things. I know you have what you need, but there are a few things I want." Benjamin said with annoyance in his voice.

"Like what?" Brad returned.

"We need modern handcuffs that look like period handcuffs. I ordered them yesterday when we were on the shuttle. Also, I got us both a Marshall's badge and credentials so we could move as we need to and not raise too much suspicion when we do something out of the ordinary."

"Whoooo…US? Out of the ordinary." Brad smiled big.

"Where did you disappear to last night?" Benjamin asked.

"I made a stop at Pluto's…" Benjamin came to a complete stop and looked directly at Brad.

"I knew I liked you for some reason." Knowing that Brad must have picked up some liquid refreshment from Mike.

Entering the room Benjamin looked at the trio and before he could say a word they all walked away and picked up items and put them on the counter.

"One last thing." The man in charge walked over to a wall and touched it, a panel opened and he keyed in a code and looked into a sensor. The wall disappeared and he picked up four stun watches. "You each get two. You will be gone for quite a while and in the event one is damaged or breaks the other may save your life. Mr. Jorgen, this one is for you, it is the original."

They put one on each wrist and a moment later they seemed to evaporate. "Test?"

The red head of the trio pointed to a patch on the wall. Since they were fired from thought all he needed to do is think and it went there. Benjamin got close and hit the target after a shot or two. Brad walked up and grinned. He took aim and fired two shots from each device, dead center.

Benjamin looked at him and cocked his head.

Brad spoke up, "Give me a break. How do you think I got meat on the trail? I am a terrible shot with a pistol or a rifle but this thing; I can stun an animal from fifty meters. The hardest part was learning to kill and clean it."

"Can we speed this up a bit? We need to fly to New York to watch the world symphony performance at the Garden."

Brad likes that style of music so his attention was perked, "Really. Madison Square Garden? I have always wanted to go there."

"Where?" Everyone exclaimed.

Brad looked at Benjamin and he had that look, "We need to leave. There are things here that are really out of whack!"

* * * * * * * * * * * * * * *

They arrived a month ago to save the signers of the Bill of Rights. It seems the Bill of Rights should have been passed and for some reason all of the people who passed it ended up dead from natural causes prior to when they were supposed to either draft or approve it. All that is left is one man then they can go forward to the 20th century.

James Madison, the main author of the Constitution of the United States, died from what appeared to be the flu on June 28, 1771.

Brad and Benjamin knew he was really supposed to die sixty-five years later of old age; not at the age of twenty.

In the last month the two travelers have popped in and out of time and amassed a great deal of information regarding what has been happening. They even discovered what was going on when Brad first started all of this and the timeline is about sixty percent restored. Once Madison is saved the Bill of Rights and the Constitution will be set in motion and the federal government will not have total and complete power over the United States, and eventually the entire planet.

Benjamin and Brad walked into a pub and sat at a table in the corner of the room, mainly so they can watch over both Madison who frequented the establishment and for any odd characters that may enter. Their Sub-Q implants were modified before they left to give them the ability to scan frequencies without letting on someone is listening.

"Benjamin, frequency 1462. I hear them. They are close and talking about Madison."

> *"Once we put a drop of this in Madison's beer, it will be lights out for him. Then we can finally get paid for knocking off all of these historical people."*
>
> *"I am so glad that this stuff works fast. If it touches his lips, he's a gonner."*

"OK, so all we need to do is figure out who they are and not let Madison drink that beer, simple!"

Madison walked in and sat at the bar. Benjamin and Brad walked over and sat on either side of him. Temporal body guards for a twenty-year-old who has no idea how important he is to history. With the way they were sitting they made small talk with him and became temporary friends. The kind of friends you meet in a bar, have a few drinks with, and never see again. They took turns buying rounds and after the fourth Madison wanted to leave. It was at that moment the two walked in and Benjamin and Brad knew instantly it was them. They walked over to the bar and ordered a drink and Benjamin saw the man put something into the drink and knew this was it. He told Brad through the link and they both were ready for anything. Benjamin activated the Sub-Q Suppressor Field and reached to shake the man's hand as an introduction. As he did he stunned him and no one knew what happened.

His partner, on the other hand, realized it and tried to jump home with no success and was shocked it did not work. He attempted to call for reinforcements and was not able to get anyone. Brad stunned him and he crumpled to the ground next to his partner.

Madison had no idea what happened so he grabbed the beer that was tainted and dumped it on the two men on the floor. Nothing happened. Benjamin and Brad heard them say if one drop touches the lips they had it, so, these two had it. This would be a good time to ask a few questions. If they allowed them to return home before the illness became severe they would survive. Excellent time to get information.....

*   *   *   *   *   *   *   *   *   *   *   *   *   *   *

"I am so glad they did not have the antidote with them." Brad started as they rode out of town on a pair of horses. Brad had been here before, as had Benjamin, but Brad had an account in the local bank with a few dollars in the event of an emergency. He said he did that everywhere he went, so he did not have to carry all of the cash with him and be the target of bandits.

"So am I. It gave them added incentive to tell us the truth, not to mention a reason for us to deactivate the Sub-Q Distortion Generator." He looked at Brad and smiled.

"The What?"

"You heard me, the Sub-Q Distortion Generator. You like it?" Benjamin asked.

"Actually, yes I do."

"OK, then it now has a new name. Getting back to business, Madison is safe so why are we still here?"

"I want to visit a couple of old and dear friends. They are just over that rise and have enough grub and spirits to make us all happy." Brad was being vague and that is not like him. What is he upto…..

As the horses walked slowly over the rise in the land Benjamin had an idea he knew exactly who these two friends are…

"Do we, or don't we?" Brad asked him.

"If we do this, there is no going back. But it would give us a real advantage in the next two jumps."

Benjamin prodded his horse toward the campfire and a few moments later he heard a familiar voice, "Hello. Can we help you?"

Benjamin looked at himself and said, "Yes you can!" His other self was stunned.

*　*　*　*　*　*　*　*　*　*　*　*　*　*　*

"OK, so it is decided then. You hold Benjamin 2 and I hold Brad 2 and we take them with us on the next jump. In theory, no matter where you are in the time stream when you activate the recall signal it gets you and takes you home. So you ---we---I---WhatEVER…should be fine."

Team 2, as they have been dubbed, turned off their implants so-as not to interfere with the transfer process. In theory, if they were in physical contact during transit they appeared with them. He cannot remember it ever being tested like this though, so this is an experiment that may end up with all four of them lost forever in history.

The process was initiated, and there was a light pop, and they appeared in the latter half of the 20th century; June 24, 1980 to be exact. The local time was 9:45pm. "We need to find a place to stay for the night and in the morning get in to speak to Bill Gates about one employee. According to our data Stete Ballmer joined the company a few weeks earlier and he will suffer a terrible viral infection and die in the next week. I am venturing to guess tomorrow is the day he contracts his illness and the person that replaced him, William Marcus Rathbone, takes over when Bill Gates steps down. All we need to do is find Rathbone and the timeline will be restored fully and the two of you should disappear because we will not need to go back and secure your assistance."

"Temporal Paradoxes give me a headache." All four of them said it out loud at the same time, and then laughed.

"OK, Team one, since you two have the ID's you go in and speak to the boss. Brad 2 and I will look for Rathbone. If we get him how can we contact you?" Their Sub-Q's are on different frequencies.

"Benjamin, think the word car, over and over as loud as you can."

After a few moments, *"OK, you can stop now."* The four of them were all on the same frequency and Benjamin pulled the Sub-Q Distortion device out and programmed it to exclude the frequency they were on. In the meantime, Brad one was scanning all Sub-Q frequencies looking for Rathbone.

Benjamin 2 asked, "Do you have an image of this Rathbone." It was sent over the link.

"I know him; he was in my class at the academy. He pressed the red button and mumbled how he could not survive under the rules he needed to live by. Never saw him again. His first name is Norman."

Benjamin 1 added, "He wasn't in my class. He must have been recruited in the alternate timeline and left the timeframe, can't wait to talk to him."

"That's what I figure." Brad 1 said

"I was gonna say that…" Brad 2 poked at himself.

*   *   *   *   *   *   *   *   *   *   *   *   *   *   *

Before team one had the chance to get to the company headquarters, Team two found Rathbone. It took them a little time to get to them but Rathbone was not going anywhere. Thankfully, the distortion device does not have a range so it killed Rathbone's ability instantly. And an added bonus it activated his homing beacon and that made it a simple task for Team 2 to locate him. Rathbone had no idea about any of these issues since he was alone in this time he did not expect anyone to be looking for him, and the distortion wave generator did not allow him to know his own beacon was lit.

Team two found and stunned him; using the stunner Brad 2 had on his wrist. Team one showed up in a taxi and in their hotel room began to question him.

"You can't leave, you can't call, you are stuck here in this time and we have the ONLY operational Sub-Q devices in this timeframe."

"You can't block me too long or any other team traveling back to this timeframe will know something is wrong and report it when they return home." Rathbone retorted.

"I can make him talk, quickly and efficiently." Brad 2 stepped over to his bag and pulled out a small bottle. Looking at it, it looked like there was dirt in the bottom. He shook it slightly and the dirt began to move.

"How about a few thousand fire ants in your pants. Will that make you talk? Here is what you are going to tell us, now, and we may let you go. What is your mission, the year and date of your departure, the location you departed from, and the person who is in charge of changing history to suit themselves."

"You gotta be kidding if you think I am going to tell you that." Brad walked over to him and shook the bottle in front of his face. The ants were pissed off now and ready to bite anything. Brad pulled the cap off the bottle and turned it upside down in the front of his pants. Then smiled at him and said, "Anything you want to say…."

A full confession came and they knew it was all the truth. Since the confession happened he would not take over as the CEO of Microsoft and turn Microsoft into the technology mecca of the planet and help them to discover temporal displacement, time travel; but rather they would be the best computer company as they were always intended to be thanks to history.

Brad stunned Rathbone again and they turned to their counter selves and told them to leave now, and they did. He held Rathbone's shoulder and they activated the recall and went home. If everything is back to normal they are going to have a long debriefing session. Benjamin is glad he had the recordings of all of the meeting so he can give them to security and their bosses and make fast work of the debriefing.

*   *   *   *   *   *   *   *   *   *   *   *   *   *   *

"Eight days of debriefing and finally they determined we did the right thing." Benjamin shook his head as he looked at Brad.

They were on the tube from the island complex on their way to the mainland, and home to their apartments, with a stop at Pluto's for some food and liquid refreshment.

"Look at it this way, they said we did the right thing, completed the mission, and we did not remember any of it as our other selves so in essence it never happened." Brad tried to calm him down since the world was fixed once again.

Rathbone, the Rathbone they brought back with them in this mission, spilled it all to the security interviewers. They found that the alternate jump location was less than one hundred miles away and was built using spare parts that Rathbone found in the facility. Security measures were increased. Since the Rathbone of this time was a maintenance worker and since they did not want him to ever meet up with himself, the archive governance board promoted him to maintenance supervisor and he was transferred to a station in Lunar orbit where the pods are developed and tested. A job well suited for him, and one he will excel at in the future.

As for Benjamin and Brad, they were given ten days off to relax from this assignment, an assignment the governance board only learned about once they returned.

"Let's find the girls." Benjamin said.

"Wait. If we never had the assignment, then did we ever go to the Moon on the weekend and meet the girls?" Brad asked him.

"Open channel to my apartment computer." Benjamin opened his portacomm. The device chirped slightly. "What was my schedule for the past 8 weekends?"

"For the past eight consecutive weekends you have hosted a party in your flat."

Benjamin looked directly at Brad and said, "Looks like we are going to the Moon!"

Brad took out his portacomm made the exact same reservations he did when this all started. The ship departed in 4 hours so lunch at Pluto's. Burger and beer.

The tube stopped and they got off and made a bee line for Pluto's. When they arrived they walked in and Barbara was surprised to see them. She walked over and handed them both a beer and asked, "Benny, you're in early today. To what do we owe the pleasure?" She turned and looked at his guest and realized who it was, "BRAD!! You're back. Welcome back to Earth. A two-year trip has to be hard to do. Where did you go, what did you see?"

"I have plenty of time to tell you everything but let's just say that for the few stops I had to make I discovered there is no finer establishment or server in the known universe. I already know what I want to order. I have been dreaming about it for months, once I knew I was on my way home. I want a Pluto Burger, all the way."

"You want fries with that order?" Barbara asked.

"Sure do." Brad nodded at Benjamin.

"Same here." Benjamin added and Barbara strolled off to get them their lunch.

"So, 'Benny' "Brad said playfully, "tell me what happened to this place again."

"Not now, not here. Somewhere when we are alone and no one can hear."

Déjà vu....

*   *   *   *   *   *   *   *   *   *   *   *   *   *   *

Their trip to the station went as planned; they already knew everything about the girls so they became fast friends. Benjamin knew how to win the contest in the dome but chose to loose and pay the price. So, for the next ten days the four were inseparable and Tiffany and Gloria chose a new restaurant on Dione, a Moon of Saturn. Scientists a few centuries ago determined it to be an asteroid that was pulled in and held in orbit around the planet. Brad knew it was a mining colony that his father owns so he made a few calls.

"Good news and bad news." Brad said.

"Good news first." Gloria said.

"OK. Good news it is. I have the reservations and travel all booked to Dione, and the restaurant has a table in the spire held for us at 9pm on Saturday. Two-day trip and we will get there nearly a full day early."

"So what's the bad news?" Tiffany asked.

"Ah...the bad news. On the day we arrive we will be having dinner with my parents. Oh, we are also going to be guests of theirs on their station in orbit of Dione for the week. They are leaving the morning after we arrive so we will have full run of the station for the next few days."

"That's the bad news?" Tiffany was excited.

"Wait till you meet my parents."

"What's the spire?" Benjamin, who had been silent so far, asked.

"Oh, the spire." Brad smiled. "Well, you see the restaurant is located on the planetoid or asteroid, whatever it is, and there is this needle looking thing that extends more than a kilometer off the surface into space, more or less. It is composed completely of duraglass so you get a full 360-degree view, of everything in every direction, except straight down I guess."

"Sounds interesting, and scary." Gloria said as she grabbed and squeezed his arm.

Benjamin added under his breath, "Another perfect vacation." Brad nodded at him.

"Can't wait to see Mom and Dad!!" Benjamin announced.

Chapter 4

New Reality – New Assignment

Brad and Benjamin had a ten-day vacation that started three weeks ago. Neither of them wanted to come home and get back to work. They deserved this break so no one fussed they were gone an additional week or so, now… as they entered their building they needed to review a lot of historical documents to catch up on the history they did not understand. When you are in the past and time changes, you remember as it was and not as the new events unfolded. Brad remembers one history, Benjamin remembers another slightly altered history, and reality has documented a third history they both need to become familiar with and learn.

Brad spoke to Tom Wolski when they returned and grabbed up the apartment above Benjamin. Since the timeline changed he had never spoke to him regarding renting or buying the place so he really had no place to live. Of course they conducted all of their business deals at their office, at table 16 in the Pluto's business center. At least that was their running joke. Tom and Benjamin liked to tell everyone that the best deals are done over a beer. Brad is not that much of a drinker, and he really likes to drink southern sweet tea. He introduced it to a few people when he was on his long-term assignment and thought about it afterwards. Did it affect history? Not really. Tea is a bit more popular but it really did not catch on so, no harm done. He kept this to himself…FOREVER!

*   *   *   *   *   *   *   *   *

As for Benjamin, he has a lot more history to relearn. When the largest changes were taking place he was in the now. Brad was on a mission so he remembers history as it was. So, for the past month their assignment is to relearn history all over again.

"Mr. Jensen, Mr. Jorgen. Please report to Matthew Sharp's office at your convenience." A disembodied voice echo'd through the building.

"Now why would they use the intercom? They could have simply called us on our portacomm or retuned to send the message directly to our heads." Brad was mystified.

"Probably just to let everyone know we are back on assignment." Benjamin replied.

The two friends strolled back to their desks to pick up a notepad. For some reason these two like to write things down. It has become a point of humor in the office, but to these two, if something happens they can tear off the sheets and put them in a pocket for later review.

They walked to the lift and pressed the ground floor. Benjamin remembered something strange, there was this old woman that annoyed him in the worst possible way but he had not seen her in a while. Perhaps she retired, or quit, or died. He thought to himself. The doors opened and He and Brad exited in silence. They walked across the plaza to another set of elevators and press the floor for Matthew Sharp. Interesting that Brad was asked to go also. Matthew Sharp is not his supervisor.

They entered the office and the receptionist pointed to the door, they entered and stood just inside the doorway. "Please sit." The voice came from the chair but the chair was turned away from them and looking out the 'window'. In reality, this window was a vid screen that can display the image of whatever you wish to look at, and it appears to be realistic enough to affect the emotional well-being of any human.

They sat.

After a moment that seemed longer than it really was, Matthew Sharp turned from the window to face them. He had his portacomm open and a privacy bud in his ear. He was speaking to someone else. "I understand.....They will be there in the morning.........Yes, both of them.......No, I am certain they will be able to teach and mentor the ten students.......Both of them have shown their capabilities, and the ability to think on their feet......6am." The connection closed and he stared at them for several seconds. Brad and Benjamin were staring at him with the greatest of intensity.

"Gentlemen, you have been chosen for a very special assignment. Not only will you be performing the research, but you will each have a team of five students which you are to train in the art of planning, and instruct in the delicate art of finesse. Think on your feet and test a new theory."

"Sir, this is rather vague. Can you be more specific?" Benjamin asked.

"I sure can. But first let me say that Brad Jorgen has been transferred to your department. He is the same level and rate as you, so neither of you is 'the boss'; am I...clear." They both nodded and smiled. "Good. Now then." Matthew Sharp pressed a control on his desk and the room got a lot darker. After a few moments the computer voice let them know that the security mode was enabled.

"OK, now I can talk. Listen carefully. There are two missions, and six objectives. Mission one, objective one; attach pods to the Malkornin scout ship in Earth orbit on or before 1700 hrs on July 1, 1947. Objective two, you will ride back to the Malkornin homeworld and enter their atmosphere. You will determine the cause for the life on that planet to all die in the coming 36-hour period." He paused for a moment to let the fact they will be several thousand light-years from Earth sink in.

"Mission two, objective one; attach your pod to the second Malkornin ship – which we believe is a battle cruiser – and fly with them to where ever it is they are going to go. According to the reports we found on their home world, that ship never returned from the survey mission on Earth. Objective two, download their computer system. Your pods are being programmed to their protocols. Objective three for both teams, come home safely. Questions?"

"Just one sir, five each?" Brad asked.

"Ah, you will each have five students for this mission. We estimate the flight will take about 2 days' travel, then on planet for three or four days. So if you are gone for a week, you will be overdue. Both teams have a seven-day present time limit. That gives you 36 hours to me, and eight days to you until you are really overdue and we will send someone back to at least make contact and try to download your information. The problem is that if you run into trouble there is no support. In theory the Sub-Q will transmit as far as necessary; we have found no distance limit on communications so far, but in actuality, no one with an implant has ever traveled out this far from Earth before. I envy your teams. You will be attached to the outside of the ships as they transition to hyper light velocities. Remember to record the experience please. The review and briefing will be … nice."

Matthew smiled and looked forward to the debriefing video's, you could see it on his face.

Pressing the control once again the room returned to normal mode. "You are to report to the school to be assigned your students in the morning. 6:00am. Please don't be late for school." He smiled.

"Yes Dad." Benjamin and Brad replied back in unison. Matthew picked up a plastic cup on his desk and threw it at them. He was laughing as he did it.

As they left the office the receptionist took their portacomms and added some data files. They walked off without saying a word.

* * * * * * * * * * * * * * * * * * * *

The time is just after 4am and Benjamin is sound asleep dreaming about various places he has seen and people he has met. All of history is in his mind, and he knows small things about famous historical figures like what Ben Franklin likes to drink on a hot summer day, or what George Washington did every afternoon just before dinner. These are the things he could never put into the research documentation. Details like this would expose the Archive Island facility to extreme scrutiny and the secret would be out. So, he dreams about his adventures. Once in a while he will talk in his sleep to these heads of state and heroes extraordinaire. On the occasion he has a companion in his bed he can simply tell them his imagination ran away with the research. But it was a fun ride! They believe him and he recounts parts of the dream to them and they listen with intense interest. He enjoys spinning a yarn or two, but what would his listeners think if they discovered that all of the stories he tells are not fiction, but fact. The historical people Benjamin talks to in his sleep are nothing more than a recounting of a real conversation or event that took place. He can never let on any of this, so he is known for spinning a tall tale. This is also the reason he is sought after for his reporting skills.

He knew he was going to do it, and next semester he is to teach a course on reporting. He has a simple plan with 5 jumps of 60 minutes of time in the past location. First jump will be to the rainforest of the Amazon before man is even on the planet. Second jump will be to the site of a battlefield in the 1700's in a pod. Third jump will be to observe Neanderthal man using a cover-suit. Fourth jump will be to witness the injury of his partner in the parking lot. The last jump will be a 10-hour jump and the student will need to secure a seat on transportation that will take them to a specific point on the planet. The last jump is the thinking on your feet jump. All flights are full, no trains are available, no cars are available to be rented.

His mind is going over the details of this class and he knows exactly how he needs to teach it so maximum benef…………………..

BEEP! "Benjamin, the time is 4:15am. You have an appointment at the Academy this morning at 6am. Benjamin, the time is 4:15am. You have an appointment at the Academy this morning at 6am. Benjamin, the time is 4:15am. You have an appointment at the Academy this morning at 6am. Benjamin, the time is 4:15am. You have..."

"COMPUTER…OFF!" Benjamin snapped. As far as he was concerned, mornings came too early in the day. "Computer, verify with Brad Jorgen's computer that he is awake."

"Mr. Jorgen is still sleeping; shall I notify his system to wake him up?" The computer would not normally permit this action but Brad and Benjamin gave each other full access to their systems.

"YES. Record the following to be played for the wake up." A small chirp, "Brad…Oh Brad….time to wake up. Rise and shine you sleepy head."

A small chirp, "Computer, after the voice is played add music. 20th century, an artist called Alice Cooper, the song is School's Out I believe. And play it a 50% volume."

Benjamin got up and was quite satisfied with the fact that he found a new and interesting way to torture Brad. The downside is that this means Brad must retaliate. Plus, if he knew Brad well at all, he knew Brad would find the appropriate….

"Nice…." Brad's voice came through the comm system and the music was playing in the background. As the song ended he said to Benjamin, "Meet you downstairs at 5:40."

"No. Meet me downstairs at 5:15, I need to eat."

"OK." Brad cut the connections and they each got ready. At exactly 5:13am, Benjamin walked through the door and into the hall. Brad was standing there.

"You're buying!" Brad smiled.

"But you're rich, why should I buy?" Benjamin responded like a hurt puppy.

"Because of the heart attack you gave me this morning, you owe me. Nice choice of song though…"

They both laughed, "OK. Seems like a fair trade."

"OK, where are we going?" Brad asked.

"There is a place I have been meaning to try on the other side of the tube. Some donut place or something. I remember someone doing the research on it just after graduation and I did the editing and review. In the previous centuries these places dotted the landscape and people used to bike, ride, drive, and walk to them by the thousands each morning to have a donut and coffee, or a biscuit or a bagel. It is supposed to be representative of these establishments. Let's find out."

They walked past Pluto's and curious, the lights were still on; but they did not stop. They past the tube station and just on the other side – a perfect location – was the Donut Hole. It looked very retro and early 21st century. As they entered they realized all of the cooking was real cooking. Nothing about this business was instant. Since they are new in the area and their company slogan is free donuts from 5:30 till 6, Brad and Benjamin walked in at twenty minutes till 6am, and received a free glazed donut; which they each devoured in three bites. They were hooked.

"I'll take a dozen and mix them up." Benjamin said.

"I'll take a dozen too." Brad said. "All like this" Pointing to the last piece of glazed as he put it into his mouth.

The woman behind the counter asked, "Anything else I can get you?"

"Coffee, very large." Brad said. Benjamin added, "Me too"

"Would you like cream or sugar?" She asked.

"Yes, triple of each." Benjamin said. Brad added, "Black for me."

* *

Before they left the donut shop they realized they were not going to the office, they were going to class. So, as they left they each picked up an extra dozen and a couple gallons of coffee. Make a good impression....maybe. Be lighthearted in the attitude department, definitely. So as they took the tube to the island they saw one of the morning professors entering at the same time.

"Good morning gentlemen, I understand you will be their sole instructors for the next week or so, then off on a field trip. I will be sitting in on the planning sessions and the debriefing; also I and one other person, whom you will meet later, will be on the assignment with you, but our mission is to evaluate the effects on the Earth, and the attitude and impressions of the people."

"I'm sorry sir, but I do not know you. What is your name?" Brad asked.

"I am Ronald Minardelli. I teach policy and protocol. The other person is from your class, a security type. He was chosen because of his familiarity with the environment."

Benjamin added quickly and quietly, "Perhaps we can hold the remainder of this discussion for arrival and over a donut and coffee."

They both understood and made small talk about nothing in general for the remainder of the ride. They walked immediately to the classroom and set the snacks down. As they entered a ghostly figure entered the room.

"Good morning children!" He said with contempt in his voice, but a playful contempt.

Without looking up, "Good morning Bob. I trust you slept well." He called him by his first name, finally. Something that was difficult to do but gets more comfortable as you practice it.

"Sure did Ben, are those donuts? They look excellent."

Benjamin turned toward him with a donut in his hand and saluted him with it, "I'll send you a hologram of a dozen." Then he took a bite.

"Funny boy…." Mr. Winchester replied.

"Actually, you will receive a dozen on the next shuttle. I will see to it personally."

"Thanks Ben, you are a good person. But I will not let that get around…."

Brad spoke first, "OK, fill us in."

* *

The class came in the room and sat in their seats like they always did. Benjamin let them know they will be sitting in the first row for a short time then break into two groups.

"OK, we will split the leadership six in half: Lead, Research Lead, and Managerial Lead is with me; Assistant Lead, Media Lead, and Paper Lead are with Brad." They talked about how to divide the class when they arrived this morning. The other four are split in two groups.

Brad continued, "You six down front please. Here…and here." He pointed to two sets of five chairs on the floor. One set in front of him, and one set in front of Brad. "Now, you last four pose something of a problem. Once your team lead has the assignment, they will decide who goes on what team. A leadership thing…" He smiled.

Benjamin spoke loudly into the air, "Maestro, if you please."

As he said that, the room went into security mode. All windows were polarized, dampening field engaged, and computer terminals were placed in secure mode.

"Mr. Winchester, can you please do that voodoo that you do." Benjamin said.

Mr. Winchester retuned Brad and Benjamin's Sub-Q to the class frequency. "Done."

"Class, I am Benjamin Jensen and this is Brad Jorgen. We are now all tuned and ready for the briefing. For some of you this is new, others it is old hand. Let me demonstrate. Brad, please transmit the files to the team." Brad transferred the files and information they had available and all of the class members looked as though they were just hit with a brick.

"You now have all of the information compiled to date. There will be two teams. I am Team Two and Benjamin is Team One. Team One will attach their pod to the exploration ship and travel to their homeworld and discover the reason for the extinction of all life on that planet. It took, from what we can tell, only thirty-six hours for an entire planet to die. Team Two, we will be attaching to the other ship, a military vessel, and find out what happened to it, where it went, what it did." Brad Paused for a moment....

...and Benjamin continued, *"This is the reason the six were split as they did. Managerial, your responsibility when we get there is to download the computer core. Research Lead, you are to fly around and research. I am leaving that up to you as to how you proceed. I am estimating you will need to play it by ear and once you get there, you will know what path you need to take. Class Lead, your role is to gather cultural information about the people, their way of life, their daily activities. Whatever else you can think of.*"

He nodded to Brad, *"OK, Team Two; the Assistant Lead will be responsible for navigation, astrogation, and annotating the surrounding environment. Media Lead your role is to download the ship's computer core. Paper Lead, your role is to maintain a vigil watch on the ships systems and in the event of trouble let us all know so we can disengage and get to safety. Benjamin, the more I think about it I need a technowiz. Wanna trade..."*

"What did you have in mind?" They spoke out loud.

"I will trade you one Paper Lead for one Research Lead."

"We're being traded, like toys!" Someone in the class, a woman, was thinking out loud.

"Yes you are. Now, who thought that?" A young woman in the front row, Benjamin's side of the room raised her hand, "Guilty. Sue me." She said.

"Ah...Ruth, right?" Benjamin inquired.

"Correct." She replied, amazed he knew her name.

"Now that you have your assignments, and the trades are complete, let's find out where the other four will be. Leads do your thing." He looked at the LEAD and the ASSISTANT LEAD. They walked over to a corner and spoke for a few minutes. Benjamin knew that corner well. When he was a student, and the LEAD of the class, that is where he used to go to make decisions with his Assistant LEAD, Bill Zorick.

They deactivated their implants so no one could eavesdrop on their conversation. Good for them. A few minutes later the Team Lead spoke.

"Monika…Wendel, you're with team two." They both looked excited. "You two are with me."

Brad raised a hand, "What is the logic behind the assignments."

"Simple. Monika and Wendel are space nuts. They can look at a group of stars and determine what they are. If we have a system error and need to determine location, they are the ones to do it, and do it fast." The assistant team lead spoke matter of fact and with great confidence.

The team lead took over, "And as for team one, Karina and Hoshi have secondary degrees in biology and genetics. If there is something on that planet that is killing them, they can figure it out."

"Great. Now, team assignment. I will be main lead of team one and I will take Ruth as my wingman." Benjamin stated flatly.

"May I ask why you are taking her as your wingman?" The team lead sounded jealous.

"Simple. Of all of the people in this room the only one to comment on the fact there was a trade in progress was Ruth. I need someone who can see my point of view, but at the same time tell me when I am being stupid." He looked over at Ruth, "You can do that, right?" Benjamin had no idea if it sounded good or not, he really did not care. She was amazing. He had to get to know her better. That, and the fact they all believed him. Ruth nodded to him and had an odd grin on her face.

"Great. Now let's get down to business. First things first, introductions. I need name, where you are from, and something unique you want me to know about you." Brad interjected into the conversation.

"I'll Start." Ruth Swisher, their first chance meeting was in an elevator just after her class started. "I am Ruth Swisher, ADMIN, I hail from Luna…the mining colony and I really think I am going to like this job."

"Mining colony. Parents miners?" Brad added

"No, Dad runs the mine on the dark side, Mom runs the company store. Wait a minute…Jorgen…are you any relation…"

"Yes. My parents are in the mining business also. Me, personally, I would MUCH rather do this. Money and fame are just money and fame; but this is FUN!!"

The whole class laughed when they realized that Brad is the heir to Jorgen mining. He is possibly the wealthiest researcher in …well, history.

Benjamin laughed also, and then, "Next." The remainder of the class all spoke up and said their piece. The Team Lead, Bradley Bentinfield III, was from the United Kingdom. Dora Guntersdottir, the Research Lead and resident wiz-kid for all technology went next. She hailed from what used to be called Iceland. The remainder of the class is Assistant Lead, William Walker, who was from Canada; Paper Lead is Drake Willis from Australia; Media Lead is LaVarr DuBois from New Orleans; Hoshi Sukiyama from Tokyo; Monika Bordow from the Mars Colony; Wendel Willis Washington who lived on the stations; and Karen Jones who simply said she was from the outer colonies.

After everyone said his or her piece, Brad spoke. "So, we will be departing in the morning for points around the globe, and throughout the solar system. Here are your location assignments."

Brad shot the roster and locations to their sub-Q and at the same instant all of them saw the image of the printout as if it were hovering in front of their face. Several of them jumped back at the sight. Brad continued.

"RUTH, you will go home for a visit to the Lunar Mining Colony, and the reason you are home in mid-semester is that you are tasked to research mining. Granted, you will not be creating a 'real' report, but it needs to look and appear as a report should look. We want to see who has writing skills and who needs assistance. As a matter of fact, each of you may pair off with the person you will be working with, your wingman, on your team during this assignment.

For the next several hours they learned about the upgrade they will all be receiving to their Sub-Q implant. It will contain a lot of extra memory capability for video recording, and the ability to transfer to five different channels with just a thought. Channel one is the mission frequency. Two is the team frequency. Three is the sub-group frequency, as in a team of two. Four is Brad and five is Benjamin. For the next several days they took the time to travel to where ever they desired, with no other purpose in mind than to get used to the new communications protocols. Brad and Benjamin's implant could be on any specific channel, but at the same time monitor their personal channel in the event someone needed them specifically.

The upgrade took roughly 90-minutes and afterwards they all had a small lunch in the school cafeteria. After lunch they returned to the classroom and back to the business at hand.

* * * * * * * * * * * * * * * * * * * *

"Security Mode Active." Brad said flatly.

Once the room was secure, "OK, how does everyone feel about the new comm protocols. Are there any issues you have noticed over the last week?"

Resounding no's and head shaking. "Good. Tomorrow we begin training in the pods. Is there any apprehension about flying a pod?"

One hand went up. "Yes and no. The flying part is fine with all of us, it's the fact we will be attached to the OUTSIDE of the hull during light speed translation. In theory, we can all be…can I use an historical phrase here, Spam in a can." This was the Research Lead, the technological contact for the class. Dora Guntersdottir seemed a bit apprehensive.

"You'll be fine…" Benjamin and Brad looked at each other and shrugged their shoulders. Instilling great confidence in this classroom of minions.

* * * * * * * * * * * * * * * * * * * *

Assignments for this weekend went as follows:

> Ruth and Benjamin will travel to the Moon Mining Colony
> Brad and Dora are also assigned to the Moon
>
> Trip and Hoshi are to travel to a tropical beach
> LaVarr and Monika are to accompany them

Will and Wendel are to travel to the asteroid belt
Drake and Karen are to join them

Each team was given enough credits to get to their location in comfort, and have a good time.

Brad looked over at Benjamin; they were sitting in the first class compartment again, only this time next to each other. "So, why did you want me to come here with you?"

"Honestly, I am really interested in the mining operation and I figure that if you were with us we would get into a lot of closed doors. Besides, it can give you a chance to visit the parents. They are here on the Moon, aren't they?"

"Actually, no they live on a station. Remember, we were there not too long ago."

"Oh, that's right. How clumsy of me to forget."

"Clumsy….are you ok?"

Brad portacomm chirped, "Brad Jorgen."

The voice on the other end was more mature, "At least you still remember your last name. Your friend, Benjamin, let slip you would be on Earth's Moon this weekend so Mother and I will be making an inspection tour of the plant. You and your friends are invited to the house for dinner. Perhaps we can get a few things out in the open."

"That may be good Dad. Can we take you and Mother out for dinner at Le Chandra? Benjamin is a personal friend of the owner and she has some really good items on her menu?"

"Sure thing son, we will be there later this afternoon, about 5pm Lunar time."

"Great, I will set up dinner for the six of us; I have two colleagues with us also, at 8:30pm."

"That would be perfect. Talk to you in a little while. Remember one thing, we both love you."

"I love you too Dad, tell Mom also."

"She heard you. See you tonight."

The connection terminated. Brad sat and looked at the device for what he thought was a really long time. In reality, it was a few moments, "Brad, you OK?"

"Yes, I'm fine."

"Want me to make the reservations?"

"Definitely, and since we were never here with the girls, Ramona will never have tested her water creatures on us, so we can get some REALLY interesting meals."

Benjamin opened his portacomm and pressed a button. Ramona was still on autodial. "Hi there."

"Hi yourself. You finally on your way up here?"

"How did you know?"

"Just look around, I have seen the inside of so many of those shuttles, I can tell you are in the first class compartment. Got a question, you like sea food?"

"Love it…why do you ask?"

"How many of you are there?"

"Four here, plus two on their way. One thing, the other two on their way to dine at your establishment this evening at 8:30pm are the owners of the Jorgen Mine."

"Oh my...I am going to kill you. OK, I got things to do. This is going to cost you Benjamin Jensen. Cost you big. I have a special dinner planned for your party. You'll love it. Gotta run. Bye."

"Is she OK?" Brad asked.

"No. But she is having fun." Benjamin smiled back at him.

Both he and Brad put their heads back in the seats and closed their eyes. Both he and Brad reactivated their implant for reception. They were both happy they did not instruct the students how to do this. It allowed them to keep tabs on everyone. Brad and Benjamin had additional frequencies or channels. One for each team under their supervision. They simply scanned through the channels to make sure the teams were playing nice, and they all were. They turned their attention to the project.

"Calling all, please select channel one." Benjamin thought.

As the teams reported in, Ruth called out 1A, Dora called out 2A, then 1B, 2B, 1C, 2C. They thought that was it, then Teams 3A and 3B called in.

"For those who are not aware, team 3A and B are the ground team and the orbit team. Their role will be to assess the local population, and monitor our orbital departure. 3A is the Orbital Team. Allow me to introduce to you Will Carter, Security Supervisor for the ground and Chun Kada, Security Technician

for the orbital team. Also, your professors need to jump; it has been a while so they will be the ground team."

Lot of hello's. Will Carter began explaining the pod to them. On Monday when they return from this fool's mission, as he put it, they would be under his guidance. Each of them would learn to fly a pod, and once they are proficient they would be sent back to the days of the dinosaur to take pictures then return. A five-minute trip, but necessary. When they jump their next jump would put them into Earth orbit. The pod could orbit and descend into the atmosphere, but not go from the ground into orbit. Not enough power capability. The orbit they would be in is just above the state of Florida on January 28, 1986; a few minutes before the shuttle Challenger disaster. A few images of this, and the disaster of Texas on February 1, 2003, would be a handy sequence in the archive no doubt. But the location each team was being assigned given the optimum video and photographic capability. One member of the team is responsible for video, the other for still images. They can determine who does what.

Benjamin had another plan. He wanted to hover down to see himself and Myra watching the shuttle explode. He would more than likely not do it, but the idea of it is appealing. The next jump would put them just off the main wing of the starship Enterprise. Science Fiction fans for more than 150 years had pressured the Space Administration into calling the first ship in a class Enterprise, and this is no different. This ship will cover the distance between Earth and Mars in less than an hour. Nearly half the speed of light. It will also provide the team with the latch on and detach experience. Since the ship is not returning the team will be able to test the long range transition theory. Brad drew the short straw, so to speak, and he will travel first back home using the final recall signal. If he returns safely, and with no issues, then he will come back to the time they are in, in an abandoned field or someplace similar, and let the rest of the team know. There should be less than an hour between when he leaves and when they hear from him again.

* * * * * * * * * * * * * * * * * * * *

"It's been three hours. Does that mean we can't get home?" Monika asked.

"No. That means three hours have passed since he sent the recall. That is all it means. You know as well as I do that time is relative." Benjamin replied. The eleven left in Mars orbit were on channel one, all talking together.

The astronauts were unaware they had guests, and since this is the first and fastest trip to the planet Mars they did not expect company. The team took advantage of the opportunity to take a LOT of pictures, and a lot of video from different angles, locations, and distances.

Benjamin got into teaching mode and the class knew it, "Ruth and I will be the last to leave. Since Mars gravity is less than the Earth's; and since the atmosphere is thinner we should be able to go from the surface back to orbit, Ruth and I will traverse down to the surface and take a lot of video and images of the colony, and of course the landing of this rocket."

"But Benjamin," Bradley, the class lead was speaking. "Is it wise to leave the two of you alone?" You could feel the jealousy in his voice. Benjamin made a mental note to ask her about it when the others left. Funny how the class lead and admin got close, just like him and Myra.

Funny, he has not thought of her in an awfully long time. The psychic therapy sessions were so much more effective than what they are doing in this century for patients with a mental issue. They cured his in just a few sessions. Time heals all wounds, they tell him. Strange how they can connect to his mind and give him the impression that an hour in the room with them is a more than a year. He will have to go thank them when he returns...

"HEY! Benjamin. You still in Mars orbit?" Brad YELLED through his Sub-Q on channel one and everyone screamed. There was a complete silence as everyone was contemplating his or her own mortality.

"You made it?" Dora asked, and then regretted it.

"Uh...yes. What gave you the first clue?" The entire class laughed

Benjamin called the class to order, *"OK, here is the plan. Brad, you stay where you are and take role as they leave the timeframe. Bradley, you determine who goes first and in what order. Leave at least a minute between each jump to clear the pad of the pod."*

Brad cut in, *"Make it 2 minutes. For some reason reentry restarts the pods systems and it takes a while to get it moving again. We need to look at that when we get home."*

"OK, two minutes it is. Dora, I need you to be last, before Bradley. You and Bradley are to film and photograph the reentry in to the Martian atmosphere of the lander while Ruth and I fly next to and in front of it doing the same thing. OK people, this is something I have dreamed of doing since I graduated, like you are getting close to doing."

"Brad, what time was it when you got back?"

"About 7pm. Why?"

"OK, here's the deal. When we get back we have a one-hour debriefing and data download, always a fun time there. After that drinks and dinner is on Brad. There is a place called Pluto's located just off the...."

"We know where it is. All of us have been there. We had to try it out after one of your classes you taught last semester, you made it sound like an oasis or nirvana or something." Karen jumped in and let him know. The entire class likes the place.

Brad asked cautiously, *"So...do you like Pluto's?"*

"Yes, all of us like it. A lot."

"Good. Brad's buying."

"What? Why?"

The whole class answered in unison in their heads, *"Because you're rich"* They had all heard this back and forth between Benjamin and Brad many times, they all chimed in and laughed.

"Oh....OK." That was all he answered. You could HEAR him shrug his shoulders through the Sub-Q.

"Here they go. Ruth, get on the starboard side of the ship, film and video need to run on auto. I'll do the same on the port side. Bradley and Dora, start filming from up here but under no circumstances are you to enter the atmosphere. Highest resolution video possible. Bradley, start sending them home. Brad, go back now and call Barbara. Tell her to get ready for an invasion."

Brad left and a few seconds later Bradley started sending the class home. In the meantime, he and Dora were witnessing a spectacular sight. Imagine sitting in a glass ball in an orbit of any planet and a landing craft begins to descend, as it heats up entering the atmosphere it generates a plasma plume for hundreds of feet behind it. Bradley and Dora were hypnotized by the visual they were witnessing first hand. The fact that someday this video may be on the news or documentary gave them the perspective they needed to do it to the best of their ability.

At the same time, they were hovering in orbit watching the silent fireball slowly descend onto a hostile Mars environment, Benjamin and Ruth were witnessing it from a different angle. Essentially, they were inside of it. Reentry was a lot worse on the Sub-Q communications than previously thought. Although they never lost contact, there were interruptions and static. The bad part was when the receiver is in your head the sound in very interesting. They made it to the surface and the craft landed exactly where they were shooting for, just like history demanded.

"Ruth, swing south slowly and get the oxygen recyclers and the O^3 mining plant. There have never been any good photos of it. It is going to blow up in about 3 months. The cause will be linked to excessive dust in the seals. Later they will determine that the dust in this area, the regolith, contains trace amounts of hydrocarbons; and as you know, put oxygen and hydrocarbons together and under pressure, and you get a BOOM! No more building. I do understand that the explosion could be seen from Earth." Benjamin got quiet. There was one more item of the pod upgrades he had not tested. The remote camera assembly.

"Got an idea, let's drop a couple cameras to keep an eye on the plant. Then you and a classmate of your choice can jump back to Earth and download the video remotely and bring it back. Remembering to autodestruct the camera assemblies."

"So, won't that leave parts lying around?" Bradley asked. He was still in orbit.

"No. The destruct is at the molecular level. There is really nothing left to see, feel, touch, or taste." Benjamin was annoyed that he cut into the conversation, but it was a valid question.

"Dora just left. I will be gone in another minute. How soon do you expect to return?"

Spoken like the class lead, "Give us another hour here and we will be home. There are a few things I want to film, we need to drop and hide the cameras, and then we will attempt to reenter orbit. If not, we will send the recall signal and leave from here."

"OK, see you in about an hour." He left. He sounded a lot less frustrated that Ruth was with him, but not completely.

"OK, all class members, sound off." Benjamin said with humor in his voice. "Benjamin...here"

"Ruth...here" She was laughing.

No one else could be heard. "OK, set your camera on the top of that ridge to take in the entire facility, I will set mine much lower and closer to get a good view of the location that is supposed to be the point of ignition."

They took off in different directions but both looking for the same thing. A secluded spot that has full view of their goal and it cannot be traveled by foot or vehicle.

"So, you and Bradley an item?"

"How did you know?"

"I'm not blind. As a matter of fact, I was the class lead…" Cutting him off she *said "I know, you told us that already"*, he cut her off this time and continued, *"But what I did not tell you is that the Admin and I were an item. She was injured on the final project and nearly died. She still works on the island, but not as a researcher."*

"I know that too. We had to review the recordings so we knew just how dangerous this job really is. After the video of the loss in your class we had a lot of good people drop out. Do you and her still see each other?"

"Not for several years, my time reference at least. She does not really know me anymore, at least what we were. The damage was permanent and rather than making her uncomfortable I let her go. It took several sessions with the psychs to get her out of my mind, but they did it. I am a lot better for it now, and every once in a while we get together, her birthday and the anniversary of that day…..the day several of our class came home for their final rest. We all meet at Pluto's and celebrate their life. We bring up funny things that happened, and discuss and reminisce. Whoever from the class is available tries to make it also. Never a one on one party."

They managed to get the cameras installed and take the rest of the video and photo's. Only one thing left, see if they can attain orbit.

"OK, on the count of three, punch it!"

Ruth started, "3…….2……1…..GO!"

Chapter 5

Space – and Beyond

"Final rehearsal for the mission was interesting. There are two shuttles leaving for the Moon in a few minutes. They will undock from the orbital port and make their way to the lunar surface as fast as possible. The class is scheduled to attach and travel to the Moon and then they have an hour or two to fly around and completely video the ENTIRE Lunar Colony.

"Uh, Benjamin," Dora was about to ask a question, you could hear it in her voice. "If the shuttle is leaving in a few minutes and we are in the classroom, how are we going to get to the pod and then to orbit in order to…..OH….never mind."

Reality hit her and she understood.

"Correct Dora, we will be jumping back to right…." He was looking at his clock on the front wall, "Now, and in orbit. As the shuttles back away from the station is what we will be waiting for, and just before they kick in the engines we will all be attached and taking the ride with them.

Benjamin thought out loud, *"Operations, please derive the precise location of the shuttles departing the station en route to the Lunar surface."*

"Precise position calculated." Came back from the operator, the voice sounded familiar but Benjamin was not able to place it.

Operations, this is Benjamin Jensen. Please pass the coordinates and temporal reference along to the chamber for departure in the morning at OH-Eight-Hundred,"

"I know who you are Benjamin. Having trouble recognizing my voice?" The operator said playfully.

Benjamin thought for just a half a second, *"Not at all Maria, just wondering what you are doing in Operations, a long way from the Data Section."*

"They are shorthanded and it gives me chance to do something a bit other than fill your head with useless information. Operations out"

The remainder of the class, including Brad, knew who she was now.

The rest of the mission went as planned. They worked out all the kinks with the latching assembly. It was a twofold process. There was a very powerful magnetic component to the connection, but in the event it was required there was also a gripping mechanism. Since the primary system was the magnet, which would provide them with the clearest and least intrusive connection, they hoped they would never need the grips. They were not certain they would work.

They appeared in orbit in a pattern around the location of where the shuttle stopped its reverse course and changed to a forward course to the moon. Similar to what they would be doing tomorrow afternoon. The class arrived in lunar orbit and split into two teams, just as they will do tomorrow. Benjamin and his team strafed the dome and took some of the best and clearest images of the colony. Ruth had an idea.

"I have an idea for a video. If each of us takes a circumference point out away from the colony, say....one kilometer; we can begin a slow approach with video running and sound off. As we approach the dome we can travel upwards and then meet in the center at the top and travel up a kilometer, rotate 180 degrees and return on the same course. Should make for a unique video for the news and media dogs."

"I love it!!" Brad was the first to exclaim.

Benjamin jumped in, *"Ruth, your idea, you lead and call out vectors and velocities and we will all follow your lead."*

They performed the maneuver perfectly. A testament to their flight ability. This would definitely make for one very interesting video and the Archives can sell this for a nice little profit.

Once they returned to the now and were sitting in the classroom again. "OK, so, let's recap..." Mr. Winchester appeared. "All 6 objectives completed, and Bradley you can get them all started on their reports. They need to be turned in to Mr. Winchester by noon tomorrow."

"One thing, Mr. Jensen. You said 6 objectives completed, did you add a number 6 on the fly?" He asked.

"As a matter of fact, sir; we did. You will see it tomorrow with the reports and I believe that sanitizing the report will be very easy and the media will buy it up for a nice profit.

"Really." He smiled a little.

* * * * * * * * * * * * * * * *

Benjamin was walking out of Pluto's around midnight. A little early for his normal Friday but this Friday was not normal. In sixteen hours he would be co-leading a team of twelve people to another solar system. This is literally the first time in history it is happening. True, there is nothing interesting about traveling to another planet or solar system, but this is not the 20th century. In less than a day, from his perspective, he will be in the mid-20th century in a low Earth orbit with a class of recruits and his best friend. They are going to attach themselves to the two alien spacecraft in orbit and travel back to the alien's home world at hyper light velocities. Once there, they need to discover what happened to end all life on that planet.

Also, Benjamin learned that the Archive Island Research and Development Committee has sanctioned a jump chamber that will house a shuttle size vehicle that can attain hyper–light speeds, but that will not be ready for several years. They are building the facility in the dessert, far outside of Las Vegas. He thought there was something familiar to the sound of that, an area in the dessert, he thought it had something to do with 1951 but he could not put his finger on it.

Ruth was correct about the video. It was a commodity and everyone wanted it to be exclusive for the first month or so. The bidding for first rights went through the roof and a very handsome profit was turned. When Ruth comes to the department Benjamin will assign her missions like this; she will end up being the biggest profit making researcher of all time, even more than himself. He was not certain if he liked that or not.

As for the new facility, the problem is they need contractors and construction workers to actually build the facility, but they cannot be aware of the facilities intended purpose. Installing the technology to allow for temporal movement will be at the leisure of the Archive Island Maintenance teams, which is how Norman was able to slip enough technology and data out to create his own jump system and nearly take over the planet.

For the construction, Benjamin recommended Tom Wolski be the prime contractor for the project. He is well known on the Island and throughout the area as a fair and honest man, he is a pleasant person to work with, and can get the job done at or below budget. They are planning to make the decision about him while he is away on this mission. They should be away from the present time for no more than seven or eight days.

When he gets back, he will find out. As for now, he needs to focus on the mission at hand. This is seriously the most dangerous mission he has ever accepted. But it is also the most historic. In the annals of the classified history of the research teams, this team will be monumental. There are truly a lot of firsts, and a lot of unknown variables.

"Hey Benny, thanks for bringing your class over, and for the heads up. We were able to restock before you got here. They diverted a cargo shuttle to us. I felt really important when I called in an emergency order for food."

"Glad to hear it. Maybe we can do this again in a month or so."

"Can you at least give us a little more warning than an hour or two?" Mike was behind the bar but he heard everything.

"No promises....but I'll try...At least I left a nice tip for you, at Brad's expense." She had not even looked at it yet. When she did she shook her head and smiled, showed it to Mike who started laughing and said, "When Brad finds out, he will find you."

"Not worried. I can handle him." He picked up a chair like he was taming a lion and cracking a whip.

"Good night. You are obviously in serious need of sleep."

"He gave Barbara a kiss on the cheek and said loud enough for Mike to hear, "Pass it on!" Winked and walked out.

* * * * * * * * * * * * * * * * * * * *

"Good morning class. Are we all rested for the week ahead of us? You have had more than a month of flight training, practice, rehearsal, and testing; you jumped in your pods and hitched a ride to the Moon and made the Island a tidy profit, thank Ms. Swisher. I think we are ready. Bradley, separate your teams and have them ready to give their assignments in the form of an oral briefing. Both team members must participate. Ruth and Dora, you will give mine and Brad's alone." Benjamin looked at Ruth and tapped his head. After so long she understood the universal sign to get online. She activated her implant and tuned to channel three, their channel, Benjamin and Ruth's personal team frequency.

Benjamin noticed Brad made a motion to Dora and he assumed they were doing the same.

"I'm here." Ruth thought to him.

"Good. When you give the briefing from our team, I need you to be exact and please do not be kind. If there is something I need to accomplish, you need to spell it out. That is the reason I chose you as a partner, you will not pull your punches...SO DON'T! This is a huge assignment and the school would not have devoted so much of this semester to it."

"I understand. I assume you will be watching expressions and gauging reactions while I am talking?"

"You do know me well but no, not just me. Brad is watching, and there are three instructors that will join us, at my request. I need to know if anyone has an issue. Personally, I can't see one. But that is why they are here."

"Understood. Please don't be too shocked at my abruptness."

"The more the better." He smiled a very small, nearly indiscernible smile, but Brad noticed it and realized he was up to something. Brad had his implant off Benjamin's frequency so he did not hear the conversation. He looked at Benjamin and touched his temple slightly. They got on the Brad/Benjamin only frequency.

"Anything I should know?" He asked Benjamin.

"Watch, discern, validate, weed out, and hope everyone is ready for this."

"Gocha."

* * * * * * * * * * * * * * * * * * *

The briefing went very well and the instructors noticed two problems. Two members of the team, Hoshi Sukiyama and Drake Willis lacked the confidence they should have possessed. They were too nervous and afraid of the pending assignment and could be a hindrance to the team and the mission.

Benjamin sent them to the psych section to see if they could help them overcome their confidence issue. They would be gone the remainder of the day and would return complete and ready to go. At least that is the hope. If not, then the teams would be rearranged. After all, these two individuals are members of each team; one on team one – Benjamin's, and the other on team two – Brad's.

A part of Ruth's briefing included Bradley. She was assigned to go and retrieve the data from the remote recorders and then ensure they were destroyed. She accomplished the mission easily. Mr. Winchester made the comment that temporal travel came easy to her, which is the reason Benjamin had selected her to jump back and collect the data. Bradley, on the other hand, appears to think of travel as something to endure. Ruth thrives in it, and seems to live for it.

Thankfully, they did not need to go to Mars, but only needed to be in Earth orbit a few months after their original trip. They downloaded the data and sent the self-disintegrate signal and it was done. They were gone from the chamber just a few moments. But it was worth it.

* * * * * * * * * * * * * * * * * * * *

The day was composed of simple historical study relating to the timeframe at hand. The year 1947 was a troubled time with the end of a major military conflict amongst other things. They will arrive on July first, but a few days before in Washington State nine lights in the sky were viewed by a pilot. Benjamin made a modification to the plan. Brad and Dora are to jump back to watch the altercation with the lights. They have no real plan as there is no account of this encounter in the computer system discovered on the Malkronian homeworld. They are very curious about this and will discover what it is.

So, initially, Brad and Dora will travel back to this event, and then in their next jump will join the team in orbit a moment after everyone else arrives, effectively losing no time.

Brad and Dora were prepared to depart. Both pods were sitting side by side on the oversized platform. One moment they were there, a bright light, and then they were gone.

As the teams entered the chamber two by two – with Benjamin and Ruth next – they would disappear in a blinding white light and vanish. Bradley was informed in private about the issue with Hoshi and Drake. He was asked to keep an eye on them and to be the last to leave. When Drake transferred to the timeframe Bradley noticed he closed his eyes as the process began. As for Hoshi, he noticed nothing out of the ordinary. She seemed to enjoy the transit. He did not know what to make of it, but reminded himself to tell Benjamin and Brad about it when he arrived.

Bradley popped into Earth orbit. The transition from light, sound, and familiar surroundings to complete isolation, absolute silence, and an ominous lack of light, not quite dark, made the appearance in this timeframe unsettling for a brief moment.

Benjamin and Bradley had a code word they set up in the event one needs to speak to the other. The reason is simple, as class leader he knew these people better than anyone, and would be the first to identify an issue or problem.

"Benjamin, that was radical." Bradley thought to Benjamin.

The counter response and subsequent transfer to the alternate channel was, *"Truly…"*

"Bradley, what's going on?"

"As Hoshi left she seemed excited, looking forward to the transit and therefore I do not think there is an issue with her at all. However, in Drake I did notice when he was about to transfer he closed his eyes tight; like he was afraid of the jump or…I'm not sure. I just thought you should know."

"Thanks. Now, let's get back to the mission. I will notify Brad when he arrives. He may use the same codeword on your second in command; did you brief William before you left?"

"Yes. He is fully aware and able to go to the lead channel."

"Lead channel, interesting term. I think if there is opportunity for another jump en masse we will use that term. Nice idea."

"Thanks..."

"Now, as for Hoshi and Drake, I will make certain Brad keeps an eye on Hoshi. Let Will know also."

They returned to the primary channel, the channel they would use until the two ships were separated enough to make a difference.

The pods grouped into their preset two's, wingmen, and attached face to face together and hovered over the point they would attach themselves to the body of the ship they were assigned to follow. About twenty minutes later Brad and Dora appeared about a kilometer away and called out.

"Man that was close. We were almost scraped by all those ships. We managed to view and follow both flights; the airplane and the space vehicles. I followed the space vehicles right into your ship you are going to follow team one. One of the ships then left there and went to the other ship."

Dora spoke up, *"Right on time everyone. They are powering up the light drive. Transition to hyper-light speed in one minute."*

"All pods, attach to your assigned positions. All team members, stay on channel one until told otherwise."

"Team one, prepare for transition in 10 seconds." Dora was monitoring Benjamin's ship and Brad's ship separately. *"Team two, 30 seconds."*

"GOOD LUCK!!" Everybody yelled at once.

Benjamin was sitting in his pod staring at Ruth who was sitting in her pod staring at him. As per assigned mission protocol, one would look forward and one aft during light transition to record the full effect. Benjamin looked forward and Ruth's gaze went to the rear of the ship where she could see the Earth in all its splendor and glory. Beautiful and blue sitting there just below them. A moment later reality distorted and Ruth watched the Earth shrink nearly instantly until it was not visible in the myriad of bright spots against the ocean of black.

She turned to look at Benjamin and had a tear in her eye.

"Are you ok?" Benjamin asked her.

"Fine. That was amazing!" She replied.

Nothing else was ever said about it.

Benjamin went into manager mode, *"All teams, report status."*

As the teams all reported in, more for mental exercise than for Benjamin needing a report, everything was going fine. Several hours into the trip both teams reported that their respective memory cores have been downloaded into the pod buffer, and Dora and Karen had accessed their respective ships systems.

A full day has passed and they have traveled farther than they thought was possible. The speeds these ships travel is a great deal more than what any human ship is capable of, in any timeframe. Karen discovered why.

"Team – this is Karen. I have discovered why their speed is so much greater than what we determined. There is an inconsistency in the engine design that we had always thought was an error in design so we removed it. I have been following and reading this design flaw and determined it creates a feedback loop of energy that multiplies with each increment of speed, whatever they call them. If we were to modify our ships to contain this design flaw, would our ship' speed increase? That is one of the questions we can bring home."

"Wonderful Karen, you and Drake are going to write that report when we get back. Drake, how are you doing?" Benjamin noticed Drake seemed to be preoccupied with something and was concerned. Karen heard the tone in Benjamin's voice and looked at Drake.

"What is it, Drake?" Karen asked with intensity.

"There seems to be a buildup of power in one of the hyperlight field pods. It appears as if there is going to be a catastrophic incident." That can only end in one way, an explosion. Benjamin wanted to fly over there and assist him with the data but if he were to disconnect from the ship he would go from a massive speed to no speed in a milisecond. He may not survive the transition. So he stayed where he was.

"Karen, what can you see?" Brad asked.

Karen replied, *"Nothing, it's going away."* And at that moment the ship reentered normal space. A couple of them began to get motion sick. Thank goodness the pods are self-cleaning and waste management is efficient.

As the ship approached the atmosphere everyone detached as per the mission protocol. Drake's pod was having a detaching problem."

"Unable to detach. Wait, I am detecting a buildup of ionizing radiation in the ship. Location......directly below my location. It is one of the fusion generators. It is building to overload. Fifteen seconds to detonation."

"Drake, jump home. NOW!!" Brad and Benjamin yelled through the Sub-Q. Then they saw the explosion of the fusion generator. It damaged the craft but it was still flying and beginning to enter the atmosphere.

"Did he jump home? Did the explosion kill him?" LaVarr asked.

"No idea. We will not know till we get home ourselves."

"Let's all assume he made it and get on with our work. We need to find out what happened. Karen, join me and Ruth, we will be a three-person team." Benjamin fell into an as-a-matter-of-fact tone and everyone took instant action when he spoke. Brad and the rest of team two were still connected and listening to the events as they transpired. No video was being sent at the moment so they were spared the horror of what happened. But they heard it all.

No one in the class had a bad thing they could say about Drake; he may be gone but they need to get back to work as soon as possible to complete the mission.

Karen Jones was now a part of Benjamin and Ruth's team. She had the job of recon with Drake, and now that is not possible. The three of them will need to work together. Karen is/was a first responder medic on the Regulus colony – Bostonia. Designed and populated as a place of peace, friendship, and isolation. Isolation from the rest of the universe. This colony would have liked nothing better than to be left alone, but a rival species, the Rhwag, from a neighboring system, found out they were there and after the colony was established for nearly two decades, they were attacked.

Thankfully, their weapons were comparable to the weapons the colonist had, and improved upon, since planet-fall. As Karen grew and matured she decided she wanted to go into the medical field, perhaps a doctor, or a nurse. Since this colony does not have an established university system, trades and professions are acquired through internship and apprenticeship. At the age of 17 Karen was learning the medical arts and at the age of 24 she graduated with the equivalent degrees of doctor of biology and medicine.

But the war was dragging on and on and she wanted to mean something in her life. When she applied for the researcher program her father was a bit upset. Her mother was killed in an attack a few years before and she was Daddy's little girl. Her mother was a colonel in the militia and was leading a battle into the heart of the enemy stronghold when the weather turned bad in a very short time. During this time of year, the weather could go from comfortable to sub-zero in minutes where they were fighting in the mountain region and they were not fully prepared. It's said she sacrificed her life for the men and women under her command by dispersing the heating units, clothing, and food rather than using them herself. She counted on a resupply shuttle to make its way from the colony, but it never made it. It was shot down just a few miles from them.

She was distanced from the other students, difficult to get to know or understand. Benjamin knew exactly how to deal with her, after all, he felt like that a lot. But this mission demanded communication and collaboration.

As they watched the ship enter the Malkornian atmosphere the plasma flame did not seem to be so bad.

"Benjamin, I am not detecting any life signs on the ship." Karen *stated.*

"Then how is it landing?" Ruth replied.

"According to the ship's computer it is in the process of an autolanding to the point of origin. That means everyone on the ship is dead already. What could have killed the entire crew while we were in transit?" Karen reported what she had discovered.

"Brad, you still on this channel" Benjamin sounded grim.

"Yes I am. All of us are." Brad chimed in.

"Dora, verify the number of life forms on your ship." He spoke directly to Dora.

"Hold on...checking..." After a few moments, *"None. All dead."*

"Then they never really reached home, they all died quickly and on the way here. Original estimate was that the contagion was brought and everyone got sick because a container or something ruptured. Not so, it seems they had a fatal reaction to the planet Earth." Brad extrapolated.

"Brad, get what you can, determine the destination, bearing and velocity of the ship, and disengage....go home. Your part of the mission is over once you feel you have done all you can do. Team one, go to channel three and get on with your mission. Brad, take

charge over there. I, Ruth, and Karen will remain on Channel one since Karen is now a part of our pair to make a trio and she cannot go to our pair frequency."

"Very good Benjamin. Team two, do the same. Infiltrate and download what you can, then as a pair disconnect and return to channel two. Once we are all hovering in the big nothing, we will go home one at a time as planned." Yes, disconnecting from the ship at hyperlight to move to another area of the ship is fatal because of the varying gravitational forces at work, but to simply let go from the vessel would mean a relatively slow transition to normal space, and then a stop. The transition would be a hard one, but survivable.

"OH, and PLEASE make sure you record the transition to hover. It is going to be amazing." Bradley added at the last second. It was a good thought.

After a few moments for everyone to leave the frequency, Benjamin continued, "Karen, are you a medical doctor or was I wrong?"

"No, you are correct, why?"

"I have a special mission for you. You need to go to their medical section and see what you can learn. Ruth will go to the spaceport and follow the activity there, I will travel to the capital and see what I can learn."

They all took off, and the others were already gone. About four hours went by and Brad broke the silence. "Benjamin, we are all disengaged from the ship and within one Astronomical unit of each other. We have already begun jumping home, LaVarr went first since he broke his nose in the transition; about five minutes later Monika followed. Before she jumped LaVarr reappeared in *our heads. He came back to tell us the best way to jump. While we were away they had the chance to inspect the pods. If you remove power, essentially shut it off, and then jump there is no power surge."*

"Thanks, we will see you at home. We are nearly complete here." A few moments he tried to contact Brad again. Nothing. If he went back already, that meant everyone else was gone too. Only team one was left.

* * * * * * * * * * * * * * * * * * * *

Team one was performing flawlessly, the data and information they were collecting was massive and sad at the same time. They had to hover over a city and watch it die. First they became ill, then vomiting and unconsciousness, then bleeding from every orifice, then death. Total time less than seven hours. Seven hours….in seven hours a person went from healthy to dead. How is this spreading around the planet at such a rapid rate?

"Karen, since you were the doctor, what can you tell us?"

"At this point, according to the medical database, the ship arrived in auto and the entire crew was dead. When they pulled the bodies out they thought it would be better to not keep them all together, so they were scatter to the four corners of the planet. Since this planet is not as large as Earth the base level gravity is much less here, and the oxygen is higher also, a perfect breeding ground for multiple bacteria to coalesce into a new strain that is nearly instantly deadly. At this point I'm not sure we are immune."

"Recommendations?"

"We need an atmospheric sample and a tissue sample from a recently deceased person. Once we run them into the computer, it should tell us what we are dealing with, and how to correct it."

"OK, Ruth, get the air sample from the area of the ship, that should be the most concentrated. I will get the tissue sample."

* * * * * * * * * * * * * * * * * * * *

"Karen, it's been nearly an hour that you have been linked up with my computer and Ruth's; in case you are not aware of it, when you have the computer tied up all we can do is hover. Although we are getting quite good at it, I need to proceed with the mission.

"Perfect timing for a rant or a rave, boss. The results are in. To these people in this environment this bacterium is as deadly as any concentrated nerve agent ever conceived on the planet Earth. But to us, it is harmless. Less symptoms than a cold. At worst, mild flu-like symptoms."

"So..."

"So, with proper decontamination we can land and walk around."

"That is not in the mission protocol. You know as well as I do that if we were to...."

"QUIET! Listen..." Ruth broke into the heated conversation between Karen and Benjamin.

"What!" They both said it at the same time.

"I hear a voice. It's coming from the next room."

"Where are you?" Benjamin asked.

118

"In the main medical center I think. Follow my beacon but first, Karen, release my computer back to me."

"Oh, sorry..."

Karen and Benjamin followed the beacon and in a few minutes they found themselves at a large and impressive building. Benjamin stopped at what appeared to be a map and somehow it looked familiar to him. He searched through his Sub-Q until he found the image in the volumes of information contained in his head.

"Got it!" Benjamin yelled out loud and broadcast it to his companions.

"WHAT?" They both yelled back.

"I just figured out what this place is. It's their version of Archive Island. We need to find a computer terminal here and connect and.....Hey, Ruth. You said you heard a voice?"

"Yes. I am hovering next to her now. She knows I am here but can't see me. I'm going to deactivate the light warping field."

"Go ahead. Also, run your visual channel so we can see and you can record."

"Done."

"Nice image. She looks like she does not have much time left. Karen, are you near her?"

"Entering the room now. Benjamin, permission to leave my pod and examine her in real-time." Karen asked but was already putting on her barrier suit.

"Do it!" Benjamin said flatly.

After a few moments Karen's pod appeared in the room next to Ruth's. The woman on the floor looked in bad shape. She was about a meter and a half tall, ash grey in color with very large black eyes. Nothing like the images and drawings of the Roswell grays, but she was stunningly beautiful. Her features were a cross between Native American and Samoan. Well defined, regal, and even in her condition difficult to turn away from…

Karen left her pod and walked over to the woman. She knelt next to her and suddenly she froze. Just for a moment or two and then began to move again.

"She just read my mind."

"Actually, Karen Jones, I did more than that. I linked my mind to yours and in this case there are two other minds linked to you, so I am connected to all three. This is very interesting. I know that you are the inhabitants of the planet Earth, a primitive planet to say the least; but you are from several hundred years in that planets future and travel back and forth in time as easily as we are speaking to each other."

All three of them were stunned and listening so intently they were unaware of anything else.

My life is nearly at an end. Karen Jones, you are correct in your atmospheric diagnosis and all life on this planet is either dead already or dying in a brief matter of time. I have one request, carry us home with you."

"Excuse me?" Benjamin said.

"Benjamin Jensen, as the leader of this expedition it is your right to refuse. But my words do not mean what you are thinking.

Karen Jones, go to that wall and press the two red crystals, then the green, and finally the blue twice."

Karen walked to the wall and pressed the crystals. As she did the wall evaporated and a hidden room was revealed. This room was a square of about twelve square meters. The walls pulsated with energy and power running the visual spectrum; it was truly beautiful to watch. In the center of the room was a pedestal. On the pedestal was a dark black cube. The blackest black any of them had ever seen.

"Go to the altar of life and press the following sequence." The woman started speaking again. Karen walked to the altar and stood there a moment looking at it in amazement. *The following sequence must be entered quickly without hesitation. Blue-red-green-green-red-blue-orange-white-blue-red-green-white-blue-blue-red-red-red-red-red. You have ten seconds to enter the sequence once you start. If you are incorrect, the system will overload and the altar of life will be destroyed. A fail safe."*

Having a photographic memory has its advantages. She pressed the crystals in the right sequence and the room darkened and the black cube disappeared and became a glowing white cube. She picked up the cube and carried it back. The woman looked at her and smiled.

"You now have in your hands the genetic material of every living creature on this planet. Take it home with you and travel back here. Place it in the altar and repeat the sequence. The machine will take over from there. Life on our dead world will be repopulated once again. We can take our place in the universe with the Humans of the planet Earth as our friends. I am the caretaker. My knowledge and experiences will be the first to appear. My new self will know you and everything that we have

discussed, and done, in this room. You call it genetic memory. We consider it as normal and easy as you breathe."

She began to cough, but this time more violently than before. Blood came from her mouth, nose, ears and eyes. After a few more minutes, she was gone.

Ruth was crying, as was Karen. Benjamin has very wet eyes and he knew they needed to do this. They would not be able to get back here in their timeframe because the distance was so massive. It would take a long time, nearly eighteen months.

Benjamin had a thought. He dropped to channel one and broadcast. *"Who is here?"*

"I am."

"Brad, where are you?"

"Arizona desert, 1947. I – we – all heard what the last member of the Malkornian race said to you and you need to get back home with that case."

"That's just it. If we come home, we will not be the one to bring it back here and reactivate the Altar of Life. I want to see this all the way through to the end."

"You have a plan?"

"Yep! I sure do"

* *

It has been a couple days and Brad is living in the desert keeping tabs on Team One. The plan was to learn to fly the Malkornian starship and travel back to Earth. Even in Benjamin's time no probe has charted the entire solar system, there are places to hide a ship this size. Brad is looking into where is the best location.

"Benjamin, I found the perfect place. Pluto!"

"But the Plutonian probes – they will see it."

"That's the beauty of it. I chose Pluto and at no point in the new history when I got back was there anything ever discovered on Pluto."

"OK, Pluto it is. I need for you to get back and set up to have the Archives send a ship to Pluto. Once we are back we can fly the ship back here and repopulate the planet."

"Consider it done. Dora, take over as the liaison for team one. If they need anything you come home next to report. The other two can remain and listen in."

For the past couple days' team one has been on channel one so everyone can hear them. They have learned to fly the ship and have launched, flown around the solar system, and landed again. Benjamin wanted to put a few items into the ship to take back. The new plan was to fly the ship to Pluto, land and hide it, and jump home leaving the ship to sit on the planetoid for several centuries. Once home, the team would take a shuttle to Pluto and man the ship once again and fly back to the Malkornian planet and reintegrate life.

"Dora, let Brad know we are about to launch and head for Pluto. This ship is surprisingly easy to fly. See you in a few days."

Dora acknowledged the request and was gone. Benjamin and team one, minus Drake, launched and began heading for the Sol system, ninth orbital body. They learned from Brad a few days ago that Drake did not survive. Where he was coupled to the ship he took such a massive amount of radiation that he nearly melted. He survived for a few minutes in the chamber but his pod was so damaged and fused they could not move it. All they could do was jumper it to another timeframe, in close orbit of the Sun. It burned up quickly and harmlessly. Drake, on the other hand, was not as fortunate. His final day was in great pain and agony, even with the drugs available to make him feel nothing.

* * * * * * * * * * * * * * * * * * *

"Benjamin, I am noticing that we can only fly at half the speed of what we did to get to the Malkornian planet. I can't figure it out; there must be a code or something missing."

"Not to worry Ruth, that will still get us home faster than we could in the pods. The only thing I am happy about is that the food dispensers on this ship provide a tasty ration. I swear it tastes like I am eating pot roast."

"That's funny because when I eat the ration packs it tastes like tomato soup."

Dora cut in, *"Alright you hungry people, I have a theory on that... The rations are designed to imitate, at least in your mind and senses, the taste and smell of whatever you want it to be. I have heard every one say it tastes like something different. So, if you want steak, it will be steak. If you want a salad, it will taste like salad. I guess it was their way of food replication."*

"Cool. Let's try it. I want Sushi!" Hoshi said, and tasted a piece of the ration bar.

"Well..."

"It does. It tasted like uni, my favorite. Now it tastes like salmon. This is going to be fun."

"What's uni?" Bradley asked.

"Sea urchin…."

"Sorry I asked."

"I think I am taking a big bite of the best Pluto's Burger, all the way of course." Benjamin bit off a piece of the bar and sure enough, it was excellent.

"WELL!" They all said in unison…

"Perfect! Barbara would be proud to call that her own."

Chapter 6

New Birth

It took them nearly a week to get to Pluto and Brad rather enjoyed camping again. It has been a while but moreover, he enjoyed camping with other people. A couple days ago he had a rattle snake crawl into camp and he stunned it. Then he proceeded to clean and cook it, not thinking anything about it. The others in the group, especially Wendel, thought it was disgusting. For some reason Dora was not affected by the site or thought of it, and was eager to taste the cooked and finished product.

Of course they brought with them provisions and equipment so they would not be seen or noticed by anyone, and so they would not need to go into town to buy food. The idea was to not be noticed. Brad figured they would be there about a week, but now that they are going on their second week, he is wondering if they will be going home anytime soon.

"Benjamin, can you determine your location and ETA?" Brad asked.

Benjamin had just woken up, as did Brad. Since in space there is no morning or night, Benjamin and team have adopted the same clock as Brad and team. This way, the teams could wake, and sleep, together. Twelve on and twelve off is the schedule. Ruth was able to gain full computer access and discover a lot about the ship and the people. The ship will fly itself, and she programmed it to fly to Pluto and land, then secure itself with tethers and clamps on the side not facing Earth.

She also discovered the medical library and began reading through some of the entries. The system, as old as it was, was centuries ahead of Ruth and her timeframe. The computer on this ship determines the race and language used and adopts itself to the user. So essentially, the computer was operating in English because that was Ruth's primary language. It made things a lot easier.

All of the ship's systems operated in this way. It was funny, when Benjamin sat in the Command chair he asked if anyone could translate the captain's console into English, and it changed itself. There was no way to crash this ship, unless you disabled the computer and programmed the collision on purpose. True, because of the nature of this vessel they were able to program the ship to go to Pluto and secure itself, power down to a minimal sustainable level and it would, without any assistance; but they wanted to see it through and get the chance to look through the ship's database, which was massive by the way.

"Estimate arrival at Pluto in six hours. According to the plan in the computer we will begin normal space in a few minutes. Then a four-hour flight past Uranus and Saturn and finally landing on Pluto. Once landed Ruth and I will return home. The others will begin departure once we return to normal space."

"Sounds like a good plan. I look forward to a Pluto burger." He heard something in the background and both got very quiet. *"Riders on horseback are coming up to the campsite. We need to hide a few things. I'll keep the link open."*

There were four people in the campsite; Brad and Dora and LaVarr and Monika. It looks like there are two couples camping and enjoying each other's company. Will and Wendel went back a few hours ago during the last shift because both were feeling ill.

Brad assumed it was the camping, which they are not used to, and the food. They may pop back in soon so they need to get these guys out of the camp fast.

"Can I ask what you folks are doing here?" One of the strangers asked.

"Camping. A few friends wanted some time away from the city to look at the stars and have some quiet time." Brad replied.

Brad noticed they all had weapons, rifles; and a couple of them had side arms. But the only one that appeared to be a danger was the one talking. The others looked like followers and he was the leader.

"Well, let's see if this trip is worth our time." One of the other men produced a revolver. "Turn over all your valuables." The leader said flatly, and then smiled. "Looks like this will not be a total waste of time. We may all have the chance to visit with your friends." He was looking at the women with a lust in his eyes that made Brad mad.

"OK, is everyone on?" Brad, and all of team one, heard this entire altercation so far and also the replies from the other three at the camp. *"Here is what is going to happen. I will stun the man with the pistol and the leader, you three fall to the ground and hide."*

"Brad, be careful." Benjamin said with intensity.

"Not a problem. I have gotten pretty good at this stunner. This is, however, the first time I have needed to fire five shots in rapid progression. Let's see if I get them in the right order and I don't get shot."

Brad pulled his sleeves up slightly to expose the location of the stunner. Mentally, he instructed the stunner to use the maximum setting which should put them out for nearly eight hours. The next few seconds were a blur.

Brad stunned the man with the pistol, then the leader, then the man furthest away and began to work his way to the other two. He managed to get them all and…

"BANG!"

A single shot rang out. Silence on the link.

"BRAD!" Benjamin yelled through the link.

No answer.

"Brad's been shot. He managed to stun everyone before they hit him." Monika's voice.

"Will, you are in charge. Do what you need to do." Benjamin stated flatly but with the greatest intensity they had ever heard.

Will began to speak almost at once, *"Monika, take Brad home and get him patched up. LaVar, I have an idea that will blow these guy's minds, and not cause any issues with present or future. How is Brad?"*

"Shot through the shoulder. He is hurt but not serious. He will be fine."

Will outlined his plan to Dora and LaVarr while Monika took Brad home and got him patched up. They should be back in a short time.

LaVar began transporting the bad guys to the future two at a time, and then the operator would send them back to the same timeframe but one hundred miles away, still in the dessert. The only issue is what to do with the horses. Do we bring them too, or do we leave them? If we leave them here, they would not survive. The final result was to have five security operatives return to the campsite and take the horses to the men and return home. So, on the last trip LaVarr returned with the security team who transported the horses and LaVarr at the same time to the location of the men.

LaVarr noticed the leader and the man with the pistol were beginning to come to, and thought it would be good if security would stun them all again so they would not remember anything about them. But the security teams popped out as soon as they appeared. The man with the pistol looked at LaVarr and started to speak but his mouth did not work yet. At that moment LaVarr had the idea to say something to him.

"That was not a smart thing to do." Then he placed his finger on the side of his nose, pointed to the man as if shooting him with his finger and dropped his thumb as if it was the hammer of a pistol and disappeared with the telltale whoosh and pop of a jump transport and the man sat there with his mouth hanging open.

He sat there in disbelief, knowing full well that if he ever mentioned it to anyone they would label him crazy and lock him away. As the rest came around no one could remember what happened, or how they got there. They attributed it to a night of drinking bad booze.

Back at the campsite Brad had returned with his arm patched up. Medical technology could patch up a simple hole easily enough but the muscle and tenderness would last a while. Brad had his arm in a sling, and Monika looked like she had been frazzled. She looked like Brad's nurse-maid, and thankfully Benjamin did not see it or he would have made some comment about it. But she looked relaxed. It had been a long night for her.

"Benjamin? Where are you?" Brad asked behind the pain killers.

"Right here, you sound like you are feeling good. How did it go?"

"They fixed the hole, I was leaking." Benjamin started laughing. *"They patched me aaaaaaaall up, told me it would be* **'sensitive'** *for a while. Everything still works though and Monika has been great. She is great. Have you ever looked into her eyes and noticed how they sparkle in the light of a campfire? I can stare into those eyes forever. She is soooooo beautiful. I would really like to get to know her better."*

Everyone started laughing and Benjamin finally said, *"Could someone down there please put that boy to bed; and remind him to shut off the Sub-Q or we will all experience whatever odd drug induced dreams he has. OH, and Monika, that stuff is like truth serum, but in the morning he may or may not remember what he said."*

"I understand." She was a little embarrassed but at the same time happy, you could see on her face she felt the same way about Brad.

"So Dora, what happened with the bad guys? We have been kinda busy here dropping back to normal space and all and were off channel for a bit. Fill us in!"

"This is LaVarr. Let me fill you in, I think you will like this and it was fun." So as he told the story about jumping forward and backward and dropping them off a hundred miles away, team one

was laughing out loud. And when he told him how the one man woke up and what he said to him, they laughed even harder."

"Can you imagine that guy waking up and seeing someone disappear before your eyes, who would you tell?" Ruth said while chuckling uncontrollably.

"That's just it, no one. You would be labeled a nut, or it would be because of the hangover." LaVarr replied.

"Definitely. Good job." Benjamin gave them a verbal pat on the back.

"OK, in a couple hours we will land on Pluto. Once there Ruth and I will transport back. Between now and then the others will all jump home one by one with 3 minutes or more between each, as their station is no longer needed essentially."

Dora began to speak before Benjamin could say anything, *"I asked LaVarr to find the highest point in the area and use visual enhancement to scan the horizon. He was able to see the edge of the horizon in all directions and there is no movement. So, I suppose we are secure in this area for a few hours. My guess is long enough for you to land and secure and all of us to get home. Before we all jump we are going to scatter the fire pit and erase any sign we were here."*

"Good thinking. Leave No Trace!" Benjamin commended her for her plan. It was something they should have accomplished every few hours while there so no one snuck up on them. But, throughout history, hindsight has always been 20/20.

Dora began taking charge of the dismantling of the base camp, while Will Walker helped to finalize the situation in space. Bradley was transmitting visual of the interior of the ship to everyone so they had the chance to see and experience it as if they were there in person. Bradley and Will coordinated on Brad's channel, since Brad was in 'another place' at the moment. They needed to coordinate the massive amount of data and the easiest way to do so would be in person.

Since the chance of hitting a moving spacecraft at the outer regions of the solar system is slim, to say the least; Bradley suggested he be used as the containment for the data. One at a time each of them connected to him on Brad's frequency and uploaded their entire database into his Sub-Q, including Benjamin. Once accomplished, he transported back to the island complex and uploaded the entire amount of data to the island computer system and returned to where team two was camped. They would all leave in the morning, a few short hours from now. He would assist in bringing all materials back since Brad was indisposed.

A few hours past and the entire campsite was vacant, with the exception of Brad, who is now awake and coherent, and Bradley, Dora, and Monika. The four of them decided to wait it out. Once they have confirmation that team one returned safely they would leave also.

"OK, the ship is secure on Pluto, all others except for Ruth and me have departed and in a moment Ruth will be leaving. She is getting into her pod now. Ruth, go home!" And Ruth vanished. "Three minutes and counting. Putting ship's systems on minimal and automatic. Reserve power levels at 100%, life support at 5%. I estimate when we return the power level will be at 22%. Encoding the ship's door to operate at voice code command only, no other access is permitted. Brad, you know my code?"

"Yes, I believe I do!" Brad laughed.

Benjamin jumped home and Brad and Monika were the last to leave this timeframe. Before they left they took the opportunity to do one thing. They deactivated their implants.

"Brad, I wanted to tell you this several weeks ago, but I have deep feelings for you and I think you feel the same way. I am not sure what we can do about them now, but after I graduate we can determine our next step."

"Monika, I care deeply for you also, and I would like to share with you something of my world. Once you graduate and take your rightful place as a researcher, we can think about the future together. In the meantime…"

"…In the meantime, we will be the best friends that two people can be." She kissed him passionately. It lasted an eternity. Brad and Monika have both thought about this moment but both of them are traditional. Neither of them wants to violate each other's belief system. Brad does not have the heart to tell his best friend, Benjamin, that Bill and Betty convinced him when they were in class together that there is a higher power, a God, which watches over us all. But for Brad and Monika this is real. Some of that information was learned when Brad was on his long-term mission to the Wild West. The preachers there are very adamant about what they say, and preach. If you are not listening to them, they get louder until you are listening and then speak directly to your heart.

They talked about it and discovered they both have the same thoughts, and once they are together in time they will request a long term assignment somewhere they can be together in spirit. A moment later all that was left of them was two sets of footprints facing each other.

* * * * * * * * * * * * * * * * * * * *

Since the ship was still attached to the surface of Pluto, which was confirmed by a probe, Benjamin told his teams to take the rest of the day off and report in the morning at 10am to the Spaceport. Twelve people started this mission; eleven will finish in memory of the twelfth. Drake will have a special place in their hearts.

Benjamin and Brad decided to go to Pluto's. They were going to sit at their normal table and when they walked in they saw the rest of the class.

"Benjamin, Brad, please join us." There were three chairs open, one on the end of the table and two between Monika and Ruth. Brad and Benjamin looked at each other and switched. Benjamin sat next to Monika and Brad next to Ruth. They did not want to appear there was anything going on between them, but Benjamin vowed when this started he would find a way some day. Ruth had no idea but thought he was rather full of himself and did not trust him. Monika, on the other hand, knew exactly how Brad felt but did not want to jeopardize her career or position in the school.

"BENNY! BRAD!" Barbara walked over and gave them both a beer. Without saying or thinking they downed that beer and handed her the empty mug. "OK, what can I get you?" She smiled and it felt like home again.

"Barbara. I need eleven Temporal Rifts, half servings." Benjamin said slowly and with meaning. The tone at the table changed completely, it all of a sudden seemed solemn.

Barbara turned and looked at Mike. "Mike, TR, eleven half glasses."

Monika touched Barbara's shoulder, "What's going on?" She asked.

"The only time Benny orders a half serving of anything is to toast a fallen friend, someone who died somewhere that he knew. A memorial. Is there someone like that?"

"Yes." And the class knew exactly what was about to happen.

"Mike ceremoniously brought the eleven glasses over to the large table and put one in front of each person starting with Benjamin. Benjamin did not move, when Mike placed the glass in front of him he stared at it with the greatest of intensity and that forced each person to do the same. Knowing what was happening each of them started to remember something funny Drake did during school.

After a moment, Benjamin stood and everyone followed. He picked up his glass and everyone did also. "To Drake, he was funny. He always had a way to make you see the humor in any situation. I only knew him a short time, but he was an all right guy."

Brad said something next while they all held their glass in the air, "The first time he tried to run up his pod he ran into the ceiling, all he said to me was OOPS! I thought I was going to lose it; his face was hilarious."

As each of them, in order, recalled something about Drake from their time together, the mood lightened. Monika was that last.

"Drake had issues keeping things to himself. I could hear…see it in his face. I believe he really enjoyed looking at shirts." All of the women smiled and nodded at the fact that Drake liked looking at their chests, and everyone understood that the hear or rather see it in his face meant that right after they received their implants Drake forgot and blurted out a few things over the link that he really intended to keep to himself. Harmless, but something everyone remembered. When she finished Benjamin continued.

"Friends of Drake Williams, classmates; I salute with you the loss of your friend, and bid you ease to make it a part of your life. TO DRAKE!" Benjamin drank it down in one gulp and threw the glass against the wall. That was when everyone noticed that Barbara had placed a container on the floor so it would catch the shards of glass. One by one they all said TO DRAKE, drank their glass and threw it at the wall. When Monika tossed hers, Barbara walked over and collected the container and pressed a button on the wall to activate the autovac to make certain there were no stray pieces.

"Barbara." Brad called out.

"Yes Brad?" She answered in what sounded like a deep southern drawl. Brad looked shocked and opened his mouth.

A moment later he continued, "Nice accent by the way. Eleven burgers, all the way, and beers all around."

"You got it." She left with a smile. She had seen this ritual a few times and when Benjamin orders half's he means in glass glasses. When the bar was redesigned no one knew what to put on that wall so Benjamin asked to put a sheet of marble or granite there. Mike asked what for and when Benjamin told him it was to honor the dead, someone who passed away or died by breaking the glass against the wall Mike thought it was a good idea. Now, each person honored at this wall has their name engraved on it for all eternity.

Tomorrow, if they come back, they will see the name Drake Williams. No dates, nothing to say what happened, just the name. That's all that's needed.

Benjamin saw the names on the wall as he took a deep cleansing breath, two names on that list he felt responsible for, Monica Brocco and Chang Mae, members of his class who perished during the class project. Much the same as the fate of Drake. No one will ever know the entire story with the exception of this group of people sitting at this table.

* * * * * * * * * * * * * * * * * * * *

"OK class. We are about to launch. The flight will last approximately 13 hours and once at Pluto, Brad and I will exit the ship and walk over to the other ship. We will enter and open the door and make ready the docking port so the rest of you can all transfer over in comfort and safety."

Brad took over, "Karen, you are to take charge of the case with the cube, and LaVarr I need for you to ensure nothing happens to either Karen or the case."

Hoshi raised her hand and asked, "So what do we do for the next thirteen hours?"

Benjamin and Brad smiled at each other but it was Monika that spoke next, "I suggest you get some rest. We all stayed out late last night and I'll tell you what, I could use a nap."

Everyone nodded, and settled into their seats. Brad and Benjamin went up to the cockpit to talk to the pilot. This was a charter flight and not a ship owned or operated by the archives. The crew had no idea where they were going or what to expect, all they knew is to file a flight plan to orbit Pluto for an hour then fly home, stopping at the Saturn Station to drop off all passengers.

"We ready to leave?" Brad asked the pilot.

"Not yet, we are waiting for the other two members of our crew to show up. Policy states we need a crew of four to operate this machine, sorry. It will only be a couple minutes."

They all looked at each other as if thinking, let's go already. But policy was policy.

A moment later the co-pilot said, "Here they are now."

Benjamin said flatly, "Gloria and Tiffany. Perfect."

"You know them?"

"Yep. They are here, let's leave." Turning to Brad. "Follow me."

"What?" Brad looked at Benjamin and asked kinda looking at him sideways.

"We need to talk to them before they see who is on board." Benjamin looked at Brad with a look of fear. Then Brad understood. These girls knew them, well. It could ruin their reputations at the school.

Benjamin and Brad stood at the airlock and intercepted the girls as they entered. "Ladies, aboard this craft are nine passengers and Brad and I. You cannot let on that you know us, nor can you ever speak of this flight as it transpires. You will be flying us around to Pluto, orbit for an hour, fly to Saturn Station and drop us all off then home. In a few weeks we will get together and tell you all about it. But for now, you have never met us and we are on a mission we cannot discuss."

"Gloria looked Benjamin square in the eyes and, "We know. We were briefed you would be here, and that we are to not speak of this flight. Oh, and we get double pay for this!"

"Great. When we get back I will spring for dinner at any restaurant on Earth." Benjamin let them know.

"We'll see." Tiffany remarked as she walked into the ship's airlock.

* * * * * * * * * * * * * * * * * * *

The ship's intercom began to buzz; the captain was about to make an announcement. "Stand by for orbital insertion of Pluto. Mr. Jensen to the cockpit."

Benjamin woke up from his nap feeling pretty good. Brad had awakened about half an hour before. They both stood and walked to the front of the craft.

As they approached the door turned red, no entry. Brad touched a pad next to the door and the chime could be heard. A few moments later the door turned green and they walked through, to see Tiffany and Gloria buttoning their blouses. Benjamin smiled and Brad looked embarrassed.

The pilot and co-pilot looked like two kids who got caught with their hand in the cookie jar, or someplace else. The girls looked totally ashamed. They left quickly and the four men were left alone in the cabin.

"It's not what you think. There was a lot of free time and…." The co-pilot started to speak.

"…and the crew needed to confer on a matter of ship's business." Benjamin finished. Dismissing the incident. "You called us up here."

"Yes, and you got here faster than I thought."

Brad snickered, "Obviously." They all laughed.

The captain continued after a moment, "Where to? I know I will need to land but I was not told where."

"How do you know that you need to land?" Brad asked.

"Let's see. Verify hard pack snow landing struts are installed on the shuttle prior to launch, install gangway and airlock assembly, take on additional fuel for the trip."

"OH....Ok. I guess 2 plus 2 equals 4." Brad smiled.

Benjamin started to outline the plan for the landing. They are to land with the airlock on the starboard side of the ship, which means the ships would be nose to nose. Brad and Benjamin will exit the craft and walk over to the other ship and make it ready for docking. Once complete the gangway will be extended and the airlock secured. Everyone will walk over to the ship and the shuttle will take off leaving the gangway and airlock on the surface. They were to proceed to Saturn and dock. Spend the night on the station, a hotel has been arranged. Pick up some cargo and return to the Moon Base Mine.

Roughly thirty minutes later they were in position to land. Benjamin directed him to where he had landed the ship about a day, or was it several hundred years, before. The science department examined the case and determined it contained – literally – the genetic material for every creature on the planet. At least all mammals anyway as far as they could tell.

Which means that if this works, all people and all animals will be returned to the point in their life when the sample was taken.

"Brad, the only thing I hope is that (a), there are directions and (b) there is enough power to accomplish what we are doing."

LANDING COMPLETE.

The voice came over the intercom and Benjamin and Brad locked up their suits and entered the airlock. Tiffany rolled the mechanism into place and the seal went red, meaning that the air was being removed from the room that Benjamin and Brad were standing in. Their suits got harder, and a little puffy, but motion was not hindered in the least.

Benjamin pressed the open panel and the outer door opened slowly. What they saw actually made them both stop and wonder if they lost their mind. This place is absolutely scary. Imagine the worst blizzard at twilight on the dessert during the worst horror movie ever made. This made that look like a children's program.

"Ready?" Benjamin asked.

"Uh…sure. Why not." Brad replied.

"Two things before you leave the ship." Dora told them through the ship's communication system and their suits. "The surface is ice. Solid ice. More solid ice than you have ever experienced in your life. Therefore, if you slip, and you will, you will fall. And two, the gravity here is about seven percent that of Earth. So if an object were to weigh one hundred kilograms on Earth, it would weigh seventeen kilograms on our Moon, and only six or seven kilograms here. If you jump high, you can go a huge distance. As for landing again, refer to point number one." Then she laughed.

"Funny." Benjamin and Brad smiled at each other.

As they stepped out of the ship both of them slipped. This was the slickest surface they had ever experienced. They turned slightly and bang, there it was. Pluto's Moon Charon. It looks like someone hung a huge picture of it over the ship.

"That is the largest Moon I have ever seen." Brad said out loud.

"Seven times larger than Earth's Moon actually, at least visually that is." Dora filled in the information.

"There seems to be a thin atmosphere, am I hallucinating?"

"Nope. We are here when the orbit puts it inside the orbit of Neptune, perigee. Same interval as before."

"Before what?" The co-pilot asked.

Dora put on her thinking cap and, "Since the interval of the orbit is 248 years, it's logical to assume this has happened before."

Benjamin spoke through his Sub-Q, *"Nice one. We all need to watch what we say here. They are cleared to see the ship, but not us. Clear!"*

Everyone responded, it was clear they had to watch what they said, and watch again.

Benjamin and Brad walked over to the ship. The door is voice operated but in a vacuum voice does not carry, at all. Brad and Benjamin looked over the entire door mechanism trying to find the external latch. They knew it had to have one but never thought to look for it before this moment. They located what they thought was the voice entry system and it looked as though it was self-contained. Benjamin placed his helmet in direct contact with the sensor and stated the pass code, in as loud of a voice as he could muster, and in as clear of speech as he could manage, "8-6-7-5-3-oh-9" and the door slid open.

Once inside the door closed again and they entered the inner chamber. Benjamin looked at the power levels before he did anything else. 99.2 percent. This ship lost only .8 percent of the power reserve in the last several hundred years, which is amazing. Benjamin thought to himself.

Life support went online the moment they entered and they removed their helmets and activated all of the ships systems. They really did not have to do much, the ship remembered Benjamin and welcomed him as Captain, and reactivated all systems that were active at the time he put the ship down for its centuries long nap. The engine core was restarted and the ship was ready to go to work. This thing is amazing.

Next step is to attach the tube from point 'A' to point 'B'. That took about two hours. When everyone arrived on board Benjamin grabbed a few of the meal bars from the ship and brought them to the crew.

"Here is a little something you may see in the next few years. They are special meal bars that whatever food you are thinking about when you put a piece in your mouth, they taste like. So, first bite can be soup, second bite is a steak, third bite is potato casserole, and the last bite can be a nice slice of apple pie with a ball of vanilla ice cream and chocolate syrup."

"No way." All of them, all four, did not believe him.

Benjamin opened the wrapper and handed them the bar in four pieces, each of them getting a piece. "OK, one at a time, tell me what food are you thinking of?"

"Cream of Mushroom soup." The Captain said.

The rest were thinking about Tuna Sushi, chili, and pot roast. Low and behold when they all put the piece in their mouth that was the exact taste they received to their brain. Benjamin handed them a dozen more bars, three each, and gave them all a wave.

He needed to get going. "Now, please do not talk about these bars or mention them and make sure you eat them or hide them before you get to the stations and vaporize the wrappers please. The last thing we would want is for them to fall into the wrong hands and someone mass producing and overcharging for them." They all agreed, and Benjamin left.

Closing the airlock on his end he sent the all clear signal and the rush of air escaping into space could be heard. Then in the ultra-thin atmosphere the low sound of the other ship lifting off resounded against the hull and then silence.

"Fifteen minutes to launch." Brad stated.

"Why wait fifteen minutes?" Monika asked.

"We need to give the other ship time to leave the area so they won't witness our rapid departure." Benjamin answered.

For the next few minutes everyone became familiar with their assigned departure area. There were only 8 chairs and Benjamin had the captain's seat, the one up a little higher and more comfortable than the rest. Brad took the seat to his left, equally as comfortable and a scan screen for every system on the ship. It also had a complete communications system in the event he needed to communicate with anyone.

The others paired off with one person from each team. The team one person showed the team two person the system, and then they took on twelve hour shifts opposite each other.

"Brad, take us up and out of the solar system." Benjamin said.

"Ruth, ahead half-light speed. Heading …. Uh…..you know where we are going." Brad started to smile and gave up on trying to look as though knew what he was doing.

"Heading two-thirty-one by three-oh-five, half-light." She pressed the button that made the ship move with the most dramatic exaggeration she could muster. "And…we're off."

"Is that really the heading?" Brad asked.

"No clue. I simply pressed the button that said return to home base, land in standard position. As for the half-light part, the button tells me that is the maximum speed at the moment."

Everyone laughed. But the ship moved and screens were changing. Once they left the solar system the ship determined the best possible speed and increased appropriately. It would let them know if they needed to be attentive to anything.

The next week was dotted with being awake and asleep, and frequent update sessions with the school. Brad and Benjamin had a private channel which Mr. Winchester and the rest of the school faculty used for such an occasion. This was, after all, a class; and participation and grades were a part of it. So they needed to provide the faculty with grade equivalents for what they were doing.

"We should be entering the Malkornian atmosphere in a few moments. Wake everyone up." Brad stated with the excitement of a kid in a candy store. He was sitting in the big chair at the moment and Benjamin was sleeping.

LaVarr looked back at Brad and smiled. His hand reaching for the alarm klaxon, a button they found a few days ago that could wake the dead. Brad and the rest of the people awake put their fingers in their ears and…

"WWWWHHHHHHHAAAAAAAA"

It lasted only a few seconds and the first time it went off the second shift was asleep. This was nothing more than payback. Plain and simple. But man was it fun.

Everyone came running into the control center blurry eyed and frazzled. Brad looked at Benjamin, "We're here!" He was really excited.

Benjamin said, "All stop. Parking orbit over the spot we launched from, begin planetary scans for life or anything else. I'll be back in 15 minutes, as will the rest of team one. I would like to complete this mission dressed, thank you." He waved a clenched fist at Brad and LaVarr.

Team one left to get dressed and ready to meet history. Team two cheered and laughed.

* * * * * * * * * * * * * * * * * * * *

"We have been hanging here in space for more than an hour. When are we going to land?"

"Brad, I just feel something is not quite right. Like we are missing a crucial element or something." Looking into the air, "Computer, analyze the surface and report."

"SPECIFY" The computer said almost immediately.

"Analyze the environment, flora and fauna; validate if hostile or incompatible with human, from Earth, life."

"SCANNING WILL BE COMPLETE IN ONE MINUTE." The computers voice sounded neither male or female, and had a duality in the sound. Very peaceful and easy to listen too in any situation.

Benjamin began looking at another screen when, "COMPLETE"

"RESULTS CONCLUSIVE. PLANTEARY ENVIRONMENT 100% COMPATIBLE WITH THAT OF THE PLANET EARTH IN THE EARLY 22nd CENTURY. POLUTION AND PARTICULATE MATTER LESS THAN .05%. POLLEN AT 22%. OXYGEN AT 34%. NITROGEN AT 61%. OTHER GASSES MAKE UP THE REMAINDER OF THE ATMOSPHERE. VIRAL AND BACTERIAL LEVELS ARE ALL WITH IN HUMAN LIMITATIONS."

"Stop. Now, using the Earth based results could a Malkornian survive in this environment?"

"NO."

"Crap, we have the altar of life and have no idea how to use it, and if we do find out how to use it the people will not survive. What are we supposed to do now?"

"ALTAR OF LIFE MUST BE MODIFIED TO HUMAN SPECIFICATIONS. THE INTRODUCTION OF HUMAN DNA TO CREATE A MODIFIED MALKORNIAN LIFEFORM WILL RESULT IN A 100% CHANCE OF MALKORNING REANIMATION AND SURVIVAL."

"Elaborate." The computer thought he was speaking to it, so it replied. Was it really telling him what he needed to do?

"THE CHOSEN MUST INTRODUCE GENETIC MATERIAL TO BE USED DURING THE REANIMATION PROCESS. THIS PROCESS IS AUTOMATIC AND CANNOT BE REVERSED. THE CHOSEN IS THE KEEPER OF THE VESSLE AND MUST INTEGRATE THE VESSLE INTO THE ALTAR AS THE TRANSMUTATION IS BEGINNING."

"OK, so Karen, I guess you are the chosen and need to become a part of the altar."

Her eyes got really wide. What did that mean?

* * * * * * * * * * * * * * * * * * *

"Landing complete." LaVarr said with a sigh of relief.

"Karen, Ruth, LaVarr with me. The rest of you do whatever Brad says."

"You have got to be kidding if you think we are staying here." Brad looked him in the eye as if you say, try me....

"OK, everyone. Follow me." Eleven people exited the ship and the planet was beautiful. When they were here a few days ago, or was it a few hundred years ago, it looked worn. Now it looked like a museum place but the plant, bird, and small animal life was abundant.

The walk to the central complex was not long and they entered the facility and went right to the room where the altar was located. The wall was closed again and Benjamin went to touch the crystals. Nothing happened. Karen wanted to try and when she touched the crystals the wall opened as it did before. She really was the chosen.

She went into the small room and placed the case in its place. Nothing happened. She touched the crystals on the table. Nothing. There was one last crystal so she touched it.

"Ouch!" Karen exclaimed.

"What happened?" Benjamin asked.

"Wait, how could a completely smooth crystal cut my finger?"

Ruth looked like she just swallowed a cow. "I got it. Karen, you have to become a part of the altar before it would activate. If not the entire you, the essence of you. It sampled your blood because the system knew you were able to survive in the environment, so it is remolding the Malkornians using your DNA." Ruth smiled and said, "I hope that doesn't mean they're all going to look like you…."

Everybody laughed.

Karen looked at the altar again and the crystal that took her blood began to light up. Slowly it became very well lit. A few moments later the other two crystals began to glow, she touched them and the object she has been guarding with her life was encased in a clear liquid. The liquid appeared at the bottom of the container and seeped up the sides to the top. When the case was completely covered it hardened. Karen touched it and it emitted a low hum as she did so. LaVarr, who was standing near to her walked over, curious. He touched it and he was shocked. Not bad but enough to let him know his touch is not welcomed. Karen touched it again and this time she received a warm feeling in her soul. Has she become a part of this civilization? Does she have a place to belong?

The room began to fill with smoke or mist or something and LaVarr ushered Karen from the room. They exited coughing slightly. They could not see anything inside the small room.

"THANK YOU. YOU HAVE REACTIVATED A DEAD WORLD"

The voice seemed to come from everywhere.

"I AM MARISHHH. IN A FEW MOMENTS I WILL BE WITH YOU IN PHYSICAL FORM AS WELL. MY PHYSICAL SELF

150

DIED HUNDREDS OF YEARS AGO AND WITH YOUR ASSISTANCE I, AND MY PLANET, WILL LIVE AGAIN."

"Can you understand us?" Karen asked.

"YES. I CAN. IN MORE WAYS THAN YOU CAN IMAGINE. DO NOT BE ALARMED, I WILL BE EXITING THE CHAMBER IN A MOMENT."

Everyone stood there with their eyes transfixed on the mist. It seemed like an eternity and she appeared.

"Benjamin Jensen. Your mission to catalog this planet has allowed for its rebirth. The Malkornian race has been extinct for millennia, but now we have returned through your good fortune, and the grace of the maker."

"You look like the person that died in this room, right there," he pointed to a spot on the floor that appeared a bit darker than the rest.

"I am. The Malkornian people do not possess the immune system that your race possesses but that problem has been remedied. Karen Jones, your essence, as Ruth so aptly worded, has mingled with our own." Marishhh looked at Ruth with a smile and the appearance of humor in her eyes as she spoke the next words. "Although, Karen, we will not look like you, we will all know of you since your genetic memory has been imprinted upon us." She turned towards Benjamin. "Benjamin, the temporal jump system is something of a mystery to us and we are willing to join with Earth, and the faculty of Archive Island, to provide additional technology and training. We have been visiting other planets for centuries before we stumbled on Earth, and in your way of speaking: we've seen a lot." She smiled back at Benjamin.

"How does this work? You were created out of the materials in the case?"

"That is correct. As I died on this floor the computer in the room took a complete scan of me. When I died it placed the essence of the scan in the case. Since I am the caretaker it reanimates me first to validate the process. I have done so and all over the planet people are returning to their lives. Yes, they all know about the twelve of you, and will memorialize Drake for his sacrifice; but they are all aware of the amount of time they have slept and are beginning to rebuild this world in their new image. With the inception of the immune system, something we did not have before, we can accomplish far more than we have in all our past millennia."

"One last thing; everything Karen knows, I know. Her memory has been implanted onto my own. Although the remainder of the inhabitants of my world will know about you, and what you did; I shall elect to not instill in them the full memory Karen has granted us. I, and a few of our leaders, shall be the only person's on this world to 'know-it-all' as you human's would say."

"OUTSTANDING!" Brad could be heard in the back of the room.

"Brad, we understand that you desire to travel to the past, the 19th century in Earth history. We will give you a discreet receiver so you can monitor the skies and note when we visit your world in that era. We have been watching your planet since it was in its … now what did you refer to it as. Kings and knights and …"

"Medieval Times?" Dora added quietly.

"YES! Thank you Dora, Medieval Times. We thought the governmental structure was very interesting so we watched. But now, my friends, I need to go to work and repopulate my planet."

* * * * * * * * * * * * * * * * * * * *

For the next few weeks the team stayed and helped as best as they could. This technology, still being centuries old, is far more advanced than they first suspected. Benjamin sat in a café on a street only a few days before looked like a bomb had decimated it. Today, it is beautiful and no matter how he or any other member of the team tries they cannot pay for a single item anywhere on the planet.

"Benjamin Jensen to Security. Please provide a link to Mr. Robert Winchester for a period of one hour – for the purpose of my daily report."

There was no approval process, it was set up in advance and he had been performing this duty daily, sometimes more than once, for a while now. Security did not even respond letting him know the connection was complete.

"Good morning my boy, how is the savior of an entire race."

"Uh, fine I guess."

"Good for you. Your report?"

"Yes sir, we have learned a great deal about their technology, and the fact they have no offensive weapons at all. Every one of their weapons is defensive. This sounds like a perfect relationship for us. They have improved the stunner and provided a schematic. The stun setting can now be set to within a few minutes, whatever time duration needed up to nine hours. Power consumption is one tenth of what it was at maximum

intensity. Our pods, since all we had was a technical diagram, were redesigned to contain a more robust computer core and engine. It is capable of point nine of light speed. So we can explore a lot more than we have been able to in the past."

"What about the culture, the people. Are they one or are there different nationalities? Cultures? Sects? Religions?"

"One for all and all for one, I guess. They all have the same deity belief system, but they differ in the way they prepare meals. The northern people like it a little spicy and the southern people blander. I prefer the north. They have some of the best food I have ever consumed. Oh, they also provided the recipe for the food bar and we have everything we need to reproduce them on Earth just never thought to mix this specific ingredient concoction before. Also, they will help us design the method they use to dispense them, this is going to be a new technology. It mixes the ingredients from storage when the person requests it. We ate quite well on the way here, and we are eating well now."

"One last thing. They want to travel back with us to meet you and the rest of the faculty. They requested that two come with us."

"Approved. I look forward to meeting them."

"Jensen out. Talk to you tomorrow."

Benjamin changed channels in his head, his Sub-Q and called out to Brad. *"Where are you?"*

"About half a kilometer from you I guess. Wait for me there. Where are you?"

"Sitting at a café enjoying some of the local cuisine. It is sorta like their version of chili I guess."

A short time later Brad and Karen joined Benjamin. They sat and something was placed in front of them. "Benjamin, Karen has something she wanted to tell you." He sipped on his refreshment. "Hey, this is good. Kinda like lemonade but not. I like it."

Benjamin looked at Brad who was concerned about a drink. When he looked back at Karen, her face was serious. Karen was slow, deliberate, and confident in her voice, "I have decided to stay here and live with these people. I am a part of them and they are a part of me."

"Before you do so let me tell you what I discussed with the school faculty yesterday evening. They decided there needs to be a permanent presence here and someone needs to be the Earth Ambassador to this world. But first that person needs to be a credentialed historian, possess an implant, and understand the people and the culture. The position will be a facet of the LT department and can last as much as three or four years."

He stared at her eyes. Beautiful and black as night. Her skin took on a glow in this light, "I recommended you for the position." She exploded. As she dove at him to give him the biggest hug of his life, they both tumbled backwards over the back of the chair.

The rest of the patrons looked concerned, for a moment. Then smiled when they realized the situation was joyous. They felt the emotions of others, they were empaths.

That is the reason for no offensive weapons. If they injured another lifeform, they would feel it also. Not something they wanted to do, ever. This is the most peaceful and tranquil place in the universe. There is no crime and just the thought of something bad is considered to be bad and the person is fixed, because they are considered broken.

* * * * * * * * * * * * * * * * * * * *

"So all you need to do is convince the school, and my boss, that Karen Jones, an untested historian, needs to be put into the diplomatic corp. That she be made the ambassador of the planet Earth to the Malkornian home world." Shaking his head, "Great. How do you plan to do it?" Brad looked at Benjamin, he had THAT grin on his face. Brad hated that grin; it meant Benjamin did something stupid.

"I have no idea…." Benjamin replied. Smiling….

Chapter 7

Back to Work

Brad and Benjamin had a meeting first thing in the next morning with Matthew Sharp. They had no idea what it was about but assumed they would be collaborating on a new assignment. Since they lived in the same building it was easy to commute together.

Entering the tube to take them to the island complex off the coast of what used to be called Chicago, Benjamin saw someone he had not seen in a long time. He refers to her simply as the 'Old Lady" and for good reason. This woman does nothing but complain and gripe about things she or anyone around her has no control over, and but she likes to hear her own voice, loudly, over and over.

This mornings discussion is a familiar one to Benjamin. Travel to other planets and we need to fix our world first before we start breaking other worlds.

Benjamin looked at Brad; this put his back to the old lady. "Man that was a great trip. How many different worlds did we land on, eight? Anyway, it doesn't matter, I would do it all over again as long as I could 'rough it' like we did. Sleeping in tents, campfire, cooking food that we found or hunted over the fire. What a great time."

Brad looked dumbfounded, he had no idea what to say back, but Benjamin gave him a sideways look as if telling him to wait a moment, and it worked, the old lady started in.

"You WHAT?" The old lady exclaimed. "You went to another world and destroyed part of an ecosystem?"

"No, we camped. Found a tree that made for great firewood, fished in a nearby stream and trapped small critters for our dinner, and discovered a whole range of plants and fruits we could eat. It was a great time.

"The destruction of that delicate system only reinforces my DIS-regard for you boy. I remember you now; you are that smart-ass with the witty comebacks. Well, let me give you a piece of my mind….

Holding up his open hand with the palm facing her disrupted her train of thought and she hesitated her speech for the briefest moment, "…please don't, you need all you have."

"Ah. Think you're funny."

"No, not really. Just trying to understand your point of view, as slanted as it is."

"SLANTED! As in Skewed?"

"As in a little off, wrong, biased, judgmental, incorrect, misinformed, did I mention wrong already?"

"Let me tell you one thing about life. It sucks. We are here in this existence for one purpose, to take up space in the universe and not make it worse for everyone else."

"Then I guess you're doing it wrong then."

The train was coming to a stop at her stop. It just happened to be the stop Benjamin and Brad needed to get off also and the only, and the last stop on the island since this mode of transportation had only two stops, one at each end of the maglev track

"My stop, I guess we need to continue this conversation later."

"Possibly, but I feel guilty."

"Guilty. For what?" The old woman snapped back.

"For engaging in a battle of wits with an unarmed opponent." Benjamin grabbed Brads arm and left the tube at a faster pace than normal. He liked leaving her without getting the last word in, he knew how it hurt her ego.

"OK, explain." Brad said as they entered the lift in Matthew Sharp's building.

"Her and I have been sparring like that since just about the first day I started working here. We never have any direct dealing with each other, but try to get under each other's skin. In actuality, she has no idea what my name is, but I know hers. If she ever learned who I was, I am pretty certain these little entertainment breaks would stop. At this point in time, we both out-rank her. I like these little verbal sparring rounds, makes life interesting."

"A hobby. Mutual hobby I see…so you are both nuts." Brad said as he laughed.

The elevator doors opened and they walked into the reception area of his office. "We are here to see Mr. Sharp." Benjamin said to the new receptionist.

"He is in a meeting and you should come back in two hours." She said without looking up.

"I believe the meeting is with us." Brad said in a tone like he was speaking to a child.

Benjamin opened his portacomm and tapped out a quick text. The reply beeped back a moment later. "I think you will want to let us in there now. He is expecting us."

"Please sit over there or I will call security." She voiced to them loudly.

Benjamin made the call, "Yes sir, we are here……..In your reception area……she will not let us in……..not sure, you will need to ask her…….OK, thank you." And he hung up. She heard the entire conversation and figured he was playing a gag on her to let them in when they clearly were not supposed to be here now. This is her office; she runs it as she sees fit.

"Right, you just spoke to Mr. Sharp and I am supposed to let you in to see him. He is in an important meeting and is NOT to be disturbed."

Matthew opened the door to his office and waved Benjamin and Brad in without a word to the receptionist. "Hard to find good help." He said to them as they entered. She heard.

"OK, I have a fun filled and exciting new assignment for the two of you." He began.

Benjamin looked at him and asked, "Can we take some time off and recharge?" Benjamin looked like a little kid and Brad had the puppy dog look in his eyes.

"Well, that is a part of it." He eyed them both. "You too are pathetic!"

"There have been reports that temporal travelers in past timeframes have been seen leaving a point to come home or to their next location. This is propagating itself in the annals of history as a phenomenon and people are beginning to create theories about time travelers visiting them, some of these people are becoming violent. We need to discover where these travelers are originating and stop them."

"Sir, we can do this one in a day or so. Why did you really call us here?" Brad asked.

"The school needs a training class in long term assignments in hostile environments and in LT data collection. That is obvious from the last thing you did with the school, and the Malkornian race sings your praises every chance they get. By the way, the new food bars should be ready for sale in a few months, can't wait to try one out."

Brad looked him in the eye, "You have never tried one?"

"No. Not yet, none available."

Benjamin and Brad both reached into their tunic and produced a bar. Benjamin tossed it to his boss, and Brad tossed a spare onto his desk. Matthew ripped it open and said, "Grilled jerk tuna steak." He took a bite and his eyes opened a little farther than either of them thought possible. "OH MAN!! That is amazing," he said as he swallowed.

"Before you take another bite, think of something else."

"OK, let's see. Pork Chop smothered in caramelized onions." He took a bite and shook his head.

"What are we going to called these when they are sold, and how much will they cost to produce, and retail for?" Brad asked. He did not want to overcharge for them.

"Brad, they will cost us one-tenth of a credit to produce, and they will sell three for a credit. That means a full day worth of sustenance for a credit. We are marketing them as field rations, or instant meals. Although we are turning a profit, it is like filling a tanker with an eyedropper. Yes, eventually it will be filled, but it will take a while. So to answer your question, no. We are not gouging the public, just providing a new and versatile product." Mr. Sharp finished and looked them each in the eye, "Now, where were we on the other matter, your next assignment?"

He thought for a second.

"Oh, right, you two seem perfect for the job." He smiled at them with a sinister smile. He was enjoying this, but they will too. "You have one week to create a lesson plan, one week to refine it with the assistance of the faculty, then you will teach the class."

Benjamin and Brad stood there staring at him. They felt like a practical joke had just been sprung, on them. They just spend several weeks with these people on a real mission, and now they need to go back and teach a real class with lesson plans and quizzes and tests?

"Is there anything else gentlemen." Mr. Sharp said, but did not wait for an answer, "You can leave now."

So the last couple minutes in the office had produced a large amount of work, but not in the sense you may think. Our temporal globe trotters now have to determine how to teach this class, a course in how to do what they do. True, Benjamin and Brad have become noted researchers and in a very short time, but to be demoted to teaching! What did they do wrong?

"Uh..Benjamin. That is not the same girl at the desk." Brad looked as he hit Benjamin in the bicep.

The new receptionist looked at them, "The previous receptionist has been reassigned. I am Tandy Bowmont. I know you two and the situation of the previous receptionist shall not be repeated."

"So, you are not going to be efficient and pay attention to detail as the last receptionist?" Benjamin poked at her. She simply stared at him with no real expression on her face.

Curious, "Where did she go?" Benjamin asked.

"She was reassigned to a wonderful supervisor, Gladys Pinchon, in building…"

Benjamin started laughing; he looked at Brad and said quietly, "The old lady on the tube."

Brad started laughing and the two of them left the floor in the elevator, still laughing.

"We'll have to send her our condolences." Brad replied when he could speak again.

The new receptionist, who obviously was quite fond of the old lady, did not see the humor. As they were entering the lift she simply stared at them; and if her eyes were fitted with lasers, they would be puddles by now.

* * * * * * * * * * * * * * * * * * * *

As they arrived back at their area they realized that yes, the classroom instruction was going to be some work; but they were issued two assignments. The first was to discover who was allowing people to view them as they departed from a timeframe.

In Benjamin's office, the two of them began planning this mission. They could fix this in a day or two, then get on the school course.

Benjamin began to speak to the computer, "Collect all data on unexplained incidents."

Brad refined, "Limit the search parameters to the appearance of a person from thin air, or the person disappearing or vanishing."

"Good idea!" Benjamin said to Brad.

After several hours they realized all visual records and written reports were on a single person. Using the date and time stamp on the video retrieved, which clearly showed a member of the Archives returning home, they set up a jump schedule to watch this person. They needed accurate visual records, and if at all possible a DNA sample so this person could be identified and properly trained.

It was obvious to Brad and Benjamin that this person was from their future. Simple logic, the record of this person does not exist, therefore either they are not born yet or his parents are not born yet.

Their plan was to jump to where this visual record was made and speak to him. When they did they waited for about 45 minutes and he showed up on schedule. Before he jumped they spoke to him and let him know they were also from the Island.

They went to a diner and had a cup of coffee and discussed their research and what needed to be done about it.

His answer was simple; he did not care who saw him. They could not do anything about it. He said that he knew who they were from their historical files but did not let on how far into the future he was from, and he would travel as he saw fit and no one can stop him. Then he vanished from the booth in the diner. Thankfully, no one saw him vanish.

Benjamin placed his coffee cup into a bag and sealed it, Brad paid the tab at the diner and left a nice tip, and they walked out of the restaurant and went around back and transferred home.

Once they arrived they called a briefing and gave Will the coffee cup. Security knew what to do. Pull DNA and fingerprints from the cup and flag them. When he applies for school ensure that he is properly trained, or at the very least, denied for training.

Now they could get on with the new course they needed to create knowing that history is safe.

***** ***** ***** ***** ***** ***** ****** ****** ****** ******

Brad and Benjamin determined the LT course had to have several, quite a few, stops. Benjamin wanted to go back to the beginning of the 21st century, he liked it there; and Brad wanted to go back to the 1700's. Making certain he went back BEFORE he arrived the first time. The last thing he wanted to do was see himself; which would be a bad thing in the long run. Or actually a more badder thing, if a preference for terrible to make a point was required.

Class starts tomorrow and the two of them were finalizing the last bit of the course. They would co-teach the course, one in the city and one in the primitive.

Benjamin and Brad are in the classroom today and have been asked to show their curriculum to the other instructors. The students received a long weekend but Benjamin and Brad had to work. The course materials are not that much, but the learning will be massive. First step is to take a seven-day camping trip to learn about camping in the wilderness. Brad will be the main instructor for this part since the actual outdoor activities will be on his part of the jump. That, compounded by the fact he has had several years of literally camping, non-stop, in the wilderness, while Benjamin simply made visits to his campsite.

Benjamin will take the class for a seven-day trip to an island paradise where they will all learn marine biology. To maximize the time spent the seven days for the training jumps will be in a temporal environment. This way the trip will be for several class weeks in the now; and they will have a few months to do what they need to do for training in the past. Therefore, camping will amount to more than 3 weeks, and the marine biology training will have duration of about 6 weeks. A real crash course but a skill that is lacking in researchers – something the faculty needed incorporated into the curriculum. But then they needed to use their new skills.

The instructors liked this plan and asked to hear the actual Long Term jump plan. Benjamin started and Brad stepped in as need be; when the discussion changed to the 1600's Brad took over.

The class would need to jump for six months of travel time, which would be about thirty-five days in the now. Funny how temporal travel has been happening for decades now and it is still difficult to talk about the past, present, and future in one context.

The trip would be first in the year 2010. There was a disaster, an oil spill and loss of 15 lives on an oil rig. They would show up in Louisiana a few weeks after the incident and stay and help clean up the beach for a while. After the first successful capping of the well occurred and the cleanup process truly began, the people of the area could see the light at the end of the tunnel.

The next three-month jump will be to Salem, Massachusetts in February of 1692. The team will be traveling back to chronicle a little of the Salem Witch Trials and just how they affected people of the day. Hardest thing about his will be the speech patterns and language. Still partially old English but polluted with the new colonial slang and inflection. Best bet for this assignment is to appear to be fresh off the boat from England, and have an accent as such.

"May I ask how you determined these two timeframes, and incidents?" One of the instructors asked.

"Simple. There are three open A-Sheets for the 2010 oil disaster. The first is visual and recorded information and data regarding the initial oil rig explosion. The second is the attitude and emotion of the cleanup crews. And the third is the emotional state of the people most affected by the loss of their ocean, the livelihood." Benjamin stopped, this was his baby.

Brad took over, "As for the 1600's, there are five open A-Sheets on the witch trials. The first is what made them start. The second is how they proved what they thought they could prove. The third is how the people, common people, felt about the trials. The fourth is 'did a government official get anything out of the trials themselves'. And the last is how did the rest of the world, or at least England, view the trials in the colonies."

"So you intend to take care of eight separate assignments with the use of the class."

"No Mam," Benjamin continued. "We intend to complete eight assignments during a teaching session over the course of five training weeks, or seven months of jump time. We also intend to ensure these students are the best prepared for not only jumping, but also upon their return to create the best possible reports. I also intend to ensure that I leave with eleven, and return with eleven."

"Mr. Jensen, you will need to draw your plan for ten students. Karen Jones is being graduated early and sent to the Malkornian homeworld as the Earth Ambassador."

"Sir, I recommend you defer her transfer for one month. I feel her talents will be very useful during the training of the class in our jumps to both the island to learn marine biology in a month, and to the camping month."

The committee conferred and their voices could not be heard by Benjamin or Brad. When the sound was reactivated, , "Very well. When do you intend to do the jumps for training?"

"Well, if you can reserve the same campsite I had used during my time here at the school, but for three weeks, and make it start this weekend that would be perfect. The last week of camping will be in a cold climate, Colorado in the Rockies during the mid-spring timeframe. I am thinking that we need to be there in the early 1600's. To see if there is an environmental issue. There is an A-sheet I remember regarding extensive video of the Rocky Mountains in the winter and a variety of Sunsets and Sunrises. Each member of the class can try their hand at video and still photography and the best of each can be folded into a report."

"You intend to camp with them this weekend?"

"Not exactly. The first jump date is scheduled for just under a month from now but I intend to make use of the temporal differentiation by jumping back to this coming weekend. Furthermore, the class will be extremely busy this weekend so they will not see themselves nor will they know anything about it until they actually jump. Since no portacomms operate in that area, and we will require all communications devices be left in the chamber as per jump protocol; they will not be able to contact themselves or anyone else, and they will not be certain when now is for them, and the training will be exemplary. If approved, I need to make the reservation for the campsites."

"Nicely thought out." It was Mr. Winchester's voice.

"How are you sir? We have not spoken in a while and I miss our chats." Benjamin said politely.

"As do I my boy, as do I. I like this plan. But there is one thing you did not mention."

Benjamin nodded and continued, "All of us will be shifted to a clean channel and each of us will have access to several optional frequencies in the event a team needs to speak during a side mission. We were thinking about expanding them to full operational frequencies with optional scan capability, but blocking their access to the current class frequency. This should give them a leg up on the use of the Sub-Q giving them an advantage through the experience after graduation. The campers will be divided into two teams, with Brad and me being the third team and separated from them. Brad and I will be wearing stealth suits so we can monitor and advise, without knowledge of our presence. Essentially, we will be educating them in the daily classes with the deficiencies we witness from the day before. "

"Thank you. That is what I thought you would say." He floated over to him and smiled.

* * * * * * * * * * * * * * * * * * *

"OK, let's recap. We worked well on a short term mission to another planet – never thought I would ever be saying that – but now we will be on a long term, or LT, mission. Why, you may ask? That is something I asked myself also. So, for the next month or so we will be learning the skills needed to go on a long term mission. Brad and I did not have that optional training when we were sitting where you are, but we made due." Benjamin paused for a moment and Brad continued.

"Me, Benjamin, and our class – or at least the portion of the class who needed to learn the camping skills – decided to go on a weekend camping trip. You ten, and us two, will be going to a location, two interesting places actually, to learn both warm and cold climate camping. You will also be learning a thing or two about marine biology. Can someone tell me, or at least guess what rustic camping skills are?"

Will opened his mouth then closed it again, Brad saw that and, "Will, you started to speak, what were you going to say?"

"Well, I am guessing you mean the old fashioned pot on a fire camping skills."

"Exactly. Cooking over a fire, making fire from nothing, trapping and cleaning what you catch.."

"Like a snake!" Dora said.

"Yes, exactly like a snake. Think of yourself as ALWAYS in preservation mode, survival instincts need to be second nature not read out of a manual as they're needed. That is what we hope to instill in the four jumps." The class got excited at the prospect of 4 consecutive jumps. "These are your final projects. This is what will make or break you."

"Four jumps. Jump one," Benjamin took over, "30 grueling days in training to become proficient in Marine Biology. I am so very sorry about the location for this, you will be camping on an island in the Caribbean and there will be an expert in Marine Biology there to train you to see and assist in a massive cleanup of crude oil." Benjamin paused, looking around from eye to eye to eye. They knew what historical event he was referring to.

"Jump two; you will spend 30 glorious days at the lovely Pangaea Hilton. Where you will bring all of your food and water, and pack out all of your trash and waste. In this session you will learn to work as a collective group. Hierarchical structure is that of the class structure. I am not in charge, Brad is not in charge, Trip is. He will assign daily duties and activities. Brad and I will hold daily training sessions designed to aid you in your missions. Cooking and fire building are among the most important."

Brad looked around and continued, "Does anyone have primitive or backwoods camping experience?"

Three hands went up. Dora, Karen, and Monika.

"Explain please. Define your experiences. Dora?" Brad offered her the floor.

"My family thought it was a good thing to learn the old ways to do things. So, every summer we camped in a different park for one month. Some were on Earth, others were on the colony planets; but all of them had one thing in common, no technology."

"And did you enjoy it?"

"As a teenager no. But as I matured and finished school and started at the university, yes. I did enjoy it. And I was, am, good at it." She smiled.

Brad looked around and got a fixed gaze with Monika. "OK, let's hear it."

"We went to the primitive campgrounds around our house. Dad and Mom thought it was fun, but none of us did. Tents or cabins, sleeping bags, open fire cooking, not for me. I need soft sheets, room service, and environmental control."

"You're gonna have fun on this trip." Looking at the last one who raised her hand. "Karen?"

"You all know about where I grew up, and what I did before I came here. Camping is simple. I find it relaxing. All you need is a good knife, some cord, and a water filtration system. Everything else can work itself out."

Benjamin liked that answer. So did Brad.

"OK, one last thing. Book training and basic skills training here for the next month, then one month at Sutter Park in sites 14, 15, and 16. You will be split into two teams; Karen leads team one in site 14, and Dora leads team two in site 15. Brad and I will be at site 16 with a couple people who will pop in as guest instructors to be named later. The goal of this trip is to learn the skills and not look like a tourist when you go on mission 4."

They watched as everyone absorbed the fact they will be camping for an entire month. What they were not told is that after three weeks they would be packing up and jumping to a very cold environment. In two days is the class break for three days. During this time Brad and Benjamin will go and scout out the areas to make certain there are no issues. Both of them will also be equipped with a stunner, as will Dora and Karen, for the duration of this education.

Everyone else will be issued a stunner in the last 4 days in the camp training and will receive an in-depth education on its use and maintenance. As much as Benjamin hates to admit it, he needs to have Will come and provide this training. The man knows his stunners.

The remainder of the day went well, the normal class schedule in lieu of this new schedule seemed to reinvigorate everyone, and Mr. Winchester kept close tabs on both Benjamin and Brad. He considers them both his progeny, and wants to give them every chance to excel.

"Alright then. Security mode off. Class dismissed. Dora and Karen, we need to see the both of you before you leave."

The rest of the class left the room after collecting all of their belongings, Dora and Karen walked to the bottom of the room, where Benjamin and Brad stood.

As they approached, they looked around to make certain no one else was in the room, Benjamin began to speak.

"Ladies, I need for the two of you to go to the Quartermaster this evening. They are expecting you for about an hour of training."

"Training, training for what?" Dora asked.

"You'll see. Just get there." Brad answered.

They both replied, "OK" and left.

* * * * * * * * * * * * * * * * * * *

"Welcome to the Quartermasters Department. Dora Guntersdottir and Karen Jones. Guntersdottir, Icelandic? One of my favorite places on this planet."

"You've been to Iceland?"

"Many times." He smiled at her and said in Icelandic, "Svo, hvar did þú býrð?"

"Ég ólst upp í Rekjavik, en fluttist til Njarðvík."

"I liked Njardvik. Especially the lamb dogs in the park."

"They have not had them in the park in years, when were you last there?"

"Mid 1980's I think it was. Research on the Regan – Gorbachev Summit. Spent some time adding temporary recording devices to the places they met at Höfði House. I played myself off as several things, one was an Islander named Guðney Gunterson. It was a blast, and my last LT assignment before I took this role as the QM. After the assignment was over, I went there with my family on vacation several times."

He looked at her and smiled, she asked, "Where do you like to go?"

"Let's see. It's been several years since I was there last, but there is a golden circle I like to make." He winked at her.

"Tourist. You actually take the Golden Circle tour?"

"Yes, but not as a tour. I rent a car and take the family on the trip by ourselves."

"OK, where do you go?"

"My favorite path is to first go to the national park at Þingvellir, the waterfall Gullfoss and the valley of Haukadalur. My favorite Geyser is Strokkur of course. I made a video of it last trip there and it is an entire wall of my house. I think the landscape is pristine. Other places we go to if we have time are Kerið volcano crater, Hveragerði greenhouse village, Höfði house for the memories; and I like to take a dive, SCUBA dive, off the back stone wall at the old aluminum plant between Keflavik and Reykjavik. You can still, to this day, pick scallops, fresh and tasty, from the floor of the sea."

"You really know the area. The last place I lived was Akureyri so I don't like to visit that area all that much. If I want to the moon, I'll go to the MOON." They both laughed. No one else in the room had any idea why they were laughing.

The Quartermaster realized and explained, "Back in the 20th century they used that area of Iceland for the training of American Astronauts going to the Moon. Keflavik, and the entire peninsula, really has a similar surface to that of the Moon and lots of open space to play with new toys and inventions."

Realizing he needed to get down to business, "OK, sorry about digressing. You two are here to learn to use the newest stunner." They both smiled and grinned, at the same time. One of them even squeeked!

Handing each of them a stunner, "You've seen the wrist watch of eons past, this is worn in the same manner. If you are right handed, put it on your left wrist, etc for the other." They both put the device on their left wrist.

"Now, take your right index finger and touch the center of the housing. Using your implant think the command SYNC." Small prick in the finger and both devices disappeared.

They were shocked. They could still feel them, but they could not see them.

"OK, now for some target practice. Just so you know. You can't leave here until you can both hit all targets."

For the next hour they practiced hitting stationary then moving targets on the range. Aiming was more a matter of visual focus than of aiming. When you directed a blast to a place, it went there. But, that meant you needed to think about that location. Then one truly scary thought.

"Last thing you need to do is shoot each other. Think Five percent setting. Right shoulder. And it needs to be at the same time."

"Why?"

"Rule is you can't carry one unless you have been shot by it. Five percent is like a little mosquito."

"I'll count back from five, and then you shoot each other. Five-four-three-two-one. Ready?"

The girls had no idea how this was important, but they did it. They stood facing each other and when the Quartermaster said one, they shot a bolt of energy at nearly the same instant and fell over together.

A moment later they started to move and "OUCH! That was no mosquito!"

"If I had told you how it really felt, either you would have flinched at the thought you were about to be shot, or you could not have shot each other. Knowing how it feels will give you a slight bit of empathy if you do need to subdue anyone."

They both were rubbing their right shoulder, but nodded. They understood. The feeling wore off quickly.

"OK, that's it. You can leave." He said.

They started to remove the stunner, "Oh no. They are now coded to you, and only you. You need to wear them until your instructor tells you to take it off and turn it in. They are everything proof so as long as you don't fall out of a three story building and land on it, you can't hurt it. And one last thing. With the exception of Jensen and Jorgen, no one else is to know you have them. Since you two are the leaders of the camping section of this mission, you need some protection in your campsite in the event a wild animal or maybe even an intruder encroaches on your encampment. This gives you security without compromising safety."

"OK….thanks" And they left.

Looking at his coworkers as they walked out the door, "I can't believe they really shot each other. I love trainee's!" All three of them shook their heads and started laughing.

* *

Since everyone in the class has an active Sub-Q, Dora and Karen were easily able to determine the remainder of the class is meeting at a club called the Rising Sun; a modern technology gathering place. As with any alcohol establishment, it has its high and low points. High points are descent food and drink; low points are the bottom feeder leeches who seem to be patrons tonight. As Dora and Karen walked in, they were touched, approached, and propositioned a record number of times before they reached the table with the rest of her class.

"We really need to find a new place to meet. I am really starting to hate the people in the place." Monika said to everyone.

Pulling out his portacomm Bradley keyed in the commands to look for a place that was quiet and affordable. "There are two here and close by. One is that place Brad and Benjamin took us to, Pluto's. The other is called The Swill and Cane, it says here it is an Old English themed Pub specializing in Fish and Chips in the traditional method." He looked at the others, "What is the traditional method?"

"Let's go find out. How far away is it?"

"Five minutes' walk."

They all stood and left at the same time. It was so crowded and busy no one noticed them leave and when their drink order appeared at the table the waiter did not realize the group sitting was not the group that ordered. The new residence of the table simply drank whatever was put in front of them.

When they arrived at the Swill and Cane the place was about half full. As they entered the patrons looked at them but did not pay them all that much attention. Sitting at a large round table the menu appeared in the air above the seating positions. They selected a drink, and ordered their meals. Pressing compete the menu dissolved.

A few minutes later a hover tray appeared being guided by a server. He did not say a word, simply placed the drinks in front of each person. When the food arrived, same fashion, the server repeated the performance. He never said a word.

When he left they all said the same thing, "I Miss Barbara!"

* *

Brad and Benjamin stopped at the Quartermaster to order a few things. Cold weather gear mostly. Enough gear for the entire class to survive for a week in the high Rockies in the dead of winter. They needed exposure to a cold environment to learn their limitations. No one would be in any real danger since they could leave if it got to that point, but the fact they needed to remain there for a week in the blinding snow and cold would help them to discover their limits and their limitations. Hopefully, this will be an asset for them in their career. It was something Benjamin and Brad had to learn on their own, but they are well suited for a position like that and thrive in that type of environment.

"Have all the gear placed in a travel pod and transported to the location in file Jensen7-30."

"Not a problem, but just be aware of one thing." The Quartermaster looked at him. "Those two women are good shots" And he laughed a sinister laugh.

Brad and Benjamin laughed also. He knew it would be ok; it was just his way of having fun. He handed each of them their personal stunners and pointed to the range, "Test fire, please."

They put the device on their wrists and each fired a test shot successfully. "OK, you can go. I will have this equipment sent to the jump point in the file." Looking at the data in the file. "According to this you are scheduled to arrive thirty minutes before the equipment, shouldn't it be the other way around?"

"No, we need to see if they can adapt or quit. Quitters never win, and winners never quit."

"OH, I like that. Who said it?"

"A man by the name of Vince Lombardi, a football coach from the 20th century. Said to be one of the greatest in all of history."

"If I remember correctly, Mr. Jensen, you did a piece on him about a year ago. I remember finding you some of the strangest clothing, but we managed to create a period looking parka using better materials, higher thermal values. I have one question; did they really play that game in a minus thirteen degree Fahrenheit ambient temperature? That is cold."

"Yes they did. And the clothing you provided was perfect for 1968."

"I know. Three others have used that jacket and thought it was perfect also."

"We need to go; got a date with history. OH, can we get a couple shovels?"

"Sure." He walked away to go retrieve the shovels, stopped dead in his tracks and said to himself under his breathe, "Now what would they need shovels for…"

* * * * * * * * * * * * * * * * * * * *

"We need to scope out the area we will be living for a week so we can prepare and plan."

"Oh, so I'm about to get cold?"

Benjamin laughed, "Yep!"

Brad turned around to go get that parka Benjamin wore in 1968.

* * * * * * * * * * * * * * * * * * * *

"How sensitive can you tune the landing?" Benjamin asked the operator.

"Normally, with in a couple hours. How tight do you need the two jumps to be?"

"I need this cargo pod to appear about thirty minutes after the class appears."

"But they will be coming from a relatively warm environment going to a sub-arctic environment and the pod contains their clothing."

"Exactly."

"If you will step onto the platform I will send you back and then momentarily send your partner back. You can determine the minimum spacing for the finest tuning I can manage."

"Better yet, send me back with this." He held up a timer. "And then I will return and you can send me to the next jump and I will retrieve the same timer."

"That is a better idea. More accurate. Let me know when you are ready."

Benjamin turned on the timer and synchronized it with the timer he handed Brad. They are identical. "Fire one."

The operator looked at him curiously, but energized the system. A moment later Benjamin was encased in energy and had become pure energy.

Appearing on a very cold and snow covered field he placed the timer inside a small rock outcropping so if the class appeared they would not discover it. As he was about to return and jump thirty minutes into the future he noticed the class arriving on the other side of the field. He made a mental note to tell the operator the class needed to appear there, and he needs to appear in this same spot. Just as he was about to jump, he appeared next to himself in the exact spot he was standing a moment ago, thankfully he walked over to the rock to deposit the timer.

"So, how did the trainings go?" Benjamin 'A' asked himself.

"Perfect. No flaws or errors or problems." Benjamin 'B' responded.

"Anything I need to know?" Benjamin 'A' asked. Handing Benjamin 'B' the shovels.

"Yes, bring an adrenalephrine injection. It seems that we have someone who is allergic to shellfish and did not know it." Benjamin 'B' replied.

Benjamin 'A' asked, "Let me guess, Wendel?"

"Nope, Karen. There are no shellfish on her home colony world and they rarely eat seafood anyway. So, have the injection with you on day three during marine biology training, at lunch. The instructor will be providing the lunch for the class using some seafood he caught the night before. It will be a lobster that nearly kills her. She is really allergic. OH, and tell Brad those leaves he is gathering on day three when in the woods, just after lunch, are Poison Ivy. It was the funniest thing I ever heard of, he needed to spend the night back in the infirmary and he was quite embarrassed about it. So, let's change the future ever so slightly."

"Thanks. Gotta run. By the way, do you remember us having this conversation when you were me?"

"Yep, I sure do."

Both versions of Benjamin Jensen spoke at the same time, "Temporal paradoxes give me a headache." They smiled and Benjamin 'A' popped out.

Benjamin walked back to the class who appeared about fifty meters away on the other side of the open field. The location was perfect for what they needed to do.

"Bradley, what is the first order of business."

"Build a fire!"

"Exactly. Get it started." Benjamin looked back one more time at the place he appeared. Mental reminder to nudge himself in a short time so he can see himself again appear and grab the timer..

The next half hour was busy starting several fires and creating snow domes they could warm up in using the shovels he handed himself. The class members had no idea the equipment would be there in a few minutes and Benjamin and Brad knew exactly when and where it would arrive. They made certain that area was clear and untouched by human traffic. Not that the item could appear and injure them, but rather to watch an area and be given advanced notice or something.

After a short time, Benjamin 'B' watched the rock area where he stood thirty-nine minutes ago and saw himself appear, grab the timer, wave to himself, and disappear. He knew the equipment would appear in a moment. And it did, right where it was supposed to be.

* *

Benjamin returned to the chamber with the timer, kinda strange to talk to yourself knowing that the next time you see the clean shaven version you won't be. After a week camping at Sutter Park, in the trees with no biological waste facilities; the embarrassed and modest shall all pass. These people are going to see the side of each other they never thought existed, and that side of themselves. Yes, after just one week. A week of little sleep, thanks to the plan of Brad and Benjamin, and a critter that is going to terrorize their campsites when they are not there.

The remainder of the education, in the classroom, went as planned. In the first aid kit Benjamin added couple A-pens, just in case someone has an allergic reaction. At the lunch that day, he plans to sit next to Karen to give her the best chance.

The timer was thirty-eight minutes and forty seconds different. Therefore, he knows when the cargo pod would appear. If he is not mistaken it was a moment after he retrieved the timer and returned home.

Time to go home for the evening and final briefing tomorrow morning and then at 10am they are off to summer camp…he laughed out loud at the thought of Benjamin and Brad's Summer Camp – Where we teach you how to survive, and not go crazy.

He was still laughing and grinning from ear to ear when he turned a corner and ran into Myra Gaylord. This was the one woman in the universe that actually made him think about settling down and raising a family. But after the terrible car accident that had destroyed a large part of her brain, she did not know him like that any longer. It took him a long time, and many sessions with the psych department to get past the feelings and the guilt. But he did it.

"Myra, hello. Sorry. I was deep in thought of a mission I am leaving for tomorrow."

"Ben, right? Jensen, I think? It has been a long time since we last spoke. I need to get to a meeting so good luck on the mission." And she disappeared down the corridor and around a corner.

Benjamin just felt a wave, not illness or dizziness, but a wave of Myra. Feelings surfaced like he has not felt in years and it was due to the fact that he was surprised by her presence. He feels like an idiot for still harboring feeling for her, but she touched him deep within his soul. The intense feeling passed and were replaced by an overwhelming wave of friendship. Yes, he still cared for her, but emotionally he was over her and could move on with his life.

Now, he needs to stop at Pluto's for a fast bite to eat, a beer or two, and then to bed. He needs to be bright eyed and bushy tailed in the morning. What a strange thing to say. How can a person be bright eyed and bushy tailed; and him without a tail at the moment.

* * * * * * * * * * * * * * * * * * * *

He walked through the door to Pluto's and sat at the bar tonight. Mike gave him a glance and dropped a beer in front of him. Took care of someone else and came back to him with a second mug. Benjamin was draining the first mug when Mike asked, "Hungry?"

"Yep. Something light tonight. I need to get to bed and get up early in the morning. Leaving for a trip in the morning at 10am, need to get in by 6am so I can get ready for the shuttle. They chartered one or something, I'll find out in the morning.. So, what soups do you have tonight?"

From the kitchen, someone yelled out, "TOMATO AND CORN CHOWDER. THAT'S ALL THAT'S LEFT"

"MMmmmm…..Tomato, and a grilled cheese sandwich, no, make it two grilled cheese sandwiches with it."

"I supposed you want pickles inside and grilled while the cheese is melting?"

"Oh yes, put the cheese and pickles between two slices of well buttered bread and cook it all together."

"You got it."

Benjamin sipped on his beer and his mind wandered a bit. He remembered the literal run-in today with Myra and the deeply rooted feeling and emotion that bubbled so quickly to the surface. He may need another session with the psych's just to be certain. Although he was not still in love with her, there was something else happening that he wanted to stop in its tracks. Silently, he made the appointment for when he returned from this two weeks – real time – camping through the Sub-Q. The telepaths will be waiting for him when he returns from this trip.

Myra liked camping too and maybe that is a part of it. After the accident when they spoke she did not remember camping ever in her life, but she would like to try it.

He has kept track of her since school and right now she is seeing someone who is like her, administration and grounded, not a researcher. She appears to be happy; at least that is how Maria describes her. They were all in school together but she has more memories of Maria than of Benjamin. He needs to set a lunch date with Maria and chat about old times. He'll have to do that in the morning if she is working. She is the person who performs the data dump and final inspection into and of the Sub-Q implant before a mission. He may see her at 7am, his appointment time, as will the rest of the class he is taking into the past and into history.

While he was thinking about all this he ate and finished his beers. Waved to Mike and started to leave, then he remembered he did not pay for anything yet. He snapped his fingers and turned around to go back to the bar, "Hit me next time. I'll add it to your tab." Mike said. "You either look like you are in really deep thought, or just like crap; so go get some rest." He smiled and waved him to get out of the bar.

Walking the short distance to his building he entered the lift and went to his floor. Used his code to unlock the door and went straight to the bedroom. Stripped and crawled into bed in one motion.

"Computer, time" He said into the air.

"Time is 10:28pm"

"Great, early night. Computer, set the alarm to wake me up at 4:30am"

"Alarm has been set for 4:30am, six hours and two minutes from now. Powering the facility down."

And the apartment joined Benjamin in sleep.

* * * * * * * * * * * * * * * * * * * *

Benjamin was standing in the middle of the parking lot where he and Myra were hit by the car and she had her catastrophic injury. He realized where he was and ran to one corner of the lot where there was a very large tree. A few moments later he saw himself and Myra leave the diner and start slowly walking across the parking lot.

As he watched himself and Myra walk across the parking lot there was a long, loud squeal. He looked over towards the street, and he saw the two cars that were racing in the street in front of the diner. As they were all watching the strange event, one of the cars had a tire explode, front right tire, and the car immediately turned and was careening toward them at an insane rate of speed.

He saw his younger self and Myra run, no real direction…just run. The car impacted Myra and threw Benjamin to the ground with a lot of force. Everyone in the diner came out and the driver stopped and was having some sort of mental breakdown. He appeared to be upset at Benjamin for getting in his way.

Then the younger Benjamin noticed Myra was not moving. He walked over to her and looked; most of the left side of her head appeared to be gone. The driver came over and was yelling at Benjamin again. The younger Benjamin stood up and punched the guy in the face so hard that he folded neatly to the ground.

Benjamin draped himself over Myra and they both disappeared. He did not care if anyone saw him or not.

"Medical has been called, decontamination is complete." The operator told Benjamin.

"Mr. Jensen, can you hear me…" A nurse was trying to wake him.

"What, yes, of course, I hear you." Then he jumped to a sitting position.

He looked around and saw that he was in a medical bay and hooked to a lot of instruments. They had no idea what happened to him and Myra, but all they could do was fix what they found. MYRA! "How is Myra!" He yelled.

"She is undergoing her 4th surgery, she is expected to survive but we are not certain how much of her mind will be intact. She has not regained consciousness yet."

"YET! 4th surgery? How long has it been?"

"Mr. Jensen, you returned from your assignment nearly a week ago. You have been in a coma, or rather in and out of a coma. This is the first time you have made it all the way conscience since you returned."

"Is anyone there?" Benjamin activated his Sub-Q.

"Mr. Jensen, welcome back to the world of the living. Class, if you are not already online, do so. Mr. Jensen is now available for conversation."

"Mr. Winchester? Do you need me to tell you what happened?"

"No my boy, while you were traveling on the nite-nite express we downloaded your video. We saw what happened and how the injuries to Myra occurred. Thank you for having an active implant

during the event. Myra will not be able to be retained in the program. Most of her brain has been violently damaged. We have determined that she can still be a useful member of the Island faculty."

"Can I speak to her?"

"No, she is being kept in an induced coma to increase the healing capability of her body. It may be another six months to a year before she will be able to talk to anyone."

Benjamin felt a very large and gaping hole in his chest. He looked into a mirror and actually saw the hole going all the way through his body. This was the hole that used to be filled with Myra.

"AAAHhhhhh....!!!!!!!!" Benjamin woke up screaming. After a moment he realized he was in his apartment, in his bed, several years after the incident he just dreamed about. "Computer, time"

"The time is 4:26am. There are four minutes until the alarm sounds."

"Computer, cancel all alarms until further notice."

He got up and showered; while he was showering he wondered if Brad was online.

He activated his implant and tuned to their private frequency, *"Brad, you there?"*

"In the shower, what's the matter, you sound, strange."

Benjamin reiterated the dream to Brad and they talked about it. They also decided that before he leaves for the training mission he needs to go to psych. They can do what they need to do in an hour or so, so they can delay the trip if necessary a couple hours.

"After you get dressed, meet me at the donut place for breakfast. Let me know when you leave."

"Will do! See you there."

And they both signed off, got dressed and left for their training mission, with a stop for breakfast.

Chapter 8

Summer Camp

Brad and Benjamin left their building and realized the air was a bit cool. They looked at each other and laughed. Both realized that a few weeks from now the temperature would be much cooler than it is now, and the snow, and the ice. But they were both looking forward to it in some weird and deranged way. Every traveler is issued two sets of environmental stabilization undergarments. Like an old Earth long sleeve T-shirt and long johns, they keep you warm when it's cold, and cool when it's hot. They are designed to fit in with the period you are jumping to but since they are moving from time period to time period, they really had no idea what needed to be made.

They opted for the first set to be designed for the trip to the island paradise, and in the pod was a set for each person – and a spare – that is designed to be normal for the witch trials. Last thing they wanted was to be called witches.

Imagine what would happen if they were burned at the stake and returned home before the flames totally engulfed them. That could, possibly, cause a historical glitch.

Brad and Benjamin walked past Pluto's and noticed the inside lights were on and there was movement inside. Brad tapped on the window and Mike walked up to the door and it went from red to green. Walking through they asked Mike why he was in so early.

"Early, what time is it?" Mike looked amazed.

"A little after 5am. Are you just packing up for the night, last night?" Brad asked.

"Uh, yes. Barbara left just about the time you came in last night" he nodded towards Benjamin, "and I have been playing catch-up ever since. She is telling me she feels run down and ill for the last few days, but last night, she was in bad shape. She is going to the medical complex this morning to see if she can narrow it down and fix the problem. You two on your way in, you have the trip you're taking. Need anything from here to help it a little?" Mike waved his arm as if he was a spokes model for alcoholic beverages.

Benjamin grinned. "Now that you mentioned it, there are a couple things we could take with us. What I need is a very large bottle of Temporal Rift, and three bottles of whiskey, and a bottle of really good vodka; and if you can put them in unbreakable bottles that would be even better."

"Give me five minutes." Mike ran behind the bar and began putting liquids into new bottles. Shortly, he had four two liter bottles standing silently on the bar like perfect little soldiers. Two a dark amber, one a kinda pastel looking redish yellow, and one nearly clear. Then he began adding liquids to the largest of the bottles, Party Size he called it.

He placed them all in what looks like a back pack lined with foam. Handed them to Benjamin, "I'll put it on your tab…." He grinned.

"Nope!" spoke Brad. "Put it on mine."

"Thanks!" Benjamin said to his best friend in the universe.

"You got it, enjoy the trip. When do you think you'll be home?" Mike asked.

"If everything we planned and hoped happens as we plan and hope, we should be back in a few weeks; then off again on another trip for a couple more weeks. Then, hopefully, home for a while."

"Good luck, and have fun!" Mike waved as they left the bar. Now for breakfast, then to the island for a data session with Maria, then…

* * * * * * * * * * * * * * * * * * * *

"All gear and personal equipment is stored and we are ready to depart." Benjamin looked at Brad, who was speaking. He smiled when he said the words personal equipment since he knew what Benjamin packed as personal equipment from Mike.

"There is a large vehicle with our gear waiting for us at Sutter Park, or more accurately it is about fifteen kilometers from Sutter Park in the woods. This is where we will be arriving. We are traveling about one month into the past to take advantage of the temporal differential. We will be in the campsite for roughly three weeks, and we are packing in, and out, all of our trash. The skills you learned in class about **Leave No Trace** will be in effect for the entire duration to help ingrain them into your mind. Leaving a piece of NOW one month in the past is not a catastrophic incident, but if you were to leave a piece of our century in the 1600's, 1700's, or even the 21 or 2300's, there could be historical implications. When you get home, home as you know it may not be there and you will be a person out of time. Therefore, minimal interaction with people and animals and everything else when traveling is highly advisable."

Ruth looked at him, square in the eye, "Nice Speech. Was it rehearsed?"

He grinned at her, "Nope. Just something off the top of my head." She grinned back and shook her head.

Benjamin looked around a bit, at each of them, remembering his class assignment when he and Myra jumped to do research on the Space Shuttle. Those feeling were there again, but they were not overwhelming like the last time. What is going on? The psych that scanned him this morning cleared his mind of the feelings and the emotion but they are back again.

"Brad, you go first and I will go last. Bradley, your call on the inbetweeners."

Brad entered the chamber and Monika followed. This was the personal chamber and a lot smaller. They could have traveled as a group all leaving and appearing at the same instant, but Benjamin liked the drama.

A moment later Brad and Monika were gone. The next pair entered the chamber and waited for the ninety second recharge of the system.

* * * * * * * * * * * * * * * * * * * *

Brad and Monika appeared next to a vehicle but there was no driver in sight. Brad looked at Monika who looked back at him, "We got about a minute." She said.

They shared an embrace and a passionate kiss. They had fallen in love and Brad was going to do everything he could to get her and himself back in the LT group. He wanted, in a bad way, to be with her for eternity.

* * * * * * * * * * * * * * * * * * * *

Power began to surge. One pair at a time they all departed. Benjamin was the only person left but he had something he needed to do first.

"I need for you to do me a favor. I need to appear a few minutes before Brad and Monika. Can you reset and send me?" Benjamin asked the operator.

"Sure thing. Give me one second……..Ready?"

"Final test of the implant. Can you hear me?"

"Yes." Benjamin replied back through the implant.

And he was gone as well.

* * * * * * * * * * * * * * * * * * * *

Benjamin appeared next to the vehicle and moved out of sight. A few minutes later he saw Brad and Monika appear, and embrace and kiss. After a minute they released each other and began their duties. Brad started the vehicle and Monika verified the gear. Two by two they all appeared and finally it should have been his time to appear. He never did and they were all thinking that something happened.

"Brad, where is Benjamin?"

"Not sure, maybe he appeared here but is injured." Brad retuned his implant to a channel reserved for only he and Benjamin, *"OK, I know you're here, where are you?"*

"About thirty meters behind you and to your left."

"Why are you doing this?"

"I had a talk with Mr. Winchester yesterday afternoon and he suggested that the class is getting too comfortable with you and I. Relying too heavily on us for guidance and they should be relying on each other and the leadership team. So, I decided to be a ghost."

"Did you bring a stealth suit?"

"Nope. Brought two!"

"Excellent. Now, we need to find you. What can we do to locate you?"

"Got that one also. I reset my jump to arrive five minutes before you arrived and have been hiding here. I will initiate the recall and the next location will be on the correct spot."

"Why five minutes before I arrived?"

"A hunch. I was right, and I am very happy for you two, but you need to keep it quiet for the next six months, until she finishes school and get an assignment. Just so you know, but don't let on please, I had contacted Matthew Sharp and requested Monika, Will and LaVarr be assigned to the LT Group, and you be reassigned there also to serve as their mentor; Ruth, Bradley and Hoshi be assigned to my area. The rest will be luck of the draw."

"I knew I liked you for a reason."

"OK, be right there."

Benjamin initiated the recall but rather than sending him home it sent him to the next location, which is the same place as everyone else appeared. It gave him the chance to hide the stealth suits in the backpack that was packed for him.

Soft pop…he was gone.

* * * * * * * * * * * * * * * * * * * *

Benjamin appeared next to the vehicle and the class seemed to be relieved. Mr. Winchester was right. This class was relying on him way too much, and Brad noticed it too.

Everyone got into the truck and Benjamin slipped into the driver's seat. It was a thirty-minute ride to the point where they needed to speak to the ranger. Will it be the same guy as it was a couple years ago? That would be funny.

As they approached the ranger station and parked they realized there were a lot of day campers. People who come up for a day and have lunch then go home. Benjamin and Brad walked into the ranger office and Benjamin was happy to see it was the same person. He knows the reservation was made and confirmed at 3pm, the time now is 2:57pm. So, allowing for system processing he figured the reservation should arrive on his screen at 3:02pm.

Brad walked in first and Benjamin followed. The ranger was finishing up with a couple who wanted to ask a lot of questions; he looked at Brad and Benjamin like they were familiar but he had no idea who they were. After a brief time, he was free and waved them to the counter. "We have a reservation for sites 14, 15, and 16 for three weeks." The time was 3:01pm exactly.

"I have no reservations to those sites, no one likes them. They are too far from everything and way too primitive for most people. You're gonna need to go home and make reservations because they are not here."

The guy was being a jerk, again. Benjamin looked at him and said, "This is the week of Ana-woka-to-knee. The reservations have been made to atone. CHECK AGAIN..."

As the ranger looked at the screen, they appeared before his eyes. He knows where he had seen them before, right here, a couple years before. Same thing happened. This time, he was ready for him. Benjamin realized the ranger remembered him, and was about to be ugly with him.

"Sir." Benjamin started to speak before the ranger could. "Complete the transaction and we will be on our way. If you attempt to spy on us, or if you attempt to do anything to our group as you tried before…" Benjamin got an evil grin on his face, "you will feel the wrath of Ana-woka-to-knee."

The ranger closed his mouth and handed them a map, Benjamin asked for six maps with high definition on the terrain. The ranger handed him six contour maps and offered a compass. Benjamin did not take the compasses, "We have our own."

Walking out of the office, Brad looked at him and asked, "You like tormenting that poor man?"

Benjamin thought about it for a moment, "Yes, everyone needs a hobby."

"OK, just thought I'd ask." Brad replied as the left the office.

* *

The weather was perfect. Clear sky and with the exception of day eleven between 2pm and 9pm, there will be no rain. Being a time traveler has its advantages. The temperature will range from a daytime high of 37°C on day 10, to a low tonight of -8°C. The average for the next few days will make the mornings cool, the days warm, and the nights somewhat cold. Perfect chance to get used to the elements, and the gear.

The hike to the sites was uneventful and fun. They took nearly four hours to get there, but they enjoyed themselves doing it. It was starting to get dark and they were split up between three separate campsites by design.

Thankfully, the first site they came to was 16, where Brad and Benjamin will be staying. They dropped their packs and set up their tent, hung some of their food in a tree and placed some in the oversized and secure cans provided. There was really no chance of a bear attack in this area, but there are a lot of other small critters, especially raccoons. They can be a playful nuisance.

Benjamin walked over to a thicket of bushes and called Brad. Brad gave him a strange look and he parted the branches. Inside was a small room used to keep tabs on the others in the class, not only that but there was a warning system that alerted their implant in the event someone was trying to sneak up on any of the three campsites. He did not want to take chances this time like the last time. That ranger was bound to try it again.

They left the room, which was climate controlled and had a case or two of the food bars from the Malkornian ship. It was going to be a special Friday night dinner, with Benjamin cooking the desserts in 20th century dutch ovens. It took him a while to find the recipes and the components, but he did manage to find them in the 20th century. It was a fast trip to a grocery store and he arrived in the very early hours of a Sunday morning. He had the cookbook from his trip with Myra; they liked experimenting and tried to make every recipe in the book.

"When did you put that there?" Brad asked him.

Shaken from his thought of Myra again, "At 3pm this afternoon. Remember a week ago I told you I needed to take care of something, this is it. I grabbed the auto-pod and set it up here. Installed the sensor net around all three sites, set up a few cameras, and even managed to get the ranger to ingest a locator tab."

"In the words of the century you are SO fond of….you Low-Jacked the ranger."

They laughed hard. Benjamin filled Brad in on how to use his Sub-Q to view information in the pod. They both had the ability to, from anywhere, keep track of everyone. A bit spooky, but that is what technology is for, after all.

Closing the curtain, he grabbed his canvas chair, and Brad followed suit. They set it up around the 'fire', but not a real fire, those are not permitted in the forest. They each, each campsite, had been equipped with two solliric camp fire rings. They look and smell like the real thing, and you can even cook on them, but there is no way to start a blade of grass on fire.

Brad got off his chair after a few minutes and sat on the ground, leaning against a fallen tree. Benjamin joined him. They watched the 'fire' appear to dance, not the same but still nice to look at. It was a fairly close holographic representation of a real fire; but both of them could see right through it.

Brad, still staring at the fire said, "You know what would be perfect right now?"

Together they both said, "Mike's whiskey."

Benjamin went to his tent and grabbed a bottle. Sitting back on the ground against the log they took turns sipping, drinking, gulping, whatever directly from the bottle.

"I miss the past." Brad said.

"So do I." Benjamin replied.

"No, you don't understand. I want to go back on another long term assignment, and this time I want to take Monika with me."

"Did I tell you there is a long term assignment in the works right now? Yes there is, the timeframe is around 1835 I think and the research team, a man and a woman posing as a married couple, is supposed to travel with someone named P.T. Barnum and his troupe. He runs a circus I think. I was thinking that with your implants the two of you could make an effective psychic team. Mind reading, who knows what else. I think you need to find him and be on the payroll before the summer, as they left in June, June 2nd of 1835 for their very first tour of the United States. I think it was a Tuesday."

"How do you know so much about P.T. Barnum?"

"About six or eight months ago I was asked to research the entertainment of the 17th through the 19th centuries. Not really knowing why and not needed to jump it took me a few days and I compiled the various forms of fun and excitement. One thing we NEED to do is go back to the 1960's and stop at an amusement park in Cleveland, Ohio. It was called Euclid Beach, and was said to be ahead of its time in what it offered to those patron's willing to risk it all. There were a lot of injuries, and a few deaths on some of the rides." Pausing for a moment.

"The really interesting thing about this Amusement Park is it was in use from October 23, 1894 through September 28, 1969. The worst time was the race riots in 1946; I think that was the year. Make a nice vacation after this assignment. Have some fun, ride some rides, do some research, and just relax."

"And since we are both white we could come and go as we wish." Brad added realizing what he meant by race riots. Blacks and whites fighting for no other reason than they were black or white. Injuries, deaths, senseless violence.

Brad was really happy. He closed his eyes for a minute and Benjamin knew he was talking to Monika. The jump plan for this trip, Benjamin noticed, had the addition of a separate frequency for Brad and Monika, for private conversations. "Monika is overjoyed. All she needs to do is graduate and it's a done deal."

"So, how far away are the other teams?" Brad asked

"That's right, you never went to the other sites. Well, the next site, 14, is about half a kilometer away in that direction. Site 15 is up a slight hill and another almost half a kilometer further yet.

"I would love to sneak up on them and see what they are doing. All of them switched off their implants so we can't eavesdrop on them." Brad mentioned.

"I do have a couple stealth suits. That could be fun." He grinned and started to get up and decided not to. "I think we are too drunk to be stealthy."

Brad tried to stand and realize they nearly drank half a liter of whiskey between them in the last twenty minutes sitting there on the ground, watching the campfire, talking about nothing in general.

"I'm going to bed." Brad said.

"mee too" Benjamin replied.

They crawled into their tents and zipped them up, and they both fell sound asleep almost instantly.

* * * * * * * * * * * * * * * * * * * *

Benjamin realized he was sitting on a park bench in front of a diner. This seemed out of place at the moment but it seemed right at the same time. He looked around and saw himself appear by a large tree. He turned and saw himself on a motorcycle. He looked behind him and saw himself putting petroleum products, gasoline, into an old car in the service station next door.

He knew what was coming next. Myra will be injured. This time he needed to stop it.

He ran to the traffic light where the cars were sitting and revving up their engines, lifted his arm, aimed and shot a pulser blast from the stunner. It hit the driver in the right shoulder and he was out cold.

He turned and looked and saw himself and Myra walk across the parking lot as if nothing happened. Then he was standing next to her and they sat on the park bench. He needed to talk to her, tell her something to get it off his chest.

He looked around and all of the other versions of him were waiting for him to tell her how he felt and ….

Benjamin woke up in his tent and tried to go back to sleep to finish the dream. He knew full well it was not possible, but nonetheless he tried anyway.

When he did finally manage to get back to sleep, he did dream about his time with Myra. All of the fun they had together. The Apollo Dome, flying like a bird; The drop ship; their camping experience; the intimacy; the closeness; that feeling in his heart that now was empty.

He looked at the portacomm, the time is 3:33am. He had a couple more hours to sleep so he rolled over and fell back to sleep. Trying to lead his dreams in a different direction he tried to remember, as he fell asleep again, something about Brad. They had great times together, and he had fun – he needed fun right now.......

*   *   *   *   *   *   *   *   *   *   *   *   *   *   *   *   *   *   *   *

Benjamin found a large dense net and someone who would give him a ride back to the cliff. When he arrived at the cliff he staked the net to the top of the cliff and tossed it over the side. Walking around the path he finally got to the bottom and stood where the group will be passing in less than 30-minutes. It appears completely different now.

Climbing back up to the top of the cliff he hid himself under the netting so he could not be seen. Tropical camoflage at its finest. After a short while he saw them coming toward him.

"Brad, you ready?" Benjamin thought.

"Yep!"

"ACTIVATE CHANNEL THREE!" Benjamin thought. He and Brad were listening to their friends over the implant, spying on them as it were. Since Brad was not a part of the original conversation he was not certain when he needed to cause the comotion. Benjamin, on the other hand was a part of the original recording and with the assistance of Mr. Winchester he learned to review his recording easily and knew exactly when he needed to divert their – HIS – attention from the inland to the water.

"……man, that is heavy."

"Natalya, I see some of the current colloquial expressions are sticking to you." The other Benjamin laughed. "So, if we remember it as it was, and we made the change, we would return to a new world. That does not sound like a good thing to me."

"Benjamin, if we were to, for example, warn NASA that the use of pure oxygen in a space capsule has a 98% probability that an explosion in the capsule will occur, and that there is a 100% chance the entire crew will be killed; what would that do? Gus Grissom first man on the Moon? Buzz Aldrin drops out of the space program? The possibilities are endless.?" The other Natalya concluded.

"What about something simple. A message in a newspaper, or a mark on a building that still exists." The other Myra asked.

Younger Benjamin added, "I get you, would the planet still exist if a mark on a building suddenly appeared? Look, I am as careful as anyone but how......."

"NOW!" Benjamin thought to Brad.

They all wanted to see if something minor could be moved in time though. Benjamin thought he recognized the cliffs they were walking near.

WWWWHHHHHAAAAAAAAAAA!!!!!

* *

Benjamin woke at the sound of the horns in his dream and started laughing out loud. He felt a lot better this morning; it was going to be a good day.

He looked at the time, 5:12am. He decided to get up and make some coffee. Once Brad smelled it he would be awake too, just like when they were in the Wild West. First one up made the coffee.

Starting the fire here and starting the fire in the 1800's was like apples and explosives. They were that different. Now, you walk over to the fire ring and press a button and it is on; in the 1800's you collected kindling, tinder, larger tinder, and finally fuel. You can use the twig, a laser ignition system from the now that is keyed to the implant of whoever is holding it, or you can use matches, or flint and steel with char cloth, or friction. Either way, the end result is HOPEFULLY fire.

Brad finally crawled out of his tent and he looked rough in the mornings, always had, always will. Benjamin handed him a cup filled with coffee, and a Malkornian food bar for breakfast. Since he was not yet awake he wasn't thinking of anything in particular, so the bar tasted like nothing. "Hey, what it this?" Brad asked.

"Eggs scrambled with cheese with a small bit of ketchup, side of bacon cooked to perfection, and fresh apples and peaches cooked in heavy syrup with a sprinkle of cinnamon and nutmeg." Benjamin said in a serious tone.

"Yea...right." A moment later Brad's eyes opened as wide as possible. "You're right. That is exactly what I taste. But, since I wasn't thinking of anything at first, it had no taste at all. Really strange." He tipped an invisible hat to Benjamin, "Thanks..."

They talked for a few minutes over the coffee pot, had a couple more cups of coffee and scanned the campsites of the teams. No one was awake yet. Benjamin had a devilish grin slowly crawl across his face.

Brad looked at him, "What?"

"Wanna have some fun?" Benjamin said mischievously, "We do have a couple stealth suits."

"And the buzz is worn off so we can be stealthy again!" Brad smiled back at him.

Brad nodded and they got into the suits. As they began walking up the path towards the closest site, Benjamin had a really strange feeling in his head.

"Hello Mr. Jensen. I hope you are doing well."

"Who is this?"

"You failed to make your appointment roughly one month from now, but we are here to serve your needs."

"Then you are the psych department of the now, not my timeframe."

"That is correct."

"How do you know…...never mind."

"Wise choice. To explain how all this works, when it cannot be experienced, would be a waste of time. You will never understand that thought is energy, and therefore once created it exists for eternity."

"Sorry I asked."

"We have given Mr. Jorgen the suggestion that you are returning to your site because you are not feeling well, and he is to go monitor the class. He will be away for ninety-three minutes at which time we will have ample opportunity to see why you are disturbed by these recurring dreams of a former incident in which you watched multiple times from multiple locations."

Benjamin found that he had already removed the stealth suit and was sitting in his chair and very comfortable. The sollaric campfire simulated the dance of living fire quite well, even in bright sunlight and he became mesmerized by it.

"Mr. Jensen, that was very productive. I believe the problem has been determined and corrected, you will experience no further incidents of dreams of that nature."

"What? I just sat down."

"Actually, that was eighty-two minutes ago. We have corrected the issue."

"Wait. What was it? Why was I having those dreams?"

"The answer is simple; the repercussions are not. Simply put, the Sub-Cutaneous Transponder in the skull of Miss Myra Gaylord was malfunctioning. There also seems to be a psychic bond *between the two of you that quite honestly has us baffled. Her Sub-Q, as you refer to them, has been repaired. In effect, you were witnessing her dreams, not your dreams. But, since you had no visual from her point of view your mind substituted your visual. Quite fascinating, I will be writing a paper on it for the medical catalog."* She paused,

"Congratulations…" Benjamin replied sarcastically.

"Sorry, when she was asleep the parts of her brain that were not functioning somehow came to life and the thoughts stored there became a part of her subconscious. She does not remember the incident, but she dreams of it. When she awakens, she does not remember anything but there is a feeling she cannot describe. We will be working with her to see if we can bring the subconscious to the conscience. It appears that you and Miss Gaylord have telepathic abilities and we would like to test you both at a later date to determine your telepathic level. I would suspect at least a 4 or 5 since this interaction took place. As for you, you may go about your assigned tasks. When you return from trip number four, please see us for a final scan."

"You got it. Thanks. Could the connection have been created when, after the accident, I placed my hand on what was left of her brain? Could I have touched the implant thereby causing a connection?"

"Possible, we will need to run a few simulations. However, to answer your next questions yes, her implant has been upgraded to the most current model. This will allow her more control and an easier time in permanent healing. Good day."

The connection to the psychic healer was terminated. *"BRAD! You there?"* Benjamin yelled into his brain.

"UH...YES! Why are you yelling?"

Benjamin reiterated the encounter and let him know all is well, he is fixed.

"Wait. You just saw a psych?"

"Yep. Sorta. They got into my head and I sat by the campfire. They found out why I was having the dreams. Myra's implant was malfunctioning, and they fixed it. Myra and I were linked somehow. It had to be the accident. I remember putting my hand where that part of her skull had been. I must have touched the Sub-Q and it imprinted on me also. At least that is the working theory. So, come back to the site and we can regroup and attack."

"Will do."

A few minutes later Brad picked up a cup and poured coffee into it, took a sip and sat on the ground.

"Uh...can you please deactivate the suit? If someone was watching a cup fill itself with coffee, they would wonder."

Brad started laughing and deactivated the suit. The cup that, a moment ago, was floating in the air was now resting on his knee.

Benjamin poured a cup of coffee and looked at Brad with a serious face. "I think we need to make a change. Three weeks here, a month in the Bahama's, one week in the Rockies."

"Why?"

"Max effect. They are expecting to go to the Rockies next, let's throw them a temporal curve."

"Nice...."

* *

The last two and a half weeks went well. Bradley stored numerous manuals in his head and it was up to Benjamin and Brad to show him what he was reading. All in all, it was a successful trip. A few days ago Brad jumped back to reset all of the jump points so they would next go to the marine biology training, then a week in the ice and snow, then to the desert for three days with nothing. While Brad was there he received a package to be hand delivered to Benjamin Jensen. He grabbed it and returned.

When he popped back in he handed the package to Benjamin. Benjamin looked at him and said, "It worked!"

"What worked?" Brad asked.

Benjamin was busy opening the box, "Survival rations from…. Mike and Barbara."

Brad got real interested. "How did you do that?"

"Let's eat, then I'll tell you."

They ate a double burger with everything, fries, and a temporal rift. Mike was generous. They were sipping on the remainder of their drinks when Brad asked, "OK, spill it. How?"

"OK. It occurred to me that if I knew the exact time you appeared in the chamber, I could go back a few hours before that and ask security to receive a package at the reception desk and bring it to the jump chamber. I called Barbara and asked her to make us a nice meal up and package it for travel. She brought it to reception where security was expecting it. A short walk to the lift, a ride down a few floors, and a few moments later Brad appears in the chamber. Now what time was it you got there?"

"14:36"

"Perfect, be right back" then he was gone.

A few moments later he reappeared on the other side of Brad.

"Welcome back. What did you do?" Brad asked

"OK, I appeared at 14:59. So I asked the operator to send me back as close to three hours as possible, then back here. When I went back three hours, it was actually 11:32, and I called Barbara and placed the order. Told security to expect a package at 14:30 at reception and it must be brought directly to this chamber and handed to you where you will take possession and return here with it. I left and reappeared here and since we just ate dinner, it must have all worked."

"You are the strangest person I know. Fun, interesting, but really strange. You did this all because you don't want to eat chili again tonight?"

"Brad, is there another dish you can cook? We still have four days here."

"Beans…"

* * * * * * * * * * * * * * * * * * * *

"Class, please assemble in site 15 at your quickest pace."
Benjamin said in his mind to the entire class. He and Brad were already there in the stealth suits. This is the last night before the next jump so it was time to break out the remainder of the booze he brought with him from Mike.

Once the entire class was there Brad began. He began to touch people on the ear, the ankle; he and Benjamin were having fun.

Brad walked over to Monika and touched her. She knew it was him by the way he did the touching.

"OK Brad. How are you doing this?" Monika said.

A second later she began floating in midair. Now, she knew there were two hands holding her under each arm but the rest of the class had no idea.

"Can you two please put me down now?" She said.

They lowered her to the ground and took a short step away from her, then deactivated the suits. They appeared and Dora snapped her fingers and yelled out, "Stealth suits!"

"Give that girl a prize." Benjamin said. "OK, on the next jump, each of you needs to become familiar with the stealth suit, but tonight, let's have a party!"

"Party, with what?"

"OH, Bradley. Jump back to the complex, there is a package waiting for you."

He stood and, "Really?" Shook his head and disappeared. A moment later he reappeared in the same spot with a REALLY large package.

Brad called the class to order, "OK, since you all did so well these last few weeks, and since tonight is effectively the last night here, Benjamin and I cooked dinner. Bradley, please open the package.

As soon as he opened the lid the smell of the burgers filled the campsite. The fries were crispy and soft at the same time, and still blazing hot. How did you do that?"

While they all ate and drank Benjamin explained how time travel worked. It is limited only by your imagination, he told them. After they all ate and the drinks were poured, he stood and, "Oh, excuse me for a moment. Bradley, what time was it when you appeared?"

"17:33, why?"

"Be right back and I'll explain" He disappeared. A few moments later he reappeared.

"OK, I just jumped back and the time was 18:16. I asked the operator to send me back four hours, where I told the operator to expect a package at reception at," he looked at the package, "17:17. That package is to be received and brought directly to the chamber where it is to be handed to Bradley Bentinfield the Third, who will take it the rest of its journey. I then returned to the moment you saw me appear."

"So, you're saying that I went back and you had no idea I was going, or when I would get there until I got back and I accepted a package that was not sent yet as far as we were concerned. Then you jumped back, went back a few hours and set it all up, then came back here. And it all worked!"

Dora remarked. "Very cool experiment."

"YEP!"

"Will, why the face?" Brad asked.

"I was just thinking. That means if I looked in my pack and there was an item missing from say this pocket, I could jump back at any time in the future and put it there, then jump back and it would be there. Basically, you are telling us that all of this camping experience is a waste of time, because we can always jump home, take a shower, have a good meal, go out on the town then jump back to the moment we left and continue on with what we need to do?"

"Sorta, but jumping take its toll on you, especially early in your career. Not a good idea to over use the jump system. Brad and I just wanted to open your minds to possibilities you never dreamed existed. That is the point of this and the next training sessions." Benjamin was not quite done. "But, off the record, it is very cool!" they all laughed.

* *

All campsites were cleaned, all litter and trash in its proper place, and everyone's pack fully packed and on their backs.

They needed to walk out of the woods and check out with the ranger, who never came near them this entire trip. The vehicle they used to get here were gone, the school picked them up Brad told them. In a few minutes they would be picked up and about a kilometer down the road they can all move on to the next timeframe.

Exiting the vehicles and putting all the trash from the packs into the cargo area, one less thing to carry around; and after adding some fresh food into the side pockets, they walked over to a large field to move on to the next phase of the assignment.

"This one is different. Everyone, stand close together and activate the jump signal in three-two-one. There were a lot of small pops, and then silence.

* *

Appearing on the beach at six in the morning was the safest place to appear, no one saw you. They found a place to camp slightly inland a bit and since it was six in the morning and they had not had breakfast they all wanted to eat. Benjamin told them they needed to get their tents set up and he would serve them breakfast.

After a half hour they all returned and he handed each of them an M-Bar, something he had been calling them for the past week or so.

They all knew what it was and thought it was a great treat. He still had enough for two or three more each, but he wanted to wait to give those out.

The next few days they found the skipper of the ship, a marine biologist, who was to teach their class. He knew they were researchers who needed to know more about marine biology, that's it. On day three he provided lunch. He did ask if anyone was allergic to seafood, no one raised their hand so he served lobster.

Karen took a few bites and loved it. A few minutes later she began wheezing and looked at Benjamin and said, as best as she could, "ana.......phylac......tic shock!"

Benjamin pulled the injector from an inside pocket and opened it, put it against her thigh and injected her with the medicine. In a few minutes she was back to normal.

"I had no idea I was allergic to anything. Benjamin, how did you know?"

"Let's just say that I am always prepared for any circumstance. Hind-sight is 20/20, but knowing the future is priceless!"

She had an idea that he knew this was going to happen, but elected to not let on that he knew. All he did was save her life but she DID get to experience lobster for the first time, and the last.

The rest of the month went as expected, they learned a lot. All of them knew all about the creatures that live both in and on the sea, and the creatures that live around the shoreline. They were ready to go back and help clean up the largest oil spill in the 21st century, in Louisiana or just off the coast.

The month ended and they needed to continue on. This time they left their packs where they were and donated the items to the marine biologist to help his charity. He received a great deal, his payment for helping them learn. Each ensured there was no technology before donating the pack, and definitely no M-Bars left inside. Benjamin and Brad gave him a monetary donation for his services, and he was very appreciative. It would go a long way to help the sea he so loved protecting.

The group walked off into the brush towards the airport and as they entered the deep thicket in a single file line they disappeared, one by one. Benjamin was first and he appeared in the snow next to the rocks where he was placing the timer.

"So, how did the trainings go?" Benjamin 'B' asked himself.

"Perfect. No flaws or errors or problems." Benjamin 'A' responded.

"Anything I need to know?" Benjamin 'B' asked. Handing the shovels to his slightly older and ragged looking self.

"Yes, bring an adrenalephrine injection. It seems that we have someone who is allergic to shellfish and did not know it." Benjamin 'A' replied.

Benjamin 'B' asked, "Let me guess, Wendel?"

"Nope, Karen. There are no shellfish on her home colony world and they rarely eat seafood anyway. So, have the injection with you on day three during marine biology training, at lunch. The instructor will be providing the lunch for the class using some seafood he caught the night before. It will be a lobster that nearly kills here. She is really allergic. OH, and tell Brad those leaves he is gathering on day three in the woods, just after lunch, are Poison Ivy. It was the funniest thing I ever heard of, he needed to spend the night back in the infirmary and he was quite embarrassed about it. So, let's change the future ever so slightly."

"Thanks. Gotta run. By the way, do you remember us having this conversation when you were me?"

"Yep, I sure do."

Both versions of Benjamin Jensen spoke at the same time, "Temporal paradoxes give me a headache." They smiled and Benjamin 'B' popped out.

Benjamin walked back to the class who appeared about fifty meters away on the other side of the open field. The location was perfect for what they needed to do.

"Bradley, what is the first order of business."

"Build a fire!"

"Exactly. Get it started." Benjamin looked back one more time at the place he appeared. Mental reminder to nudge himself in a short time.

* *

They found things to do and everyone was asking where the cold weather equipment was. "Bradley, what temporal coordinates did you tell the operator to jump them to?" Benjamin knew that about a half an hour had just past, since he just saw and waved to himself picking up the timer. He waited a few more minutes knowing when the package would arrive.

Bradley looked at him like he was a blank slate. He had no idea what he was talking about.

"Well class, come with me…" They followed him into the center of the field. Form a very large circle….bigger……bigger…..OK, good. Now count backwards from ten."

And like good lemmings they did so. As they hit the count of one the package appeared in the center of the circle.

"How did you do that?" Brad asked.

He turned and looked at the rocks; Brad followed his gaze where he saw someone vanish. He turned back and smiled at Brad. Then he said, "Thank you! What time is it?" Brad knew exactly what he was doing, and he made a note of the exact time and location.

The winter camping experience was easier than the camping in the woods. They all had to start real fires using multiple methods, and cook their food over the fire.

The next jump would take them back to the classroom for a few days, then on to the real assignments as far as the class knew. They had no idea about the three days in the dessert, YET!

Benjamin had not had any recurrence of the dreams that bothered him. He did dream of other things in his past, and a few in his future. He especially liked to dream about his grandson, and wonder what ever happened to him as a researcher. Who was the woman he would have a child with, and when? All of these questions will be answered in the future. It was interesting to be a leaf on the river of time, but you never fully get the entire story. He would just have to wait till it all happens in real life. But, the real question was could he wait.

* *

The time to return to the classroom has come. Everything is packed and when Benjamin departs he will be touching the cargo pod.

"OK, everyone returns two by two."

Brad left first. As they all left Benjamin watched. They had all progressed so far. Only he was left. He placed both hands on the cargo pod and vanished.

He appeared in the cargo chamber and quickly moved to the personal chamber where he continued on to the dessert where everyone else was already waiting for him.

He arrived a few minutes before Brad, and when Brad saw him he shook his head and said, "I hate you. You just love playing with time, don't you?"

"My new favorite toy!" Benjamin replied.

As the others appeared in the dessert they were wearing essentially their street cloths, leaving all the winter gear in the pod. When he left the cargo pod to move to the personal pod he told the operator to transfer this cardboard box to his temporal coordinates plus 30-minutes. And yes, they arrived right on time, as the Sun was rising.

There was no shade anywhere to be seen, and in the box was a container, 2 liters of water for each person, and one M-Bar to be used only if absolutely necessary.

You could not starve to death in three days, so he hoped each person would be able to gather enough food to maintain for the three days.

He handed each set of two a three-meter square tarp they could use as shade … One side white, one side reflective silver.

There was no chance of anyone dropping in on them this time in the dessert, since he let them all know that the year was 100 BC. There were some very unique life forms present, called bugs. Something they would ALL, Benjamin and Brad included, need to get used to over the next couple days.

As the Sun rose on day one and climbed into the sky, Benjamin looked and Brad and said flatly, "Hope I make it, it's hotter than I thought it would be."

Brad replied, "And coming from the deep freeze to the oven only makes it worse.

Everyone learned to catch, clean, and cook a variety of snakes and critters. They learned that some of the plants could be eaten raw thereby utilizing their internal water content, others needed to be cooked and eaten to make them palatable or to remove toxins. Thankfully, Karen had a scanner to determine the safety of anything before they ate it, raw or cooked. She had asked the Quartermaster Corp to design it to look like a nondescript item that could be from nearly any timeframe. Their result was a small square of wood with an engraved design on the top. A family keepsake. Once she touched it, she could activate and since it sent all data directly to the brain of the person holing it, only someone with a Sub-Q could use it. A medical and environmental scanner. When she set it down, or in general was not touching it any longer, it reverted back to the piece of wood.

On the third day he asked everyone to show him their Malk bars. Everyone held it up, and he instructed them to eat it now. That is when they discovered a hidden secret; it provides rehydration to the body. How it works they had no idea, but it did. Either that or it makes them feel like it did. That would be something for the science teams to discover when they returned.

Chapter 9

Class Final Project

Benjamin stood in front of the class, they had been through a lot and had a lot of fun and education in the past couple months together. Actual class real-time was a great deal shorter.

"OK, welcome home everyone. I trust you all slept well, had a good meal, refreshments, and are ready to finalize the projects you have. Bradley, do you have the assignment sheet?"

"Yes." He answered tentatively. Benjamin did not tell him how it needed to be done, just what needed to be done. It was up to him and his second to figure out how to accomplish that goal.

"Please let them know what they will be doing in each timeframe."

"OK, let's see. For the Witch Hunt assignment." Bradley began. "The teams will be four groups of mostly three. Group one will consist of myself, Ruth, and Wendel. Group two will consist of Hoshi, Monika, and Will. Group three is Dora, LaVarr, and Karen. Group four is Benjamin and Brad. Benjamin and Brad will be floaters and observers, and troubleshooters."

Benjamin nodded in agreement and Bradley continued. "In the 20th century, the oil spill, Benjamin and Brad will be our college professors and we are a group of student's part way into a marine biology degree. This way, we can look like fools in some cases but they will need to be experts. Thankfully, they will be able to use the excuse that it's been a long time since they were in the field, and we can use the excuse that we are just students." Everyone laughed. "As for the Witch Hunt jump, Benjamin and Brad will take on the role of a VIP from a neighboring county or settlement or possibly from England depending on the tone of the town when we all arrive. Their goal is to infiltrate the town government to see if they can learn motives from that side. The rest of us will move around as inconspicuously as possible to see what we can see from our vantage points, with a couple of hurdles. Number One: Hoshi and LaVarr. We can all pose as townspeople, but oriental and black cannot be hidden easily in this timeframe. In this instance, I'm sorry to say, the two of you will need to stay out of the project directly. Your influence and assistance may hinder the progress, and be deadly to you or someone involved. Therefore, you will maintain a vigil of our base camp, which will be hidden in the woods a few kilometers from the town. You will also be given the stealth suits to wear under your cloaks. In the event of a problem, remove your cloak, hide it, and activate the stealth suit. Get back to camp. If the situation becomes deadly for you or someone else, depart, come home. Activate the suit and send the jump signal."

"Well, put. Yes, I think the suit is a good idea. Base camp is perfect. We will bring a proximity scanner and place it high in a tree. Set the signal to the class channel, video will be on channel 9 so everyone can monitor and be alerted in the event of a perimeter breech, use a model 30 proximity scanner. In the event you need to leave the 1600's timeframe, send out a mayday and that you are jumping, and then go. Don't wait for permission to leave but also, DO NOT BE SEEN EVAPORATING!" Benjamin paused for effect, "UNDERSTOOD!!"

A chorus of, "yes" could be heard.

"I have one question." Bradley raised his hand, and his voice. "I was planning to use a model 100 scanner, better range and clarity and very stable. Why do you want to use an older model, the model 30?"

"Simple. A model 30 has a range of about a kilometer in the woodland areas we will be making camp. That is a large enough perimeter for what we need since walking up on us in the woods is not exactly something that can be considered fast. Also, 40 days after activation the mode 30 disintegrates, where-as the model 100 has an active life of nearly a decade; meaning if the tree fell with your model it could be discovered by someone looking for firewood. Lastly, the model 30 can transmit alarms and video on multiple frequencies over a greater range." Benjamin smiled. "But that's just my opinion; you're in charge of this mission."

Bradley thought for a second, dramatic pause more than anything else, "I agree. Model 30 is a better device for this mission."

"Thank you" Benjamin said. Brad, on the other hand, was in the back of the room, behind all the students, shaking his head and rolling his eyes. Benjamin and Bradley saw him and nearly started laughing. They both had to turn around and look like they were getting something off the table.

"OK, the day is nearly over and you leave in five days for your mission. You have the next four days off, early break. Now get out of here and relax, because for the next six months, it is seriously going to be a hard life."

The class started to leave but Ruth stayed behind for a minute. Monika was with her but she waited near the back door.

She approached Benjamin and Brad, who had walked down the stairs to stand next to him. "Gentlemen, the class is starting off this break session with dinner at your place Benjamin, Pluto's. After that, we are all going our separate ways and meet back at Pluto's the night before class resumes. We would like it if the two of you joined us for the kick off."

"I believe I speak for Brad; we would be honored."

The girls left and Brad and Benjamin were standing in the room alone. "You two think you're teaching them something. You're not. What kind of skills are camping and hiking, and building fires?"

"I hear a voice but no Mr. Winchester….where are you?" Benjamin said into the air.

As if on cue he appeared about an inch from Benjamin's nose; he did not flinch when he appeared. Holograms can be quite annoying at time.

"Mr. Jensen, Mr. Jorgen, we need to talk. Face to face."

"That means zero G. I hate zero G." Brad whined on purpose. He actually loved being weightless in orbit. But he wanted to see what kind of look he could muster, and it was a look he wished he had not created.

"Be here tomorrow on the noon shuttle. You are already booked, be at the port at 11am. See you for lunch boys." He disappeared.

"Now what?" Brad asked.

"Who knows, I'm hungry."

"Me too."

They left the room and walked out of the school and went back to their desks and checked messages. Since he had been gone so much his supervisory work was backing up on him. He sent a message to one of his coworkers and asked if she could help in keeping up with the reviews. She would get it in the morning and acknowledge the message.

They stood at the same time and looked at each other with a look on their face like it was unique, but shrugged it off since they do that a lot recently. They entered the lift and went to the ground level, leaving the building they walked to the tube and waited for the car to arrive and open so they could get back to the mainland.

Their conversation was light and filled with discussions about women, and parties. Party, Benjamin thought. He had not had a party in a while. Maybe a party tomorrow tonight. Wait, I'll be in orbit. Never mind, he told himself.

The tube arrived and they both walked in and sat down in the seats that are facing each other. They talk a lot but they like to talk.

"Hang on a sec, I have an idea." Benjamin ducked into a florist and disappeared behind the reflective glass of the shop. Brad was wondering who was getting flowers.

Brad stood there on the street just looking around for about a minute and went in after him. "What are you doing?" He asked Benjamin.

"Having my hair cut, what do you think I'm doing, I'm buying flowers?"

"Why? For who? Not me I hope?" shaking his hands in front of him in a 'get away from me' motion he laughed.

"No, actually, I was thinking about Barbara and Mike. They were great on this last trip. I wanted to say thanks."

"Then don't give Mike flowers." Looking towards the clerk who just reappeared from the back of the shop. "Do you make any kind of fruit baskets?"

"Yes we do. The book is right there in front of you, the red one." Brad opened it up and selected a basket that looked interesting.

"I'll take this one." He pointed to a basket that was about mid-range in price, but more than the flowers.

"Nice choice." The clerk responded back. "I'll make it up now, give me a few minutes."

"Also," Benjamin added. "Put a little more into that flower arrangement."

"You know," The clerk started walking back towards the backroom, "I really enjoy the jab and thrust of two friends arguing over whose gift is better. Kinda gets you right here." The last sentence was said as if it were a touching experience and on the verge of tears, but she was tapping the old fashioned cash register that obviously was nothing more than a museum piece, art work. But the impression was made perfectly.

They all laughed. But they still each increased their gift one more time.

Another twenty minutes in the shop and they had their gifts, Benjamin with a bouquet of real and artificial flowers and Brad with enough fruit to make a horse shy away. But by golly, they were truly glad that these two people were more than simple bar employees, or owners even. They were friends.

Brad held the fruit basket behind his back, and it hurt his shoulders. That thing was heavy. Benjamin put the flowers behind his back, but it looked like he was trying to hide a redwood tree in his pocket.

They walked over to the bar, the rest of the class saw them, and gave Barbara and Mike their gifts. Both were ecstatic, Mike loved fruit and this was some of the best in the city from what he could see. Barbara broke into tears and hugged them both, and the guy at the bar, and Mike, then another guy who walked in to ask directions and…well…you get the picture. Flowers are her favorite thing.

After all the hugging, the delivery boys went to the table. Barbara brought them both a beer. Ice cold and perfect. They drained it in one breath. The rest of the class looked at them in amazement.

"PERFECT! Now, please do that again. Better yet, redo the whole table."

Barbara looked at Mike and yelled. "Benny's buying a round!" The whole bar yelled and applauded. All 5 other people. "Oh well, five more beers won't break the bank." She said as she smiled at him,

After a bit Barbara returned with all of their drinks. "Benny, I'm so sorry. You had to buy those people a drink because of me."

"Not a problem Barbara. As long as you make those burgers and have them shipped to us, I'll do that every night. If you knew the cooking I had to put up with…"

"HEY!" Brad chimed in and the entire table erupted in laughter.

"I did notice you bought him one too, the first time. Judging by the number we sent in the second batch, and the number at this table, I am gonna guess you bought dinner for this entire motley crew."

"He sure did!" Bradley answered. "And it was truly wonderful. Like manna from heaven."

When Bradley said that Benjamin and Ruth looked at him in shock. They both understood the reference, to an ancient Earth religious practice. But he had not heard it since he was in school, from Bill and Betty. The others shrugged it off as a cliché or something. Monika, Dora and Brad understood it all too well. Brad read the entire Bible while he was in the Wild West. Dora, on the other hand, grew up in that environment. Their house was used weekly for a home Bible Study meeting. Monika attended a school that was wrapped in religion. Something that stuck in her mind, but she is not all that active any longer. But it is still something that affects her life in subtle ways.

The rest of the evening they talked with the class. They would be talking an awful lot over the next few months but this was a good time.

They all left early knowing they had somewhere to be in the morning. Some were going home, some on vacation; others were going to the orbital station to visit in zero G with an old professor. Now, what would he want? Why face to face?"

* * * * * * * * * * * * * * * * * * * *

It was an interesting meeting on the space station.

"Security, this is Benjamin Jensen. Please link my implant with that of Brad Jorgen for twenty-four hours."

"Link established. It will dissolve in twenty-four hours, be advised you are scheduled to depart from chamber alpha in twenty-six hours."

"Acknowledged, and thank you."

At the moment, Brad and Benjamin are sitting in the coach seats on their way to the Moon for an encounter with someone who claims to be from the past. He claims he was accidently brought here without the knowledge of the person who brought him. They are attempting to ascertain if this person is a threat, or an extortionist, or simply a man out of time.

"OK, so when we get to this rendezvous what do we do?"

Benjamin answered, "Simple. We play twenty questions. You and I know a lot about the time period he is claiming to come from, and we also know we add a few things in a report that are close to correct to circumvent an instance such as this. Terminology, mannerism, memories; it all comes into play here."

"So what, we buy him dinner and chit-chat about history?"

"No, he knows as well as we do that if time is changed, it changes for always. Unless we go back to correct it. Our goal is to go back to the point he claims to have traveled into our time from and delay him from doing whatever it was he did to get caught up in the temporal wave. It still bugs me though, how did security, and the operator, not notice he was there and not supposed to be?"

Benjamin looked at Brad, square in the eye, for an answer, *"as if I know…"*

"Sorry, I was hoping you had a clue or something. This has me bothered."

The remainder of the trip was as usual, boring. When they arrived they checked in at the hotel and had roughly an hour before they needed to meet this man, Andrew Carlssin. One thing for certain, Mr. Carlssin has no intention of stepping foot in the facility of Archive Island, but Benjamin and Brad had a trick up their sleeves.

Benjamin opened his portacomm and tapped out a text message to Bradley Bentinfield the third. He sent the message and put the unit away. Resting his head on the back of the seat he closed his eyes and drifted off to that place just before sleep.

"EXCUSE ME!! But I have no intention of living out your fantasies…"

Benjamin sat up and opened his eyes laughing out loud. "Sorry, I forgot."

He had to wait to daydream until Bradley contacted him with the result of the search.

* *

Benjamin and Brad sat in the bar waiting for the third member of this dinner meeting. Why such a public location as this had them curious at first, but after thinking about when he is supposed to be from, the year 2010, he remembered people then were suspicious and careful when in this situation. So, they opted to stroke his ego and play along to see what he wanted to maintain his silence.

"Benjamin, and Brad. Did not expect to see you again so soon." A man approached them and offered his hand.

Shaking hands with Benjamin and Brad, he sat at the small bar table. Now that the third guest had arrived Benjamin signaled the hostess who was looking for a table.

"You are?" Brad asked.

"Andrew Carlssin, a man out of time." He mused.

"Mr. Jensen, your table is ready." The hostess stood between Brad and Benjamin and made a 'follow me' motion.

"Hold that thought" Brad told him.

They made their way to the table in the back of the establishment. A group was being ushered to the spire table; they were in for a treat!

As soon as they were seated, a waitress came up, "Drinks, appetizer?"

Brad spoke first, "The appetizer sample platter, bottle of a nice wine, something good, and three glasses." She walked away, Benjamin laughed to himself.

"OK, prove to me you're not from here."

"Or better yet, prove I'm not from now."

"Whatever. Continue."

For the next few minutes he told them all about his life before he left 2003. The houses where he lived in PIKEVILLE, KY; his occupations; friends he had; historical incidents from that and recent history from his point of view. It all sounded real enough.

"All I want to do is get back to my time. I really don't care how, or if you drop me off in 2003 or 2010. I left in 2003 on the coattail of someone from, I believe, fifty years in your future. He was doing a research project on the signing of the truce between the Hatfield family and the McCoy family. As he was leaving I jumped him, I was a not too nice person in that time. I was hoping to nab some of that money he seemed to be toting around with him. But, a moment later we appeared here. In a field outside what I knew as Cleveland. I got up and ran, as fast as I could, in any direction. I managed to conceal myself on a shuttle and came here where I have been performing odd jobs for room and board, and some food. But I'm getting tired of the whole mess; send me back to my time.

"Mr. Jensen, there is a Bradley Bentinfield wishing to connect to you for a period of five minutes. Do I have your permission to connect?"

Brad and Benjamin looked at each other, since they were tuned to the same frequency, they both heard the message. *"Yes, five minutes is sufficient."*

"What did you find out?" Benjamin asked.

"From all historical references we could locate that this man claimed to be from the future. He knew a lot about the stock market and a few interesting things that happened during his life but in no way is he any harm to history if we return him to 2003 were it seems he was already returned to, since we found him in the archives during the research, it needs to be around the beginning of March. On March 19 he will be arrested by the Securities and Exchange Commission for insider trading, but he will claim that his insight was due to his being from the future. No one believes him. Nothing else is heard from him. He does not impact history as far as we could determine."

"Bradley" Brad asked *"Do me one more favor. Look up to see if there are any images of the signing of the truce between the Hatfield and the McCoy families in June of 2003. We are looking for anything or anyone out of the ordinary. Send them to my portacomm if you find anything."*

"Will do. Have a nice dinner." And the connection was broken.

"Well, we are prepared to listen, why should we do as you ask?" Brad asked.

"If you don't, I go to the news. I have proof and they will believe me. I want to go home. I have no ties here and I am ready to go."

While they were speaking to Bradley the appetizer arrived, as did the wine. It was a sparkling wine, and very tasty. Brad looked towards the kitchen door and saw Ramona peeking out. She waved, he nodded. He knew why he got such a good tasting and flavorful bottle. She made it!

They ordered dinner and ate and drank another bottle of wine. When it was time to leave Brad paid the check and the three of them left together. As they were walking Brad invited them in for a nightcap, a phrase Andrew was very familiar with.

While they were eating Brad received a photo of the signing. It seems Andrew WAS from 2003, his image was captured at the June 2003 festival. Earlier, when Bradley was connected to Brad and Benjamin with the Sub-Q, Brad sent Bradley an image of Andrew's face, and he was able to match it to a person in a photo. But, Bradley also found an image of him from a January 2003 news story about the crash of an aircraft in Charlotte, North Carolina. So, Bradley, distilling a little of the information into a cause and effect determined he departed from early 2003, but was returned to near the same time and then was arrested in March, released and all charges were dropped, then went to the festival. There was one previous access to this event in the database, from a few days ago. He is assuming it was this person attempting to learn information about the past, his future. So when he returned he could be rich.

As they entered Brad's Suite, Andrew walked over to the bar and poured a drink for each of them. They toasted to time travel.

Andrew went over to a chair and sat down. Brad and Benjamin sat on chairs next to and opposite him. Benjamin pulled his sleeve back on his left arm and a moment later Andrew was sleeping.

Brad picked him up and disappeared. Benjamin paid for the rooms and took the shuttle back. When he arrived at Pluto's there was a beer and a burger waiting for him at the table.

"So, what happened?"

"We appeared in the chamber and he was sound asleep. The operator sent us back to Louisville, KY on February 1, 2003 where I dropped him off at an emergency room after hitting him again with the strongest jolt I could get from the pulser. He would have been out cold for another 20 hours or so. Before they could speak to me I vanished. They said he was in a coma and put him on a bed. So, they already think he is cracked. Now, he is going to prove he is cracked even deeper."

They ate their burgers, drank a beer and toasted to Andrew. Maybe one day they would go back and follow him, to see what he did. But not today.

"Oh, before I forget. Mr. Winchester let me know four things on the trip back on the shuttle. ONE: according to security there has been no temporal differential, so we did it correctly. TWO: The class jump is still on for two days from now, and thanks for taking this assignment on. He did not want to leave it to security to strong arm the guy. He liked our method. THREE: When the assignment is over you can go back to the LT department to train a new team member. The circus thing I mentioned. FOUR:

Miss Monika Bordow will be joining us after graduation, and she has been assigned to you for her training.

Brad started to cry. Just a little. "BARBARA! CHAMPAGNE!"

Barbara yelled to Mike to get Brad a bottle of Champagne.

* * * * * * * * * * * * * * * * * * * *

The class was ready to depart, t minus four hours. Departure is scheduled for eleven this morning. Time for the headache. As Benjamin walked in to have his Sub-Q filled with all the data and information he would need for these two consecutive trips, he knew he needed one last thing. So he added some new data early this morning and a slight addition to his and LaVarr's jump plan.

He and LaVarr would jump with everyone else but they would leave after a day or so and jump to a couple days prior to the accident on the Oil Rig. Benjamin and LaVar would pose as movie scouts looking for the set of the next big block buster, and would charter a helicopter and go to speak to the rig boss twenty-four hours before the explosion. The next day, timed to get there about fifteen minutes before the explosion, they would film and take images using cameras they purchased when they arrived. This way, they would have real live footage of the actual incident. Using the recording and image enhancement in the implant would allow them greater resolution and zoom capability than is possible with any camera in the year 2010.

LaVarr was impressed that he was asked, and questioned the decision. Benjamin's answer was, "You're a likeable person. How could anyone say no to a guy as nice as you who has a boss as self-centered and egotistical as I will be? It is the Hollywood way. Trust me. I have experienced it."

"OK" is all LaVarr could answer. Bradley laughed.

"I wish I could see that!" Bradley said. Laughing at the thought of these two portraying some duo of comedy.

"You will. We'll show you the visuals when we return to where you are."

"Great"

"BENJAMIN JENSEN, you…are next. Time for your headache." Maria came out to get him. She noticed he and Brad were the oldest ones in the waiting area so she had fun. "Can I get you a wheelchair grandpa? I see you are going out with all these kids, hope you got your nap in." Everyone laughed, including Brad. She turned to Brad, "Oh, old timer. Your wheelchair is on its way." Everyone laughed again.

Benjamin stood up slowly, very slowly, and gave the impression he was hunched over and very old. Looking at Maria he said loud enough for everyone to hear, "Kids today….what can you do?"

Maria wrapped an arm around him as if helping him walk and replied, "I understand gramps, I hear the mind is the second thing to go."

"WOW! I hope she really knows you two?" Monika added as if taken aback by the comments.

At that moment Benjamin scooped Maria up in his arms and started walking toward the data transfer room.

"Not a problem, she was in the same class as Benjamin and I. She opted out of the program after her and I finished the class project of Buffalo hunter in the 1800's. That's where I fell in love with the Wild West, and Maria decided to opt out just before graduation. She became a travel agent for the rich, but she had this place in her blood. With her skills, she was perfect for data implantation and retrieval. If she needs to go and get data in the past, she knows how to jump and still has her implant; it's just not fully active most of the time, and she jumps every few months just to stay current."

Brad smiled a really broad and happy smile as if remembering something that brought a lot of joy in his life.

"So, she and I spent a long time together in the past. We portrayed a brother and sister and had a lot of fun playing poker. All in all, I would not give up the experience. We had the most grueling assignment, and it turned out the safest. Benjamin and his partner Myra were hit by a car and he was in a coma for a long time, she suffered irreparable brain injury and needed to have the implant modified to take over some of her higher brain functions. A couple others died, one in the twin tower destruction of the United States on 9/11. Another died at a Civil War battle, cannon ball exploded into the building they were in. We had a good class and we lost a lot of good people. This is why the class assignment policy has changed to a moderated and instructed extended session with at least two seasoned researchers. A couple years from now, some of you may be in our place." He paused momentarily. "You grab a few interesting A-Sheets and try to merge them into a longer term multi-jump class assignment."

A few minutes went by and they chatted about the past assignments Brad had, something they enjoyed doing in the 1947 dessert while waiting for team 1 to fly home. A short time later Maria walked up to the remaining group.

"BRAD! Can I stick a hot poker in your eye?" Maria asked with a smile.

"Anything for you sis!" he replied and followed her into the room, after the prerequisite welcome hug.

When he sat in the chair it reclined slightly. She was looking in the computer to make certain it would all fit OK. "How you been? I have not had the chance to see you in a while."

"I took an LT back to the wild west. I have been gone for about two years my time."

"You look good though. Need any medical before you jump?"

"Nope. Good to go."

"OK, all that's left is me giving you a headache."

"Sounds like fuuuu…..." As he said it, she pressed the button and he froze in mid word. When the process ended, Brad finished the word, "…uuun!"

* * * * * * * * * * * * * * * * * * * *

The rest of the class filed in to the room two by two and had their data uploaded. They were all sitting in the waiting room again until the headache past, usually about fifteen minutes or so.

"All of you are clear to go." Maria said.

"Thanks." Benjamin got up and gave Maria a big hug and kiss, leaning her back in the process. "When I get back we'll have to have dinner and catch up on things."

"I'll like that." She did not even appear phased by the show of emotion, but it was obvious that the emotion was not of romance, but of close friendship and fun.

Brad walked over and gave her a hug. "Do you trust him?" He pointed to Benjamin.

"Are you kidding?" All three of them laughed and gave a three-way hug. The rest of the class looked at them.

Ruth said something so perfect they all laughed again, "Old people!"

*   *   *   *   *   *   *   *   *   *   *   *   *   *   *   *   *   *   *   *

"OK. The time is five in the morning and the date is May 13, 2010. LaVarr and I will be going back tomorrow to watch the explosion. We will be gone from your reference for about a week. While we are gone, the Brad's are in charge of the two teams. Remember, Brad is your instructor / professor. Talk to him like he is teaching you. And BRAD! Act responsible. Ruth, Dora, please TRY to keep him in line. Now, we need to find a place to live."

They walked into town and were hoping to get a hotel as close as possible to the water. After a couple kilometers they found a place. They landed in Slidell, Louisiana and found a hotel called the Holiday Inn Express. They have a restaurant and a bar. Around the corner is a diner called Waffle House. Benjamin could not wait to try it out.

Benjamin walked into the hotel and up to the counter. By the time they arrived the time was 7am. The day was starting. "Good morning. I would like to get several rooms for a month? How many do you have available?"

The clerk tapped a few keys and, "We have only 8 rooms left. Two luxury king, one king executive, and five double queens. Cost is $140 for the Luxury King and $130 for the others. If you book the rooms for two months, I can knock some off the rate."

"OK, two months. Here is a credit card but I will pay in cash."

"I'll need to get the manager. Please wait."

After a moment the manager appeared, "Can I help you?"

"Good question." Benjamin stared at him.

"I understand you want to pay cash. Is there a reason for that?"

"Yes. The school gave us cash and I do not bank in this area. Do you accept cash or not? If not, is there a reputable hotel where a couple marine biology professors and their students can live at for a couple months while we are helping out in any way we can?"

"Well you don't have to be rude. May I see the credit card?"

Benjamin handed him the card. It was encoded in such a way that it always was approved for whatever amount was run against it. This is why they pay cash for everything. The card machine beeped.

They completed the transaction and got their key. "Oh, one last thing. Do any of the rooms have an area where we can all sit and talk in the evenings?"

"Yes, the Luxury kings do."

"Thanks." Benjamin passed out the electronic keys and they all made their way to the rooms. Thankfully, they were all close together. Benjamin and Brad took the Luxury, and since Bradley was class leader he got the other king and a room to himself. The rest had to determine who was going to share with whom.

The room assignments were fast and simple; Ruth and Dora, Hoshi and Monika, LaVarr and Wendel. Karen and Will got rooms to themselves. Today they would determine what was going on in the area. Learn about the people in teams of two or three and generally do nothing. Tomorrow they would get to work. In a couple days, when everything is running smooth, Benjamin and LaVarr would jump to the previous time and do the video.

Everyone was in their rooms unpacking, watching the news and getting use to a less technological time in Earth's history.

"Class....Please meet in the bar in fifteen minutes." Benjamin said into his implant.

Everyone acknowledged.

"Benjamin, can you and Brad stop by my room on your way?"

"Not a problem!" Brad replied. Benjamin just said sure.

They knocked on Karen's door and when she opened it she looked scared, or terrified of something.

"What's wrong?" Brad asked.

"The moment we entered this time I had the feeling of dread, emptiness, desolation, aloneness. It is driving me nuts."

Benjamin said, "I have an idea, be right back!" and he popped out.

Returning a moment later he said, "Karen, return to the school and visit with the psych's. I have a feeling that the instant you enter the home timeframe you will feel better. But, the psych's can help. Return back here to this moment when you are through."

She popped out of this timeframe to return home. A few seconds later she returned smiling. "They figured it out! They fixed it!"

"Fixed what", Brad asked. She was gone only a few seconds, but to her it was a lot longer.

"They determined that I have a psychic link to the Malkornian race. I can always feel the general feeling of the planet. Now, in this year, there are no Malkornian's and my mind was missing them terribly. The psych's asked the representative on the Island to help. They came over and sat with me for a few hours and essentially put a piece of them into me so I would not be alone."

"COOL!" Brad and Benjamin said in unison.

"So what does that mean?" Benjamin asked.

"What it means is that I have a small part of the knowledge of that race living in my mind. I can access it and tell you some very interesting things about several subjects. Also, I am not quite a telepath, but I am now an empath; like them. I feel what others feel." She smiled and looked at each of them. Then continued, "So that's what dumbfounded feels like?" She smiled, and they laughed at the thought.

* * * * * * * * * * * * * * * * * * * *

They sat at the bar for several hours, then sat outside on the deck. The weather was warm and humid, but it was a nice change from inside sterility and the stifling outside of home.

"Brad, the volunteer coordinator will contact you tomorrow using this portacomm…" Benjamin started to explain.

"…Uh, I believe that is referred to as a cell phone." Lavarr said, with an air of authority in his voice.

"…Uhmmmm…right…cell phone. With the exception of Ruth, Karen, and Wendel, the rest of you, follow Brad's lead. You will be washing the crude oil off shore and ocean creatures and helping to clean the beaches of the oil deposits. Don't work with each other; try to work with other volunteers. Now, Ruth and Wendel, the reason you will not be doing this is you will be providing assistance to the local population in filling out the forms to get financial assistance. You will be essentially on your own. I chose you because of your background," he said to Ruth and Wendel, "you both seem to like paperwork so much, so here's your chance to make your mark, hopefully not in history." He smiled at them.

Turning to Karen, "As for you….because of this new ability of yours I do not think it would be wise to put you into a position where you can feel fear, pain, anguish, or any other negative emotion. So, Bradley and I were talking about making a new A-Sheet for you, and you would be responsible for the report on this one yourself." He paused for a moment in thought but Bradley took over.

"The one thing we have been trying to determine is how the people here are feeling; now we can seriously find out. An empath walking around the area or helping at a shelter or feeding station can get a good overall impression of the people, and the happenstance…is that a word?" he chuckled.

Benjamin took over, "Bradley is going to go with you to provide support and assistance as needed. This is not exactly the safest environment right now, but if you are smart you will be fine."

Brad chimed in, "If you two pulled a cart of some kind and carried cool – refreshing – clean water, you could seriously make a lot of friends. And just think of the information you could gather!"

"Good idea. We will talk to the volunteer coordinator about it when we see her. LaVarr and I will leave tomorrow after lunch. I need to take care of something here first. We'll see you when we arrive back.

The rest of the evening went well. The sun finally dipped below the horizon and the air began to cool, slightly. They sat at the bar and were talking about getting something to eat. It was about 9pm so most of the fast food places they discovered were closed or closing, but Benjamin remembered about Denny's.

As the waitress walked back for a drink order, "We do have a question for you. Is there a Denny's close by?"

"Sure there is. Walk through the building and out the back, five minutes' walk down the street and there ya are. Go out the other direction and you have Waffle House. I like Waffle House better, more fun, faster, and cheaper."

"THANKS!" Benjamin replied. "One more round also and then put the total on room 123."

She returned with the drinks, and they talked about school and the future, being cryptic or discussing the topic through their implants.

The class was getting comfortable with Benjamin and Brad and were starting to open up to them. A short while later the entire class walked in single file through the building and out the back door. They saw the sign and walked toward it like it was a beacon of survival.

Entering the door everyone wrinkled their nose. It was food but there were so many smells, not aromas, in the place they thought it was a bad smell. Benjamin and Brad took in a deep whiff and an over exaggerated AAHHH came out afterwards.

"Now that's cooking!"

No one was sure which of them said it, but they were both nodding in agreement.

The staff saw the group walking to the restaurant and set up a very large area for them. What they did was put together five or six tables to make a large long table. Benjamin at one end, Brad at the other, the class in the middle.

"What can I get you to drink?" Barb asked, Barb looked like a sister of Barbara, and everyone noticed too.

"Uh, you look almost identical to the waitress who serves us at home." Dora said to her.

"Well then, she must be one fine example of a woman, what's her name?"

The entire table answered in unison, "Barbara"

"Great name" and she walked away to get everyone's drinks.

"Mr. Jensen, Mr. Jorgen. This is security operative Alpha Six. Please respond."

"We're here Alpha, what can we do for you?"

"We need for you and LaVarr to not make your secondary jump a few hours from now. Where are you currently? We need to meet so I can provide you with additional information."

"We are eating a meal, activate your beacon."

As he did the implant picked him up and bringing up the GPS he was able to determine where he was located. *"You are three kilometers from our location. Sending you some files, activate them and you will have a better idea."*

"Received, I shall be there in fifteen minutes. Save me a cup of coffee please. Black."

"Can we order you something to eat also?"

"I have no idea what to order, so can I trust you to order something good?"

"Do you eat meat, vegeterian, vegan?"

"No. meat is just fine."

"Then Meatloaf it is. It will be here when you arrive."

"Thank you. I am jogging, and will be there shortly. Alpha out."

"Did all of you hear that, or only Brad and I?"

"No, we all heard that. He was on the class channel."

"I thought so."

Barb returned to deliver drinks and take food orders. She brought reinforcements.

"Oh, Barb, there is another joining us in about ten minutes, he needs a black coffee and a meatloaf platter. I need the meatloaf also."

They talked quietly and waited for their meals. Most ordered a sandwich, Benjamin and Brad ordered the meatloaf platter, as did the member of security through Benjamin.

"Mr. Jensen." A young man asked.

"Yes. You are?"

"My name is Brian and we need to speak privately. The three of us," he pointed to LaVarr. As he said those words the food started to arrive. "After dinner. In this instance, time is on our side." The Security man, Brian, nodded in agreement.

Everyone ate and when they saw the meatloaf platter they all wanted to taste it. They all loved it so Benjamin ordered another double order to pass around the table.

After dinner, Brian used the implant to speak to everyone at the table.

"Here is the video feed we received a short time ago from a security operative."

As they watched the video they saw Benjamin and LaVar in a helicopter. The video feed was a live web feed from the Oil Rig. At the moment of explosion, a very large shard of metal was propelled into the helicopter and it burst into flames. LaVarr gasped, Benjamin sat there and looked at the time index on the display.

"OK, we need to do this, but since we know we will not be injured. At that time, we will increase altitude and avoid the explosion all together."

The security man was about to leave, "I did not bring currency."

"We got it. You owe me a beer when we get back."

"I will never have met you. If you are not killed I will have no reason to come back, therefore, goodbye."

He walked out the door never to be seen again.

"LaVarr…wait, I'm sorry. Bradley, I need two of your students to return and bring back orbital pods. Although I would love to go up in a helicopter, I think we will be safer in the pods."

"Dora, Hoshi. You two fly better than any of the rest. Return and get the pods this evening after you get back to your room and return with them. Where should we park them?"

Brad voiced up, "I got the perfect place. The dumpster is a place no one likes to be around, so how about behind the dumpster. Flat field and no traffic, or foot traffic, for that matter."

"Great. It's a plan. LaVarr, meet me in the lobby at 5:45am. We'll eat breakfast and then jump. Ladies, activate the stealth skin and code it to the class frequency so we can find the pods in the morning." With the cloak coded to the class frequency the implant will detect and uncover the pod so they can see and find them easier.

"Will that be one tab, or separate?"

"One please." Brad told her.

Barb handed him the bill, he and the rest of the class laughed and all pointed to Benjamin. She walked to the other end of the table and handed it to him. He looked at it and peeled off $150 from his wallet and handed it all to her. "Keep the change" He told her. "You may just be seeing a lot of us over the next month or two."

"Thank you, and let me know when you will be here and I will have things ready."

As Benjamin was leaving he saw a business card at the register. He picked one up and asked, "Is this where I can get in touch with you?"

"Sure is" The manager told him.

"Great. I will call you about half an hour before we arrive every day. We will be here for a couple months and this just became our favorite place to eat. The hotel is nice, but you really don't get much for the price. How are your breakfasts?"

"Best around. Stop by in the morning, we're always open!"

Benjamin waved and left. They all needed to get some sleep. In the morning there will be a couple pods out in the back that he and LaVarr will use. They will be able to go a lot closer and see in a greater resolution. Better bet in the long run, but he really wanted to fly in a helicopter. Rotary wing aircraft. A lot different than a hovercopter. Put grav plating on the bottom of anything and it can fly.

Benjamin had a thought for an experiment again. Go back in time say… to the early to mid-21st century, introduce grav plating and flying transportation, pop home and see what the outcome is. If he did it, he would get in a lot of trouble, but it was one of the things a researcher always thought about.

Benjamin crawled into his bed. Not really comfortable, he missed his bed. It self-adjusts to your body. Firmness, temperature, everything. This was a bag filled with foam. And used by a lot of people. He is oh so glad that researchers are required to be vaccinated against all known past and present bacteria and viruses. Then he fell sound asleep and began dreaming of Brad.

"So the timeline is restored."

Brad watched the visual of the team of con men and women. "Hey, I know them. They bought me dinner one evening at a local saloon when I arrived." Reality began to sink in, "OH…that is how my name got into the history books."

"Well then, I guess you are cleared of all charges." Benjamin said happily.

"Sir, our mission is complete. A success. Should we not be returning home?"

"Kid, relax. These times are few and far between. We have no assignment, no worries, and nothing that needs to be done; and our lives are not in peril." He tossed Roger a blanket and a cup for coffee. "Relax, you deserve a good night's rest and a good breakfast before we go home."

Roger said nothing. He was getting chilly so he poured a cup of coffee and wrapped up in the blanket. Sitting on the ground with his back against a log he looked at Brad and asked a very straight question.

"Brad, has he always been like that?"

"Yep! Benjamin is driven by dedication to history as rule number one."

"Then what's rule two and three?" Roger asked, kinda half joking.

"Rule two is loyalty to friends, and rule three is the pursuit of happiness."

Benjamin added, "Rule four; choose your friends wisely and trust your friends completely, and if it ain't fun, why do it!"

They enjoyed the evening together and all three slept very well. Brad pulled out a bottle of whiskey, vintage…yesterday. As he was sitting there on the ground leaning against the log he looked around the fire and saw all of the people he once thought of as family. Myra, Tsa, Maria, Natalya, even Will. He looked at them all and began to tear up.

"I really miss all of you. I wish we were all still friends."

Myra responded, "Can't ever be, Ben. You have become a real loner, self-centered and full of yourself."

Maria continued, "I don't think there's room in your heart for anything but that ego of yours."

Brad spoke next, "I know you like to see me a lot, but why is that, really. True, you are my best friend in the entire universe and all of time. But shouldn't you be looking for a long term female companion?"

Ruth spoke next, where had she came from, "I knew from the moment we met you had your eye on me. Conquest? or something deeper? I want a relationship, not an acquaintance. Remember that when you wake up!"

It just turned to morning and everyone was gone except for Brad and Roger.

"Well, we will leave you our horses Brad since we can't take them home with us." Benjamin grinned as did Brad. They both looked at Roger who was staring at them with a giant question mark. When it dawned on him what they were laughing at inside, he laughed out loud, "That would be funny!"

"So, you wanna keep anything we brought with us?" Benjamin asked Brad.

Brad glanced through their personal belongings like he was at a flea market. Picking out a few things he placed them near his pack. Then he looked at Benjamin and said, "There is one other thing I may need."

Benjamin replied, "And what would that be?"

Brad stood there for a moment in total silence, after Benjamin figured it out; he did not say a word.

"Well kid….time to go home and do some real work." He turned back to Brad. "See you in a few months when I need a vacation!"

They hugged and so did Brad and Roger. Roger evaporated and they both knew he was already home.

Benjamin pulled his soul from inside his body and handed it to Brad. "Do you know how to use that thing?"

Brad nodded; "I took the liberty to grab the user manual from your brain when we were exchanging information a few nights ago. Thanks to the whiskey, you didn't even notice I had it."

"Yes I did. But I was planning to leave it for you anyway. I have no further use for it anyway."

Benjamin waved and began to evaporate but jumped into the air as high as he could before he disappeared.

As he appeared in the chamber he looked at the operator whose eyes were as large as pie plates.

Benjamin, without a soul, spoke in a mean spirited voice at the operator, "WHAT ARE YOU LOOKING AT?!"

Benjamin woke up, not in a cold sweat but rather with a satisfied feeling. He had returned to a point on his continuum where he was happy. OK, some of the people who were with him were not happy about or with him, but he could get over it.

He had entrusted Brad with his soul. "Can't wait for the psych's to hear about that one. That should keep us talking for a while." Benjamin muttered to himself.

He looked at the cell phone he bought at the gift shop earlier that day and the time was 3am. He had a couple hours before he and LaVarr met for breakfast. There was no way he was getting back to sleep, so he decided to use the internet. As slow and cumbersome as it is, he may enjoy the diversion.

He got dressed and went downstairs to the front desk, "Is there a computer I can use to check my … uh…Email."

"Yes sir, in the business center, over there." She pointed behind and left of Benjamin.

"Thanks"

Benjamin was getting frustrated, this thing was slow. According to the speed it was less than one gigabyte transfer rate. How is that lack of speed possible?

"You up already?" LaVarr startled Benjamin.

"Yes, you ready to go."

"I am."

"Let's go to Denny's for breakfast, and then we'll get on the road." He used local timeframe terms in case someone overheard them.

They left for the Denny's to experiment with breakfast. Benjamin was an old hand at this; he really liked eating at Denny's but he also liked to try new things. LaVarr, on the other hand; well, this is a new experience for him. Let's have some fun.

Chapter 10

Side Trip to Oblivion

Breakfast was really good, but LaVarr asked why it was so wet. When Benjamin told him it was cooked in oil, or rather fat, LaVarr did not really understand. Then he saw that the bacon was cooked first, and the eggs were then cooked in the same pan. Then he understood. He was not used to that much grease in his diet, but Benjamin did not have a problem with it.

After they ate, LaVarr made the comment he liked bacon and wondered how it was made. Benjamin made a side note to himself to create an A-Sheet for a mission, and assign it to LaVarr, that will research the history of bacon. He knew LaVarr would work under him eventually, he requested it. This could be his first solo assignment and something which would benefit the archives. But for now they have another mission to accomplish.

Benjamin stood in front of the pods, LaVarr to his left. They opened and entered the pods, the hatch closing behind them as they settled into the seats. A few moments later a slight hum could be heard if you knew what you were listening for; if not, then it sounded like some sort of background noise from the highway.

They lifted off and the hum grew softer and softer, till it was gone.

* * * * * * * * * * * * * * * * * * * *

Benjamin and LaVarr appeared on the beach as they were supposed to, but their pods were implanted in the sand. The moment they appeared, the pods shot up like a champagne cork. There were a couple of joggers on the beach and the sound and site of the materialization made them stop their run and look around wondering where it was coming from, you could see it in their faces and the fact they were looking from left to right as fast as their head would allow them to move.

"Benjamin, since we now have pods, are we going to hover within the zone of the explosion?"

Speaking through the pod communications system rather than the implant allowed them to have their own thoughts and speak to each other. "Yes, we'll take opposite positions from the location of the explosion, full video and run at high speed for max capability. We know the explosion begins at 9:36pm, so we have a few hours till we need to be out there. Let's take a trip there now and document the rig, the area, and all ships with in fifty miles of the rig; once complete, we will go under the water and record. I want a few good shots of the well at the bottom as the explosion begins, and of the explosion itself. This is much better than the helicopter."

"I agree. So, do you want the above or below surface piece?"

Benjamin thought for a second, "Which would you like?"

"If I had a choice, I would like the below surface."

"Then you got it."

Traveling out to the rig was uneventful, and to make it safer they went at less than max speed and at an altitude of three hundred feet. Higher than any part of a boat, and lower than any aircraft.

The rig was roughly 60 miles away and the pod could get there in ten minutes or so, but they flew more slowly than needed and recorded all of the activity up to and including the rig.

As they approached the rig they recorded everything. They stayed 180 degrees away from each other and began a medium speed spiral that would visually record every square centimeter of the water between the rig and fifty miles out. Once complete, Benjamin made a bee line for the rig and LaVarr was also racing for the target. As they approached the rig itself Benjamin stopped short and began filming, LaVarr went under water and began his run. Benjamin tried to record every square millimeter of the rig itself as did LaVarr only from the underside. The time was approaching when they needed to move clear, but they still had some time.

The next few hours they went above and below the surface and recorded every inch of the rig, and the well. Throughout history, this time period has been known as the beginning of the ecological disasters that nearly destroyed the Earth. First the ozone depletion, then this massive oil spill, then oxygen generating rainforests are systematically cut down; what were humans thinking? Thankfully, once man decided to go back to the Moon to live, and survive, they discovered the Moon was not a wasteland. No sir, it was a mineralogical soup waiting to be tasted. The regolith alone provided enough usable oxygen to begin correcting the ozone, and all the breathable gas needed by those first pioneers who arrived, set up a home, and lived in the danger of being exposed to any number of interesting ways to die.

After the radiation dome was created it provided a wonderful shield to the dangers of space for the inhabitants of the lunar colony. Benjamin loved the Moon and daydreamed of it often, but this was not the time or the place…..

Shaking himself from his imagination he got back to the business at hand. If they were instructed to do so, they could initiate a beam on the well head to contain the crude, and another force shield to permanently seal the well. Top kill, bottom kill, none of them worked. It was months till the oil company got the well-sealed and began to get the area to recover slightly. But the people here, the fishermen and women of this area, would never fully recover. Some have, and will, lose everything.

People as far away as North Carolina relied on their seafood for their livelihood, and if it was tainted by crude or so expensive that they could not sell a finished product, most had no option but to close their restaurants and find a new source of income.

"Benjamin, the time is 9:33. I will make my way to the ocean floor."

"I am nearly in position to record the start of the rig exploding."

* * * * * * * * * * * *

Returning to the chamber they left the pods and let the security teams put them away and downloaded the data to the mainframe. They initiated the jump and arrived back at the dumpster. Benjamin had no idea what day it was or the time. They were supposed to arrive on the beach at sunrise several days after they left, but they seemed to be at the back of the hotel, behind the dumpster where the pods were waiting for them initially.

"Someone's coming." LaVarr said.

"Do not let them see you." Benjamin replied. They both took cover and watched as they saw themselves approach, get into the pods, and take off.

"OK, that was odd. I just saw me leave." LaVarr had a funny smile on his face. He found this humorous.

"We were not supposed to return to the point of departure. Something it different." Benjamin opened his Sub-Q link to the Brad frequency, *"You awake?"*

"Yep! Sure am. Welcome back buddy." Brad laughed.

"OK, I need an explanation…" Benjamin retorted!

"OK, meet me at Denny's in 10. Bring LaVarr, he will find this interesting also." Brad cut the link but got on the Bradley frequency and told him to get everyone else up. He knew Bradley was awake already, or rather he had just woken up. He forgot to turn off his Sub-Q last night before he fell asleep and Brad caught a glimpse of his dream. He watched a couple movies on the television in his room, something called Superman. He dreamed he could fly. Brad jarred him awake and reminded him that he really needs to be more careful about his off and on – it could get him into a pickle if he was not careful.

Brad threw on some clothes and made his way to the restaurant. Bradley woke up the rest and let them all know to meet there in 30-minutes or less.

As Brad walked in, he sat at the four seat table between Benjamin and LaVarr, Benjamin on his left. He ordered a cup of coffee for himself and looked Benjamin dead in the eye and said, "Was that cool or what?"

"What are you talking about?" Benjamin was really confused.

"OK, I did my own temporal experiment. I knew the moment you two departed and as soon as you did I popped home and reconfigured your parameters to reappear a minute before you left."

"You did this?" Benjamin was somewhat irritated.

"Not exactly. I had a request from Mr. W; he wanted you to have a taste of your own medicine, as in playing with time and all. You do know that they are monitoring us at just about every minute as long as we are within range of the Archives. He wanted to see YOUR reaction." Benjamin laughed. He needed to get them both back one day, but it was rather funny.

They ordered their breakfast, a second breakfast for two of them, and a first for Brad. The server walked over and looked at them, LaVarr and Benjamin, and, "You two back already?"

"Yep!" LaVarr replied

"Anything I can get you?" She asked them both.

LaVarr jumped in first, "Give me what I had a few minutes ago, that was good."

"You mean you want to order another entire breakfast?" She was smiling but looking at LaVarr like he had an arm growing out of their ear.

"Sounds good!" Benjamin exclaimed. Now she was in shock.

Looking at Brad, "You? I supposed you want one of everything on the menu to catch up?" Now she was playing with them.

"No, not this morning. Just give me what he is having." Pointing to Benjamin.

"Coffee all around?" They all nodded. She walked away shaking her head, "You guys just ain't gonna believe this one." She said to the staff.

As they finished eating the rest of the team began filing in and sitting at tables around them. It was still really early so the staff was not 100% yet, but they were making due. This was their busiest morning in a long time.

* * * * * * * * * * * * *

The next few months were both eventful and uneventful. They cleaned fish, birds, turtles, and any other creature they found that was covered in gunk. They vacuumed the beach and the ocean at times. They wore hazmat suits and swimsuits. They helped the area recover in more ways than cleaning the beach. The paperwork was monumental and their assistance made it easier for the people to receive help. They filled out reports each day in their own minds to compile when they returned home, that is what Benjamin reminded them of each night. This is the reason each of them had their own channel they could connect to, privacy but with an active implant so they could review and report in their own minds.

Karen learned to use her empathic ability and really made a difference in the emotional well-being of those she met. She knew for a fact she was going to like her assignment after graduation.

Their time here was up. In the morning they would leave. After a good night's rest and a shower, they would change into their 1600's garb and leave for their next adventure.

* * * * * * * * * * * * *

The group found a nice field to make camp when they arrived and installed the sensor net around them. They would be notified if anyone approached. The base camp monitors had a third person, thanks to a twisted ankle. So they each sat watch in the camp one third of the day. Benjamin ensured they all remembered how to use their stunner, and since it was a nonlethal force weapon it could be used as needed…when needed…without worrying about the outcome. Providing the target was not about to fall on something which in not conducive to human life.

They had been here nearly a week and were sitting around the fire eating a meal. Several of them went into town and picked up food, but Brad and Benjamin liked to cook. On occasion, they had people stumble upon their camp. Hoshi and LaVarr would sit up against a bush with the suit activated and just listen. They could always ask anyone anything through the implant, but it was not necessary.

When a stranger arrived, Dora and Ruth quickly took over the food prep and the rest of the women tended to woman's work. The men sat around and rested, of course. They went out during the day and hunted.

Several days ago Benjamin and Brad went to the town center and introduced themselves as representatives of the Crown. They were accepted without question thanks to their dress, demeanor and wealth.

They quickly became a major force in the local government and discovered that the local pastor, and the leader of Salem, was in league to make the town a safe place that was free of witches.

It seems it all started with three girls who appeared to bark and fall on to all fours and vomit. They called it witchcraft. Benjamin knew what had happened thanks to a report he remembered reading before they left. It seems that in 1976 a psychologist by the name of Linnda Caporael discovered that the abnormal habits of the accused were caused by the fungus ergot, which can be found in rye, wheat and other cereal grasses. Toxicologists of that timeframe say that eating ergot-contaminated foods can lead to muscle spasms, vomiting, delusions and hallucinations. Also, the fungus thrives in warm and damp climates — not too unlike the swampy meadows in Salem Village where they are now, and where rye was the staple grain during the spring and summer months. Lastly, cooking the bread in the oven does not kill all the bacteria, thereby making the bread the means to infect others.

"Benjamin, I cannot believe that these people can really believe that an illness can be witchcraft. How can they be so foolish, so closed minded, so ignorant?" Dora was speaking to the group gathered around the fire.

"Think of it this way, how can one person or a group of people consider someone or some group who thinks differently than them a threat?" Benjamin replied. He found a teaching moment.

"Come on, are you saying that happened?" Will chimed in.

Benjamin continued, "Think about the 1950's. Senator McCarthy and his witch hunt. He was not looking for witches; he was looking for Communists. And if you did not agree with what he was doing, you were then considered a Communist and on his list. You were accused and it did not matter if there was any evidence or not. Just being accused was enough to end your career, and quite possibly your life."

Brad responded next, "...and look at the Luna's Group in the early 22nd Century. They tried to give the Moon back to the Moon and because of it they were ridiculed and berated in public, and their names and reputations were destroyed all in the name of preservation for the future. They never reaped what they sowed, but less than 100 years later, in 2230 I believe, the world government was established and declared the lunar surface an ecosystem. Building and use was strictly limited and regulated, proper use was enforced and there is a lot to be said for what they accomplished."

Benjamin looked at Brad with a....'RIGHT?' look on his face. Brad simply smiled back at him. "The Lunar Surface, I love that place. It is really a sparse and beautiful place to visit." Everyone agreed with Benjamin.

As if in unison they all heard a ringing in their head, which they all became accustomed to, but not used to hearing. It was the proximity alarm announcing uninvited guests. They instinctively turned to the video channel and watched an enhanced image of three men approaching their campsite as quietly as possible.

As if on cue everyone stood and got about their business or sat and did what they were supposed to do. They had a few minutes since these three was just under a kilometer away, but moving towards the camp at quite a fast pace.

Ruth and Dora took over the food prep and Benjamin and Brad sat and began sharpening their knives while sitting on a log near the fire. A few minutes later the men were at the edge of the clearing watching them. With the implants it was easy to talk and see what was going on while at the same time appearing to ignore them, or maybe not see them at all.

As there were two members of this group who were essentially invisible, they followed them and recorded their movements and sounds and transmitted it all to everyone.

The goal of this mission was to talk to the town's people, not have them talk to this group. The last thing they wanted was to inject unfamiliar ideas into these somewhat scrambled heads, who knows what repercussions that may have on posterity. The three men walked into the camp and were welcomed with a warm hand of friendship and a seat at the table for evening meal. They stayed and learned about them, realizing that Benjamin and Brad were the leaders of this group. Since Brad had so much familiarity with divine 'things' from a few hundred years in these people's future, Benjamin deferred to him when the topic broached on the religious.

This opened them up to the witch hunt, trial, and execution line of questioning. Brad learned that the vicar of the local church had ideas that if you are not normal then you are possessed. This went out on a limb and fell off the cliff when the three men made the accusation that Ruth and Dora were witches and they were using their charms and incantations to have their way with these three men. Benjamin started laughing, but Brad stayed stoic in his demeanor. He realized these men had an agenda of their own and needed to discover what it was before this escalated out of hand.

After another 30-minutes Brad discovered they were nothing more than con artists looking for an easy mark. By portraying themselves as victims of witches they would be treated by the town well enough, but by allowing Brad to buy their silence, they could acquire so much more.

They did not believe there were witches, but the people of the town would. It was at that moment that Benjamin, Brad, and Dora fired their stunners at the same moment, coordinating it all through the Sub-Q. Benjamin disappeared for a few minutes and popped back in with three auto injecting syringes. Handing one to Brad and one to Dora, they pressed it against the right thigh of the men and listened to the hissssssss as it dispensed the medicine into their body.

"What are we giving them?" Dora asked.

"Alcohol. Not straight alcohol but enough and partially broken down so they will appear to have been drunk all day and yes, they will have one amazing hang over when it wears off." Benjamin answered.

They were hit with a 7-hour stunner blast so they still had a while to sleep; and since it was still before midnight they knew these men would wake up before sunrise. They would not remember anything about approaching the camp, dinner, the conversation, or even meeting anyone in this group.

The three of them held the men and popped back to the chamber, the destination was reset, and they reappeared several miles away on the other side of the village of Salem. A secluded area that was just far enough away so-as to appear a likely place for the men to imbibe, but close enough to the town so they would have thought this is where they came from with their bottle. Dora broke a half filled bottle of a locally brewed spirits near them, so when they woke they would think they had a good time.

This class has been on several extended, long range, and technical missions. But this was not one of them. This was an impromptu and seat-of-the-pants mission needed to maintain the integrity of the timeline. This is the reason they are here. This is the reason Benjamin and Brad were asked, every so nicely, to teach this class. This is the class that is the first to learn what it is like when you are on a long-term mission and need to ensure you are not spotted as a temporal agent or a target of bad people. This is a class in how to fit in and be invisible in plain sight. This is the mark of a good researcher. Something Benjamin and Brad excel in on a minute by minute basis when they are not in their present timeframe.

The group had enough data collected on this time and situation to compile a thorough report, so in the morning Benjamin would let them go into town, Salem, one last time. He and Brad had worked it out. When he appeared in the chamber to get the autoinjectors, he requested a location change. The new jump point for each person would be relocated to Salem; but in the year 2007, not 1793. A moment after they appear a transport bin would appear near them with local clothing, and since they were not bringing anything back with them, it would not be out of place. The bin was one that was purchased in the 1990's at a general type store on a previous mission by another researcher, so leaving the bin with the clothing 200 years out of date would seem as though a theater group lost some of its costumes.

The bin also contained enough currency to complete this assignment, a mini-vacation.

They wandered around Salem as a single or in couples for a few days, knowing full well that if they needed anything all they had to do was yell.

About the 5th day Benjamin contacted everyone and asked them all to meet with him on Derby Street in Salem, in the lobby of the Marina Hotel. After spending a week in the early 21st Century the group was all decompressed and ready to return home. But Benjamin and Brad had another idea.

Brad and Dora jumped back and picked up a few portable data terminals that looked like present timeframe laptops, but the guts were definitely anything but 20th Century technology. They stayed in a really first class hotel in the heart of Salem, on the waterfront. They each had a very nice suite, and Benjamin and Brad retaining the last two Deluxe King Suites with Wet Bars. The others in the group either shared a very nice suite, or had a suite of their own; it was left up to them with a 'what happens here…stays here' mentality. Monika took a smaller room near Brad, so they could grow their relationship in a subtle and quite moral way. The entire class knew what was happening but said nothing. They had every intention of getting closer and becoming a married couple, something Benjamin snickered and shook his head at when Brad told him.

Bradley and Ruth opted to take a large suite together, to which Benjamin felt a bit jealous and that made him nervous – did he have feelings for Ruth! Impossible!!

They spent nearly a month here at the hotel and the manager gave them the use of one of the training rooms, they called it the Compass Room, so they could write their reports and save them to the "laptop" computers. Dora was smart enough to return home one morning to retrieve a portable security screen. Enabling them to openly discuss, work, and complete their reports with no prying eyes able to see, or ears able to hear.

When not in TRAINING, they walked around the town and went to the marina and chartered water craft, fished, or simply sat and watched people. The group on the other hand opted to take water taxi rides, compliments of the hotel, to the harbor dock near the aquarium. Not the fastest mode of transportation, and at times not conducive to a fancy hair style, but still a lot of fun.

Benjamin became friendly with a woman he met at a local bar, she worked there. She was the best server in the place, and her name just HAD to be Barb; which as everyone knows is short for Barbara.

The place was located on Derby Street and had only been open for a year or so, and Barb had been there from the beginning. It was a short walk from where they were living, in the waterfront hotel and marina. Left out of the hotel, cross Congress Street and in less than 2 minutes there it was – happiness and joy. Benjamin realized he could make a great life for himself here, if he decided to take on a long term assignment.

That also made him nervous; was he starting to think about settling down, starting a family, a life. Something is wrong with him, at least he thought so.

One evening everyone was calling him, and he discovered this when he remembered his implant was turned off. When he turned it on he was inundated by a wave of mental yelling that almost hurt. He shouted back to them all and Brad quietly inquired as to his location. He let them know he was at the Beer Place about 500 feet from the hotel. They were all on their way to meet him, they had an idea they wanted to share and get his opinion.

Barb brought him another beer and he stopped her before she could leave with his former mug which was drained of its contents. He had a standing request to her to never bring him the same beer twice. He had cycled through all the beers in the place several times, and was nearly complete with this pass, his third.

"Barb, in a few minutes I have about a dozen colleagues stopping by for a few beers and some food. I told them all about the Lobster Mac and they all want to try it. Can we push a few of the tables together and turn this into an event?"

"Sure thing, the one thing the boss likes is a large party, give us all job security ya-know!" She smiled back at him. "…and an 18% gratuity added to the bill!" She winked at him.

They had grown close over the last few weeks and he had spent nights with her in both his hotel, and in her apartment. They were not serious, except for the fact they were both simply looking for a fun and exciting time. Something they both had.

Benjamin handed her his credit card, "Put everything for tonight on this. Consider the drinks and foods open to all in the party. No limits." He handed her the card, and it was wrapped in a $20 bill. "Pre-tip" he said, "I hear if you are a big tipper you get great service here?" He grinned at her.

She slapped him playfully on the back of the shoulder, bent down so they were nose to nose and said to him, "Do I look like I'm laughing?"

"Uh, no. Actually you don't." Benjamin said back to here. A moment later she realized he was not looking her in the eye as she had planned, he was looking nearly straight ahead and directly down the flopped open gap in her blouse. "But may I commend you on the view?"

She stood and popped him on the shoulder again and took a step away, walked back over to him and gave him a quick peck on the lips. Turned and walked back to the bar. A few seconds later the group walked in the door and Brad was the only one to see the kiss. She had met Brad a couple times and she was fun to be around. Brad and Monika, Barb and Benjamin had had a nice dinner a few times on the river. They had even chartered a boat once for a day on the water. That was when Brad and Barb learned they got sea-sick. Benjamin handed them each a motion sickness pill which they took without question, and in a few minutes they both began to feel better.

Later Barb wanted to know the name so she could buy more; she had never had one work that fast, that well, or that long.

Benjamin told her he had no idea since he lost the packaging, but they were given to him by a pharmacist when he was in San Francisco last year. All he remembered was that it was a grocery store he was at and the pharmacist was a beautiful, dirty blond, and two inches taller than he was; she was also married and had three children, two girls and a boy. Her husband did something on the cruise ships but he could not remember what it was that he did. She was disappointed, but it was not as if he could tell her that this combination of medicines has not been discovered yet, and will not be discovered for a few hundred years.

One thing you learn after time in his profession is to spin a realistic yarn. The sad part was that if he took a polygraph test, something they had in the 20th and 21st Century before telepaths, he would pass it with flying colors. He referred to it as the art of deception. Something he really enjoyed about his life. And with the memory capacity of the Sub-Q he remembered not only each and every fib, but the date and time it first passed through his lips.

The remainder of the week was just as much fun, and educational. By day the reports were completed and the class could resume their training losing no more than a few weeks. Even though the time for them that passed was a great deal more. Saturday morning, they were all at breakfast and Brad stood to let the class know it was time to go home and continue their studies. It was a nice break from the monotony of class, but they all knew it had to end sometime, and the sometime was now.

Benjamin continued, "I have one last gift for you all. We are going to attend a Boston Red Sox baseball game tomorrow. I used most of the remaining funds but we will also be sitting on top of the scoreboard. A coveted seat for sure."

The WOWS!...and the OH MANS!...were yelled in the final minutes of the report creation as Benjamin passed on this information. Brad, who never really considered himself a sports fanatic, really enjoyed watching baseball, and especially the Boston Red Sox for some reason. He even ordered and received a bumper sticker that read:

I root for two teams, the Boston Red Sox and anyone playing the Yankee's

*   *   *   *   *   *   *   *

Benjamin paid more than $1,000 for each Green Monster ticket, and managed to get the entire front row after some creative bargaining with the ticket holders he found. The class was extremely excited and was acting like kids, especially Brad! He had a grin on his face that started just behind his left ear and sailed across his face all the way to just behind his right ear.

They all met in the lobby of the hotel and were about to hail two large taxi cabs when the manager of the Marina hotel yelled to Benjamin.

"Sir, Mr. Jensen." He walked up to Benjamin smiling himself. Robert Isabell had not only become a friend to this group who had made this hotel their home for so long, but he, and they, felt as though the term FRIEND was not quite enough to explain how he felt.

"Hi Bob, what's up?"

"I hear tell that you and your group scored seats on the Green Monster!"

"Yep! That we did. All of us are going to sit on row one."

"Well, I know that cost you a pretty penny. I hope the scalpers did not take you for too much?"

"They did, but it was worth it to see the excitement on the faces of this group after all the hard work they put in."

"Can I offer you our shuttle van? We can drop you off at Gate 'C' and pick you up after the game."

"EXCELLENT! Yes, thank you."

*   *   *   *   *   *   *   *

As the van arrived at Gate C, Lansdowne was one very crowded street. The group entered the gate and showed their GM pass. They had to climb a LOT of steps but it paid off as they once again saw the sky. Taking their seats in row number one, no one could believe it; even Brad and Benjamin were excited.

This entire group knew the outcome of the game as well as any highlights, but still, just being here was exciting. Wendel and Will asked everyone to record what they see, hear, smell, and experience. They had a side report they wanted to write on the FAN-atics of sports fans in the early 21st century, focusing on team sports with baseball as the main theme. So, everyone turned on their brain camera's and had as much fun as possible. The footage of the game would be edited later.

During the game Mike Lowell, third baseman, collided with Doug Mientkiewicz, first baseman for the Yankee's. Doug Mientkiewicz was trying to catch a throw from Derek Jeter, short stop, and he and Lowell crashed into each other. Mientkiewicz suffered a mild concussion and a fractured bone in his right wrist; he was placed on the disabled list and ended up missing three months of the season.

Lowell was no worse for incident and went on to have his best season in 2007, topping off the year with the distinction of being the 2007 World Series MVP when the Red Sox won their seventh World Series title.

After the game they found their way to the field and just looked at it. Nothing exists like it in their world, so this is a tremendous example of what Earth needs to return to, a simpler and greener time…greener lifestyle.

A few of the players were walking around on the field and they asked if they could take a picture with them. Thankfully, Wendel bought a digital camera during one side trip he was making; he wanted to NOT appear odd staring at people, places and things. He still used the camera on images so he can get the realistic grain effect in the image, to bring some realism to his report. He passed the camera around and everyone took pictures with the players.

As they left Gate 'C' the van was waiting for them on the crowded street. They all piled in and the driver that delivered them to the stadium picked them up and brought them to the Salem Hotel in less than an hour. The ride was only about 25 miles, but traffic after the game was intense.

As they each piled out of the van they each shook the hand of the driver. In their palm was a nice tip. Each of the 11 passengers gave him a $50 bill and a heartfelt thank you. They really had no need for the cash any longer so they wanted to either spend it or give it away. The driver made nearly $800 in tips since Benjamin and Brad each gave him double of the rest of the class members.

The driver never looked at the bills he was receiving, simply said thank you and put them into a pocket to be viewed and counted at a later time when he was alone. Brad wanted to be a fly on the wall when he looked at his tips. The man was gonna scream!

They had come to know most of the staff, at least a little and opted for a final meal at the hotel restaurant. Class members ordered their favorite foods, such as Traditional Fish and Chips, Grilled Mahi Mahi, Potato Encrusted Salmon, Waterfront Mac & Cheese, and full racks of BBQ Babyback Rack of Ribs. The appetizer, of course, was 11 orders of the Crock of Wharf "Chowda".

Afterwards Brad paid the tab and everyone left a Twenty Dollar bill next to their plate. True the 18% gratuity was already added on to the bill, so the three servers who serviced that group did manage to make out quite well.

Bob stopped by the table while they were enjoying their coffee and dessert and sat with them for a few minutes.

"We are going to miss you all a lot! Some of the best and oddest visitors we have had in a while. I am very glad I took the chance on Mr. I-Want-To-Pay-In-Cash over here," Pointing at Benjamin, "You people are nuts." The whole table erupted in laughter.

Benjamin handed him two envelopes. One marked housekeeping and one marked desk.

"Bob, please deliver this envelope to the housekeeping leader, and when the desk staff is all assembled you can open this envelope. Just a little something as a thank you from all of us to all of you."

The hotel manager accepted the envelopes and put them into an inside pocket of his suite jacket and nodded to everyone and asked Brad, "So what did you order for dessert?"

Brad grinned at him, "Everything…..twice"

"Pardon?" Bob asked.

"Well, the menu had six dessert choices on it so we ordered two of each. Everyone will get a little taste of each one if they desire, with the exception of Benjamin over here that is. He ordered an additional Fried Cheesecake for himself."

Benjamin winked, "I know what I like already!! Also, I ordered an extra Espresso Crème Brule, what I don't finish I'll pass on to the vultures." After everyone heard that he was pelted with balled up napkins.

"You do realize that this is the hardest the cooks have worked in a while?" Bob smiled at Benjamin.

"Yep, took care of them already. And believe me, it was worth it!"

Chapter 11

Welcome Home

Brad and Benjamin left their building and realized the air was downright cold. They looked at each other and laughed, both were thinking about their sub-arctic campout. The reports had all been filed, the class has resumed its standard training program, and Mr. Winchester deemed this experimental course a complete success and asked Benjamin and Brad if they would like to be a regular instructor for this course, the Art of Impromptu Thinking and not getting noticed.

Brad suggested that one seasoned researcher, such as Benjamin, should partner with someone in the current class who graduates and becomes a skillful researcher to instruct the next class. That person from the current class will become the lead in the subsequent class, thereby creating a permanent base of additional instructors, and fresh ideas and capabilities. It was adopted and Benjamin was teaching in two years again, but the question is who will he be teaching with? Ruth? Hoshi? Will? LaVarr? Trip? He would not know until that time comes, so for now he did nothing.

For the next few months Brad was just about attached at the hip to Benjamin, and visa versa. They received assignments… both very short, and not so short. Orbital Pod jumps to catch a ride to the Moon, Mars, Jupiter, and other points; jumps to follow and chronicle a specific day of John Wilkes Booth, Babe Ruth, Adolph Hitler, Lee Harvey Oswald, Jack Ruby, Amelia Earhart, and Christa McAuliffe. There was also a series of assignments to research Kareem Abdul Jabbar, Magic Johnson, Tim Tebow, Doug Mientkiewicz, and Derek Jeter. All sports figures and all for different reasons. Biggest research question that needed to be answered was, what do you do when you are on the disabled list?

He and Brad were at the same game when he and the gang all sat on the Green Monster. He saw them all up there having fun, but stayed out of their camera view. They were there for another purpose and were sitting in the bleachers.

But after spending so much time with the group that is just about ready to complete their training, Benjamin discovered he truly missed teaching, or rather imparting his knowledge and experience to the younger class. Brad, on the other hand, disliked technology and would rather be back anywhere on the first longest term assignment he could find.

The beep that emanated from the desk seemed as though it was breaking the trance they both seemed to be in, staring off to a place only they could see. Pressing the toggle, "Jorgen here."

"Mr. Jorgen, is Mr. Jensen with you?"

"Yes I am." Benjamin added.

"Good, please report to security. We have two assignments that need to be completed before dawn." The channel closed.

Brad and Benjamin looked at each other for a second. Not a question but that look a dog will give you when you think he is trying to ask you just what on Earth you are?

Rising, they left their now joined walled office and headed for the lift. Not realizing it was headed up, and they needed to go down, they pressed the override and scanned their ID card. The lift stopped, and began to descend. Bypassing all floors on its way.

"HEY! What the hell is going on, I have a meeting I am going to be late for!" The voice from the back of the lift yelled.

Benjamin knew that voice and a small, sinister smile creeped over his face. Brad saw it and got scared. He knew that look, it was bad…..someone was going to get pissed off at him….US….before it was over.

"Ma'am, we need to commandeer this lift. Archive business." Without turning around, Benjamin spoke to the front of the car.

"What the hell do you think I am doing, my nails?" The old woman yelled back.

As the car slowed to a stop at the lowest floor in the building, the woman realized she was dealing with someone who was more important than she was; after all, her clearance did not authorize her to go to this level.

The doors opened and Brad and Benjamin exited the car. As he did, Benjamin said to her, "Ma'am, I now return the use of this car to you." He pressed the top floor button, where she was originally heading, but his hand slid down the panel and a dozen or so other floors illuminated. "Oops…!" he uttered in a low voice.

"Asshole!" She cried back as the doors began to close.

Benjamin turned around at that moment and gave an ever so slight grin and wave to her. Her head followed the doors as they closed; she had the look of disbelief in her eyes.

"Was that nice….." Brad asked Benjamin as they approached the security entrance.

"No," Benjamin responded. "But it was fun! I think she recognized me…."

Entering the security briefing room Benjamin and Brad saw the table had only two empty seats. Taking it as a sign they sat in those two empty seats.

Will was in attendance and spoke first, after a nod from his supervisor, the director of Security, "Activating Security Systems." The room was buttoned up tightly, not even a stray electron could escape unless it was supposed to, "The following information is classified and cannot be divulged outside this room."

"Gentlemen, there has been a breech in the timeline and you two may be the only ones who can verify. What do you know about the early 21st Century space program?"

Benjamin opened his mouth to speak at the same time Brad gestured to him as-if to take the floor, "Everything." He said it plainly, clearly, and with no arrogance in his voice. It was a simple fact, not bragging.

"I am aware of that, but I wanted validation. What can you tell me about an astronaut by the name of Lisa Nowak?"

Brad looked at Benjamin, "You got this one?"

Nodding to his best friend, "Yep." Turning to the table he began, "Lisa Maria Nowak, born May 10, 1963, she flew aboard a July 2006 Space Shuttle mission I believe, a robotics mission specialist if I remember correctly. But in early February of 2007 she was arrested in Orlando, Florida for the attempted kidnapping of another astronaut – Captain….uh….Shipman, can't remember her first name at the moment. Shipman was romantically involved with astronaut Bill Oefelein and Nowak had a jealous streak and was obsessed to the point of wearing an astronaut diaper and driving non-stop from Texas to Orlando to kidnap Shipman. The news media focused on the fact she wore the space diaper for some odd reason and referenced it at the drop of a hat. She was booted out of the Navy in 2010."

Will started to speak, "Close enough. Here is the problem. Nowak was an astronaut in 2015 and finagles her way to the first Mars Mission a few years later…."

"She was not even an astronaut in 2015, and never was associated with NASA after the incident, nor was she EVER associated with the Planet Mars." Brad interjected.

"….IF…I may continue…" Brad nodded in apology to Will who essentially ignored the gesture, "Captain Shipman seems to have fallen off the face of the Earth, as in there is no record of her being born. Someone, somewhere in time, saw fit to delete her. Your assignment is to correct this error in the timeline. You have prudence, and an open authorization. Depart at your discretion, but fix this as soon as possible."

The remainder of the briefing consisted of the normal importance, and rhetoric; Will was listed as the operator / control for this assignment so the three of them would need to work together.

"One last thing," Brad asked, "You said there were two assignments?"

"You will receive the second assignment when you return from this one."

It appears that Will, Brad, and Benjamin were all in transit when the timeline change occurred so the three of them all remember history in the same way. The room emptied out and only Brad, Benjamin, and Will were left in the room.

Benjamin smiled and said, "Well Mr. Jorgen, shall we go save all of history again?"

Brad looked at Benjamin and smiled back, "Sure thing Mr. Jensen. One more time just for fun!"

Will stood up and glared at them both, "Idiots!"

Benjamin and Brad nodded in agreement, and followed it with a few "YUP's". Hurrying to catch up to Will, they were following him out of the room. Will turned left and they turned right, in the elevator. As the doors closed Brad looked at Benjamin with a playful, but serious, look.

"You got any idea how we are going to pull this off?"

"Nope! You?"

"No clue" Brad replied

For the next several weeks Brad and Benjamin performed a great deal of research on the Shipman family and discovered that it was due to a kidnapping in the hospital shortly after she was born. The baby was never found and the parents never had other children after the incident.

Brad and Benjamin discovered the exact date and time of the kidnapping and were dressed as police officers visiting a friend on another floor. They just happen to be in the exact right place at the exact right time and using the Sub-Q to scan all frequencies they tapped into the kidnapper's conversation. There were three of them. Brad and Benjamin each wore a stunner on their wrist, but the service revolver they each carried contained the same stun capability.

Once they knew they were in the hospital and about to perform the deed, they activated the anti-jump device so they were trapped in this timeframe. Brad stood in the nursery and waited, dressed as though he was a doctor or a male nurse or something.

Benjamin was dressed like a cop, but off duty and very casual about it. He saw them approaching the nursery and let Brad in on the conversation and the video so he knew who to look for when they entered the nursery.

The moment they entered Brad approached the trio and identified himself as a Temporal Agent. The look on their face told him they were trying to jump but the block was working perfectly. Once they realized it was futile, they began to run out of the room and that is when Benjamin drew his revolver and fired three rapid shots. Since it was not a real pistol, there was nothing but a soft thud as the plasma impacted their bodies and scrambled their neural pathways for about eight hours.

Brad came strolling out with a couple gurneys and they put the smaller two guys on one, and the woman on the other. They draped a sheet over their faces and began to roll them down the hall.

Rolling them down to the morgue they commandeered an ambulance and departed for a place where they could talk freely.

Six hours later they were in a wooded area with no one around for a hundred miles. They lit a small campfire and started cooking, only after removing three metal chairs they grabbed at the hospital from the ambulance and a coil of rope. They proceeded to tie them to the chairs and there was absolutely no way they were going to escape from this confinement.

After they ate a nice dinner, the bad guys started to come around. The woman was the first. She was mad, mad enough to gnaw through her arm to get away if she could reach it.

"Good morning Sunshine!" Brad said in a VERY jovial manner.

She looked at him and if she had lasers in her eyes, he would be a puddle right now. She glanced over to her partners and saw them still unconscious. She was starting to contact her home base but something appeared to be wrong with her temporal communications device. She did not know that her captors could listen in on her conversations.

She attempted to place a call through her SubQ to someone named Rufus Willicot, and he replied to her.

"Where are you?"

"No idea. Some jerk has us tied to chairs around a campfire but has not said a word to us yet, just looks at us as if waiting for us to say the first word."

"Good. Keep quiet, I'll be right there. I am homing in on your signal. See you in ten minutes." She smiled at Benjamin, not a happy smile but the odd smile you see when a sadistic boy is about to pull the wings off a fly.

Benjamin smiled back and stood to get another cup of coffee. As he sat back in the comfy camp chair he and Brad were using, he heard something behind him. Thankfully, the woman did not consider they were temporal agents, or more precisely the short term memory of the moment or so before the stun blast hit them was obliterated from her mind.

A few seconds later a man walked into the campsite and held an interesting looking weapon on Benjamin. Benjamin said, "Hello, can I help you?"

The man looked at him and pointed to the woman and the other two and said, "Release them, now. Or I will have to shoot you!"

Benjamin resettled into his chair and appeared to get more comfortable, and then he spoke softly. "Mr. Willicot, may I call you Rufus?" Both the woman and Rufus were taken with shock that he knew his name. "I am going to give you the count of three to lower and put the thing away, or you will be as unconscious as your henchmen over there?"

Rufus looked at him with sever scrutiny, he raised the pistol thing and leveled it at Benjamin. That was the last thing he did before he crumpled to the ground in a mangled mess, like the puppet master simply let go of the stings on the marionette.

Brad appeared out of thin air, removed the stealth suit, and sat in his place next to Benjamin. The woman then looked at him and asked, "What timeframe are you from?"

"Funny" Benjamin said, "I was about to ask you the exact same thing."

They spent nearly four days in that campsite and with the exception of providing the four a bit of water, Benjamin and Brad ate and drank well. Steak, pork chops, baked potato, plenty of coffee and snacks galore.

Their prisoners, on the other hand, received a slice of bread every 6 hours, 32 ounces of water during the course of the day, and were never released from the chairs so, they smelled ripe.

Finally, Rufus cracked and let it all out. The four of them were contracted to get the baby and pop home with no one seeing them either do it, or depart. For the task they would each be set up for life somewhere safe, secluded, and comfortable.

Brad asked why that particular child. One of the other two added that the boss wanted a very smart kid, genius level. Obviously, this guy's IQ just above that of a single celled organism. Once they had all the information Brad departed and returned a moment later. Will was with him and he brought a few friends. Since they had no idea why their retrieval signal was not working, the moment when Brad departed Benjamin deactivated the dampening field, they did not leave and if they had any brains they could have done so.

Will and his three friends walked over to the bad guys and stunned then with a maximum blast. Brad deactivated the field and the eight of them departed. Brad and Benjamin spent the night and brought the ambulance back and parked it right where they got it from, even putting the key in its place above the driver's visor and filling the gas tank.

They left the parking area and walked down the street and into an alley. Once out of site, they returned home.

* * * * * * * * * * * * * * *

As they appeared in the chamber, security instantly sprang into action. Will opened the communication channel and asked, "So where were you two?"

Brad and Benjamin laughed a small laugh at the irony of it all, "Scan this person and deactivate their Sub-Q until further notice. Authorization 4-4-2."

Will was about to protest Benjamin giving him an order, but when he heard the 4-4-2 he stopped and did as he was instructed. They had knowledge about history or specific events that he did not, therefore, unless he was instructed otherwise, what they said in this matter was law.

"The person is Simon Cratorinni, according to the archive database; he was born about an hour ago." Using the genetic imprint, the SubQ takes and downloading it made for easy work to ID the person. Verifying Identity was standard procedure when returning from a jump. After all, the missions are stored by your trace readings and not filenames in the event you were returned in a less than talkative manner, or worse. "I need to log the mission since the two of you are supposedly not on an assignment at the moment."

"Standby..." Brad transmitted the files to Will's console.

"Holy crap, a 4-4-2 for this? This guy is in trouble." Will said jokingly.

It was the first time in a long time he heard Will say anything humorous and he wondered what was going on. Brad looked at Benjamin and said, "A joke?"

Walking out of the chamber Benjamin handed Will the prisoner. He also handed him an old fashioned handcuff key and smiled.

As they walked off, they talked between themselves, "So, you can add it to your reports, his SubQ has been adminkeyed, he is on his way to the penal facility orbiting Uranus, and there is a briefing in 30-minutes in the Security Conference Room. Who needs to be there?

Brad began, "Let's see, your boss, My boss….."

Benjamin took over, "Us, you," Talking to Will Carter, "the files in the upload, perhaps the committee." He smiled at Will who smiled back at him. "See you there in thirty." Benjamin and Brad turned and left, the prisoner was placed in a transport tube after being stunned with a maximum charge. Safer for all concerned. With his SubQ placed in an off state, there was nothing he could do anyway.

After a shower and a change of clothes, Brad and Benjamin left the locker room and headed for the elevator on their way to Security. Stopping for a quick bite to eat they grabbed a meat pie and a soft drink from the lobby cart.

Martha was back, "How is your daughter?" Benjamin asked.

"Fine I guess. Her third child is due this month, and after the birth they all plan to visit poor old grandma for a few days."

"Where is she living?" Benjamin asked.

"Lunar surface. She works in Admin and Johnny works are some kind of maintenance person of something for Jorgen Mining. He really hates his boss."

Brad piped in, "Why's that?"

She opened up to him, as if all she was waiting for was someone to ask. "That boss of his, Joseph Bartholomew Relensky. He gets his workers involved with a project and just before it's finished he turns it in like he did all the work. Johnny should have been promoted but this guy, he goes by the name R-sky seemed to find a weak link in the Jorgen family and weaseled his way into the cushy position. Huge raise, lots of bennies, and no labor. Johnny on the other hand is no spring chicken and was looking forward to leading the team, same he has been with for almost 10 years. They know and respect him. Believe me; if all those people had a choice of pushing a button to stop this Rsky guy from being blown into space or something, they may need to sleep on it before they make the decision, if you hear what I'm saying."

"I do, believe me, I do. Let me see what I can do." Brad said to her. "But never tell him you said anything to me about it, OK?"

"Sure, but what can you do?"

"Let's just say I have some clout with the Jorgen family. I will see if they will look into the matter discreetly. What is your son-in-laws name?"

"Jonathon Walters"

She nodded and handed them their food, Benjamin dropped some currency on the cart and she tried to hand it back, thanking them for the chance to just listen to her. Benjamin put it into her apron pocket, smiled, and walked off fast enough so she was not able to give it back. She pulled the cash out and looked at it, 100 credits, for a three-credit purchase. She always liked Ben and Brad, but now she knew they thought a lot of her.

Brad, on the other hand, pulled out his portacomm and made the call. Speaking to his father, Brad filled him in on the situation he heard from Martha regarding this R-sky fellow and Johnny. His father let Brad know he would look into it in the morning. Brad knew for a fact he would, his dad was a man of his word.

* * * * * * * * * * * * * * *

The briefing went well; Simon had gone back and changed time so Colleen Shipman was never born. He did not kill anyone but rather ensured that her parents never met. In temporal law, creating a situation that negates the life of a person either directly or indirectly by the manipulation of historical events thereby an individual is not born is a crime of manslaughter under extreme circumstances. Simon was sentenced to life in the prison, and when he applies for a position, they would know.

He was from about 45 years in the future and after he was sentenced, he told all. He worked on the island and got bored. Therefore, he would pick an event in history and make a minor change just to see what it does. Then if the new version is worse than the old, he would go back and undo what he did. He was about to undo this 'What If' when he was caught.

For the next couple of days, the temporal friends had no duties, no assignments, nothing to do. Benjamin decided to have a party and Brad attended, at least for a little while. The class was on break and a few of them made an appearance at the event.

Brad showed them all a new holo he just designed; it was a space flight scene. They all instantly recognized it as the transition from normal to hyper light velocities. No one said anything but they looked at him and smiled. He understood they knew what it was, and was thankful they stayed silent.

Brad had a chirp from his portacomm and read the message. Mom and Dad want him on the Moon, at the mine, tomorrow at 10pm. They are promoting Johnny to director of the section and since he helped to discover the situation they wanted him there also.

A few of the other guests asked where he found this holo, and his answer was he discovered it during research. One of the class members opened the information about the image and noticed Benjamin had removed all of the original location and

294

localization data, and replaced it with data that made it appear it was created in a room on solid ground.

The party was great; everyone had a blast and left about three in the morning. Brad did not feel like going back to his place so he crashed on Benjamin's couch. It was very comfortable after all. On Sunday morning the automaids crew entered and did not see him right away, at least not until they pulled the blanket off him, he was covered from head to toe after all. The young woman that pulled it off to fold it up literally jumped back a good solid meter, and since Brad was already awake, all he did was smile.

"OH! Sorry sir. I was not aware there was anyone sleeping on the sofa."

"Not a problem. I really need to get upstairs to my place anyway. I have a few things I need to do today."

"Ok, is there anything you need us to take care of?"

"No, except…" looking up at the ceiling slightly, "Computer, activate program annoy Benjamin."

The young ladies looked baffled.

PROGRAM RUNNING, the computer responded.

A moment later Benjamin emerged from the bedroom and walked directly over to the couch where he saw Brad. Brad was sitting there in the middle of the couch laughing and the two young ladies were standing on either side of the couch. Benjamin was standing directly in from of Brad.

"OK, WHY!! ??" Benjamin yelled. After a few moments, Brad broke into uncontrolled, fall of the couch, laughter. Benjamin just stared at him for a second then realized there were two very beautiful women standing in his apartment, or actually cleaning up his apartment. A moment went by then he realized he was completely, absolutely, stark naked. The moment he realized it, the women started laughing also. The situation was very odd, "Uh, well, I will be right back." He walked back into the bedroom and got dressed. The three in the living room simply continued to laugh.

As he departed the women applauded and whistled.

* * * * * * * * * * * * * * *

Benjamin was now cleaned, dressed, and less vulnerable so to speak. Brad was still dressed in what he had on the night before; the women had finished cleaning up and were putting away what arrived from the auto fill of the refrigerator and the cabinets. They were just about finished with their work when Benjamin returned. Brad was still sitting on the couch watching an old western drama about a single father and his three son's exploits in the Wild West. He really needed to get back there.

"Better?" Benjamin asked.

"Yes." All three responded.

"Well, we are finished and we need to move on to our next location. Thanks for the laugh. And just so you know we were laughing at the situation, but I can honestly say we were impressed." The last part she put a hand on her hip and slowly looked him up and down. Benjamin smiled, shook his head, and started to say something but nothing came out.

All he managed to say was, "Thanks" and the girls left.

Looking at Brad, who turned off the screen and was watching this whole interaction as if watching a strange comedy program, he said to him, "Happy?"

Brad replied, "Uh huh!" and smiled again.

"So, what are we doing today?"

"Well, I need to go upstairs and shower and change, then we have an appointment on the Moon."

"We do?"

"Yep. My dad let me know last night that he fired the manager and will be promoting Johnny to the position and he wants me…or rather us…there. He thinks you are his long lost son or something. Oh crap, that kinda makes us related or something."

"Let's see, that either makes you my younger brother by calendar age, or my older brother by temporal age." Benjamin was three days older than Brad if you strictly go by the date they were born, but Brad has spent a great deal more time in the past and therefore experienced a lot more actual time than Benjamin.

"One last thing I need to do," Brad said into the air, "Computer, contact Maria at the travel agency and put it on the screen."

"Hello. Brad…Benjamin…..to what do I owe this pleasure?"

Brad outlined that he wanted to buy a ticket to the Moon for Martha, transportation to the terminal and first class seating and accommodations once she arrived on the Moon. She needed to NOT have any idea as to who paid for this trip. Brad wanted her there at the promotion party knowing full well she would not be able to get there on her own. Ticket prices are a bit more than she could afford. He also needed two seats, for him and Benjamin, on the next flight. All seats First Class.

Maria terminated the connection and while Brad was getting dressed, he received a message it was all taken care of. Limo to the terminal, priority seating on the shuttle at 6pm tonight, best room available in the main dome, and private drive on the Moon to the mine – about an hour ride – to surprise her daughter and son-in-law.

No one knows what the gala event is for tomorrow night, which all employees and family are invited to a dinner and discussion at the cafeteria at the mine at 7pm. Brad was satisfied with what Mom and Dad had planned. A full round of awards to the employees, recognition of certain teams and milestones, then three promotions.

In the process of investigating the situation with Johnny and his former manager, they learned of the same situation in two other work areas and after everyone left for the evening terminated the employment of the three who are not conducive to a good and healthy work environment. At this point, none of the employees are aware the three were let go, who are already on their way back to Earth. Everyone was given time off until the day after the Annual Gala Event, as they are referring to it as.

When Martha knocked on her daughter's door, she was nervous, and excited. Her baby girl – extremely pregnant – opened the door and nearly screamed. "MOMMY!"

They had a great visit that afternoon and dressed for the event. She had no clue how she got there and did not look a gift horse in the mouth. One of the other people who were being promoted at the party, Julie Williams, also received her parents as a gift, but no one had any idea as to how or why they received a ticket. The third person being promoted, Marcia Reynolds sadly had no family. She also lacked any real friends so essentially she was alone.

When Benjamin and Brad arrived at the Jorgen residence, Brad's mother threw her arms out and yelled SON! She hugged Benjamin and Brad stood there shaking his head. "OH! You too…" She said to him in jest.

They had a great visit and when it came time for the dinner, Benjamin invited Marcia to sit at his table. She really had no idea who they were, only that they worked at the archives and were very nice. Ramona was there, catering of course.

Each table had seating for four, six, or eight diners. The table where Brad and Benjamin were sitting was up front, close to the stage. Marcia felt a bit uncomfortable but it went away after a glass of wine. Ramona put several bottles on each table to be used as they saw fit.

Dinner was served and was very good. Three choices, meat choices were beef or chicken, fish, or vegetarian. No one took her up on the vegetarian choice and she was somewhat shocked at that. The meat and fish meals were divided evenly among everyone.

At Benjamin and Brad's table, Brad had the steak, Marcia had the chicken, and Benjamin had the fish. They all shared a piece of their meal with each other and talked and became friends in a way. She still had no real clue as to who Brad was or why he was here. She would shortly…..

Brad and Benjamin walked over and said hello to Martha and her family. She wondered why they were there but never asked. She introduced her daughter Margaret and her son-in-law Jonathon Walters to Brad and Benjamin, her favorite customers.

"Ladies, gentlemen, and honored guests." Brad's father stood at the podium. "I would like to welcome you all to this first of many company events. I plan to do this twice a year if for no other reason than to give you all a chance to relax, have a good meal and have a good time." He paused for a moment then continued when the light applause died off. Brad and Benjamin took their seats again.

"First and foremost, I am giving each person, each employee, in this room a 500 credit bonus in the next pay check." The room bust into hoot, hollers, and very intense applause. "Don't count on that at every meeting though." Everyone laughed.

Mr. Jorgen put his hands up and everyone quieted. Allow me to introduce you to my family. This is my wife Rebecca, My son Billy….oh, I mean William." They all laughed at the joke. "My daughter Rhonda. The four of us all work here at this mine and at other mining locations around the solar system. But, I also have one other son, Brad. Stand up and admit you know me son." He said it jokingly. Brad stood and waved to everyone. Martha looked him in the eye; a complete state of shock was on her face. "He chose to not be a part of the mine, but rather took a different route. He is a researcher at Archive Island and, from what I hear, a pretty damn good one. Lastly, there is a young man that has become like a son to me, Benjamin Jensen. He is a bad influence on my wonderful son Brad, but hopefully Brad can keep him out of trouble." Benjamin stood and waved to everyone, then blew 'DAD' a kiss. Dad shook his head and the crowd laughed softly.

Brad and Benjamin looked at Marcia and had no idea why the odd look on her face was so, odd. Looking at Brad, "Jorgen?"

She said slowly. Brad nodded. She was in shock at the idea she was at a table with one of the Jorgen family.

"OK, now the real reason I am here. This morning I terminated three employees because they were not conducive to a productive environment. I terminated Ralph Watson, Dennis Floyd, and Katrina Stepsin. They are already back on Earth looking for work. My son, Brad, brought to my attention that there may be issues in management and that the people in charge may not be the best person for the job. My son and daughter did some investigating and discovered some sad news. The three that were terminated were not looking out for their people, and had no other goal but to make themselves look good, and collect a profit for themselves, therefore, they are no longer employed with Jorgen Mining. So that leaves a hole in management."

Pausing again to collect his thoughts and make things more dramatic, "Marcia Reynolds, can you please come up here." She walked up to the front. "I want everyone in this room to know that you are being promoted not to supervisor, but to director of your department. Everyone we spoke to said you were the best. So, as an accounting director, you will need to promote and hire a replacement for not only your old position, but also the person who you will need to promote to supervisor. I understand no one has had that position and the previous director was essentially micromanaging the department. Therefore, you are the new accounting director. Congratulations!" Everyone applauded and Marcia looked in shock. He motioned for her to step to the side but stay up front for the time being.

"Julie Williams, can you please join me." She stood and walked to the front, equally in shock as Marcia was a few moments earlier. "My understanding is that you kept the logistics department operating under some very tight budgetary constraints. Did you know the restraints you were working under were that of your former director? Not us…" Motioning to his family. "As such, we are in dire need of people with your talents, therefore, I am making you a…no scratch that, THEE Logistics Director for Jorgen Mining. My son will be glad to step aside in this department and give this duty up to you. He has enough things on his plate as it is." His son appeared to look relieved, and Julie stared out at the crowd without seeing anyone. He congratulated her and she stepped back next to Marcia.

"We have one more promotion, and yes, it is the director of mining operations. John Walters, your turn." Johnny walked up to the front to receive his honors.

"Johnny, we spoke to a lot of people that worked WITH you, and they all admitted that they would not mind it so much if they were able to work FOR you. So, you are now the Mining Practice Manager, Director of Mining Operations.

"You all do realize that with this new position you are forced to move. Since the three of you are now directors and not regular employees any longer, you will be living in Hab One, which is connected to the Admin complex where your offices will be located. You will each have at your disposal a hover car so you can get around on the surface as you need to, checking up on things and making sure everything runs smoothly. Also, each quarter you will be required to take a 10-day trip Earth-side for the quarterly conference where you will provide a report to the stockholders. And yes, since the shuttle there and back is owned by us, families are included. Lastly, and sadly, I am so sorry to inform you, all three of you are required to attend an annual banquet for prospective customers and vendors on our station orbiting Saturn. There are times during that banquet I would rather be digging myself. But, what can you say. Someone has to pay the piper. Now, the three of you will be right alongside of me offering your time and sacrificing your valued brain cells to the happiness and joy of the investors." Applause and laughter filled the room.

As Marcia returned to the table, Brad and Benjamin stood and made a Marcia sandwich. It was a big hug and she really needed it at that moment. Benjamin thought she was a very nice person and he thought he would like to get to know her better, as a friend actually and not a lover.

The rest of the evening was music, drink, dancing, and fun. Brad and Benjamin walked over to Martha and her family to congratulate Johnny, and Martha stood first as they walked over and popped them both on the arm.

"So, a Jorgen huh! Do I need to start calling you sir now?" She said playfully. Her daughter was shocked that she spoke to them in this way. That was evident by the looks on her, and her husbands, face.

"If you do I'll never eat at your cart again…" Brad laughed back at her.

They talked for a few minutes and Benjamin spoke to the group, "Can I invite all of you for lunch a La Chandra tomorrow? The owner is a really close friend, and Brad and I need to get back to work soon. Besides, Brad's buying!" That took them all by surprise.

"I am. Why am I buying?" Brad asked, knowing full well what the answer was going to be.

"Because you're rich!" Benjamin said flatly.

"Oh, OK." Was all Brad answered. The other three at the table were truly amazed at the way these two talked to each other, they really did seem like they were brothers.

* * * * * * * * * * * * * * *

Lunch went well. Ramona brought a few bottles of Ben's Friendship out for the table and just had to let everyone know how she came up with the name for the wine, and one extra special bottle out for the pregnant woman. "Margaret, this bottle tastes exactly like the other bottles but with one very important exception, it contains no alcohol. A new line I am bringing out in a couple months. Now that you are here and not able to imbibe in the normal drink, I am hoping you will test this out for me and let me know what you think." Margaret was amazed that she was getting something so new, and that her opinion counted so highly by this woman. The owner of not only this establishment, but many more.

"Not sure what qualifies me for such an honor. But, sure. I'll give it a try."

"Well, if you are here with Benjamin and Brad, you have got to be someone to be trusted. I know these two, and although THEY can't be trusted as far as I can throw Benjamin….uh, except on the Moon that is….then you must be a wonderful person."

Ramona poured her a glass of the alcohol free wine and she tasted it. "This is good!"

She passed the glass to her husband and he had a taste. "This tastes exactly like the this one" pointing to his "But it has no alcohol?"

"Nope!" Ramona nodded to them and walked away.

The others around the table all wanted to taste it but did not ask for the glass. Brad decided that the three promoted people and their families should also be invited to this meal, with Brad and Benjamin to escort Marcia since she had no family.

Ramona asked, "So Margaret, I am having trouble thinking up a name for this stuff, any ideas?"

She thought for a moment, "Mom's Delight!" She replied.

"Hey, I like that!!" Ramona looked at her. "Well then, Mom's Delight it is. I'll give it a subtitle of 'Endorsed by Margaret Walters and Mom's everywhere', what do you think?"

"You want to put my name on a bottle of wine? Really?"

"Sure. I put his on a bottle." Pointing to Benjamin and then to the bottle of Ben's Friendship on the table that everyone was drinking. Now she had to explain the name of the wine again.

Dinner was wonderful, and afterwards Benjamin had a great idea. "How about some dome time?"

After lunch Brad paid the check, Ramona walked over with the check and looked at Benjamin but handed the check directly to Brad. "I had an idea this was all your idea" she said to Benjamin "So I figured that Brad would be paying the bill. Now, YOU need to leave a tip for your server, she put up with a lot from you."

"Touché" The others at the table laughed at the way these people played off each other. Benjamin pulled a bunch of credits out of his pocket and began counting it off. Ramona just grabbed the entire thing and said to him, "That should do!" He nodded and "OK".

Marcia asked, "How much was that?"

"No clue, but I think it was more than enough. Now, let's go fly!"

"I have never done this before." Marcia admitted

"Neither have I" Several of the others also added.

They were walking to the flight dome as they were talking. When they entered Benjamin yelled at the man in the place.

"TIM!"

Tim walked over to the group and as he was approaching he looked at Benjamin, "SON!"

"Son?" Benjamin replied.

"Sure, I call you son cause you're so bright" The group laughed. Jan, on the other hand, saw Benjamin and left the snack bar and ran over to him. Since it was low gravity she leapt and flew like supergirl and hit Benjamin like a sack of rice, knocking them both to the ground.

Standing, Benjamin looked at Tim and said, "Can you please remove this?" Pointing to Jan who had him in an arms and legs bear hug. Tim grabbed Jan and pulled, "OK honey, you need to let go of the strange man now." Jan let go and laughed.

Benjamin introduced the group and Tim and Jan. Jan spoke first, "Uh, I really don't think you should be flying right now." Pointing to Margaret's belly. "we don't have a set of wings for two yet."

"I have no intention of flying at the moment, although some day I would love to try it."

"After the baby is born and you are ready, you get a flight on me." Jan told her. "But for now, let me get you a nice cool glass of lemonade and you can watch these lunatics act like children."

They had a blast. Margaret and Jan sat and chatted; Benjamin and Brad played chicken and got everyone else to join in on the game. Martha had fun and it was her first time. She did really well.

While Benjamin was showing off his portacomm rang, as did Brad's. It threw off their concentration and they ended up crashing into each other. Everyone heard the ringing, and saw the collision, and cringed!

They landed on ledges on opposite sides of the dome about midway up and answered the call. They had to leave; they needed to go back to work.

Chapter 12

Fresh Meat

Brad and Benjamin left their building and made their way to the school auditorium, where graduations took place. The class that Ruth and Monika and all the rest of their new friends were in were finally done with school, and ready to take their place as employees of the Island.

Brad was preparing for a long-term assignment and used Benjamin's circus research as the basis for his jump plan. He would need to select one other person to join him on the mission, and Benjamin knew exactly who that would be.

Benjamin had just returned from a trip, it only lasted an hour. He had to go forward in time a few months. He landed in the same chamber he departed from and asked the operator for the date. Correct target arrival and the door opened.

He walked out of the chamber and walked over to the school, a few minutes away. He entered the school campus and up to the receptionist. "You have an envelope for me, Benjamin Jensen. It should be a Blue One Control."

The receptionist handed him a blue envelope and he accepted it and walked away. Looking around he thought he would see himself since he really wanted to see if he could. Where on Earth am I? He wondered.

He entered a conference room, it was empty and activated a terminal. Punching in his name as a search he saw he was away on an assignment, a long assignment. No specifics there in the file but that was no surprise since he was not logged into the system as himself, he logged in as a generic user, therefore, the file only contained unclassified information. He thought this would be an interesting assignment and could not wait to see what it was going to be. He reset the terminal and popped home.

Leaving the chamber again, he walked up to the same receptionist and handed her the blue envelope. She knew exactly what it was. Thanked him and he left.

He handed her the list of the next class leadership, as voted on and elected the previous evening. These people would get the six rooms reserved for the leadership six. The school had voted and passed the annual referendum a few years ago, which meant that a new class was to begin every year. This should increase the number of researchers, but it also meant that the instructors would be stretched thin. This is the reason a few of the better researchers are, or have been, given the duties of an instructor; like Benjamin Jensen, Brad Jorgen and Will Carter.

Returning to his office to see what else needed to be done he sat and activated his terminal. A message from his mother, she is fine and in the asteroid field have a blast. Finishing up reading the headers of his messages Brad stopped in front of his open door. Without saying a word, he logged off and stood to join his best friend.

Brad and he were on their way to the school to watch their class, the class they helped teach, graduate. He felt proud of them, and happy that he, and Brad, had some small part in their education.

Benjamin heard through the grapevine that Ruth and Bradley were no longer an item. Not sure what happened and he really did not care all that much, just happy that she was available.

Matthew and Ariana were there to take the responsibility for their newest team members. Matthew was receiving Bradley Bentinfield III, Ruth Swisher, and Hoshi Sukiyama. Ariana was receiving LaVarr DuBois, Monika Bordow, and William Walker into the long-term departments. The sad part was that the LT group, outside of the departments, was known as the deep studies group. After all, what could be long term of reading and researching a topic. The last two went to Matthews's group, but not under or near Benjamin; they would be one floor up and considered the instant researchers. Drake Willis and Wendel Willis Washington were in the instant department, slang for the real name of the group; rapid research.

This group, relatively new, did fast and intense research, less than 48 hours from start to finish. The next level was Benjamin, where it was normally a week to several months. The last was Brad's group, several months to several years.

All that was left was Karen Jones. Since the knowledge of the Malkornian race was now common and universal, Karen was accepted into the LT department and given a permanent assignment to the ambassadorial staff. She was named, at the request of the Malkornian Ambassador, as Earth's ambassador to the planet. Her Sub-Q would be an asset since with it she has the ability to telepathically communicate to the people of the planet, or home to upload reports.

The graduation went well, and afterwards the reception was spectacular. Maria Martinez and Will Carter came up to Dora Guntersdottir and asked to speak to her in private. Brad and Benjamin knew exactly what they wanted, and thought Dora would be a perfect addition to Security. In the last four classes, eight years, they acquired a grand total of two new security operatives. The most recent being Dora and the other is …was…

Will Carter. More good people is exactly what security needs, but it is hard to find the right person.

The gathering went on for several more hours, and pretty much everyone was there, except for Mr. Winchester. The last trip he made to a graduation was two classes ago, when Benjamin and Brad's class graduated. No one has been able to exceed Benjamin's reading speed until now.

Benjamin had the honor of passing on the reading trinket. True, it was only a little fob, but it signified that the person in possession of this trinket was and is the fastest reader currently at the academy.

After he was introduced he began, "Two classes ago I received this doodad from the person whom I beat in reading speed. That person is physically not here today, but he is always here." He tapped his chest. "And here." Spreading his arms to encompass the entire room. He continued. "When I received this fob, this token, I received it from the current fastest reader in the history of the school, Mr. Robert Winchester. I am not certain how long he was at the top of the pile, but it had to be a while. When I surpassed his reading speed he actually came to the graduation to pass this little thing on to me, and I really appreciated the fact he did it in person and not by proxy."

He paused for a moment, and then continued, "Mr. Bradley Bentinfield the Third, TRIP as I normally call you. Please come to the front." He waited for Trip to walk from his seat and stand next to him. He looked nervous.

Continuing, "It is also my deep honor to inform you that you have surpassed me in reading capability. According to the last evaluation you had in the class room, your reading capability is 686 words per minute more than mine. I am passing to you the golden novel. This trinket has been a part of this program since its inception. This is a priceless keepsake. Street value is about $3.00; historical value is… who knows. Each person engraves their signature into this award once they receive it." He paused.

"It is the duty of those who possess it to pass it to their successor when their record has been surpassed. I cannot tell you what your actual speed is at this time; you will learn that tomorrow during your school debriefing and employment indoctrination. Suffice it to say, you beat me and I am truly honored to be beaten by you."

He shook Trip's hand and applauded as did the entire room.

* * * * * * * * * * * * * *

"Benjamin Jensen here" Benjamin said as he answered his portacomm. He was on the train on his way to the Island Complex on this wonderfully beautiful Monday morning. The sky was blue and there were no clouds, the air was cool but not cold, T-shirt weather he called it, about 12 or 15 degrees C or so. Knowing that later in the day, it would warm up considerably.

"Yes…..Yes….in about 15 minutes……OK…….I shall be right in once I get to the Island." They terminated the connection.

About ten minutes later the train arrived at the Island station and Benjamin exited quickly. Setting a course for the lift in the next building, not his, he entered that car and pressed the needed floor and went up. He needed to be at Matthews office as fast as possible. He had an assignment for him.

Exiting the elevator on Matthews floor the receptionist simply touched a button and Matthew Sharp's office door slid open and Benjamin went through. As he passed her desk, he gave her a wink and she winked back at him. But this was one time he had not noticed.

As he entered the room, he saw that Matthew was on a call. Benjamin sat in the seat on the 'guest' side of his desk and waited. When Matthew finished the call, "OK, really quick. You got three new recruits last week and you need to make them into functional members as fast as possible. Here are the 4 more critical A-Sheets we have open that seem as though they can be accomplished in the shortest timeframe. Next Monday each of these people under your wing will need to report to a group on their findings."

"You said four?" Benjamin asked.

"Yep, you get one also. Now, I have you on top. The other three you can dole out as you see fit."

Looking at the sheet on top he saw what his next assignment is and realized it was a LOT more than a weeks' worth of work, while at the same time teaching the new people how to do what he did. Thankfully, they had a good start with the class he and Brad taught so there is a good base already laid.

Benjamin looked over the other three assignment sheets and decided at that moment who received which assignment. All four of them were about current events, and nothing in the past need be researched. These were not easy assignments by any stretch of the imagination, but seemed as though they are important.

Matthew received another call and motioned to Benjamin to leave. He did and walked out and into the elevator and down to the ground level. Exiting the car, he walked across the lobby and toward the elevator set that would take him to his office area, but he saw Brad entering the building from the terminal. Benjamin motioned over to Martha's cart and he nodded.

Benjamin arrived at the cart a moment before Brad did, and Martha said hello.

"Benjamin! Good morning. Coffee and an éclair?" Martha asked.

"Coffee yes, but what do you have in the way of a breakfast sandwich?"

"Egg and cheese, egg/cheese/meat is all I have left."

"Egg and cheese, coffee, and yes throw in the éclair."

Brad arrived and Martha perked up a bit. "Mr. Jorgen Sir!" She said with a smile.

"Is my Dad here? If you call me that again, no more tips!" She gave Brad a hug.

"HEY! What am I?" Benjamin said in a sad voice. She gave him a hug also.

"What can I get you?" She winked. "Mr. Brad Sir!" Brad shook his head.

"Whatever he is having is fine." He pointed at Benjamin.

Brad asked, "How's that family?"

She responded, "A lot better. He likes being in charge and actually has an 'open door' policy. If someone has an idea as to how to do something better, they can bring it to him. They'll try it out and evaluate it, it is works, they keep it; if not, they scrap it or modify it."

She handed him his food. "So far, they have all done really well. Lots of new ideas, and the Jorgen's, you know, your family, gets a report on the things and stuff. They love it and are thinking about putting him in charge of the Mining Operations Suggestion Office. He implements stuff all over the place and travels a bit too to see it through."

She paused for a moment, "Although the new job is great, this is a lot of work away from the family but it looks as though it is going to taper off." She winked, "He put in a suggestion for a MOSO at each location. Once they are all filled, all he would need to do is have a weekly call to get reports. Now, he is loving it."

Brad and Benjamin smiled at her and left for their offices.

* * * * * * * * * * * * * * * * *

Arriving at their office Brad realized he needed to move his desk when maintenance arrived a few minutes later to bring his personal stuff to his new office where he will supervise his new recruits. Before he left the shared area Benjamin and he worked in, his portacomm went off. The conversation sounded like the conversation he and Matthew had earlier that morning, and Benjamin knew he was talking to Ariana Kimber.

Brad left to get his new people started on their first assignments. Benjamin called everyone that worked for him into his office and told them to bring a chair. Ruth, Bradley, Hoshi, and Roger all filed in. The other two people assigned to Benjamin had been reassigned to the other teams in Matthews's department. Benjamin had done such a great job training them; they had been promoted and led a couple people now. Roger was the only one left and he was ready to move up as soon as a slot opened.

Benjamin started, "OK, we have 4 assignments, and 5 of us. I was instructed I need to accomplish this one," He pulled and put the sheet on the table, "and you three get the other three. Ruth, here is your assignment."

Ruth accepted the sheet and read it to herself and started laughing. She read it aloud, "You are to find evidence as to if the Earth has been visited by extraterrestrials." They all laughed.

Bradley was next, Benjamin handed him his sheet, "You are to discover if there is evidence of excessive orbital debris in space."

Handing Hoshi her sheet, "You are to search for evidence of interesting items in our solar orbit."

"What's yours?" They all look at Benjamin as Ruth asked.

"Mine is simple. I am to verify and validate the work and reports of the three of you; and in actuality, it is Roger and I on this one. Roger will take Ruth; I will take Bradley and Hoshi. The reports need to be orated next Monday morning at 9am in conference room Delta.

The planning and execution for the jumps were set and they all jumped alone. No one was scheduled to last more than an hour or so, and when Bradley did not return after 11 hours Security was sent back to find him. They discovered he was in the hospital. He appeared in the middle of a large field and was struck by a small motorized vehicle. The driver, or rather rider, immediately called an ambulance and when it arrived they scooped him up and brought him to a medical facility. They saw he had some sort of implanted device in his head, since they took an x-ray of him.

Security walked into his room and removed the IV's and the cardiac monitor, and activated the recall signal. A moment later they were in the chamber and Bradley was being placed on a medical bed and moved to the medical facility. He would be fine in a few hours, just a few broken bones and bruises. He will be sore for a while, but he can live with that.

Another security operative was sent to acquire the recordings made by the hospital staff of the implant. They got them and jumped home. No record of his accident or treatment was left to be seen. Only verbal accounts for the law enforcement officers to focus on, then they will close the case as unsolved a few months later. Bradley cannot jump back to the year 2018 again since if his face is scanned by a camera, and recognized, it could become complicated.

The rest of the reports went well, no incidents were reported, no issues.

The biggest revelation was that there were countless reports of extraterrestrial visits, but very little evidence. A snapshot or two, people with odd burns, stories to be passed on from one generation to another. But nothing hard and conclusive.

Until Roger pointed out a theme in all three reports. All three reports had information about the 1947 Roswell incident and all separate and independent accounts of the same event. Matthew asked Benjamin to look into this incident to see if they could determine if it was the Malkornians; or some other space faring race visiting and exploring the planet Earth.

Benjamin, a millisecond later, looked at Roger and said, "You found it, you take it. Keep me informed and remember one thing, remember our standard."

Matthew looked surprised at Benjamin's passing off of this assignment. He knew how much Benjamin enjoyed the pods and the idea of finding perhaps another new race of beings was appealing to Benjamin, but he also knew that someday Roger would be in charge of this group and Benjamin would be retired, teaching, or not able to continue his work for a variety of reasons.

"I will" Replied Roger.

Roger kept Benjamin updated on the progress of the research, and he pulled Bradley, who was fully recovered, and Ruth into the process. They found everything available on the incident, the moment in history the event occurred, and even some hear-say they needed to check out or filter through. Making a short jump in pods to the timeframe they were concealed and in orbit when the Malkornian ships made their departure with the entire class and Benjamin and Brad attached. A couple hours later they watched another ship phase into being several hundred kilometers away. This ship looked like a large tube and had no indication of propulsion. Since it did not 'fly' into Earth orbit, the assumption was that it phased into being from another place.

The consensus was it traveled interdimensionally, which as far as they are concerned was not possible. A smaller craft exited the cylinder and made its way into the atmosphere. A couple of the pods followed and one stayed up with the larger craft. The larger craft spun and scanned the area of space all around the planet Earth, including an intense scan of the lunar surface.

The scan beam passed over Roger's pod and the systems blinked out for a moment. A minute later the scan beam concentrated a scan directly on the pod. The stealth mode disengaged and the pod was visible, but the systems all appear to be fine. The ship moved physically closer to the pod and Roger got a bit nervous. He could not be caught.

"Bradley! The mothership sees me and is moving towards me. I need to jump home so I am not caught." Roger told Bradley through the Sub-Q.

A second later Roger was gone and the mothership knew it, and returned to its original position. At that moment the smaller craft changed course and grazed Ruth's pod. Ruth was able to maintain control but the alien craft was not able to make it into orbit again and crashed in the dessert over New Mexico.

That was the instant that both Bradley and Ruth realized they were a part of history, and they have just fulfilled their role in time. They scanned the area and found two aliens, so different that any being known even in their time. The aliens had very large eyes, and long slender bodies. Longer arms and fingers than you would expect, but you were drawn back to the eyes. They were the size of a human hand when made into a fist, and they were silently still and lifeless. Ruth felt horrible. This was her fault.

They stayed a bit longer but noticed the mothership had a buildup of energy and vanished. Leaving their 'people' behind. The alien craft disintegrated and the wreckage was strewn over the area. Ruth watched as the being in the craft were either ejected and their bodies thrashed as they hit both solid rock and hard packed Earth; or the concussive force of the instantaneous change in momentum causing fatal internal injuries.

Hovering less than one thousand meters off the dessert floor Bradley and Ruth watched as the military carefully picked up the aliens and made the area appear as though it was not what it was....

The sole witness was coerced into silence and all bodies and pieces were taken to a classified military facility deep in the dessert. This area, in a few decades, would become known as Area 51. Following the convoy to the facility was a simple task, but one of the vehicles in the convoy was setup as an electronics or detection vehicle. The operator kept looking up at the sky in the area of where the pods were actually located, but they did not see anything, and Bradley estimated the operators attributed this to a fault in the system, rather than an invisible and hovering silent pod tracking their every movement.

Once at the facility they watched as the cargo was removed and then waited a short time in case anything else happens, then returned home one at a time, Ruth first.

As Ruth vanished Bradley waited a few minutes so the pad could be cleared. While he waited he took continuous scans of the area and determined the aliens were emitting a high frequency tone. This tone was of a higher pitch than anything that could be produced or for that matter heard on the planet Earth. He refined the receiver and after playing with it for a minute he detected two distinct tones, one ever so slightly higher than the other. With the tone he was able to determine the location in the building and in doing so discovered that the aliens, as they were dying, must have set off their homing beacons.

Since there was nothing else to do here, he sent the recall signal and returned home.

 Upon arrival in the chamber he was still receiving the homing signal from the alien spacecraft. Talking to the operator through the Sub-Q, *"Open frequency 39-Beta, home in on a direction…bearing and distance…from this point."* The operator did as instructed and discovered the exact location.

Responding through the Sub-Q, the operator informed Bradley as to the point where the signal was originating. *"Approximately* seventeen hundred and eighty-three point six miles, in the Nevada dessert, just south of Little Fish Lake. I will inform security to send a team."

"NO! It will take too long. Jump me there. Send me back fifteen minutes and at an altitude of 1,000 meters."

The operator was a bit taken aback by the request, but it would be the best and fastest way to get there, and also since Bradley was still in his pod it was safe. "I will comply. But you cannot use your implant to communicate until I contact you, understood."

"Yes." Bradley was transported back in time 15 minutes and a thousand meters above the dessert. He heard the entire conversation he had with the operator, but had his implant in standby mode, so he was listening only. Once the operator sent him back the operator contacted him through the implant.

"Gamma 934, your status!" He spoke into his mind and Bradley heard and replied.

"Safe and Secure. Altitude 500 meters and descending, slowly. The signal is very strong. Has my team been informed?"

"Yes, they are in transit to your location as is a security detachment. At the request of Mr. Jensen their implants are being tuned to your frequency."

"Good....Benja...."

"We are all here Trip. Report!"

"In a nutshell we went and witnessed the alien craft appear in orbit a few minutes after all of you and the Malkornian ships departed from Earth orbit. Roger stayed in orbit and watched the mothership, for lack of a better term, while I and Ruth followed *the smaller craft to the surface. It was fast and maneuverable. The orbital ship was able to detect our presence and as it approached Roger, he jumped home to avoid unneeded scrutiny. The vessel must have contacted Ruth and I while we were following because it changed directions and ascended rapidly, faster than we were able to get out of the way. A wingtip of the craft scraped Ruth's pod and the vessel careened to the surface, impacting with a violent force. Ruth jumped home slightly damaged. I stayed to see the outcome. The government concealed the incident and took the pilots to a facility in the dessert. They did not survive the crash. I performed a complete scan and detected what seemed to be a homing signal. I jumped home and was still receiving the homing signal and instructed the operator to jump me here, as it was faster than a transport. You all were informed and here we all are."*

"OK, since you are there what are you seeing?" Ruth asked.

"A lot of sand."

Benjamin spoke next," Bradley, *jump home and take the pod to this location. We should all get there about the same time since the pod is considerably faster. See you in an hour or so."*

"Jumping..." and he was gone. Fifteen minutes later, *"Benjamin, I returned and am in transit to your location. I am at 1500 meters AGL and at maximum velocity. See you shortly."*

Chapter 13

Alien Welcome Party

About an hour later Bradley showed up and landed near the transport Benjamin, Matthew, Ruth, Roger, Will Carter, and the security pilots used to get there. The pod was a lot faster than the transport so when Bradley arrived they were still getting out of the transport, and getting their gear together.

Everyone heard the light hum as the pod descended and landed next to them, even though it was essentially invisible. Since they were all tuned to the same frequency, Ruth let him know he was not able to be seen. A moment later the pod appeared and the hatch opened to let Bradley get out.

Will Carter, Benjamin's former classmate and evidently his nemesis or adversary used a hand scanner to determine the location of the signal. Will made a sweeping motion around him and started walking off in a direction. A few minutes later he stopped and said the signal is coming from here, and pointed to the ground.

The other security team pulled out a portable excavator and trained the beam on the spot and initiated the system. A few minutes later the dirt and rock that covered the door were gone and what was left was a steel door with no handle.

Benjamin noticed there was an electronic lock next to the door. Will walked in front of it and looked over. "No power." He removed a small cube from his pouch and attached it to the mechanism, a second later it illuminated.

Will tried a multitude of keystrokes and after a few minutes Benjamin became slightly annoyed. He wanted to get inside and did not have time for this nonsense.

He stepped in front of Will and eyed the keypad over. Looking at the sides he noticed it had a seam. He selected a flat spoon looking instrument and pried the side off. Scanning the inside now he cross-circuited the circuit and there was an audible thump.

Ruth pulled on the heavy door and it opened. As the group examined the door they realized the thump they heard were actually steel rods being retracted into the door frame. They seem to have come out of the frame and into the door. A very good thing Benjamin found a way to retract the rods. He looks at Will and smiled, nodded his head, and made an 'after you' motion with his arm to Will and the security team.

They entered the darkness and used portable lamps to see where they were going. There were a LOT of stairs and when they hit the bottom they were in a very large hallway. They were on one end and the other end was at least 200 meters away. Between them were only 4 doors, 2 on either side of the hall, and some very low level lighting that was hardly working at all. The impression they had was that of the by gone days' thriller vid, where something jumps out and scares the crap out of you. They all looked at each other, a few times, and started walking towards the other end of the hall.

As they walked, their steps...footfalls...took on an eerie reverberating echo. This was unnerving for one of the security guys; you could see it on his face. His partner put her hand on his shoulder to help keep his emotions in check. It works, at least for now.

Benjamin, Roger, Ruth and Bradley were at point, with Will Carter in the middle and the two security operatives taking up the tail position. Never in his wildest imagination did Benjamin feel as though a simple mission such as this could have such an historical outcome. This building has layer upon layer of dust on the floor and the door frames. This facility has to be more than a few hundred years old, possibly dating back to the early twentieth century.

As they approached the first door Benjamin reached out and grasped the door knob. Turning he discovered it moved freely, so it was not locked. He pushed the door open to see a small room with eight bunks, four sets of bunk beds. He also saw there were uniforms laying on the bed as though the residents died instantly, there were no bones or other discernable component of the human anatomy present, but there was an excessive amount of residue on the bed, and in the uniform.

Benjamin reached down and picked up the metal tag on the metal chain. He read the information and then read it aloud, "Bernard Trwolski, it has a number also and stated he is a Christian. This must be his….ah…."

"Dog Tag." Roger added.

"Yes, correct." Benjamin remembered that Roger had an affinity for the early war period of the United States.

Roger asked, "Does the number have 3 numbers, 2 numbers, 3 numbers separated by dashes?"

Benjamin looked again and "No. a single number"

"Then," Continued Roger, "These tags are from before the mid 1960's. That's when they converted from serial number to social security number."

They glanced around, Security looking in the lockers the inhabitants used to store their belongings. Finding nothing of interest outside a few old weapons, they emptied out of the room and back into the hall. Will opened the next door. It appeared to be more of the same, but there were two beds in this room.

"Officer Quarters." Roger added. Everyone agreed.

Making their way to the next room, Ruth opened the door. She had to hold back a scream and everyone else saw her face. Security jumped to the front and peered inside. When they entered they all knew why. The gray aliens were in what looked like hermetically sealed vertical glass tubes and seemed to be suspended in the center. One of them looked as though an autopsy had been performed, telltale by the incisions, and the gaping hole in the abdominal cavity. Next to him was another cylinder with what looked like could have been the parts this individual was missing.

"Go check out the rest of the facility." Will said to the two security people.

As they left, Will scanned the room and determined the signal was not coming from a piece of equipment, but from the bodies of the aliens.

Matthew walked into the room as Will made the discovery.

"Mr. Carter, please elaborate." Everyone turned to look at Matthew Sharp. He was accompanied by one of the pilots, since they worked for the Security detachment.

"Well sir. These two alien bodies seem to be emanating an extreme high frequency signal, and as far as we can detect, it is organic in nature. If this is correct, then this signal has been broadcasting for centuries. The frequencies of the two signals are close, but not exact. From that I am making the assumption that everyone in their universe emanates a frequency upon death. They may not even be able to hear, or rather receive the signal so they may not know of its existence. If so, can you imagine the noise? Perhaps the emanation is due to their presence in our universe.... dimension, whatever."

"Understandable." Mr. Sharp paused for a moment considering his next question. "Therefore, can we use this signal to our advantage?" Inwardly smiling he had to ask the question. "Can we follow this type signal back to its source? Can we visit their universe? If so, can the jump signal be initiated from another universe?" A very large smile stretched across his face. "In all the years I have been doing this, never did I anticipate asking that last question." Then he shook his head.

"Sir. This is not your typical mission, therefore, Ms. Martinez has instructed me that any mission related to this discovery has been deemed the sole responsibility of the Security Detachment. We will answer those questions." Will was standing tall as he said it. Benjamin actually looked on him as though Will had authority for the first time.

"Good." Matthew said, turned and walked out into the corridor.

As he was walking through the door, "Mr. Carter, please come to the far room on the right." One of the security types, the woman, yelled into the hall and her voice carried into the tomb where they were all having their discussion.

As they all entered the room, last door on the right, they noticed a file cabinet seemed to be randomly place on an empty wall. Looking at it closely they saw the dust was a centimeter thick, but it had a gap. There was an opening there. Benjamin and Roger moved it out of the way while Ruth found the latch. It opened rather easily like it was balanced properly; not bad for the 20th century.

As the trap door opened they saw a flight of spiral steps leading down into the darkness. Even the light from their personal torches did not seem to find the bottom. Will tested the steps and headed down. His footfalls could be heard quite easily, and for longer than any of them thought possible. Benjamin and Ruth were counting the steps. 296 of them if they counted correctly.

The rest of them headed down two at a time. The sound echoed as if they were in a very large cave. As they all hit the bottom, Benjamin noticed a series of switches on one wall. He flipped a few of them and nothing happened. The Security team walked over to where Benjamin was standing and attached a portable power unit to the wall. Through inductance it should provide at least a little power to the room so they can turn on a few lights.

As soon as they attached the PPU, several very bright spotlights lit from the switches that were flipped on a moment ago and their attention was directed to the craft on the other side of the room. It was the ship Roger had seen, and Ruth had damaged. It was either intact, or rebuilt. But was it flyable?

*   *   *   *   *   *   *   *   *   *   *   *   *

As Benjamin, Roger, Bradley, and Ruth stood in the elevator with Matthew, it was dead silent. Everyone was looking straight ahead and appeared as though they were in the elevator alone. The door slid to its open position and Matthew exited the car first.

Followed by Benjamin, then Roger, then Bradley, the Ruth. Ruth thought to herself that the elevator emptied in rank order, with Matthew Sharp at one end and herself at the other.

As they entered the door to his office his receptionist, Tandy, opened the door, not saying a word. Matthew took his seat at his desk, with the other taking the seats on the visitor side of the antique looking desk. Ruth noticed, for the first time, that it was not really made of wood but a plastic that appeared to resemble wood. Still beautiful, and practical at the same time.

Matthew looked at the visitors and started to speak. Benjamin stopped him before he could make a sound. Reaching towards his desk he tapped the surface and the room suddenly became silent. It was not noisy in the first place but there was a kind of white noise that suddenly disappeared. Ruth remembered the sound quite well, or was it a lack of sound. Security mode had been activated.

"Ben, I need you to take as many people as you need and get to the bottom of this, find out everything you can on the facility. Who, what, where, when, why, and how… Roger, you need to learn what you can about the visitors we found. I need to know everything, and I need to know it yesterday."

Matthew paused for a minute as he considered Bradley and Ruth. The only other two people in the current universe who had knowledge of these trans-dimensional beings.

"Ruth, you are to work with Roger and Bradley, you are to work with Benjamin." Looking at Benjamin and Roger, "Gentlemen, let them work it up, you follow their lead on this; let's see how their training is progressing." He smiled at them, turning to Bradley and Ruth, with a more sinister grin, "You two seem to be the new Ben and Roger, your one job in this is to make Ben and

Roger feel like they just got out of school, and you are teaching them what they need to do to complete an assignment....completely! Make me proud you two." Turning back to Benjamin and Roger, "Is it even possible for you two to let someone else lead? I guess we will find out."

Matthew smiled a playful smile. He knew what he just did, and he did it for a threefold purpose. ONE: He truly wanted to see what Bradley and Ruth were capable of, TWO: He wanted to let Benjamin and Roger take second seat for once since Benjamin finished his training and Matthew made Roger a team lead, and THREE: He thought it would be fun to make the new guys try as hard as they could to make the old guys look bad.

"Yes sir," all four of them said simultaneously.

Matthew motioned to the door and they all stood, Matthew returned the room to normal and they left the room. As they entered the elevator and the doors closed, "Bradley, meet me in the book library in 15 minutes." Benjamin said. He looked at Roger who said, "Same for you Ruth. Only make it 13 minutes." He grinned at Benjamin. Ruth and Bradley looked at each other and rolled their eyes. They were both thinking, this is going to be interesting.

* * * * * * * * * * * * *

After a week of intense research, Benjamin and Bradley jumped back to a few minutes before the appearance of the dimensional ship, watching the altercation with Roger on their sensors and hearing the chatter between them on the communication frequency their Sub-Q was tuned to for that mission. They saw the ship appear and as it was suspended in orbit it began to move towards Roger, who was about to vanish from this timeframe and return home as he had already done in their past. As it focused on

Roger, Benjamin and Bradley both fired a microscopic dart that bonded itself to the skin of the ship. If the ship ever appeared again Earth would be warned or notified. But the people of Earth would need to first know how to receive this signal. This dart set, perfectly spaced and positioned, would set up a harmonic which would reverberate and amplify so the people of Earth in the future, Benjamin's future, would know if the ship ever appeared.

Once satisfied the darts were in place, they popped out, and reappeared at the same moment as before only at positions to witness the collision with Ruth, that was Bradley's assignment; and the crash of the alien scout ship, which was Benjamin's assignment.

Everything went as history recorded it the first time. Ruth grazed the alien vessel, and the ship crashed, and the government types showed up less than an hour later to collect everything. They tried to tell people it was a weather balloon, yea….right…..

Benjamin was following the path of destruction, as he called it, from the point of impact to the point of collision. Bradley was doing the same only in reverse. They met somewhere in the middle and both flew to the crash site and waited. The military showed up, lots of armed security and lots of very large trucks. It took them several hours to pile the debris on the trucks and leave the area. A cleanup team had begun returning the surface of the dessert to a pre-crash appearance, and several miles away made the sand and surface appear as if a weather balloon had crashed, and a flammable gas payload had exploded. Scorching the surface with very large backpack type torches they scorched the area, and burned…partially…the weather balloon and it payload.

Bradley followed the convoy from about a thousand meters as they left the highway and went into the high dessert. Benjamin stayed and watched the team make the area look like a lie to humanity. Once they left the area, Benjamin went at max speed to the facility they discovered in their time.

Moving up the mountain side facing the facility, Benjamin recovered a probe he had placed their 25 years earlier, or was it three hours. Needless to say, the recording buffer was 57% filled in that time. Time travel can be confusing and difficult to understand, unless to can keep a concise temporal reference in your head as to what happened, and when.

As he approached the probe he downloaded its memory, which was a video and scanner log of everything in that direction for nearly a quarter of a century. He wanted to know when the facility was built, who constructed it, and when it went into operation.

Afterwards he initialized the probe and set it back to automatic, allowing it to continue its monitoring of the facility with an empty recording buffer.

Rejoining Bradley he passed on a copy of the recording which they reviewed, Benjamin watched the video in high speed and Bradley watching the scanner results.

They discovered the bunker was built ten years earlier as a fallback command post. The hanger where the ship was discovered actually held tanks and ordinance to be used as a last resort. A few hours prior to the aliens occupying the facility the entire facility was emptied and restocked.

As they watched they saw a very bright and powerful pulse emanate from the facility. Scanners thankfully were not overloaded, or maybe the probe was far enough away to not be affected.

"Benjamin, the scanner shows a very intense pulse of radiation a few weeks after the aliens were brought here."

"Radiation, what type?" Benjamin asked, expecting it to be gamma or some other terrestrial radiation.

"Unknown!" Bradley looked at Benjamin, and as soon as that registered in his mind they met eyes, and Benjamin opened his Sub-Q.

"Security, scan the area for ionizing radiation pattern 4-Delta. Unknown type."

Security complied and did not find anything. But the ship seemed to be a hot bed of this radiation. They need to look at the ships systems and database before the scientists destroy it.

"Bradley, we need to jump back to the moment of impact and scan the ship and the database before these scientists have a chance to set off what seems to be either a booby trap in the system or a cascade of the reactor"

Bradley and Benjamin jumped back to the impact and the death of the aliens. They did learn they were both killed on impact. They went into the ship knowing they had several hours before the first intruder showed up to see what happened.

They downloaded the database after spending an hour trying to determine where it was and how to connect to it. When they left they popped out as the first military officer crawled through the hatch.

At home Security took over the investigation, so Benjamin and Bradley never heard about the project again, bureaucracy at its finest. They did hear that the ship was accidentally activated and went home to its universe. The only problem was there was someone on the ship at the time. They have no idea if she survived the transition.

Chapter 14

Loose Ends

It has been more than six months' present time since the dessert event, and Ruth and Bradley have drifted further apart. Benjamin was not as focused on her any longer, but then again, neither was Bradley.

Ruth found her place in the department, a valued member of the research team, and someone who would…on occasion…be more than willing to jump if for no other reason than to experience something new. She was always looking for something, like there was a large void with in her being she was trying to fill in; but then again, Benjamin realized that he, too, had that same empty feeling. Like a part of him, a very important part of him was missing. Perhaps, more accurately, it was not missing but rather he has not discovered the square peg that will fill in the empty round hole.

He would keep looking, and perhaps on his next assignment he would discover what he needed to learn.

Bradley, finally, requested a transfer to Security and it was approved. He liked the work, but disliked the research. He told Benjamin one evening at Pluto's, in an extremely inebriated state, that he wanted to go to Security so he could work on the alien project. He wanted to be the one to crack the database. But it took him months to get up the nerve to actually do it.

Benjamin passed this information on to Matthew the next morning in confidence, and when the request finally showed up all those few weeks later, it was approved instantly.

Brad and Monika were about to depart for the Wild West again. Brad looked like a kid in the proverbial candy store. Monika had gotten close to Ruth after the breakup with Bradley, and Benjamin and Brad strengthened their brotherness, if that was a word in some past or future timeframe.

Brad, Monika, Ruth, and Benjamin were on an assignment, two actually. Brad and Monika were working for Ariana Kimber in the LT department and were assigned to experience the first year or three of the Ricketts' Circus. They did some research on the circus and quickly realized it was going to be a LOT of fun. They were posing as a husband and wife team, billing themselves as Mr. and Mrs. Brain.

Ruth and Benjamin had an assignment in the same timeframe. They were jumping back to follow the presidency of George Washington from April 30, 1789 through the end of 1794. What Brad and Monika are not aware of is that their research collides with their assignment on April 22, 1793, when George Washington, the President, attends the circus.

First to enter the chamber were Monika and Brad, saying their goodbyes to life as they knew it. The two women gave a long hug, as did the two men, then they switched. They were jumping back to March 28, 1793 so they could contact Ricketts and when the Circus idea comes up, provide him some means of getting the people interested in the circus, and the fun carnival atmosphere that surrounds the name circus.

The chamber filled with a soft glow that became brighter in mere moments. At the point when the intensity of the light was about to hurt the viewer, it dissipated to nothing and they were gone. They were now in the past, immersed in their research.

Benjamin walked over to the security operative and requested that his and Ruth's implant be set so they could tune to Brad and Monika's frequency. Their research will collide at jump point three in their temporal reference, and it may provide a safety and data retrieval instance for Brad and Monika. The security woman agreed and they received the secondary frequency.

They entered the chamber and a few moments later they too were on their way to meet up with history.

* * * * * * * * * * * * * * * *

Arrival in 1793 was a bit bumpier than they were used to, it seems they appeared above a small lake or large pond and sank to their knees in the water. These were the correct coordinates, but with all of the rain recently the shore of this body of water appears to have expanded a bit more than expected.

Ruth started laughing, as did Benjamin. Without saying a word, they extricated themselves from the muck, mire, and very chilly water and onto dry land. They were roughly three miles from town, and certain this was the location of their friends.

Ruth looked at Benjamin and made an announcement. "I'm cold!"

Benjamin smiled and said, "Me too!"

They found a dry place to sit on a fallen log. Benjamin pulled his twig from an internal pocket of his jacket and made a small fire to warm their bodies and dry their clothing as much as possible. They decided to spend the night here as it was just about completely dark. They were not afraid of the local critters, since they were both wearing stunners, but the creepy crawlies, as Ruth put it, made her jumpy.

Setting up camp was rather rudimentary. All they had was a canvas tarp and their clothing. Adding a few additional large pieces of wood to the flames, but in such a way as to extend the burn time in a small fire, rather than a larger fire, Benjamin took the tarp and laid it flat, doubling it at the ground.

"OK, lay down." He told Ruth, who was rather wary of his intentions.

She did, and he lay next to her, making certain she was between him and the fire to give her the maximum warmth. He flipped the canvas over the two of them and settled in to a restful sleeping position. Rather, as comfortable a position as was possible under the circumstances.

Confidentially, to himself, he thought this was really nice and comforting. As he dozed off he realized he was beginning to get emotionally attached to her and this woke him up from the almost asleep stage he was in.

The next morning, they were much warmer and dry. They each had a Malk bar in their pockets. Something they really should not have had with them but who in this time would chance eating something that looked like a brick of yeast? They did remove the wrappers and wrap the bars in what looked like butcher paper or something similar.

Benjamin went to the water and scooped up a one-half liter cup of the murky liquid. He added a PureTab he pulled from the left heel of his boot, and waited a minute or so, then took a sip.

"AH! Good clean water." He handed it to Ruth who used it to wash down her breakfast.

Ruth asked, "So, what did you have for breakfast?"

"Eggs scrambled with cheese, grilled pork chops, hash brown potatoes, and grits. YOU?"

"A big bowl of yogurt filled with a honey granola." She replied.

"Let's take inventory." Benjamin asked, "I have 18 PureTabs, 9 Malk bars, 2 twigs, 2 stunners still fully charged," He fired a shot off from each to verify operation, opened his right heel he pulled the items out and counted. "Also, 4 minicams and 13 med packs." Opening the small pack he carried on his back. "And one canvas sheet, 3 bottles of the elixir of life…namely three different types of alcoholic beverages in period specific bottles, 1 knife and our cooking and eating stuff. You?"

Ruth recited her inventory. "Since you have been cleaning the water most of the time on this assignment, I still have 50 PureTabs left, I have 9 Malk bars also, 1 twig since I lost one of them in the campfire that night a week or so ago, 2 minicams and 13 med packs, and 2 stunners." She tested her stunners and they both worked fine.

"Well, I believe we should get moving. No telling just how far it will be until we meet up with Brad and Monika."

"We could just call them you know." Ruth said.

"But that would spoil the surprise!" Benjamin said with a devilish grin.

They began walking towards the city where Monika and Brad lived, and planned to be in the audience at the show before letting their presence be known.

Benjamin and Ruth walked the lonely road in near silence. They really did not have all that much in common, except for work. Benjamin did have the infatuation with her at first, but that had worn off by now. He was beginning to think of her as his wife though, they had been together day and night for the past 45 days. Strange, how in all that time he never thought about her sexually. Yes, she was very beautiful, but he respected her.

She, on the other hand, felt as though she had known him all her life. For some reason she thought they were becoming better friends and who knows where it may lead in the future.

There was something they both had in common. Interjecting temporal references and puns into their conversation to lighten the mood, make a joke or at the very least....get a groan!

As they were walking down the road they saw a buckboard approaching from behind them. They paid no mind to it, but moved to the edge of the road so the driver could pass easier. As the horse drawn conveyance got closer the driver stopped next to them, "Can I offer you a ride into town?" He asked.

That voice, it was familiar, it was Brad.

Ruth looked at Benjamin and gave him a sly grin. He looked at her and shook his head so-as to tell her to not say a word. Which he reiterated through the Sub-Q.

Turning towards him, but keeping the hat in such a way to conceal his face he replied, "That would be mighty fine stranger, and in return we will share with you a bottle of Temporal Rift."

Before Benjamin could say another word Brad leapt from the cart and landed on him and Ruth, giving them the biggest bear hug possible, and knocking them to the ground in the process.

After a few minutes, he permitted them to start breathing again by releasing them. Looking them over, "So what have you been up to for the last few month or so?"

"Uh, Brad, for us it has been less than two months, 45 days to be exact." Ruth replied.

"Well, anyway, Monika will be happy to see you in any case." He smiled a huge smile.

Climbing into the cart, Ruth and Benjamin took their seat on either side of Brad. As Brad flicked the reins a tad to get the horses moving, he asked a simple but important question.

"So, seriously, you did bring some Temporal Rift with you, right?"

Benjamin smiled back, "Yep!"

"OUTSTANDING!" Then he spurred the horses to travel at a slightly faster pace.

As they approached the town, people waved cordially to Brad and eyed his passengers with a curious eye. Not to say friendly, but more on the side of caution. Brad stopped at the General Store and picked up a few things. He put them on the counter and the proprietor pulled out a book. Flipping a few pages, he folded it back and added up what Brad had picked up.

"Well Brad, it seems you have about a dollar and a half remaining on your tab."

"Thanks Zeb, I appreciate that. If there is ever anything else that you need let me know. I am quite handy with mechanical things and can get just about anything to work in one way or another."

Brad exchanged a few more words with Zeb, the owner of the store and walked toward the door. Benjamin and Ruth fell into pace behind him, but Brad stopped short of the door without warning. Which meant that Benjamin, then Ruth, collided into the back of the person in front of them.

Zeb let out a chuckle but Brad said, "Let me introduce a few friends on mine from back home. They are here for just a few days. Benjamin Jensen and his cousin Ruth Swisher. This is Zebulon Walken, the owner of this store and the man that really needs my assistance in fixing mechanical gadgets."

Benjamin and Ruth said 'nice to meet you' at the same time. Since they were now considered cousins, there was closeness between them, but not too close... that was to be expected. They were family, but nothing more. Benjamin saw through Brad on this, and so did Ruth. The morality clause.....Benjamin simply smiled in return. Brad saw it and realized Benjamin realized what he did....

"Nice to meet you both. Any friend of Brad is a friend of mine. Brad makes me a considerable side income, and in return I give him a little to help defray his costs when he purchases from me. You got any talents Mr. Jensen?"

"Call me Benjamin and yes, I too have a knack fixing things also. Something Brad and I share, and how we met. You'll have to ask Brad about it sometime over a nice cool beverage."

Brad winced, he hated making up a story from beginning to end, and Benjamin knew it. His way of a payback for the cousin thing.

Zeb asked, "How long will you be in town?"

"Not that long, a few days maybe." Ruth replied.

"Well, nice to have you here anyway."

They said their goodbyes and left the store. After they were out of town, Brad looked at Benjamin, "How we met? You know how I hate making up stories.... what could have prompted you to say that?"

"Cousins?" Was all Benjamin said to Brad.

Ruth realized the implication at that moment. It meant they had to sleep in separate rooms, no open affection, and no intimacy. Something she was not sure would have been the norm if the scenario had been written a different way. At first she was annoyed, but after a few miles on the road thinking about it, she liked the idea of just getting to know him better with no expectations.

As they pulled up to the house Brad and Monika were living in, Monika came outside. She was obviously curious at the sight of two people on either side of her husband. But, as soon as she realized who it was, she yelled a good old Texas cheer and ran to meet them.

After dinner, Benjamin pulled the bottle of Temporal Rift from his pack. Brad looked like a kid in a candy store. Monika was happy there was something tasty to imbibe in, and Ruth was just happy to be with her favorite couple.

Brad and Benjamin were in the same graduating class, as were Ruth and Monika. Ruth and Benjamin were urgent and short term assignments researchers; while Brad and Monika were Long Term researchers. The difference, well, that is the difference between watching a sporting event on the vid, and being one of the players in the game. Both looking at the same thing, but in a completely different light, and a fresh mindset and depth of knowledge.

They sat on the front porch on four identical rocking chairs, handmade by some local craftsman. Sipping on their drinks and making idle chatter. It was nice to be together again, but they only had a few days.

Shortly, Brad and Monika would go off with the Circus and Benjamin and Ruth needed to head home to write their reports. Before they left, Brad would make a data dump to Benjamin, and Monika would make a data dump to Ruth. At least a little of their research so far could be analyzed.

But for tonight, Brad and Monika slept in their room; Ruth had the spare room and the bed, while Benjamin slept on the living room floor. He spread out the canvas over the top of a bunch of hay from the barn and it made for a very comfortable bed. Monika gave him an extra blanket and all four of them had a wonderful night's rest.

Ruth had a dream she was walking in a dessert next to Benjamin, but she called him Ben. They were dressed in flowing robes and sandals. They were both very happy she knew, but she had no idea where they were so when she woke up she chalked it up to the TR, she did have a bit more than she should have last night.

Benjamin awoke when he heard noise in the kitchen area. It was about ten feet away, and there were no doors to muffle the sound.

He saw that the Sun was rising, barely, and realized that this was a farm after all and Brad and Monika had work that really needed to be done.

He stood and asked, "Coffee?"

Monika nodded an enthusiastic yes and he smiled back at her. "YEP! After we finish the chores, about an hour usually. But if you help, we can cut that to about thirty minutes."

Brad and Ruth walked into the living room at the same time, from opposite sides of the room. "So, if all four of us do the chores, we should already be done!" Ruth said jokingly.

"OUTSTANDING!" Brad exclaimed. And the four best friends left for the barn to tend the animals, the chickens and the pigs, and do whatever else needed to be done.

As they walked out the door and into the brisk morning air, Ruth stopped abruptly and looked at the sky, "That is a beautiful Sunrise."

"Yes it is." Monika agreed.

"Chickens and Pigs, makes me hungry for breakfast." Brad said quietly, but they all heard him well enough.

Benjamin got that grin on his face and Ruth saw it first. "I think we are about to hear some words of wisdom…"

They all looked at Benjamin, so he said, "A chicken makes a contribution to a bacon and eggs breakfast, but a pig gives his all."

The groans were expected, and without malice, but Benjamin put his hand to his chest, and said to them all, "In all you do, in all you strive to achieve, be the pig!" and he bowed slightly to the group.

Brad shook his head, and slapped Benjamin playfully on his shoulder. Monika and Ruth looked at each other and at the same time said, "MEN!"

They managed to get the chores finished in record time and headed back to the house for breakfast. Brad stopped to pick up some of his homemade sausage, and Monika picked up a dozen or so eggs.

Ruth experimented with a Malk bar. She essentially melted it and then liquefied it in some water. She handed everyone a glass and asked them to take a sip while she made a toast, not telling them what she did. Before they all drank, she made a toast to the best tasting orange juice you have ever had; when they drank they all tasted the orange juice and were completely surprised. Then she got mean, she made another toast to the worst fish dish and watched everyone take a sip and nearly gag. It was really funny and they all laughed a lot. The rest of the drink they each took turns grossing each other out. When the glass was empty they had breakfast, a wonderful meal and a wonderful time.

They needed to leave and return home.

After arriving at home Ruth and Benjamin did not have a lot of time to spend together for a while, but they looked at each other a lot. He was, after all, her boss so there was a level of propriety that needed to be maintained. Once in a while they met at Pluto's and talked over a drink or some food. They managed a trip to the Lunar Colony once, and had a really good time. Ramona treated them right as did Tim and Jan.

But now they needed to work. There was history that needed to be researched and historical figures that needed to be watched.

-- THE END --

Chris Cancilla was born in Cleveland, Ohio, the East Side, in an area known as Collinwood; near East 158th and St. Clair. He really liked growing up there and would not trade it for anything. The friendships he made in Elementary School at Holy Redeemer School, and in High School at St. Joseph (now called Villa Angela – St. Joseph's) are priceless and some of them are still in force. For most of his youth, he worked in the family business, DiLillo Brothers Dry Cleaners, for his grandfather, and DiLillo Brothers Men's Wear for his uncle. He also "apprenticed" with his Uncle Duke who had a radio and TV repair shop smack-dab between the men's wear store and the dry cleaners. But, he enjoyed working in the dry cleaners for his Grandfather, Carmen DiLillo, the most.

In his youth he really enjoyed Scouting. Spending a great portion of it in multiple Scout Troops and Explorer Posts, Scouting influenced his life in a very positive way, and the training, knowledge, and education he gained during his youth in the troop is still influencing his decisions as an adult. The ideals of Scouting, especially the Oath and Law, serve him today like a moral compass, guiding his actions to be a man his family can be proud of in all aspects of his life.

After high school, Chris spent 14 years in the U.S. Air Force where he managed to see a fairly large chunk of this 3rd stone from our star, but his only regret was that he never made it below the equator, so he never got to see the toilet swirl the other way. During his Air Force career his favorite assignment was to Lowry Air Force Base in Denver, Colorado where he was able to ride motorcycles and camp in the Rocky Mountains. This is a close second to the 2 years he was assigned to, and lived in, Keflavik, Iceland; a place where he and his wife Tammy became the best of friends and experienced some really odd and unique adventures.

Currently, he and his wife Tammy, along with their daughter Allison and son Gregory, all live in a western suburb of the Atlanta area of Georgia. You cannot forget to mention his cat, Snip, who is like a little buddy. Snip follows Chris around from room to room, you may or may not see him all the time, but he is always close by. When guests arrive however, Snip is there at the door to greet them, sitting patiently until the new arrival acknowledges he is there, then he stays in whatever room the most humans are inhabiting.

The Boy Scouts of America is still a very large part of his life, especially teaching new adults the skills needed to not just survive outdoors, but to reinforce the way these outdoor skills and habits need to be taught to the leaders of tomorrow. Leave No Trace camping is a major part of his instruction and is a philosophy in the conservative style of camping, if not the only way to ensure a great time for not only you, but for future campers. Wilderness camping is a great way to decompress and gain insight into what is hidden in the inner recesses of your mind. Sitting around a campfire on a cool or cold night watching the flames dance and watching the wood that has given its all to the beauty of the moment, allowing you to reflect inside your own thoughts and be honest with yourself. Nature has a way of bringing all things into clarity; even when you spend all night arguing with a 50 pound raccoon about cobbler residue in the Dutch Oven on the picnic table, the same Dutch Oven you said you would clean up in the morning. Sometimes, the raccoon wins!

Chris' day job is as an EDI B2B Integration Specialist, or an EDI Developer. Take your pick, they both mean the same thing. That's a fancy way to tell someone that you work with computers to translate data from one format to another. He calls himself a digital mailman. He moves the data and information files from one place to another, but he does not own or is not responsible for the data in any way. So, a mailman! After all – the mailman doesn't write the letters, only moves them from point A to point B. What is EDI, well, it stands for Electronic Data Interchange. It is a method to efficiently communicate with a trading partner and electronically transfer documents such as Purchase Orders and Invoices using a national standard format. All done with computers so the chance of humans screwing it up is minimized greatly.

If you are connected to Facebook and you LIKE the ACHIVES Novel page, or the Christopher E. Cancilla Author page; you will then be the first to know when other works of fiction are available from this author. Chris also has a passion for cooking, and the creation of several cookbooks not only gives him the opportunity to experience new cuisine and cooking methods, but it also provides him with the means to share and teach cooking to those who are less experienced and knowledgeable. By no means does he consider himself a chef, but he does consider himself a cook, both in the home and in the woods.

Cooking in the wilderness is a skill that not too many people have and one that Chris enjoys teaching to Scout Leaders, both old and new, in the classes that he teaches for Scouters (Adult Boy Scout Leaders) and also to the Scouts themselves during the COOKING Merit Badge course. Chris was happy that the BSA finally made cooking a required merit badge for the Eagle Scout rank. It is a skill that will be valuable for the rest of your life. Especially if you want to prepare a romantic meal for a date, or simply provide a meal for yourself that you actually enjoy.

Whenever Chris develops or finishes a new story or cookbook, he permits a couple of people to read his book and offer ideas to improve the storyline or the text in general. Who knows, he may allow you to be the next editor for which he will definitely give you kudos in the beginning of the book.

I hoped that you enjoyed reading this book. Please read the others in the Archive series or, if you are interested in cooking, check out the cookbooks. Let Chris know what you think of the book and if you liked either the stories or the recipes.

Additional Works by Christopher E. Cancilla

The ARCHIVES: Education

Book One in the Archives Series.

Benjamin Jensen is a man destined for greatness and a friend to all. Read the story of how it all began. His earliest Research Academy days and how he nearly destroyed time as we know it. Be with him as he loses the love of his life to a senseless and tragic accident, an accident that later in his career he can avert.

The ARCHIVES: Fixing Time

Book Two in the Archives Series.

Benjamin's best friend in all of time returns from a long term mission before he is supposed to return, but the reason causes the archive staff to worry. Someone, from the future, is traveling back to points on the timeline to strategically change history to their advantage. Changing the balance of power and collecting priceless artifacts to sell as antiques several hundred years later. Brad and Benjamin are dispatched to make all needed corrections to get the history books, setting time right once and for all while not appearing in the history books themselves.

The ARCHIVES: Salvation

Book Three in the Archives Series.

Several places on the Earth, the orbital facilities, the Lunar Colonies, and the far reaching corners of the human populated universe, Christianity is beginning to grow, and spread. The world government is concerned it may over shadow their power, or their ability to lead the people into their vision of what the future needs to look like. Benjamin is sent back to a place he feels he needs to travel to determine if Christianity is detrimental to society in general. Is this mind altering or brainwashing? Do Christians want to control everything? Is there a reason to fear Christians, or all religion in general? This is what he is tasked to learn, and fix, if necessary. On the way, he discovers a unique reality and brings that information back to his boss at Archive Island, in the form of a very interesting, honest and convincing report.

The ARCHIVES: Family

Book Four in the Archives Series.

Benjamin Jensen is selected to take over as the Director of the entire Archive Island complex. With that promotion comes both amazing responsibility in the guise of becoming one of the most powerful men in history, and a danger so terrifying it has never before surfaced. With his promotion means that each of his compatriots are promoted to fill in the void as he and Brad Jorgen are propelled into intrigue and mystery. The big questions on everyone's lips, will Benjamin measure up to match the job? Can Brad avert a disaster that could mean an end to the Jensen lineage? Why a reporter is permitted free run of the Archive Island complex is baffling to some, but allowed to happen by all? Come and take this journey with us to explore the dark areas of space and the human condition, and the soft spots in our Family.

The ARCHIVES: Fresh Start

Book Five in the Archives Series.

Benjamin Jensen is the Director of the Island Complex for nearly two decades now, and his best friend Brad Jorgen is his second-in-command. Their sons are students in the Academy and already well on their way to becoming influential and experienced members of the Archive Island Complex Temporal Research team. But, is there danger? Can they trust a non-TR with the secrets of temporal research? Will they need to correct time so history can flow as it is intended? Join the journey....join the excitement.

Bus Route 40-A

A novel

The life of a planetary bus driver can be mundane, repetitious, sedate, and of course unique, interesting, exciting and spontaneous. Driving your whale around the planet picking people up and dropping them off is a lot of fun, sure. But at the same time it is good to get a break in the monotonous time you call your day. So when Walt was asked to take a charter trip for a few days, he jumped all over it, and knowing he had a good friend to ride shotgun, he felt like it would be a good thing. Plus, you get double pay and less work time so he could be home more after the trip was over. No could ever imagine what was about to happen, Walt would either survive the incident, or he would die. Either way, he would be hailed a hero.

The Cancilla Collection

A collection of short stories, essays, and ideas.

Chris Cancilla enjoys…no, he LOVES to write. And to that end he has an opinion on just about everything. You can enjoy an eclectic sampling of a small collection of some of the pros he has penned throughout his life.

Camp Menu Planning

A cookbook

Designed essentially for Boy Scouts to learn the art – if not
the technique – of cooking. Contains a lot of recipes, but
more importantly the recipes are more a method or style than
a road map to a meal. Borrowing one recipe and using the
technique of another and possibly ingredients of a third is
what real cooking is all about, and this book instills that
knowledge in whoever reads, and uses it to learn or learn
something new. The additional information contained in the
book are highly useful in the troop cooking experience. This
book, along with the Camp Cooking workbook, will give
your Scouts the arrows in his culinary quiver to make his
friends and his family happy. Gaining the knowledge and
experience to impress his fellow patrol members with each
meal in the woods, and provide the Scout with the
ammunition to cook an amazing meal for his family in the
home.

Camp Cooking

A cooking workbook

This is a workbook designed essentially for youth to use as a
guide to cooking. This is where they have instant access to a
variety of recipes and cooking techniques to learn the art – if
not the technique – of cooking. The book contains 45 pages
of recipes and if they cook all of the recipes in the workbook,
they will know how to cook, and cook well. This workbook
is a very small version of the larger cookbook. The recipes
in this workbook are extracted from the cookbook, Camp
Menu Planning.

Made in the USA
San Bernardino, CA
03 June 2016